Land of the Frontier Saints

A novel by Jamie McDuell

Dedicated to my mother, Olive.

"Sweet little sleep, my dreams are yours to keep."

Chapters

1. Ending

Though the Sun will be turned into darkness, and the Moon into blood, it is not the Lord's Day. I am here to repay evil, for God takes too long. He could not save Jackson Tait, and He will not save me. Heaven has no place in my heart and no space for my soul. My anger, my rage is of this world. I cannot turn my cheek, nor rest until eyes and teeth are taken. The devil that built this house left his mark upon me when I was only eight years old and now I'll return it. The pillars of smoke are the sign of his end, and the flames the things we shall all become. It is I who am clothed with the Sun, with the Moon beneath her feet. It is not the Lord's Day. This day is mine, and mine alone.

Frank Marlin, my grandfather, has governed this church as if he was the Word made flesh. Yet today he will become human. I will reduce his sermons to ashes, and the Sodom he has built to rubble. It is beneath that wreckage that I wish to find my grandfather. His bones smashed, his blood draining away, his last breath slipping from his throat. As I cover his mouth, his eyes fixed in terror, he will know that I am the rider upon the white horse. With scales in my hands, I will place the mark upon his head, and he will at last suffer for every vile act he has committed. And when Frank Marlin finds the darkness that has been reserved especially for him, I will find my redemption, my moment of freedom. No heavenly reward will grant me that.

The syrupy contents of the can of gasoline in my hand splash onto my dress and run down my legs as I force open the only window I can see. I make my way into the long courtyard and watch the fire engulf the church adjoining the west wing of the compound. The flames spiral upwards behind the high ground floor windows, until the timber arches upon the ceiling begin to flare with shimmering fury. Half-formed figures dance amid the choking air, their desperate hands scraping in vain against the glass. I feel no pity for them. Clawing its way across the roof, the fire's deep orange hues fade gently into the darkening colors of the early evening sky. I stand here transfixed, astonished at the beauty and horror of it all.

Easterly winds bring the smell of jasmine, its perfume quickly overpowered by the stench of burning flesh. A low boom ricochets around the buildings as the support structure of the main sleeping quarters begin to bend, bow and finally break. The heavy oak beams plummet two stories down, crushing the once grand veranda as if it were made of leaves. The river at the north end of the compound has swollen to the point of bursting. The currents swirl as I watch the charred remains of a small child become entangled in water reeds. There is no way to cross without drowning, no option but to follow the spread of the flames towards the main entrance of the compound.

Through the fading light I can just make out three objects on the ground in the middle of the courtyard. I tentatively begin to move towards them but freeze after only a few steps. A sharp, splintering sound comes from the window to my right; the paint around it bubbles and dissolves as the glass expands and contracts like a lung. When it finally explodes, a swarm of vicious shards pierce the right side of my body and face. Tiny red carnations blossom though my dress. The iron-rich taste of blood fills my mouth as I plead with myself to keep walking. Instead I step forward into a recurrent nightmare: the form of Cousin John comes staggering into view. Every inch of his body is alight as he stumbles through the now empty window. His clothes have almost burnt away, leaving his skin to feed the flames. John lurches towards me, his arms outstretched as if crucified. He attempts to summon the meekest of sounds.

"Laura Jo...Laura Jo."

The Laura Jo he knew is dead. I am the resurrection. The hate-filled, godless soul that will destroy the things that John holds dear. He is Moses' burnt offering of sin.

The fire silences him. He drops like a stone onto his knees, then hard onto his dripping-wax face. The dry crab-grass around him begins to pop as it ignites. In seconds it has formed a circle of light around him. His contorted hands twitch like a rattlesnake as I move past him, the great wheezing frame of his body finally coming to a halt. John has not found salvation or mercy. But I have the blood I've longed for upon my hands. When the flames die down I pour more gasoline onto him in the hope of prolonging his suffering.

Past John, the three prone objects gradually come into focus. There is no sense of surprise or shock; I instinctively knew what I would find here from the moment I first glimpsed these spectral shapes. The lifeless bodies of my mother, Josephine, and sisters, Beth and Ann, rest three feet apart from each other. Their eyes stare blankly into the ink-blot sky, hands clasped together, locked in prayer. Deep purple bruises run like rivers across the throats of Ann and Beth. Their silver-blonde hair splays out behind them, the burning light of the buildings trickling off its ghostly sheen. Bitter tears fall over my lips. I separate their fingers one by one and softly lay their hands by their side.

Mother's head is surrounded by a slowly expanding red halo. The blood glistens in the grass as I bend down to close her remaining eye. One side of her face is no longer there. For her the tears will never flow. Though she may not have been the root of our family's sickness, she was its ripe, rancid fruit.

Smoke drifts in great waves around me, and I can barely see beyond the end of the compound. Panic begins to spread through me as I realize the fire has encroached upon nearly every exit. Even now a part of me does not wish to die. The one route left open to me is past the room in which we stored and framed the history of our congregation. I summon what small amount of energy remains in my body and begin to press on towards the gate. A voice echoes out into the courtyard and stops me dead.

"Laura Jo Marlin!"

Every sinew in my body strains as if it is ready to snap. Ten feet beyond the veranda doors sits Frank Marlin, slowly rocking back and forth in his chair. His sallow skin glows like a Halloween pumpkin in an arch of fire. A sickness courses through me as my grandfather reaches for the shotgun that lies at his feet. In one flowing action he slides back the bolt of the gun and aims the long black barrels straight at me. He jerks the weapon twice, beckoning me forward.

"And the sheep returns to its flock. Did you think you'd be spared, Laura Jo? I should never have let you leave your mother's womb. We are all going. This end must be shared, shared between me and you, as we as a family have shared everything else."

I can no longer hold on to the can of gasoline. It slips from my fingers and hits the ground with a dull, metal thud. The sepia liquid empties around my feet. The heady odor of the gas drifts up to my head, leaving me dizzy, and my nerves tingling.

The wall behind him is covered with pictures and clippings. In the center of everything is a blown-up newspaper image of my grandfather, his remorseless gaze condemning us all. A picture of my mother slips from the wall and shatters as an image of my nine year-old self draped in virginal white starts to burn, sweat and blacken, my innocence destroyed one final time.

Yet I no longer am controlled by the fear which Frank Marlin spread through us. My salvation came in the form of a boy. An hour ago, Jackson Tait drew his last breath. Grandfather quickly thrusts a knife into that open wound.

"Such a shame about the boy…such a shame. More's the pity his parents could not join him. It seems that I, alone, was chosen."

He cannot resist a smile.

"Oh, Laura Jo. You're proof ever-lasting that He has never entered your heart, that you were formed for a more…common use."

He makes the sign of the cross with the gun.

"His rod. His staff. His shepherd. Goodnight, Laura Jo. You will not sleep well."

Frank Marlin's lines of scripture sear out into blackness around me, his conviction still unfaltering, his anger absolute. But where once these words were divine, I now laugh at the sound of a dying, bedeviled old man. I will not bow before him, nor place my hands in prayer.

As my grandfather releases the safety on his shotgun I hear the distant wail of sirens. They will be far too late to save me. In a few seconds, death will steal me away from the land of the Frontier Saints.

2. Fall of a Sparrow

In the moment before death, my world comes flooding back to me. I am eight years old and am hiding in our neighbor's wheat field. The voice of my mother is weakened against the endless afternoon breeze as she calls my name. The rippling spears of wheat hide my tiny frame as I lay against the cool, dusty earth. As the tips of the crop above me bend and sway I feel the sun sneaking through, trying to parch the ground. Patches of flickering light dance like mayflies across my body. I push my ear to the ground and hear what I think is the heartbeat of the land thumping against my own. The sound grows ever louder, ever more repetitive and mechanical. Down there, among the dirt and the insects, I decide that I won't be going back home again anytime soon. I know I can't explain away the smashed glass and the broken doll's head as easily to my mother as I could to my father. And he won't be back for another whole day. Laying there it seems as if I could be swallowed by the soil and drowned by the air. My mother's voice grows more frantic as the whirring and scything reverberates through the ground beneath me.

"Laura Jo, Laura Jo…come on now darlin', I got a surprise for you, don't do this to me now!"

I cover my ears and squeeze my eyes tight to cut myself off from the world beyond the fields, and as I do, I feel a great presence looming across my curled-up body. The land has stopped shuddering and only a noise like the sea plays behind my hands. I slowly open my eyes to see the shaded outline of a man. His body is lean and sinewy, with a face that looks as if it has been crafted from the granite mountains that border our town. The wheat seems to bow before him, as if Solomon had returned. At once he is both a stranger and yet somehow familiar. He stretches out an arm towards me.

"Stand up, girl. Stand up".

Stricken with fear, I dare not move. The insistence and command in his voice is so different to that of my mother.

"Girl, for the last time, stand. Take your grandfather's hand."

I can't resist any longer, and place my hand in his. He pulled me to my feet in one hard, fluid motion, like I'm a rabbit who's wandered into a hair-trigger trap.

Sighing deeply, he cups his left hand under my chin then moves my face up into the sunlight, assessing me as if he has pulled a relic from the earth.

"Turn yourself around, my girl. Witness how you've been spared."

Slowly, I turn into the breeze. Ten feet from me is a giant harvesting machine, its engine fans faintly whirring in a vain attempt to cool itself down. The sun bounces off the steel blades of its outstretched arms. Inside sits a young man, white as a sheet and hands clawing either side of his disbelieving face. Looking me straight in the eye, he bellows through the thick glass, "I couldn't see you, I couldn't see you," before turning to my grandfather and exclaiming "Thank you, sir, thank you." My grandfather raises a colossal palm and a wry smile to try to soothe the man.

"Now don't you worry son, I got her safe and sound right here. You go ahead and jump down from there and go fix yourself something stiff, take your mind off it."

Once the man has begun to walk unsteadily back through the field, my grandfather leads me in the opposite direction towards home. Grasshoppers leap around, loosened from the wheat, before we move onto a broad path cut between two fields. In the distance I see my mother, her arms drawn tightly up around her bosom. Her pregnant stomach bulges through her blue checked dress. Beside her stands my little sister Ann, her head solemnly bowed.

As we continue along the path, something twists and turns manically in the air in front of us. It struggles for a few seconds before plummeting onto the dry earth. We walk over and see a tiny sparrow flipping and flailing around in small circles, still trying to fly. One of its wings is partly torn and traces of blood stain some of its feathers. The bird's will to live, however, has clearly not deserted it. Its black eyes are still bright and furiously alive. The instinct to fly and soar still floods every part of its being. When I try to bend down and take the bird in my hands, my grandfather grips me by the shoulder and moves me aside. Standing over the bird, he steps firmly down on it and from beneath his foot I hear the smallest of cracks. He turns towards me and strokes my hair, his face as emotionless as a weathered waxwork.

"Only some of us are chosen, Laura Jo. Only some of us get to choose. He will acknowledge our mercy. It was He who chose *us*."

The horizon in front of me always appeared limitless, as if it stretched towards heaven. After I had risen from the wheat, new borders and boundaries would reshape the world I once knew. In time they would reshape me too.

***

My grandfather walked permanently into our lives less than a day before we found out that my father, James Carter, and my elder sister, Beth, had been taken from us. It was while walking back with my grandfather from the field, looking up intently into his face, that I realized that I met him only once previously. Father had taken me the summer before to visit a local farmer, as he had been considering rearing a few lambs on the small plot of land we owned. He let me pick three and they were loaded onto an open-back truck Father had borrowed from a neighbor. Though I was allowed to pick them, he explained that I was not to name them, as they were being reared for a specific purpose - to be killed, butchered and eaten. Despite his attempts to dampen my ardor I had been unable to take my eyes off the lambs the entire way home. My face flinched every time we hit a bump and they crashed into each other then quickly separated like great balls of cotton floating apart. When we pulled into the side track that led to the house I finally turned around. In front of us stood my grandfather and a woman slumped gracelessly in a wheelchair. Her appearance terrified me. Though it made my flesh prickle I could look away from her. The clothes she had been dressed in, as she clearly could not dress herself, were ill-fitting and seemed drained of color. My mother nervously twitched in the background as she stroked the hair of the woman I now know was my grandmother, Emmy. It was the one time I ever saw my father fly into a rage, his usually calm, forgiving ways momentarily thrown to the wind. He slammed on the brakes and was out of the vehicle before it had fully stopped moving.

"Take your damn sermons and your bullshit holiness and get the hell off of my property, Marlin."

"Can a man not visit his own flesh and blood? Is this what it's come to?"

"Oh, now she's your flesh and blood is she? You've driven six hundred miles to play Daddy? "

Mother tried vainly to interject.

"James please, Daddy just wants to see the babies, and I'll get to spend some time with Mom."

"Did you call him down here? Tell me you didn't. Please tell me you didn't. Have you forgotten the things this man has put you through? And now the sanctimonious bastard rolls up here and wants to see our children? He goes near them, I'll split him in two."

"James, she hasn't got long, look at her for God's sake, she can barely move."

"And she didn't move a damn finger to protect you, did she? And she sure as hell could move well enough then."

When Grandfather began to laugh to himself and murmur under his breath, Father leapt forward and grabbed him by his collar, almost lifting him from his shoes. This only encouraged him more. A low sarcastic growl shook from his body.

"You believe all that nonsense she told you, boy? You don't even know your own wife, after all these years under your 'protection.' You were pathetic then and you're pathetic now. Look at what you're doing in front of your children."

I'd soon learn that Grandfather had an extraordinary knack for making the perfectly innocent look guilty, for turning any situation to his advantage. Though I went unnoticed, he had seen Beth and Ann returning from an errand, walking hand in hand along the path. When they had almost reached us, he had provoked my father into a reaction. Now they stood still with shock at the sight of their father half throttling a stranger. Upon seeing his girls he let him go, backed off a few paces before bending over with his hands on his knees. I desired nothing more than to run to him, to hold him tightly, to make him feel better like he always made me whenever I was upset or scared. It was simply fear that stopped me. Raising himself up, he came to the truck and lifted me from it. He beckoned over Beth and Ann.

"Girls, inside the house with me. Now."

They ran as fast as their legs would carry them to his side. He turned to my grandfather.

"If you're not gone in two minutes, I'll make you gone myself. There's no undoing the damage you've done."

It would be years before I understand what he meant by 'damage.' From behind the door we heard a car engine start and moments later the sound of gravel being spat out from beneath tires. Father hugged us three girls together as we listened. In the following days there were no great rows between my parents, and no sense of animosity. This came as a surprise given my mother's volcanic temperament. The only protests my mother made were quiet ones: she begged my father to let her parents back into our lives, to move on from the past, to find forgiveness in his heart. But the mere mention of my grandfather was like injecting venom into the room. When she brought him up his reply was always the same – he would never let Frank Marlin near enough to ruin his daughters. She ultimately knew her pleading was futile, that Father's mind would never be turned on the subject, and so she gave up trying almost as quickly as she started. Though in the two months that followed, our life would carry on along on the simple trajectory it had always done, never could we have envisaged that that our grandfather would take Father's place at our table.

It was to be my father's line of work that would ultimately lead him to his death. Being a craftsman and carpenter of some repute, my father had clients all over the state. At weekends he would often take one of us girls along with him to deliver a piece of furniture or to discuss a customer's ideas face to face with them. He said that people loved the personal touch, and it did his business no harm at all if he brought one of his beautiful little blue-eyed, snow-haired daughters along to melt a client's heart. The contrast of us girls against the jet black hair and dark eyes of my father must have been something. The well-heeled, genteel ladies we visited would be bowled over by our ready smiles and delightful manners for ones so young. I recall long afternoons playing in highly manicured gardens or standing on the banks of sleepy backyard bayous, a home-made lemonade or biscuit in my hand and a client's own children or dogs dashing around beside me. Father would wave at me from a table shaded by trees as he sketched out perfect designs of bureaus, beds, cabinets, wardrobes, and vanity boxes. There was nothing that could be made of wood that he could not produce.

James Carter's skills as a craftsman were only bettered by his abilities as a father. Though my memories of him are dim and hazy, I remember his gentleness, and that his temperament was both even and fair. When we would misbehave it was he who would first calm my mother's fitful histrionics before telling us exactly why what we did was wrong. He spoke to us knowing we would understand his reasoning; he treated us as if we were already fully grown and this sign of respect was not lost upon us even at those most tender ages. When alone with him, he would always tell us just how much he appreciated our company on his trips out of town, that it would never be the same without us. Our father was the very center of our universe.

It was a sweltering Saturday in July when my father and Beth set off on a two day visit to a client named Florine, who lived in a small town at the end of the northern state lines. I kicked the dust up from the ground into great billowing waves, sorely disappointed that it was not my turn to accompany him. My sense of annoyance was greater than usual, knowing they'd be staying in a motel that evening. Seeing my tantrum in the rear view mirror, Father turned the engine off, got out of the truck and walked slowly over to me. From his pocket he produced a small wooden cross with Christ laid out upon it. I had never seen anything so beautiful. Father was not a religious man, but perhaps he believed in his own way. He respected, at least, the things that the figure on that tiny cross represented, but he was never bothered or concerned by anyone else's faith or indeed their lack of it, as far as I can recall.

"Now, little Miss Carter, I want you to do your daddy a favor and varnish this for me so it's ready and dry for when I get back. It'll need two coats for sure, one coat for each day I'm gone, so you're just going to have some patience with it. That's what's called for in this life sometimes, Laura Jo. I know you're a patient girl. Take care of it for me – it's one of my finer pieces. You keep it real close."

Seeing my satisfaction and delight at assisting him, he kissed me on the forehead, told me to be a good girl for my mother, before he drove off with Beth. I can still see her pulling faces at me through the back window of the truck until her image became no more than a shimmering blur. It was only a few hours after they set off that my grandfather appeared, and consequently saved me from the jaws of the harvester in the wheat field. Less than twenty-four hours later, my father would lose his life to another machine. I long ago gave up believing in the idea of coincidence.

Father and Beth met their end rounding a sharp turn half way up Mount Chesapow as they returned home to us. It was concluded that the brakes on my father's truck had completely failed, causing it to veer straight into the ravine that separated the mountainside from the elevated section of the road. Their death was instantaneous: the weight of the engine in the front of the truck made it tilt 90 degrees during its fall and it struck the carpet of jagged rocks and boulders below with such force that the front half of the vehicle concertinaed, crushing the passengers inside. These were the details I overheard state troopers proclaim to the local police. Hiding under the back porch, I listened carefully as they informed their colleagues that if the fall hadn't killed my father and Beth, then the great shards of glass from the windscreen sure as hell would have. That image would haunt me forever.

Though it would be a decade before I would truly understand the horror of their passing, it was the impact it had upon my mother that really affected me then. Before my father died, my mother had been a largely good-natured and attentive woman and I loved her dearly. We'd all been home schooled by her since we were babes as she held the firm belief that no state or government institution would ever be good enough for her girls. We would never get the attention we needed or deserved. I suppose my father had agreed to this for the sake of an easy life and there was no doubt Mother had taught us well; we could read and write long before our few friends of the same age.

While mother was never the type to be declared homecoming queen, she was attractive in her own way. She radiated an electric presence and personality that my father seemed magnetically drawn to. When she laughed it was a thing to behold; a manic, warming cackle that would rebound off the walls of whatever room she graced. She did, however, have a troublesome temper and went up like a tinder box just about once a week. It might have been that the milk was off early, that someone had jumped the line at the corner store in town, or that we'd failed to clean our hands properly for the thousandth time. Her anger would uncoil in an instant and shake the foundations of the house. After years of practice, father was something of an expert when it came to getting her down from the ceiling; she would soon be laughing at her own performance and the trigger for her fury quickly forgotten.

Mother had always been a woman of opinions and woe betide you if you should ever contradict a single one. She had readily distanced and differentiated herself from the folks on neighboring farms, especially those who lived further into town as there was always something about their manner, their attitude, their beliefs or their dress that she took issue with. But she was always polite and courteous to them nevertheless, and it was rare that her famous temper would be unleashed in anyone's presence except her own family: Josephine Carter was good at storing up her frustrations and resentments to expel in the privacy of her home. She only allowed people to see one side of her.

It was fortunate then that my father was very good at making her laugh and was either ignorant of, or simply didn't care about, her faults. I guess you would never have picked them to be a match; but whatever existed between them undeniably worked, and however differently we were raised to that point, once my father was gone it would soon become clear that we would not get close to being 'normal' again.

Ann and I had been drawing faces in the ground by the side of the house when the police first arrived. The flashing blue and red lights of their cars immediately gave the evening a strange, spectral air. A scream came from the house shortly after they entered which sent a chill straight through us. It was as if every ounce of rage within my mother had been condensed and transformed into raw, animal sound. Ann began to cry before she even knew what it meant, her tiny arms fastening around me as tightly as she could manage. I covered her ears and tried to block out the deep sobbing that now seeped through the walls and windows. I instinctively knew two things at this moment: something had happened to my father and Beth, and I would never see them again. A female officer came and took us by the hand and led us towards our bedroom. She fought back tears as she explained in the best way she could that Daddy and Beth had been in an accident. Ann was simply too young to understand the implications of what she was being told, as we sat gripping each other upon the bed, conjoined twins born two years apart. The officer knelt before us as Ann spoke to her.

"Is Daddy in pain?"

"No darling, your daddy will never feel any pain ever again. He's gone to a place where he and your sister won't know what it is to hurt."

"But when's he coming back?"

"He's not coming back sweet girl, he's in Heaven now."

"Can I go and see him?"

"You'll see him again someday darlin', but it's just not your time yet. Hopefully it won't be your time to go visit him for a long, long while. But hey, your daddy's part of you, he's all around you and inside of you...your parents never really leave you."

How wrong that officer was. Though, unlike my father, she didn't physically leave us that day, something within my mother left us immediately. Once the officer had backed gently out of the room, a smile of pity etched upon her face, I quietly slipped behind her into the darkening hallway. The door of my parents' room was ajar. Inside, my mother thrashed around the bed, eyes ablaze, and pregnant belly bulging as if it were about to burst. Two already distressed state troopers attempted to restrain her. Almost inaudibly she whispered "God, God,

God" to herself, over and over again. I hadn't noticed that my grandfather was in the room until he slowly left a shadow-filled corner, leant down and began to speak into my mother's ear.

"How, then, can they call on the one they have not believed in?"

"Sir, I'm not sure that's such a good idea at this moment."

"And how can they believe in the one that they have not heard?"

My mother's body contorted and twisted as if a toxin had been administered and had begun to take effect.

"Ma'am, you need to listen to me, you're putting too much strain on your body. You're putting your own and your child's well-being at risk. Please ma'am, the doc's on his way."

"And how can they hear without someone preaching to them?"

"Listen now, we're trying to help your daughter here and you're inflaming an already difficult situation, just back off and let us do our job. Christ Jerod, where the heck has the doc got to, she needs sedating."

"And how can they preach unless they are sent?"

"I'm going to have to ask you to leave the room, sir."

The door swung open and a doctor, an ocean of sweat dripping from his brow, moved quickly to my mother's side.

"Sorry I'm late gentlemen, hell of a thing isn't it?"

My grandfather looked intensely at the doctor as he lifted out a syringe from his medical bag.

"As it is written, 'How beautiful are the feet of those who bring good news!'"

He smiled to himself and walked out of the room as the doctor pierced the needle point into the arm of my mother, the two troopers using all their strength to render her temporarily motionless. I ran to the other end of the hallway and out the back door, hurled myself down the porch steps before crawling back underneath them. There I lay as if I were dead myself, watching and listening as assorted law enforcement officers came outside to discuss the wretched details of the accident.

The days that followed were lived in near silence. Mother remained in her bed, her eyes transfixed on the same point on the ceiling. While my grandfather fed Ann and me, he did not otherwise acknowledge us. I was left to dress and wash Ann, to read her a story before bed, to comfort her when she began to shake with fear each day, terrified that Mother would never be well again. At least three times a day my grandfather would enter my mother's room and lock the door behind him. Through the wall I could hear him talk to my mother relentlessly for almost an hour. He would begin quietly, his voice deep and even, before building to a fearsome crescendo. When he left the room, sweat clung to his reddened face, his knuckles seemingly bursting through his clenched fists.

Memories of my father flooded my mind, taunting me with moments of tenderness, affection and togetherness. Mother remained prostrate and lifeless, her room taking on an institutional air. In the stolen moments I had with her, mainly when my grandfather went to get provisions, I would sit at the foot of bed and ask her how she was feeling. Never once did I get a response.

In the weeks that followed I was desperate to be acknowledged and seen. I longed to be told what to do, to be asked to brush my teeth and comb my hair, finish my food and complete my arithmetic. I wanted to be guided, and loved, and chastened. But when people would ask how my mother was doing and ask who was looking after me, a constant undercurrent of sadness and pity pervaded their voice. To my despair they chose to keep a respectful distance whenever they could.

That isolation ended abruptly. The appearance of Bibles by the side of our beds coincided with our mother's re-entry into the world. When I awoke on this nameless summer day, I felt so used to the apprehension and loneliness that everything seemed in its rightful place. The thick curtains in our room meant morning still seemed like night. I got out of bed and stood on something, almost losing my footing. As if blind, I ran my hands over the floor around me before eventually finding the object. On picking it up, I felt the solemn weight of a book in my hands. Climbing over Ann's bed and waking her in the process, I pulled back the curtains to be greeted by a dazzling blue sky, and the sun's rays streaming straight through the window with such force that I had to avert my eyes. The light glinted off the shiny embossed gold cross on the black leather-bound cover. It throbbed hypnotically before me as if it were about to detach itself from the book. On opening it I found a sheet of paper containing a single reference to a passage of scripture. Timothy 3:4. I searched uncertainly through the pages until I found the correct passage, which I read in a whisper to Ann.

"He must manage his own family well and see that his children obey him with proper respect."

We began to understand the true meaning of these words when we were called to the table for dinner that evening. As we entered the kitchen Ann froze with shock and moved behind me. It was not just the sight of our mother sitting at the table that scared us so. After weeks of seeing her prostrate, her hair matted and wild, her bedclothes turning grey and stained, we were taken aback by how immaculately groomed she looked. The only thing new was her dress. It was chaste, dour and pattern-less in its design. Her pregnant belly was barely noticeable beneath it. Upon seeing our fear, she beckoned us towards her. As we edged nearer, Ann began to cry.

"Hey now girls, there's no need for tears. I'm here now, you don't need to worry anymore."

"But Daddy's gone and-"

She raised her finger to her lips to silence me.

"There are things you girls are going to find hard to understand. Your daddy was a fallen man. God declined to change his heart, to bestow mercy upon him. He wasn't able to save himself, he wasn't chosen. But your grandfather's going to show us the way."

"He didn't fall, he drove off-"

"Be quiet girl! It was *not* his destiny to be saved. But it is ours, children. It *is* ours."

"What about Beth?!"

Mother clasped her stomach.

"She's here now."

The room spun and my legs shook beneath me. My grandfather pointed for us to take our seats. Across the table sat a woman that was at once my mother and not my mother. Her informalities and inflections seemed to have been stripped away and replaced by a language and demeanor so radically singular and unwavering. Her old self had been stripped away, it existed only in my memories and Ann's. Grandfather took his seat and placed his huge hands, his fingers spread open, upon the table.

"Now I know these words of destiny, God, and salvation mean little to you. This is natural. It's natural because people aren't inclined to believe in God. It's not even up to us to choose to follow and believe in God. That is down to Him. Sin is our natural state. It is our master and companion until God declares its end. We cannot save ourselves from this state. No act of goodness, of virtue or righteousness we undertake will lead us to our redemption or salvation. We can only wait and pray that His irresistible grace enters our lives and He will elect us. Children, I have been elected. Unconditionally elected. Through me, my family has been elected too. Your minds may be young but a single day in this world is enough for a thousand bites of the apple. But through me you will no longer be objects of wrath, like your father was: our election has set you apart."

Though beset by confusion and fear, the certainty and conviction is his voice was thrilling. A child without boundaries is ultimately an unhappy one, and I could see them now being lain down before me. Though I did not understand the meaning of his proclamations, they had a warm narcotic air that drew me intently in. My father and sister were gone, my mother was a stranger, and I yearned for a sense of permanence and purpose. Those were the very things my grandfather seemed to offer. For so long he had barely acknowledged my presence and here he now sat, his eyes rarely leaving mine, his words directed to me.

The question that now begged to be asked was how he, how we, had been chosen. He smiled, satisfied that I had asked the right thing. Once our plates were clean, he moved to the lounge and sat in the large oak chair. Ann and I were ushered over by my mother to sit at his feet. He placed his huge hands upon the tops of our heads and asked if we were ready to listen. Even though we professed our eagerness to hear him, he began to press his fingers into our skulls to the point where we felt the need to cry out in both pain and ecstasy. When he finally removed his hands it was as if we could still feel them there.

3. The Story of Election

That first meal with my grandfather and mother would prove to be our very own Eucharist. It was from here that our family would be reborn, and our relationship with the world would change forever.

Kneeling upon the floor, we gazed expectantly at Grandfather. His hair seemed to tumble across his head like great grey waves as he steeling himself for the rendition of his life. He scanned the room as if a crowd were before him, jostling for every inch of space and waiting upon every breath to escape his body. Mother sat to his right, her face expressionless and numb. Yet her pregnant belly seemed more like a barren void than a nourishing womb. Raising a palm to the invisible masses before him, he finally began.

"Perhaps I will spare you every detail of my younger life. Though, it would seem, looking how the years have worn upon this old face, the details did not spare me. I was born in a town at the edge of the desert in a house unfit for animals, the second of the seven children that Henry and Violet Marlin bore. My conception was the last act my father performed before he was sent to fight in the jungles of the east. An unskilled laborer by trade, he returned to us a disease-ridden drunk with no prospect of suitable employment. When the bourbon began to flow in his veins by late morning, he would make use of his time by beating my mother instead. The threat of his belt buckle was constant. Henry Marlin would fill us with tales of his bravery abroad while we looked on terrified at his cowardice at home. In the evenings he would sob and curse in the corner of the house as he drank each of his long dead friends under the table once more, Mother fretting as she cooked him a dinner from the meagre scraps he provided. She would rather his wrath visit her than me or my older brother Jimmy. The sound of her muffled screams would still penetrate the walls as we tried to sleep in the freezing desert night. As she fell time and again with one child after another, the bruises on my mother's tired face would change color as slowly as the seasons.

"As for work, Henry could not hold a saw steady until the demon drink had passed his lips, and neither could he hold it at all once too much had passed, though the townsfolk of Little Rock mostly turned a blind eye to the misgivings of a hero of the war and gave him irregular jobs fixing up their properties. The small amount he made from this did not reflect his circumstances; by 1953 I had five more brothers and sisters, each barely ten months apart. Seven children shared two beds in one room, the house slowly falling apart around us. My brother Jimmy and I tried to help the family financially from a young age. By the time I was eight I was cutting lawns with a pair of rusting sheers, or standing on corners with a filthy rag in my hand offering to shine the shoes of anyone who walked past. We became the sole source of income for the family in 1954. Drunk out of his mind, my father had been attempting to patch up a roof when he knocked his tool box off the edge of the gutter. As he tried to descend the ladder, a bottle of Tennessee's finest swirling around in his overalls, he slipped and fell to earth, his neck snapping as if it were a rubber band. Apart from his wife and children, his funeral was attended by just one member of his old platoon who stood and quietly shook as my father's body was lowered into the ground. He knew and missed my father like we never could.

Prosperity grew everywhere around us, while we lived as if from a different century. mother could not help but turn hard and bitter, for time and experience had brought little else but struggle and cruelty. The eldest of the children were left with little option but to fend for the family in any way we could and I admit to you now that there are very few things that I have not stolen. Jimmy and I lifted tins of fruit from store shelves, snatched chickens from their coops, took coins from the pockets of drunks, freed tools from the sheds of our neighbors. In the dead of night we would raid and ransack properties of all descriptions and leave with anything we could carry. We were caught and beat more times than I can remember, but no punishment or retribution was ever strong enough to make us quit."

Rising from his chair, my grandfather turned around and lifted up his shirt. On the left side of his back were a dozen round, thick scars. He turned so the stretched skin of the scars glinted in the dim light. A shiver of excitement pulsed through me.

"I received these emblems of ill-gotten gain while running across open farm land. Reeking with sweat and fear, a stolen transistor radio in my hand and someone's medical prescription in my pocket; the farmer whose house I had broken into hit me from some distance with a blast of buckshot. Once I picked myself up, tears streaming down my face and blood staining my clothes, I simply continued to run. As the local doctor sat removing the shot from my skin, Mother never asked what I had been doing or how Jimmy and I came by the money we did. Even the doctor knew it was a fool's errand to ask why I wasn't in school with the rest of the town's children. The stench of poverty clung to you as soon as you walked through the front door. But it never left me, whether I was in the house or not.

"What money we made from selling what we stole was never enough. By my late teenage years two of my siblings died from a combination of malnutrition and pneumonia. Their deaths fed the guilt that came from my inability to provide for my family. From that point on, the nature of my crimes would escalate, each one outstripping the last in its immorality. I broke the jaws of men who had stumbled out of late night bars and made the mistake of taking a darkened path home. Sometimes we would take the very shoes from their feet and leave them whimpering or unconscious on the sidewalk. We flagged down pick-ups on back roads, pretending to need a lift into neighboring towns. If they were kind enough to stop we would pull them from the vehicle, drag them kicking and screaming to the verge and make off with their vehicle. The only schooling we received was from men whose foundations were dishonesty and deception; as the seriousness of our crimes grew, we began to associate with those who took their crime seriously. It was all too easy to find someone to take a stolen car off our hands, or to ship the liquor we'd robbed from a wholesaler's yard. Given the number of terrible acts we committed it was surprising that we were not caught during those years of disgrace. That, at least, was one of the advantages to living in a town in the middle of nowhere in particular, a town of no importance to anyone of importance. I am ashamed to admit that not only were we good at what we did, but we took every pleasure in our actions. Though the money troubles of our family were eased and we could afford to bring my mother a small taste of the luxuries she had previously been denied, the tendency for wrongdoing was now deep inside us. It flowed alongside the ice in our veins. When Jimmy and I first embraced the criminal life it was a means to an end, a means to get money, a means to keep our family alive. But it is often said that you become what you do, and being a criminal became an end in itself.

"There was, however, a big difference between myself and my brother Jimmy; the first time the police caught up with us and entered our family home a sense of shame ran through me like it never had before. Heart racing and knuckles whitening as they gripped the armrest of the chair, I could not look my mother in the face. But when they began to question us Jimmy sat there brimming with pride. He knew they had nothing concrete on us, and set about taking advantage of this. My brother stretched out his long body and clasped his hands behind his head as if he were ready to sleep, a smile as wide as a slice of watermelon on his face. The officers did not take kindly to his casual, sarcastic manner. The senior of the two stood there, a holstered gun at his side, his impatience growing at the silence that had greeted his inquiries.

"He kicked Jimmy's legs apart and said 'I asked you a question.' 'Ask me again,' replied Jimmy. The officer looked across at my mother who sat there as if a ghost, a half-remembered thought of the human being she once was. Life had stripped her of all surprise and care. The officer turned back to Jimmy.

'This is your Mother's house boy, so I've cut you some slack here, but your answers better start coming thick and fast. Now where were you?'

"Jimmy looked him straight in the eye and said 'We were both here. It was milk and cookies night. We never miss milk and cookies night, ain't that right, Ma?!' Well girls, panic spread through me like a fever, and I wanted to bolt for the door. Jimmy sat there laughing to himself as if this were a stage show put on for his benefit. The officer, rage now simmering beneath his calm exterior, did not take kindly to being an unwilling actor in this scene.

'Boy, we might not fit you for this but your card is marked, you hear me? You're just too dumb to not get caught eventually. What's so damn funny about that?' he snapped at Jimmy.

'Well' drawled Jimmy, "It's your badge officer, it's on upside down. Looks like Russian. Maybe you're a Commie.'

"The younger officer strode towards Jimmy, his Billy club clenched in his fist. I jumped in between them and tried to reason with them.

'Please, he's sorry officer, he's just playing with you, being an ass, and really he's sorry. It wasn't us, we were out of town that night, we got witnesses if you need them.'

"The older officer dragged his colleague back.

'I bet your witnesses are real reputable types too. Like I said, you boys are marked. There's gonna be eyes on you wherever you go. You'll be getting written up if you so much as breathe near a place you shouldn't be.'

"And girls, that officer was as good as his word. Patrol cars seemed to haunt every step Jimmy and I took after that day. We found ourselves face down on pavements, hands cuffed behind our backs on suspicion of every unaccounted-for felony in Little Rock, spent nights in the drunk tank when we hadn't touched a drop of liquor. On several occasions we were driven out to the desert and left to spend the day walking home, our skin red and blistered from the unforgiving sun. The soles of our feet became intimate with the clubs of every local officer. We were harried and hounded from morning until night. The noise of sirens even seemed to seep into our dreams.

"Not only did this harassment mean that money dried up quicker than a creek in a heat wave, but it led to Jimmy becoming more determined than ever to up the stakes of our lives and go for the biggest score we could imagine. The pride that often overwhelmed him meant that he could not face being outwitted by the law. Jimmy needed to show superiority over those that chased him. I tried at first to talk him out of this grand act of revenge but there was no moving him. What else would or could we do, he reasoned. What education or chance did we have?

"I carried on refusing right up until our mother died. When she was late rising one morning, Jimmy walked in to her room to find her kneeling by the side of bed, her hands in prayer and eyes staring into the hereafter. She had died a long time before this. My father had in reality killed her long ago and her body had somehow kept on, a mere memory of movement. Our two youngest brothers and our sister were whisked away to the state's child protection service almost as soon as my mother's casket was lowered into the earth, patrol cars lying in wait on the gravel drive of the cemetery. We would never see them again. What had we left but a derelict home within which to lead our derelict lives?

"Jimmy and I both felt like animals. We were backed into a corner, starving and ready to bite anything that provoked us. This was the life we had chosen and it seemed that this life led only one way. Knowing my brother was going to do this with or without me, I had no choice but to be there with him. So it was that at seventeen years of age I agreed with my brother to rob the First National bank in the middle of our little town. And in agreeing to this I knew it would mean, in one way or another, the end of our life there.

"Being high on adrenaline and ignorance, we did not plan the robbery beyond walking into the bank and demanding they give us every bit of cash they had. All we needed was a car and a gun. When clearing out my mother's room, Jimmy had found my father's old army issue revolver stashed beneath the mattress, a solitary bullet lodged in its barrel. We would take the first car we found with a full gas tank. It was a bright July morning when we walked from the house for the final time, desperate young men ready to perform a desperate act. As we looked back upon the crumbling edifice of our home, nothing surrounding it but bush and dirt, Jimmy reached into his pocket and pulled out a box of matches. He walked back into the house, doused the parlor with a bottle of booze that had sat there untouched since our father died, and set the place alight. Jimmy joined me back outside and we watched the flames quickly strangle and suffocate its flimsy frame. No one else would be able to enter our home, to sift through our past, and glimpse that snapshot of our misery. Turning away, we walked towards the road that led to town. After a few hundred yards we found a sky blue Chevrolet with white fins parked on the shoulder of the road. Looking to the grassy plane that led from the road we could see the owner of the vehicle in the distance, a woman moving beneath him on the ground. The keys hung limply in the ignition, inviting us to take control. In seconds we were hurtling along the empty road, heat rising off it as we headed towards our fate. As we hit the edge of Little Rock we slowed to a steady pace. People passed by us in a dream-like state on every sidewalk, their orderliness and civility like the strange customs of another country.

"Upon reaching the bank, the enormity of what we were about to undertake began to dawn upon me. It was the grandest building in town, its marble columns reaching up twenty feet and glistening in the morning sun. A security guard stood smoking outside, laughing and joking with customers about matters we could never understand as they went in and out about their business. Jimmy passed me a paper bag and whispered quietly into my ear.

'So brother, here we are. Now I'm going to keep the gun, you just put you hand inside this and give the impression you've got one too. When they see mine they won't question yours.'

"I asked him what we'd do about the security guard.

33

'Don't worry about him either. I'll deal with him. When we're inside you go for the tellers and I'll make nice with the manager see if we can't come to an agreement about an interest-free lifetime loan.'

"Sweat had begun to roll down the side of my face. Jimmy wiped it away and gripped my shoulder with his hand, telling me everything was going to turn out fine. Once the guard went inside we slipped from the car and followed him. A tide of air-conditioned cool wrapped itself around us as soon as we were inside. People waited patiently in line to cash checks, withdraw money, and discuss mortgages. The domed ceiling above me seemed to spin like a Ferris wheel, the figures in the frieze coming alive as it span and knocked my breath out of step. I watched as Jimmy moved to the guard and tapped him upon the shoulder, revolver now out of his waistband. As the guard looked around, Jimmy cocked him across his nose with the butt of the gun, blood gushing onto the cold white floor. He bellowed at the top of his voice as the guard lay moaning at his feet.

'Good morning ladies and gents! If you'd be so kind as to get your behinds down on the floor, what's just happened to this fella here won't happen to you. Now believe me when I say that my brother and I don't want to use the nasty things in our hands. But if you step out of place, we won't have any choice but to.'

"Jimmy pointed for me to move towards the tellers. It appeared my legs had frozen and no act of will could make them move at that moment. Women had begun to cry as Jimmy repeated his threats, the pool of blood at his feet a warning to all. Men murmured insults and swore retribution under their breath. The alarm had probably already been triggered, but we figured to be gone before anyone could react to it. Jimmy waved me ever more fervently towards the tellers at the counter, my hand trembling inside the paper bag. He called out for the bank manager to come forward. The manager, a grossly overweight man in an ill-fitting suit, raised himself like a wrecking ball from the floor, but only after Jimmy threatened to shoot the guard in the back. Taking my first furtive steps towards the counter I noticed a man still standing amid the human detritus upon the floor. Fear drove me quickly over to him; after asking the tellers to load whatever cash they had in a sack I threw at them, I calmly requested he sat himself upon the floor alongside everybody else. Instead of acting upon my command he simply smiled at me and took a glance at his watch as if we were waiting at a bus stop together. I raised my voice and said 'Mister, didn't you hear me? I'm not gonna ask you nicely next time, don't be a hero now.'

"As Jimmy dragged the manager behind the counter towards the vault, the man before me continued to act as if all was right with the world. Dressed head to toe in black, his dark hair slicked sideward across his head, he radiated a serenity I could barely imagine. Reaching out his hand towards me, his palm to the heavens, he began to address me.

'You think you're in control here, don't you son? Well here's some good news for you: you're not. And what's more, you can't save yourself here. That's not up to anyone but the Lord above. But maybe you should think about letting these good folk here go. I'll hang around, you can tell me what it is you think you're achieving by this and I'll just sit and listen. Maybe I can help. Besides, what are you going to do – shoot me with the bag you brought your lunch in?'

"Stunned by his defiance and the way his words, delivered in such melodic southern tones, seemed to penetrate the furthest recesses of my mind, the bag slipped from hand and lay pathetically upon the ground. He took that hand in his and continued.

'I've a feeling there's something special about you son. Like, in the year of our Lord 1961, we've been brought together on this today for a purpose. I had a most peculiar sense about the day as soon as I opened my eyes this morning. Now I know why. Come on, son – look at the fear and anguish you've created in this room. Have these good folk at your feet done anything to deserve that? I think you're here for me, not them. Now let's put a stop to this.'

"At that moment I wanted nothing more than for it all to be over. The police were sure to be close, and as the head teller passed me back the sack, I looked quickly inside to see only a fistful of notes resting at its bottom. Confused, I looked up at the teller.

'It's Friday, hon. Jesus, even my kids know every Thursday night we ship out most of our funds. Your friend won't find barely a bean in the main vault either. This is Little Rock, not Vegas. You listen to Minister Earl here.'

"The man who stood before me was indeed a man of God. He took me by the shoulders, looked me straight in my eyes and introduced himself.

'I'm Minister Earl Peaks, son. Now from that fact alone I think you'll comprehend that I'm a serious man, that I don't say a single word lightly. Why don't you tell me your name and we can go from there?'

"Before I could answer, Jimmy reappeared, shouting and cussing behind the counter. He kicked the manager, now sporting a large open gash above his eye, under the counter hatch before vaulting over the top of it himself. Surveying the odd scene before him, he began to unravel.

'Frank, what the hell are you doing?! There's hardly a damn cent back there and this fat piece of garbage won't tell me where it's all hiding. And why the hell are these people still standing up?! Get down on the floor now or I'll put a hole in your faces that's bigger than a fist, so help me God. I turn my back for a minute and the world goes crazy.'

"While the teller dropped to the ground when Jimmy kicked the manager once more, Minister Earl stood even taller. Jimmy's reaction was one of disbelief.

"Mother Mary, we got no damn money but we got ourselves a hero. I said get the hell on the ground!"

"He pointed the gun square at Minister Earl's head, but the minister's only reaction was to sigh as if he were mildly disappointed. As I sat there, sure that my brother was about to take this man's life, I was taken by the most extraordinary feeling, like God himself was whispering in my ear. This was not my path, not my place, and not my fate. Neither was it the fate of Minister Earl to die. I implored my brother to stop.

'Jimmy, we've gone too far. Let's just end this; we ain't got barely a dollar between us for crying out loud – it's not worth it. This minister here, he's just trying to help us, leave him be, please. Jimmy, we still got time to get out of here.'

'God damn you Frank Joseph Marlin, you're listening to a stranger before your own brother! I'm not leaving here until the minister here gets his holy ass down on the floor, or I put him down. And besides we're not leaving without the money we came for.'

"Seeing that Minister Earl was never going to comply, Jimmy cocked back the stiff hammer of the old service revolver

'I guess you get to talk to your boss a bit sooner than you thought.'

"Before he could squeeze out the round I lunged forward and forced his arm up towards the ceiling. Hearing my own brother scream that I was Judas was like a knife to the gut. It will echo through the rest of my days. Now as we struggled he began to overpower me, and with the barrel of the gun pointing at my face I watched as he point blank pulled the trigger. The only sound however was the click of the hammer. He had not aligned the barrel with the one bullet the chamber of the gun held. I summoned up the energy to throw Jimmy a few feet from me, and as he stood there, shamed and startled that he almost killed his own brother, a hail of shotgun blasts from the back of the bank ripped his body apart.

"As the sound of the shots reverberated around the room and slowly faded, I surrendered myself to the police. They flooded the room like a swarm of ants. I lay myself face down upon the floor, placed my hands behind my back and waited to be cuffed. Assured I was going nowhere, they left me to see to others in the bank, not least the manager, whose vast body they struggled to heave to its feet. Closing my eyes as tightly as I could, I lay there in the blood that drained from the body of my brother and the wreckage of what was once my life. It was then that Minister Earl knelt by my side, placed his hand upon my head and told me that I, Frank Joseph Marlin, had been unconditionally elected by God. Yet all I could do was reach out for my Jimmy.

'My brother. My *brother*. He called me Judas...Judas!'

'Oh, son. It's your brother who's Judas. And if he is Judas then you...you're the one who he's betrayed.'

"As he raised his hands in prayer toward the ceiling of the bank a strange sense of elation and righteousness swept through me. It was as if a door to another existence had been opened, its heat and light dazzling enough to burn the very eyes from my head. It was as if everything I had done – each vicious, criminal act – had merely been the means to get me to that point. I knew unequivocally that I had been spared, just like you were in that wheat field, Laura Jo. Do you see that sacred thread that runs between us all in this room? For it is not only blood that binds us, but the absolute will of God himself."

Ann and I sat motionless at Grandfather's feet , entranced by every sound and syllable he had uttered. Before us now stood an emissary of the almighty, the word made ragged flesh.

4. With the Same Lump of Clay

Grandfather's story was not yet done. As the months fell past us, we slowly learnt of his strange journey from bank robber to ordained minister, from non-believer to devout follower of the Calvinist faith. We, as a family, were transformed as the tale unfolded, its lessons and rules becoming the very foundations of our existence. Every thought in ours heads and word from our mouths was slowly reshaped by the beliefs that my grandfather instilled deep within us. As this new family took shape from the ashes of the old, we were taught to adhere to one absolute, unquestionable truth: life is religion, religion is life. There was no part in our waking lives that God did not play a role in, no aspect that He did not ultimately control. And my grandfather became the vessel through which God Himself spoke, planned and governed.

Grandfather may have established the rules by which we lived, but it was my mother who vigorously enforced them. Any deviation from them would bring the swiftest reprimand, or threat to retract the love she had for us. Having already lost my father, the thought of losing her in any way was enough to ensure an unswerving obedience. Her transformation in this time had been the greatest. She was no longer capable of any real warmth and her capacity for joy had been stripped bare. In their place was a fierce, unrelenting devotion to my grandfather and a conviction that our lives had a higher, greater purpose.

Beyond this, we were lonely, impressionable girls, too young to properly reason and question, whose minds were ripe for molding. Our grandfather was a powerful, charismatic man and the story he put before us was unimaginably alluring. All children want to feel special and his story, and its consequences for our family, meant that we were perhaps more special than anyone we knew. In time, we became nourished by the thought that God, in His great wisdom, had set us apart; that we were the few that had been chosen.

Now at the head of our table sat my grandfather, a small town Moses returned from the mountain with a tablet of stone burned into his heart. The Shepherd had been reunited with his wayward flock, and he set about reconstructing our family's past to remodel our future. Every previous experience and situation was refracted through the lens of his Calvinistic doctrine until it did not reflect the reality of the moments we had lived and shared in any way. It began with my father: who we thought he was, how he spoke, and what he stood for would gradually be altered. Memory turned out to be the most malleable of things, an untrustworthy source of information that should be conditioned and feared. In the months following his death, the image of our father still haunted Ann and me. We instinctively expected him to return at any moment; to hear the sound of his truck tires churning and spitting out the gravel outside; his boots scraping on the mat that no longer read 'welcome'; the deep timbre of his voice calling us towards him. Ann would frequently ask Mother to make sure she saved some food for when he came home. At first Mother would not even respond to her plea, but I could sense the anger inside her beginning to scrape and crawl its way to the surface. Her fists would clench so tightly it seemed as if her very knuckles were about to break through the thin white skin of her hands. I was certain that she would strike out at us should the talk of our father continue in this manner.

The tipping point was reached one early autumn evening. As dusk descended upon us, the skies swirling with virulent purples and oranges, I saw Mother and Grandfather carrying armfuls of my father's clothing and assorted belongings out of the back of the house. I followed them out onto the porch and came across the pyre of his possessions they were assembling. The creaking sound of the swing seat swaying as the breeze tipped it to and fro was the only noise that pierced the silence. I began to cry before rushing towards the heap and attempting to scoop up as much as I could in my small arms. Mother screamed 'Enough!' as she fiercely ripped the garments away from me and threw them disdainfully back onto the terrible flaming altar of belongings.

"These are my daddy's things!"

"Laura Jo Marlin, I've warned you for the last time. I will not have you near me if you carry on seeing fit to mention him!"

Even father's name 'Carter' had been erased from our family. Now 'Marlin' was forced upon us by Mother. It was an alien, parasitic word that gradually soaked its way deep into your consciousness through the sheer force of repetition. As the standoff between my mother and I intensified, Grandfather strode quickly between us and intervened.

"Josephine, go and get Ann. I think it's time we let them recognize the truth of the matter, let them know how you were all wronged by this man."

Ann was brought forth, her arm straining as Mother dragged her unceremoniously down the porch steps which we were both then made to sit down upon. Standing high above us my grandfather turned and pointed towards the pyre.

"The man who wore those clothes, who used those objects, and lived in this house, was enslaved to the service of sin, as are we all. It was his master from the moment he first drew breath, to the moment the last air slipped from his lungs. He was not capable of choosing God, of servicing the interests of anyone but himself. His heart and head were never houses in which God would reside."

Crouching down low, he placed his huge hands upon my and Ann's chests, his gaze searing straight through us.

"But he does reside in here. Because you, like I, have been chosen. Your father was not. Christ's death upon the cross did not atone for everyone's sins. It atoned for the sins of those who God elects, who God *chooses* to be saved. Now when James Carter's truck left that road it was God's will, God's plan. The Almighty predestined this to happen, as He does for all things. Your father would leave your mother and you girls for days at a time; he would leave you to fall into the arms of women who were not his wife, to be with women barely old enough to bear children. He would even use you children as the bait with which to capture the affections of those he wished to visit his lust upon. So God let his lust lead him to his fate upon that mountain. As it is written: "All have turned away, they have together become worthless; there is no one who does good, not even one." But God chooses both those who will be saved, and those who will meet unending death. And in death he abandoned your mother and you once more. This had to happen for our family to find its way back to the path that the elect must walk. To bring you back to me."

In that moment the innocent way I had looked upon my father's relationships with his clients melted into thin air, and corrosive, poisonous thoughts began to quietly blossom in their place. I did not understand the physical nature of relationships at the time, but I did understand the notion of betrayal. While I could not or did not truly believe my father's dealings were anything more than business, a single drop of doubt was enough to begin undermining the past, and our family as we knew it; the mental picture of my father greeting Cordelia Jones with a kiss, a kiss to an old client and friend, became something altogether more sinister and meaningful; a shoulder around the arm of Janey Tullow as she thanked him for building her a new bureau became a sign post of other, hidden intimacies. James Carter's transition from martyred saint to Godless pawn had begun.

Having already been schooled in the notion of Unconditional Election, my grandfather now used my father's death to begin to teach us to believe in what was termed Total Depravity and Limited Atonement. He then used my mother to teach us one more doctrine. Taking her by the shoulders he turned her to face the pyre. From his pocket he removed a box of matches and handed it to her. As he poured a bottle of white spirit over my father's possessions, my mother threw lit match after lit match upon it. Toxic fumes began to tarnish the air around us. On the top of the pyre sat a box in which I thought I had last placed the tiny carving of Jesus upon the cross which my father had me varnish. When the flames reached the box it fell down the face of the burning blackening mass beneath it, spilling its contents. Mother turned around and came to embrace Ann and I, her mood radically altered by the sight of her husband's smoldering shirts and shoes, records and memorabilia.

"It's for our own good, my sweet babies. These things have no place in our home, no place in the Lord's plan for us. You've got to realize you're not ordinary children. We were always supposed to be at my father's side."

As she spoke to us she tenderly held her pregnant belly. When the baby that resided inside was mentioned it was always called Beth; my mother and grandfather spoke of the impending birth as her 'reawakening.' Ann and I unreservedly believed that it was our sister returned to be with us. It was easier for a child to accept this as fact than to accept the reality of her death or, worse still, imagine her buried beneath the cold, hard cemetery ground. No funeral was ever held for either her or my father.

Around us, night had begun to usurp the day and the pyre before us took on the air of a primitive sacrifice, the last memories of my father surrendered to a terrible, unconsecrated hell. Grandfather beckoned us all closer to watch and feel the heat of its flames.

"Girls, you cannot run from the Lord. If He has deemed fit to work His way inside your heart there is no escape, no exit. His Irresistible Grace is more powerful than anything you can imagine. For years your mother was led away from the path He designed for her, but look at her before you now. See the strength of her faith, her courage to concede her will to that of God. She could not ultimately turn her face away from her true calling; no human has a resolution strong enough to overcome God's desire. His seeds simply lay dormant within her, ready to grow at the time of His choosing."

At that instant, with his words circling like vultures above us and his eyes shining with an intensity that was almost too much to bear, he looked as if he was connected to something beyond mere flesh. Despite my growing reverence for my grandfather, I felt compelled to slip back outside before dinner and feel blindly around in the dark until I found the tiny figure my father had given me. I took it to my room, and found a safe hiding place for it, this last remnant of the father I had known.

***

We began our days with an hour of Bible study, my grandfather selecting parts of both the Old and New Testaments for us to read. He would then go into great detail as to their meaning, and often use them to show the failings, flaws and godless faults of a wide variety of local and public people, from a man he knew who worked at a local sawmill to the President of the United States himself. In the middle of his fervor he would actively encourage us to rebuke them, to not be afraid of voicing our disdain for their wretched, unelected existence. We were far too inhibited at that tender age to do so. Sometimes he would even highlight the special significance of Bible stories to our own family. One such occasion stuck in my mind more than most. He had chosen the story of Abraham and he asked us to pay close attention to his binding of Isaac. After we had gone through the passages, his huge frame toppled the chair as he rose from it in one fierce movement. To an outsider, Grandfather would no doubt have seemed extremely aloof, his intentional coldness and distance designed to prickle the hairs on your neck. But when it came to discussing scripture or the place of our family in the order of God's world he was energy incarnate, seemingly possessed by the very Spirit himself.

"You see, Abraham was given the terrible duty of sacrificing his own son, to show his devotion to the Lord. He bound his son Isaac to the altar and was willing to strike him down with the knife that burned in his hand."

"He wouldn't have really though, would he?"

Ann's face was ashen. Since my father had passed, any mention of death or dying saw her physically recoil.

"Yes, he would not have hesitated to do so. How could he resist the grace, the will of God? When your father first met your mother I struggled in vain to keep them apart, as I knew that all he had to offer was certain ruin. But my cause was a fruitless one, for it began to interfere with the things that God himself wanted me to accomplish in this world. So I sacrificed both your mother, and therefore you, by allowing James Carter to raise you."

"But Daddy loved us!"

"James Carter may have professed he loved you, but he did not love God, and he could therefore not love you truly. Now as Abraham was about to deal a mortal blow to Isaac, an angel appeared and revealed to him that God had been testing him, and that Isaac was not to be sacrificed. In the bush nearby he found the ram, which took the place of Isaac and was offered up to God. I believe that God in His way had tested me, to part me from my family to show my devotion. In my dreams I began to see your faces over and over again and I knew this was a sign that we should be reunited. When I returned to this house God's real plan unfolded; I was to save you, Laura Jo, from the jaws of that harvester, as well as the very soul of this family. It was your father, like the ram in the bushes, who was to be the true sacrifice."

After he had finished with us, his strange, alluring logic burrowing ever further inside our heads, we would take breakfast and then complete any outstanding chores. Mother would then home school us as she had done previously. Except that everything we now learnt, or re-learnt, was through the gaze of her re-established Calvinist beliefs. Strict rules were also established by my mother as to the color, style and nature of our clothing. Gone were the bright blue or red summer dresses I once adored and in their place were now long, pattern-less white ones. This, she told us, was a symbol of our purity, of our connection to God. She herself would only ever dress in grey. When we had finished our evening meal, my grandfather would then begin to recount his Story of Election, and refused our pleas to take the tale beyond his arrest at the bank. He would simply tell us we were not yet ready, that we did not yet know enough about our fledgling faith to truly comprehend the consequences of what had taken place.

Ann and I were sent on a rare trip beyond the grounds of our family home. Usually it was Grandfather who would make regular trips to town or to local stores to bring back the domestic goods we needed, for though she was no longer bed-ridden, Mother had yet to venture further than our garden. As Grandfather had left the house straight after Bible study that morning, Ann and I had been tasked to walk to a neighboring farm to buy a dozen eggs. Money in hand, we began the half mile walk to Ms. Simmons' sprawling homestead. Instead of taking the long, twisting road to her property we decided to cut directly across the grassy plain that stretched for miles to the east. Once you crossed the narrow willow-strewn river that ran adjacent to the road, it was almost a straight journey to the gates of the farm. Upon approaching the gate we saw a Mexican man sleeping in a fold-out chair, and a make-shift stall laden with fruit and vegetables for sale to his side. His feet were bare, his shirt half open and the straw hat he sported looked half-eaten. It was no fit guard against the unrelenting sun. Sensing our presence, he stirred from his morning slumber.

"Oh, hey girls. Good morning to you. Just resting my eyes for a minute there. I guess you're looking to buy some fruit? Or vegetables maybe – we've got some beautiful sugar-beets here this season."

His smile was so broad it almost annexed the rest of his face.

"No sir, our mother sent us for some eggs."

"Ah, eggs. None right here. Run on up to the house and June will shake those chickens down for you."

"June?"

He laughed good-naturedly at our confusion.

"Ms. Simmons. Her name is June. You can call her that, she won't mind at all. She only makes me call her Ms. Simmons when I'm in trouble. Which is more often than I'd like!"

Pulling himself up from his chair, he opened the gate and ushered us up the sloping path to the house. When we were halfway along it, he called out.

"And while you're there, tell her I'm getting a little parched down here – I could do with a nice, cold sarsaparilla."

We waved our consent and continued up the path. The house itself had seen better days; the paint flaked all across its façade, the insect mesh curled away from the windows like lemon peel, and gaps plagued the roof where slates should have been. Just as we reached the porch the door was flung open and four children of different ages ran shouting and screaming through it. They fled past Ann and I down into the garden, and all leapt straight into the large plastic canvas paddling pool that swallowed up the lawn. As they splashed and cavorted around, Ms. Simmons came to the door.

"Well, hey there girls! I've not seen your pretty selves since your daddy... since before you and your daddy delivered that garden swing over there. Now, how's your poor mother holding up? Everyone in the neighborhood is always wondering, always fretting about her."

"She's fine, thank you Ms. Simmons. My grandfather's looking after us. He's looking after us all."

"Gosh, now there's no need for you young ladies to be so formal. June's my name. You pass Josephine on our love. How can I help you, anyway?"

When she went to her kitchen to retrieve our order of a dozen eggs, I noticed that her two youngest boys were far darker-skinned than her two girls. She returned with a bag not only stuffed with eggs, but with an assortment of tomatoes as well.

"We've got more than we can eat. I'm sure your mother will put them to far better use."

After paying for the eggs and thanking her, I turned to go. Ann remained rooted to the spot and tugged at the side of my dress.

"What about the man? He was thirsty."

I had completely forgotten about his request. Looking anywhere but at her, I awkwardly broached the issue with Ms. Simmons.

"Oh, the man down there, the man by the gate, he asked if he could have a drink. He wanted sarsaparilla. We don't want to get him in trouble. Does he work for you?"

"Work for me? Ha! Chance would be a fine thing, Laura Jo. I think he was born bone idle. Tells me he's upholding a family tradition, and yet his brothers are the most energetic, hard-working men I've ever seen, so I don't buy that line. So no, he doesn't work for me. Paulo is my partner, we live here together."

"He's your husband?"

"I'm afraid we're both no longer the marrying kind, darlin'. We've been there before and it didn't best suit us – the two girls, Boxy and Ruth, are from my first. They were the only good things that came out of it. The youngest little terrors there are mine and Paulo's. He might be a little on the lazy side, but he's a good man when all's said and done. I just like to moan about him – it's a woman's privilege, isn't it? Well, you'll know what I'm talking about when you get a little older."

I stood there upon this kind, gentle woman's porch, her beautiful, happy children chasing each other in and out of the water, her partner contentedly dozing in his chair. As I looked back at her through the open door, I narrowed my eyes, and saw nothing but sin. It crawled over her face, her arms, her apron, knotting like snakes below her hips. Her boys, born without God's anointing, born out of wedlock and into unholy power. The cool balm of my own superiority pulsed through me, made me stiffen my spine. I took my hand off the doorframe, feeling it might contaminate me suddenly. It seemed to me that their ragged, crumbling house was a sign, a reflection of those who lived within it. Thanking her once again, I pulled Ann down the porch steps and whispered to Ann not to look back at Ms. Simmons. She called after us to let Paulo know that she would soon bring down his drink. We did not acknowledge her. On the way back home we stopped by the river and sat on the bank. As the branches of the willows danced rhythmically before me, and the sun lent our skins a luminous glow, I felt there was an order and power to the world far beyond what we could simply see and feel, and that my family was deeply connected to that.

"Ann, those people who we just met. You know we're different to them, don't you?"

She shrugged and nodded at the same time. "I liked their pool. We haven't got a pool."

We left the bank and moved on to the gravel path that led to the bridge. Ann had asked if she could carry the bag of eggs and tomatoes and I had reluctantly agreed. As we walked she began to swing the bag slightly. The bottom of the bag tore open, scattering half of the goods all over the gravel beneath and half down the sloping bank. As I voiced my annoyance at Ann's lack of care and we desperately clambered to pick up the strewn goods, I suddenly stopped, utterly amazed at what I saw. Not a single egg had been broken, but each tomato had been damaged in some way; their skins torn and juices seeping out on to the earth. I made Ann collect only the eggs, which she then placed in my folded-up dress.

"You see, don't you? He only wants us to have these. We didn't ask for anything else that she gave us."

When our grandfather returned home later that afternoon he came into our bedroom to find me reading out a passage of scripture to Ann. He asked us what and why I was reading and I explained in great detail what had happened during our visit to Ms. Simmons that's afternoon. Grandfather did not say a word, but simply smiled, ran his hand through my hair and left us to our reading. I knew then that he would finally continue the tale of his election by God.

***

After his arrest, the authorities were unable to throw the full force of the law at Frank Marlin, due to the fact that he was technically still classed as a minor. But it was Minister Earl's standing and influence in the local community that saw the charges significantly watered down; the police, an array of witnesses, the prosecuting attorney and the judge were all harangued, cajoled and mollified by the minister and his associates until a conviction and sentence amenable to all was agreed upon. Though he never once contested his guilt, Frank served only thirty days in county lock-up, before being placed into the care of the minister, who would, for the next three years, become his official guardian. It was, as my grandfather would tell me, as if the whole world had been ripped from its axis and spun the wrong way.

"On the morning of my release from jail, Minister Earl was waiting to meet me, along with his wife Isabelle and their five children.

The children, the eldest of whom was only fourteen, stood in a line, all immaculately dressed and silent as the desert night. There I stood in the filthy clothes given back to me by the state, the smell of damp and rusting iron clinging to me. As Earl introduced me, though polite in their manner, they looked at me as if I had just fallen to earth, a reaction for which I could not blame them. I rode in the front passenger seat next to Minister Earl, whose questions about my welfare were unrelenting. The excitement my presence generated in him seemed more apt for a visiting dignitary than a newly evicted juvenile delinquent.

"As disorientating as the experience was, nothing could prepare me for the sight of the Minister's family home. When the shops and business on the fringes of town gave way to the greenery and orderliness of suburban dwellings, and the rows of houses themselves gave way to the parched fields beyond, the sprawling edifice of my new home gradually came into view. Ornate and mock-colonial in style, it looked as if it had been left there by a tornado that had lifted it straight from New Orleans. Waiting to greet us was a small army of housekeepers, cooks and gardeners, each of whom already knew my name.

"The inside of the house was just as palatial; a grand, arching stairway un-spooled in the center of the main entrance, and the deep, rich wood upon the floors, door archways and windows looked as if it grown from the very foundations of the house itself. I was taken to the bedroom that would be mine alone. It had been freshly painted white, ready for me to decorate in a color and style of my own choosing. Fearing this all to be a grand ruse, a terrible joke that would end with me being thrown out and deserted, I lay on the bed for hours, too scared to move. Mary, the head housekeeper, came later that evening to collect me for dinner. The entire Peaks family was waiting for me once more, standing up in unison as I entered the dining room, ready for me to take my place next to Minister Earl. Seven sets of eyes burned into me as I sat down. As the dinner was brought to the table, Minister Earl readied himself to speak, the air around him bristling with electricity.

'I need not tell my own family about sin, for it lays among us now. Always present, always waiting to spread destruction inside and around us. But though it is our ever-present companion, there are times when sin itself is the means by which someone will be saved by God. When Frank entered the bank two months ago, he believed he was there for one purpose alone – to take money from the pockets of the town. Little did he know that he was there by the will of God, to save me and also himself from the terrible intentions of his own brother, his closest kin. Children, this boy has been sent as a living testimony to God's word, he is a lightning rod that will harness the faith of our community and will channel it to God's own end. Frank will need your care and your prayers to help in this most important of times.'

"It was all too much. I sat looking at the food, not knowing which fork or knife to use, the dizzying beauty of the crystal lights on the walls, and Minister Earl's foreign, harrowing kindness fighting within me against a lifetime of anger and mistreatment. Knocking the chair flying as I rose, I ran towards the entrance hall and tried in vain to open the great bolts and deadlocks upon the door, all the while hearing the minister's calm, steady steps walking towards me. Scratching at the door like a rabid wolf, tears half blinding me, he placed his hand upon my shoulder.

'Easy son, take it easy. I'm sorry. I know this must all be very daunting. Please forgive us for our being so overzealous. We're all just so excited to have you here.'

'What do you want from me? I didn't ask for this. I can take care of myself!'

'It's not what I want, son. It's what the Maker Himself wants. Our paths were intertwined for a purpose, and we neither of us can escape that. In our religion, in Calvinism, there is such a thing called "The Perseverance of the Saints." It means you can't outrun the Lord, wherever you go. If He wants you, He will take you. I can undo that door for you, and you can run from me now. But you cannot second guess the Lord. You'll find yourself once more at my doorstop soon enough.'

'Why would He choose me? Why would He do that? I'm nothing, I'm no one. I've robbed, and fought, and cheated and lied, there's nothing else out there I'm much good for. I ain't been to school, I can barely read, and now I'm sitting at your table and I don't even know what damn fork to pick up. Just let me go!'

"And with that, he let me go. I walked out into the night, left the grounds of the house and carried on in a straight line until I found a road. With nothing but moonlight bearing down upon the tar and the low hum of cicadas in the bush beside me, I continued, tired and weary, for mile after mile. Until, in the distance, at the edge of the county line, I saw a great many flashing blue and red lights. As I neared the illuminations I realized that across the road there lay a metal barrier of police cars. Having nothing hanging over me, I walked up to them and tried to pass. An officer stepped before me, a shotgun held horizontally against his chest.

'What's your name, son? Where do you think you're going?'

"I was going nowhere. A mere hour earlier, a prison transit with a cargo of two inmates had broken down on an empty stretch of highway. While one guard went for help, and the other tried to fix the problem himself, the prisoners managed to free themselves, overpower the guard and flee into the night. Having nothing to prove my identity, I was driven back to Minister Earl, the only man for miles who knew who I was. The door of the minister's great house had been left wide open, and the troopers and I walked straight in. Minister Earl sat at the now empty dining room table. He had been patiently awaiting my return, for there was not a doubt in his mind that I would come back. When the officer had left, I stood, head bowed, before him.

'Raise up that chin, boy. Look at me. It's natural that you're going to question. That very human part of you, the part that fights for your very survival, is always going to make you want to run, to protect yourself. But the power of what we're dealing with is beyond the base desires of your own flesh and blood. And you ask "why me? Why me?" You look at the wrongdoing you've entertained and see no reflection of God's work within you. But this is where you do not understand that God chooses you regardless of sin, for reasons often unknown to us. As the scripture tells us, "Does not the potter have the right to make out of the same lump of clay some pottery for noble purposes and some for common use?" You see, my boy, it was through your common use that, ultimately, your noble purpose has become clear. Either way, this was not your decision, not yours at all.'

"I was instructed by Minister Earl and his wife to spend the next week resting and preparing for what was to come. Other than eating and reading the brand new Bible the Minister had given to me, I had little to do but sleep. Taking to my bed almost as soon as the sun set, I began to dream the same dream, night after night: unbolting the door to the Peaks' household, I would walk out and take to the road, a road that stretched out in a straight line into the infinite distance. For mile after mile, nothing on the road was familiar to me, each field different, each house a different height, the sky ever shifting. Yet always at the same point I saw another man walking towards me, his movements reflecting my own. As we drew nearer I could not fail to recognize him, for the man was me. And as I stood there facing myself, feeling God's very breath upon my neck, I realized that I had returned once more to the minister's house. The first six nights I had the dream I would wake in a cold sweat, my bones aching as if I had physically walked the road itself. But on the seventh evening, the dream changed. As I reached the door it was already open, the road beckoning beyond. It was I who then shut the door and slipped the bolt across. I awoke in a state of serenity, that same calmness that had flooded through me as I lay upon the floor in the bank. To run from them, to leave there would have been like trying to turn back the tide with my bare hands. Though it was my hands upon the door, it was God's will that I close it. When Isabelle, the minister's wife, entered my room that morning to bring me breakfast, she was somewhat surprised when I began to talk freely with her. To that point I had only ever given short, direct answers to her many, many questions. When I told her about my dream, and how it had finally changed, she did not respond. Sitting on the edge of the bed, she began searching through my Bible. After passing her finger across a line of text, she tenderly kissed me upon the head and left my room. The words seemed to fall from the page as I read: 'it is hard for thee to kick against the pricks.'

"Though I had truly begun to accept that my place lay with the minister, my neatly groomed hair, the new suits I had been bought, and the attention I received from the Peaks made me feel as if I were an imposter. Emmy, the eldest and prettiest of Minister Earl's daughters, was especially kind to me. Before she left for school each morning she would sit beside me while Minister Earl began teaching me the values and ways of the Calvinism faith. As I have a disease that sometimes causes me to misunderstand certain letters, Emmy would help to explain exactly what Minister Earl meant or how to pronounce words. She would nervously smile, brush the thick curls of hair from her eyes, and wait for her father to signal for her to assist me. He actively encouraged all his children to dote upon me, each of them readily accepting that in the pecking order of the family I, a stranger in the nest, had usurped them all.

"The entire family would leave me on Sunday mornings, Minister Earl having told me I was not yet ready to be introduced to church life. He would practice his sermons throughout the week, standing in front of a mirror, watching, tweaking and changing every gesture as he went. He would often ask me to recite parts of it back to him if he forgot, or to see what it sounded like as he strove to find the words that would inspire the hearts of his congregation. By Sunday he was at fever pitch, the words impatient to spill out of him. I longed to be with them as they walked off towards the church and would watch them until they were nothing but hazy blurs upon the horizon.

"While they were gone I would furiously re-read the Bible passages I had been taught, and in no time at all I had learnt whole sections off by heart. Minister Earl would always return in a state of near euphoria, his shirt drenched with sweat beneath his black church robes. The children would circle him like a pack of dogs, listening as he detailed how various members of his flock had been electrified by his words, or how donations kept flooding in towards the restoration of parts of the church. In his heightened state he would pace up and down and test me, quick firing the names and numbers of lines of scripture at me, which as time wore on I was expected to know word for word, without a pause for breath. He would often then make me write, with the studious help of Emmy, about the things that had happened in my life, and to answer specifically why I thought they had happened. Sunday after Sunday he would read my words, a look of disappointment appearing on his face at my failure to answer correctly. Everything I wrote was bound to the earth and bound to logic: I stole because we were poor. I fought because I was angry. My brother died because he tried to rob a bank.

"Though as I became ever more immersed in my new found faith, and nourished by the attention and affection of the Peak's family, that sense of earthly logic began to melt away. Two months after my arrival I was charged with answering the question of why some of my brothers and sisters had perished. My written response was short, simple and I felt a firm belief in the words that I committed to the page: 'because this was the will of God, the destiny He had planned for them. Proverbs 21: 1 -The king's heart is in the hand of the Lord; he directs it like a watercourse wherever He pleases.' When Minister Earl read my response he fell to his knees, and gripped my arms as his eyes fixed upwards on some heavenly point.

'Lord, in your wisdom you have granted understanding to the ones you have chosen, for the cherished few who your son, Jesus Christ, purchased redemption for as he withered upon the cross. Frank, my dearest boy, I believe you are finally ready to join my crusade, my crusade to revitalize this community, to show them the depth of the power of the Lord. Look at how this nation has changed around us, look at the transgressions that have become so commonplace in our lives, how those once righteously vilified and condemned are now leading us towards the very edge of the cliff. Together we'll lead them back to safety.'

"The entire family was taken out to have lunch upon the lawn on a large wooden table beneath the shade of a grand, looming oak. I sat at the head of the table with Minister Earl, who made toast upon toast about me, his arm around my shoulder, pulling me ever closer to him. I had never felt happiness like that before, and vowed to dedicate my life to our faith."

"When Sunday morning came around, I felt an immense pride as I walked with the Peaks family to church. It was, however, still hard to not feel like a fish out of water. Sensing my nervousness, Emmy walked next to me the entire way, her small hand clasped in mine. As we hit the edge of town and began passing houses people came out to join our procession towards the church. The warmth with which they greeted Minister Earl was something to behold. The men acted as if he was their long-time drinking buddy, the women and children as if he were a much-loved relative returned to the fold after years away and yet it was merely days since he had last seen them. He knew all the intimate details of their lives; what jobs they did, if they had sickly family members, whether they had got their cars fixed, who was having trouble with their taxes, which of the children were doing well at school. Our group was thirty strong by the time we came upon the grand structure of the old church, the west side of which was draped in scaffolding and dark netting. Filing in among the rest of the congregation, we took our place in the front row as Minister Earl readied himself in the pulpit. Every seat in the church was taken and I had never seen so many finely dressed people in one place. Minister Earl raised a hand to silence everybody.

'Folks, I'd like to thank you all once again for attending our Sunday service. Seeing all your faces out there makes me so proud to be a part of this community. And today we're here in part to welcome a new person to our flock. Now I've spoken to you many times about what fate means, about the grand play the Lord has written that each and every one of us has a role in. But I see and I hear you. For while you kindly nod your heads in agreement when I speak of these things, I know there's that part you that thinks 'I'm in control, I'm shaping my own future.' Every day you pick up a newspaper and read about ever more extraordinary things that 'man' has created; a cure for some terrible disease, a new generation of faster, slicker automobiles, even rockets that will orbit the earth. Gives you a sense of progress, doesn't it? That 'man' is on the right path - the path he made with his own hard, uncompromising labor. So let me say it now: the progress of man is aligned to the will of God. When a scientist toils away for years in a laboratory and at last makes the breakthrough he seeks, that's because God Himself wanted this to happen. When an electrical storm destroys your house and possessions, that too was God's will, part of His plan for you. For you see, if we are born enslaved into the service of sin, and have no natural goodness within us, how can any of man's works of wonder truly be his own? They cannot. Many of you consider yourselves people of faith. But I see and I hear you. Though you loyally attend this service week upon week, year upon year, do you practice your faith away from the hallowed walls of this institution? Do you ensure that your children are raised within the boundaries of that faith? That our five central principles are as much a part of them as the five fingers on each of their hands? God works outside of these walls. He's invested his spirit in every part of our lives, be it politics, or sport, or business. There is no separation. For those whose idea of faith is in fact merely habit and duty, you will fall away. God has not chosen you, for it is He and He only who deems who is fit to be saved, to grant them access to the world beyond this one. As the scripture tells us; you cannot save yourself. No deed, no matter how good, will be your saving grace. Now I have served this community for many years, I have humbly struggled to nourish this flock with the word of God. And yet five months ago, I found myself only moments from death - a terrible, merciless end. Now you've all no doubt heard and read about what happened in the bank that day. But the truth is somewhat different, and it sits within this very building. Frank son, I'd like you to join me up here.'

"As the congregation twitched and whispered in their seats, the low hum of their voices echoing all around, I sat petrified in my seat. At his second time of asking I rose to my feet and walked to stand beside the pulpit, facing out towards the seated mass. Like an actor readying himself before the curtain, Minister Earl stepped down from the pulpit. He reached out his hand towards the audience, his head bowed, sighing deeply. After a crushing pause he began, his voice louder than I had ever heard it.

'My son, before our paths crossed, how would you describe your life to the good folks before you?'

'You could say I spent years taking things that didn't belong to me.'

'You stole from people, you robbed them?'

'There's a good chance that I've stolen something from many of the good folk in this room, that my brother and I broke into their houses, farms and outhouses and laid our hands upon whatever we could.'

'And why did you do these things?'

'I suppose desperation at first, our daddy was gone and our family couldn't survive on what we had. Felt like we had no choice, sir. But as things went on… you could say it felt natural to us, like it was always meant to be. I'm ashamed to say it excited me... it sort of defined who I was.'

'You felt compelled?'

'Yes sir, I felt compelled in every way.'

'As if something beyond you, something far more powerful than yourself was guiding your every action?'

'Well, yes sir, I suppose you could describe it that way. It never seemed as if we had a choice.'

"The congregation had been roused from its Sunday morning slumber. People craned forward over every row, hands gripping the pew in front of them, determined they would not miss a word of what was being said. The only time I had felt so many eyes boring into me was court. At first I tried to look anywhere but at those sitting before me, but a voice deep inside seemed to tell me to gaze at each and every person in the room. The minister continued on.

'*Compelled.* Now folks, I'm sure you realize the power of that word. This boy before you felt little more than a marionette. He could not see the strings that dragged and pulled him through life, and he did not understand whose hands grasped and manipulated those strings. It was those very hands that led him and his brother to one more fatal act. Backed into a corner by the circumstance that was chosen *for* them, they descended upon the First National with an unbridled, destructive intent. The first time I saw this boy, a notion that we had always been destined to meet ran through my heart. I felt as if we had been commandeered by the Lord above to save each other. Now, Frank and his brother Jimmy stood before me, a gun in his hand. Even then I knew no harm would come of me. Frank, my son, what did you feel at that moment? Was it plain fear? Were you simply scared? Scared of getting hurt, or going to jail?'

'No sir. It's hard to explain. It wasn't anything as simple as that. It was like everything had been leading to that moment, you seemed so familiar to me. It was as if I was flooded with a sense of serenity, and inside that… I could hear a voice telling me what I was doing was no longer my path.'

'And what did you do then?'

'I turned upon my own brother, the person I was closest to in the world.'

'You felt compelled?'

'Yes… but it was as if this time something beyond me was directly speaking, sort of guiding my actions.'

'So I say now to you all before me once again: God chooses who He saves, and if He chooses to save you, then it's impossible to fight against it. His Irresistible Grace will sweep through every part of you. This boy here before you is living proof of God's will, His predestination of all things. His own brother was to die that day, his own brother. He was not chosen to be saved.'

"A cacophony of noise erupted around us. Several people rose to their feet shouting 'Me' and 'I want to be saved,' or sat looking stricken in their seats, clearly moved by the power of the story they had heard.

'Know this,' said the minister. 'God will not save you all. *Few* will be elected. There is no saving yourself – so open your hearts, be *willing* to be saved. Let me, and let this church help guide you to a place where salvation may occur. Like Frank Joseph Marlin has been called to do, let all those under this roof walk with me too.'

5. The Shipwrecks

And so it began. My grandfather was enrolled in a program of ordination to become a Calvinist minister. For eight hours a day, for the next two years, he would learn the intricacies and boundaries of his calling. This was no formal education, for all other books and learning, bar those of a holy nature, were banned and the playing of, or listening to the music of stringed instruments was strictly frowned upon. His faith became an ever deepening shadow, and the world beyond it ceased to exist. Through the window in the room he studied, Frank would fail to notice the seasons falling and blossoming and the shifting colors of the sky. He was immune to any sound bar the voices of his teachers, who ever so patiently erected a fortress of Calvinist ideas around him. Within the warm cocoon of the Peaks family, my grandfather's life gained purpose and direction. To Minister Earl he became as good as a son, a younger, brighter mirror image of himself. To those outside of it, their bond was at once inexplicable and enticing; my grandfather was the means by which Minister Earl could re-connect with his congregation and set about engaging and sharpening their beliefs.

Every night before dinner they would set off into the community. In the parlor or kitchen of the family they had chosen to visit, their sacred stage-play would unfold. The tale of Frank's life and his grand epiphany in the bank would be retold, while Minister Earl, in his role as the arbiter of God's will, prodded and pulled his audience towards their own Damascene moment. Every aspect of their lives would be pored over, scoured for traces of the divine, for signs of election. Should those signs be found, Minister Earl and my grandfather would conclude their act with an emotional declaration of salvation. Rarely would they leave a household without an upsurge in the faith of their congregation and a handsome donation towards the restoration of the west wing of the church.

Within a year Frank's prominence and status in the community was assured. Though he was not yet ordained, he was treated as if he were. His celebrity was such that delegations of believers and ministers from adjoining towns would frequently visit to bear witness to the walking proof of their faith. The congregation had swollen rapidly, with the Sunday service attendance so large that the pews resembled a river about to burst its banks. Frank would gaze out upon them and see a clear line between those who had been declared chosen and those who had not: the elected would tranquilly take their place on the front few rows, certain of their place in God's order, while an air of growing desperation clung to those behind them who had not yet received word from on high.

Frank had also been tasked by Minister Earl to work upon the hearts of the children of the town. Every Sunday after service, he and Emmy would gather a group of local children together for Bible study, or more often a trip out into the fields beyond, where the world would be re-appraised through the eyes of a believer. All the children sought Frank's friendship and attention and like a holy piper he would use the promise of this to lead their minds to a place of belief. By the bank of a stream they would sit, Frank attempting to steal their imaginations away from whatever television shows and comic books they had been watching and reading that week. They would ask him to describe in the smallest detail what it had felt like to rob from people, to break into peoples' homes, and what it felt like to be shot. He would duly oblige by giving them the kind of graphic descriptions that only children truly appreciate. Every trace of blood and dirt was accounted for. When asked just 'why' he had done the things he had, his answer was always the same: that this was the will of the Lord, predestined to be so. Then Frank would throw a branch into the stream and ask everyone to watch as the flow of the water took it, against its will, to an unknown point of its choosing. The Lord, he would remind them, was not somebody who could be resisted. It was during these Sunday outings that he and Emmy began to grow closer. Her complete and utter deference to his knowledge and standing no doubt thrilled him. She would kneel patiently by his side, her eyes never leaving him. Such beauty and devotion could surely not fail to affect a man. And should any of the children question the authority of Frank's word, she would tersely remind them of just who they were talking too; a living example of the faith their parents wished them to belong to. Of course, the children of parents who had already been declared chosen were far more easily persuaded as to the true order of the world. The instinctive desire for your circumstance to be better than that of your neighbors was at its most naked here, amid the minds of the young.

To this point, Frank Marlin's tale was one of ascendancy and growth, of spiritual fulfilment and personal enlightenment. He had found a new family and a new life and a future had been mapped out before him. With Minister Earl a father in all but name, it would be right to assume that he would have felt a sense of completeness for the first time in his young life. Yet Frank did not. Despite the respect and adoration of those around him, there were questions circling around his head that had begun to eat away at him. While his convictions were steadfast, fissures of doubt, which would slowly grow to the size of canyons, had opened up where the beliefs of other's were concerned. The uncertainties were to surface as a result of Minister Earl and Frank deciding to visit, unannounced, a leading member of the local community, one Eldridge St. Clair.

Both men had started the journey to his secluded house in high spirits, certain that St. Clair - a wealthy businessmen and generous benefactor to all the town's most deserving causes - would no doubt fit the bill as one who would be saved. An extremely healthy donation towards the restoration, to Minister Earl at least, felt as guaranteed as a banker's check. St. Clair was a large and flamboyant man in his early fifties and had himself been pushing for weeks for his nominal election, certain in his own head that a man of his prominence would surely not be left aside.

As they neared the house, Frank had his usual wealth of questions about the person they would be assessing, but became quickly puzzled at the unusually vague responses given by Minister Earl; before abruptly returning each time to eulogize about St. Clair's wonderful sense of civic pride, he would only remark that he was as 'confirmed' a bachelor as there ever could be. The dusk had long set in, turning the ivy that clambered its way over the façade of St. Clair's house a moonlit blue. It seemed at first that St. Clair was home, a light flickering among shadows in one of the second floor rooms. But repeated rings of the bell brought nobody, not even his housekeeper, to the door. Frank had turned to leave when Minister Earl rang for what would be the last time, and a voice finally calling out from beyond the door.

"Now, who wants something at this time of the evening?"

"Is that you, Eldridge? It's Earl Peaks and young Frank. Is everything OK? Maybe we should return on a more convenient occasion."

Frank could hear the faint undertow of cursing, dulled by the oak door.

"Earl! No sir, you just wait right there, I just wasn't expecting any company tonight. You should have called ahead. Let me just fix myself up here a second; I could've been ready and proper for you all."

When the door finally opened, a disheveled Eldridge St. Clair stood before them. Dark patches of sweat stuck his creased pink shirt to his body; hairs shot a hundred different ways on the back of his head; and his shoes did their best to hide his sock-less feet. Ushering them through to the lounge, he excused the state of himself and of the house. Though it was clearly the housekeeper's night off, it was obvious to Frank that something deeper was amiss. Minister Earl must have noticed too, but was doing his best to gloss over that fact; idle small talk filled the air as a clearly apprehensive St. Clair glanced nervously around, his eyes never settling on the minister or Frank.

"I make you right there, Eldridge. Something's got to be done about those yahoos. Every darn week they're falling out of McGinley's and causing some kind of trouble. Rumor has it there's a lot of bad blood over some card games. The fools get liquored up and take their grievances out on each other in a public square of all places."

"That's what I'm saying Earl, it does the reputation of this town a great disservice. If we wanted a bunch of cowboys running loose, we could all have moved down to Missouri."

Disinterested in their talk, Frank studied the room to get a firm idea of just who this man was. On a small table filled with bottles of alcohol stood two glasses, both with a little whiskey still in them. His sense that Minister Earl had company beside them was heightened further still when two low, muted thuds echoed across the ceiling, freezing the conversation. St. Clair attempted to break the awkward pause.

"Sounds like I've gone and left that damn window open again. Honestly, I'd forget my head if it wasn't attached to my neck."

Frank was to make St. Clair more nervous still with his next question.

"Sir, may I use your bathroom?"

"Well… sure, sure son. It's the third door on the left as you go up the stairs. The third door. You'll have to excuse the mess up there, dear old Maria isn't what she was in the cleaning stakes and she's on a leave of absence this evening."

As St. Clair's hollow laughter rang around the room, Frank made his way up the stairs. Behind him St. Clair called out 'the third door' once again. As he reached the top he paused and waited until banal chit-chat once again filled the lounge. Quietly as he could, he began to open each door on the left hand side, finding nothing each time but darkness and finally the bathroom. He turned to face the series of doors on his right and entered the one directly opposite the bathroom. Hearing the rustle of sheets, he blindly felt across the wall for a light switch. When light struck the room, he was confronted with the sight of a man, perhaps in his late twenties, sitting bolt upright in the bed, his back against the cushioned headboard. His torso was bare and it seemed to Frank that he was naked beneath the sheets too. They gazed at each other for what to Frank seemed an eternity, so confounded was he by what he saw before him. The man did not seem flustered, the near empty bottle of bourbon beside him clearly having chased off any sense of fear. Brushing the hair off of his forehead, he casually rested one arm behind his head. With the other hand he slowly patted the empty side of the bed next to him. Frank moved backwards, but was unable to look away. Before he left the room the man raised an index finger to his lips and made a calm shushing sound.

Frank closed the door, waves of panic, anger and shock colliding within him as he did so. He knew what this meant, knew that it had nothing to with the housekeeper, knew that this wasn't a relative come to stay. It simply meant that St. Clair was 'queer,' that this fine, upstanding member of the parish had intimate physical relations with men. Young men. What it also meant was that their journey had been a wasted one. St. Clair, as yet, was clearly not one of the chosen. He would need to be ostracized, held up as an example of the total depravity of man, until he renounced his homosexual endeavors, stopped bucking the very laws of nature themselves. Once he had gathered himself and got his breathing under control, Frank began to descend the stairs, desperately wondering how he should prize Minister Earl away from St. Clair so he could tell him. Amid the mess of thoughts, a terrible one came forward. Stopping halfway down the stairs, he replayed the conversations he had had with Minister Earl on the way there. 'As confirmed a bachelor as there can be. As confirmed a *bachelor* as there can be.' It seemed that Minister Earl already knew about St. Clair's errant ways. And if the minister knew, then reason had it that most of the congregation would know too. Given the immense popularity and standing of St. Clair, it was likely an open secret among everyone. Though confused and troubled as to why they had come here at all, he reasoned that this whole trip had been merely planned as a courtesy, a way of putting off St. Clair, of quietly discrediting any chance of election. Why else would the minister engage with such a man?

Back down in the lounge, the minister and St. Clair were getting on famously, regaling each other with old tales they'd no doubt heard a thousand times before, any sense of worry in St. Clair seeming to have vanished. Frank sheepishly sat back down, his head bowed, unsure of just what to do. Almost on cue, Minister Earl swung the conversation around to the story of Frank's election, expecting Frank to assume the role he had performed a hundred times before. Though he did this, he did it as if programmed, the passion and fire stripped from him. He kept telling himself that this was just for show, just to keep St. Clair happy, but it stood counter to the enthusiasm shown by Minister Earl for the whole charade. When the story of Frank's salvation ended, they began to go through St. Clair's own life story. While the minister sat and listened intently, Frank could not fail to think that everything he heard was little more than a string of lies, half-truths and outright falsehoods.

"Of course my greatest regret was that I never took a wife. There were a few who came close to being Mrs. St. Clair, but I guess it was never the right time or place. I mean look around you, it's pretty obvious that this place lacks a woman's touch. No, sir, it seems it was never meant to be."

"Well, Eldridge, I guess this was the plan, the path God set out for you. Though that's clearly unfortunate on your behalf, I'm certain that the Lord decided to keep your distractions to a minimum. I mean how would you find time for a wife with all the work you do for this town? Your businesses would have gone under years ago. You'd have been too busy running around after that lady, right?"

As they both sat there chuckling, three words begged to let go from Frank's lips: Faggot, queer, homosexual. He summoned up every last piece of willpower not to do let them out.

"You see I've always felt I had a great connection with the spiritual, like many of the things I've done I was truly compelled to do so. Guided by some higher force, as they say."

Frank clenched his fists, his unease showing itself upon his face. Still the words *faggot, queer, homosexual*, pleaded within him to be released. He looked despairingly at Minister Earl, desperate for him to bring this purgatory to a close. And yet the Minister was clearly building up towards a declaration of election on the behalf of St. Clair.

"It seems obvious to me Eldridge that the Lord rests within your heart, which he has set-"

"Wait!"

"Frank?"

St. Clair had raised slightly from his chair, clearly perturbed by the interruption, his head turning briefly to look towards the stairs, afraid that the drunken stranger in his bed had made himself known.

"Whatever is the matter, young fellow?"

"I...I need to speak with the minister, sir."

"Son, I don't think there's anything to say right now. Now let's conclude our business with Eldridge. I'm sure it's nothing so important that it can't wait a while."

"But Minister, I..."

Minister Earl shot Frank a look that bordered on fury. Crestfallen, he bowed to the will of his elder.

"Yes, sir, I guess it can wait."

He was forced to sit and watch in sickened silence as Minister Earl deemed Eldridge St. Clair elected, a man saved by Christ through his death and absorption of sin. A sadness deeper than the bed of the ocean swept through Frank as he watched Minister Earl hold up check for $25,000, written with a grand flourish by a proud, beaming St. Clair. Talk had moved swiftly on to the restoration of the church and St. Clair had suggested he make a donation almost as soon as the minister brought it up.

"So Earl, you're doing a fine job with this young man. It's rare to see such dedication. Now, I really do appreciate that kind of commitment to a cause."

"Why thank you, Eldridge. As you've seen, he can be a little impatient, but, I think the whole town recognizes he brings something special to our community."

They made their way through the hall to the front door, Frank opening it as fast as he could as the minister and St. Clair bad each other fond farewells behind him.

"So, this is good night then son, and a good night it has been indeed. Now you folks drop by any time now, but let me know next time and I'll have Maria fix us all up something nice."

When St. Clair held out his hand, Frank did not want to touch him. It took everything in him not to make a scene and refuse him. St. Clair gripped his hand far too tightly, a quizzical, challenging look upon his face. When they finally left, Frank looked back towards the now totally dark house. In an upper window he thought he could make out part of a face, peering out from behind a curtain and a hand waving a mocking goodbye.

Bar the sound of the engine of Minister Earl's Lincoln as they drove homeward, an uneasy silence hung between the two men. My grandfather told us many times that he had stared out into the dark distance, longing for some divine indication of what to do or say, but was merely blinded by the lights of the oncoming traffic. Every time a U-turn sign flashed past he hoped that the minister would swing the car around, head back to the St. Clair residence and explain that there had been a misunderstanding, that he had got it all very wrong. When they eventually turned off onto the long private drive of the Peaks' home, Frank's sense of defeat and betrayal was complete. He knew something had changed between them that evening, that intangible bond distorted and broken. When Frank attempted to get out of the car, Minister Earl stopped him.

"I know what you want to say and I'm guessing you're a little confused right now."

"You have no idea what I'm feeling right now."

"Eldridge is a little different is all and-"

"Different?! There was man, a man in his bed. In his own damn bed, Minister!"

"While we were there? Oh Jesus Christ our Lord above, I guess that complicates what's happening here a little. Why tonight of all nights, Eldridge?"

"You're going to go back and explain why he's not chosen?"

"No, no. I'm not going to do that. I mean it was an unfortunate set of circumstances this evening. Where Eldridge is concerned, everyone knows that he's always had certain... proclivities. But these aren't the kind of things that polite folk discuss, bring up in general conversation."

"They turn a blind eye? Ignore the fact that he's a queer, that he does disgusting things to men?"

"Now there's no need for that kind of talk! The personal life of somebody like Eldridge is something that has to be tolerated, understood for what it is. This church, this community simply can't afford to make enemies of a man like St. Clair, given his prominence in all matters civil and the fact that he owns half the darn real estate and businesses in town."

"Even if he's the enemy of God himself? Scripture says that-"

"You're going to quote scripture at me?! I know darn well what the book has to say on those matters and it doesn't make for easy reading. But down here, right now there are certain situations where an ungenerous attitude and a head full of naivety will cause more trouble than it would ever be worth and derail us from the good work that the Lord wants us to complete."

"Is that check burning in your pocket yet?"

"Son, before you say another word, something you may live to regret, you better stop and go think about just what you're suggesting here."

***

Whenever my grandfather reached this point of his story he would unfailingly describe the next few weeks as some of the most fraught and conflicted of his young life. He acknowledged that Minister Earl had given him everything; a home, a family, an education, and a purpose. The Peaks family had nourished and fed him so well that the face of the man he saw in the mirror each day seemed only a distant echo of the crooked, lost boy he once knew. The feelings of safety and contentment that stirred inside him when he compared his old life to his new were enough to overwhelm him with happiness. Minister Earl had become his touchstone, his mentor, his friend, and the very yardstick by which he would endeavor to be measured. No man he had ever met had been as straight and true and reliable.

But the incident at St. Clair's seemed to stand in direct

opposition to so much of what Frank had been taught and had completely embraced. An almost physical sense of pain swept through Frank every time he considered that the minister had betrayed the word of God, that his actions were both traitorous and self-serving. Watching the Sunday service it could not escape his notice that very soon almost everybody in the congregation had now been declared 'elected'; soon there would be no one left who was not. This struck Frank as entirely false. The chances that Jesus' death saved everybody in that room were simply improbable. There were those who God clearly had created for a more common use, and those who would never be saved from the debauchery of the acts they committed. He could not bear to watch St. Clair as he took his place in the front few pews, pompousness and a freshly enhanced sense of importance etched upon his face. When the minister had condoned his web of lies and deceit he had therefore made a mockery of all those who had been 'chosen' before him.

Though both the congregation of the church and its assets grew, it seemed to Frank that it became more empty and hollow with each passing week. The funds at Minister Earl's disposal were now so great that he was able to have people work upon the crumbling west wing of the church for fourteen hours a day, six days a week. Yet the more repaired and solid the edifice of the church became, the more his image of the minister and his relationship with him fell to pieces.

To temporarily punish Frank for his disobedience, Minister Earl had stopped taking him out into the community with him. The last few 'elections' had occurred without him. The minister had also made it clear that he would not take kindly to him bringing up the issue with any of the other ministers who taught Frank during the week and that Frank was to trust his judgment on the matter absolutely. The free time he now had he spent with Emmy, who knew something was wrong, but tried as best she could to ignore the simmering conflict between the two men. But her presence there seemed to confirm that her loyalty to her father was at the very least a little divided. There were indeed allusions in the things she said that made Frank feel that the attention and adulation she bestowed upon him was perhaps down to more than her love of his devoutness and his standing within the church.

"Frank, you remember little Marty Holt don't you, one of the kids we spoke to after service last Sunday?"

"The one who never takes that red cap off, like it's glued to his head?"

"Yeah, that's the very one."

"Well what about him?"

"I saw his parents in town last week. Mother and I were ordering in some groceries from Jefferson's and I noticed them across the road, inside the little kids' playground, next to the bank."

"They weren't robbing it, were they?"

"No! Silly."

"What then? Were they busking or hawking their possessions, collecting money in that red cap of his?"

"Frank, be serious. It's just that… when I was watching them, it struck me how different they are together. How different they are from my own folks."

"Most folk are different from Minister Peaks and Mrs. Isabelle. He's a leader in this-"

"I know what he is. It's not the way that I mean. I mean the way that they act with each other, the way they touch and look at each other. Like there's no distance between them."

"I wouldn't know about things like that."

"It just seems to me that it would be a nice way to be with someone."

"We've got other things to dedicate our minds and time to though, haven't we?"

"I'm just saying, is all. I'm just saying."

Though Frank did indeed know about 'things like that' and could not help but notice the beauty and charm that Emmy possessed, he simply could not reconcile the pull towards those qualities with the stipulations of his faith. It was as if a sheet of glass had been placed between them, through which, though they could place their hands together, any true connection seemed impossible. Anything that would distract him from his path towards becoming ordained, or that would dilute his faith in God was to be avoided.

From the confines of Frank's own devotion, Minister Earl's choices and actions were brought into the sharpest of contrasts. He had either fallen from the path constructed for him by the Lord or he was never chosen in the first place. Most of the congregation was complicit in the problem. The minister could stand there happily before them because they were purposely blind to or openly tolerant of the corruption in their presence. Perhaps being 'elected' meant no more to them than having a better fridge freezer, a bigger television, or at least that their neighbors were no more special or better than they were. Either way, Frank knew this could not go on, that if he believed, truly believed with every fiber of his being, that this situation could not stand. Knowing there was nowhere else to turn, he fell to his knees and began to ask the Lord to re-invigorate his purpose and plan, to bring forth a day of reckoning that would separate the truly elected from those unworthy. He hoped too that

Minister Earl would find a way back into his own heart, so desperate was he to have his faith in him restored.

That day came sooner that he had dared dream. Frank had awoken on a bitter and stormy Sunday morning, the rain lashing down without relent like buckshot against the flapping shutters of the house. Outside it seemed almost like night, the sky a mass of black and grey. Once dressed, he headed down for breakfast before they were all due to leave for church. At the bottom of the stairs sat the five Peaks children, the youngest of whom, Raylan, sat clutching onto Emmy's legs. In her hand was a note which she held up to Frank.

"Where are Minister Earl and Mrs. Isabelle?"

"It's my grandmother. Daddy's mother. She's been taken ill. They think it's pneumonia. Mother said they aren't sure if she's going to make it through. Daddy says to prepare for the worst. They left in the middle of the night to be with her."

"And they're still not back?"

She shook her head and handed the note to Frank. Within the note Minister Earl had left strict instructions for Frank to go ahead to church, and should he not make it back in time, to cancel that day's service and explain the unforeseen circumstances. Frank ordered all of the children into the dining room for breakfast, after which they were all told to wash and dress to prepare for that morning's service.

The gardener, Michael, had been assigned that day to drive them to church; with seven of them crammed into his vehicle he slowly navigated through the decaying, older roads on the outskirts of town which were quickly flooding. Frank had expected the attendance at service to be greatly reduced due to the near Biblical downpour, and yet through the constantly steamed-up glass he could make out dozens of vehicles filled with congregation members waiting for the doors of the church to open. Michael pulled up as close to the private back entrance as they could, but still they were drenched in the short run from car door to church door.

Once Frank had opened the main doors, the congregation, half of them sodden and all of them freezing, began to make their way into the church and take their seats, the water from their clothes collecting in pools at their feet. As the time for the start of service came and went, the town's folk sat there shivering and growing ever more impatient. Frank stood by the pulpit, nervously glancing up at the clock as it ticked past nine thirty, the cut-off point at which he was supposed to bring a halt to the day's proceedings. But Frank had no intention of doing so. It was clear to him that should Minister Earl have even left in time, there was no way by this point that he would make it to the church; he was sure to be thwarted by the torrents of rain that would make every entry road into town practically impassable.

Sweat began to cascade from his brow, every nerve in his body twitching as he tried to steel himself to address those before him. But Frank could not quite find the final impulse to climb the steps of the pulpit. It was almost as if gravity itself was chaining him to the spot on which he stood. In the oppressive gloom of the church and the growing crescendo of discontent from the congregation, the entrance doors swung slowly open. Fully expecting to see Minister Earl appear and race along the aisle, Frank began a slow, disconsolate walk back to his seat, his plan killed in its birth. To his surprise, it was the drenched and harried figure of Eldridge St. Clair that came towards him. Swearing under his breath and apologizing for his tardiness in equal measure, he emptied his large brimmed hat, that had collected water like a bucket, onto the cold concrete of the floor before squeezing his generous frame into the remaining space in one of the front pews. Frank knew this was a sign to continue, knew that the Lord had needed him to wait for the arrival of St. Clair. He walked to Emmy and spoke quietly in her ear.

"Do you believe in me?"

"What do you mean, Frank? Daddy is going to be so mad at us, all these people-"

"Just answer the question."

"You know I do, but we've got to explain, send people home."

"They need to stay right here. I'm going to speak. There are things they need to hear."

"Frank?! You can't, the Minister will be furious, it's… it's not your place yet."

"This has happened for a reason, Emmy. It's the Lord's will that I speak today. St. Clair is here. He's the signal. Now you just said you believed in me. Did you mean it or was it just what I wanted to hear?"

"You *know* I do… I'm scared Frank. Scared of what Daddy will do. What about St. Clair, what's he done to you?"

"He's everything that's wrong with this town, everything that's wrong with this congregation."

Turning quickly away, he walked towards the pulpit. He gripped the rails on the stairs for dear life as he walked up them. He tapped the old microphone to see if it was on and a jarring high-pitched squeal echoed off the walls, immediately gaining him the attention of everyone in the room. Frank could feel a sense of righteousness and authority begin to flow through him as he stood above the townsfolk, staring out at their expectant, puzzled faces. After raising his hand for order and silence, he began.

"I must first apologize for the absence of Minister Earl today. As some of you are already aware, both he and Mrs. Isabelle have been called away to the bedside of his ailing mother. Now, I know you're also cold and wet and, given that the minister is not present, no doubt wondering why you're still sitting here. Well, it was the distinct wish of the minister himself that today's service would go ahead and he has therefore entrusted today's proceedings to me. For it occurred to us that like the rain that is coming down so unrelentingly outside, our commitment to learning the word of God must be just as unceasing. So both the minister and I thank you for being here on this most treacherous of mornings.

"And it is another form of treachery I want to discuss with you today. Now most of you good folk will know me, or know of me. I have sat in many of your houses and apartments. I have drunk from your cups and eaten from your plates, while you kindly related the stories of your lives. You will have heard from my own lips the terrible details of the wickedness which I was once in the service of. We know that we here are all sinners and have been from the second our tiny lungs sucked in that first breath of earthly air. We know too that it is God who chooses the exact path of our lives and in His benevolence gave the life of His only son so that some of us, *some of us...* would be saved. We in this church have come to the realization that some of you may be laboring under the knowledge that you have indeed been elected. There are those among you who have not and never will be."

A flurry of conversation swept through the congregation, each person looking apprehensively around at their friends and neighbors, unsure of what Frank meant. Emmy sat stunned before him in the front row, gripped by both fear and adulation. He raised his hand for silence once more.

"For there are those here that, by the lowest means of deceit and deception, have not been truthful as to their history or to the vile nature of the acts they commit. These acts could not be committed by anyone who has truly been chosen, by anyone who was set to inherit the kingdom of God. The truth is that these people are the shipwrecks of humanity, who ran aground upon the rocks of sin and have remained there ever since."

St. Clair sat rigid in his seat, his mouth open and face drained of all color. It had begun to dawn upon some of those who knew him just what Frank was alluding to and they began to shift uncomfortably around him, to watch him closely for any reaction. Yet the only noise now to be heard was the flapping of the plastic sheets against the scaffolding that dressed the west wing of church as the wind whipped into it with an unbridled fury. Frank could sense that he had the congregation in the palm of his hand, and that his words were beginning to pull some of the audience in his direction.

"But I am not here to be cryptic or plain obtuse, for the scripture upon this matter is as clear and true as can be. For I know you are now wondering to which 'acts' I refer, which sin has snuck in among us and poisoned the well that we all drink from? I ask you to take the good book in front of you. Turn to Romans 1:26-27. Now read, please *read*: 'For this reason God gave them up to passions of dishonor; for even their females exchanged their natural use for that which is contrary to nature, and likewise also the males…were inflamed by their lust for one another, males with males committing what is shameful, and receiving in themselves the recompense which was fitting for their error.' Or Genesis 19:1-13, Leviticus 18:22, 20:13, 1 Corinthians 6:9, Colossians 3:5-6.

Time and again you will see the Lord's rejection of those who seek the flesh of the same sex, his casting aside to the purgatory that awaits them."

Gasps ricocheted back and forth between the townsfolk, the air thick and infected around them.

"Now the men that covet men in this very room do not belong among us. They are *unfit* to sit at the table of the chosen, to parade their false face to the world."

A cry of 'that's right' came up from the back of the church and was swiftly followed by two more from the east side of the church. A general wave of consent seemed to flow through the audience. Yet there were those who began to call for an end to Frank's performance: whole families who, regardless of their own belief, took his stance as an affront to the goodwill and stability of the community, and began to leave the storm inside the church for the one outside. It was if, my grandfather would often say, he could see the town dividing before his very eyes. He took no small pleasure in seeing St. Clair overwhelmed by anger, those sympathetic to his plight attempting to calm him down and stop him and his fury from fleeing this scene of indignation.

"We, as a community, as a congregation, as individuals, do not have choice. If God has chosen you to believe then you cannot try to fight His Irresistible Grace. And for those I see before me already walking away it only means one thing: God was never truly in your hearts. You have no place here. Those that stay must condemn the behavior of those who seek to spread this disease. We must tolerate it no more. God has brought us here together to worship, to be bound by our common election and belief – and we must not let it be diluted or destroyed by the unnatural treachery of the few. I ask one thing from those you who remain: stand with me."

Ripples of rising applause broke out across the room as ever more seats were vacated, including that of St. Clair who finally broke free of the human constraints around him and bellowed towards Frank.

"You, sir, are a disgrace. If this wasn't a place of worship I'd tear you limb from limb. You may have your damned audience now, but this is not done. No, sir, you have more than crossed a line here today. God *damn* you."

A group of men several rows behind St. Clair began calling out: 'Sit the old queen down,' and 'tell him to leave if he doesn't like the truth' echoed down the church. Every shred of enmity they had stored for years towards the rich and powerful landowner and businessman seemed to be finally finding its way to the surface. St. Clair duly left, with those he passed unable to look him in the eye.

Frank descended the steps of the pulpit and was immediately surrounded by congregation members all wanting to congratulate him on such a fine and stirring sermon. Others shouted insults into the backs of the throng around him, reprimanding him for the dishonor they thought he had brought upon Minister Earl and the church.

As the din that had drowned the room dissipated and the last few churchgoers closed its doors behind them, Frank felt consumed by a sense of elation and relief, as if he had purged himself of the burdens that had haunted and plagued him for weeks. Still in the front row were Emmy and her brothers and sisters. Knowing he had to get them home, he summoned Michael the gardener to ready the car, telling everyone but Emmy to wait by the door. Overwhelmed by what had happened, she fought hard not to lose control of her emotions.

"Oh Frank, what have we done? I've never seen anything like

this before."

"I've done what needed to be done. I've done what I've been taught to do; what Minister Earl should have done a long time ago. There's no blame on you."

"I sat here, didn't I? I sat here and clapped and never left. Don't you think Daddy will find that out?"

"So let him find out. It isn't about me, you or the minister. It's about our faith and how true we are to it."

He took her hand and walked her to the door of the church. Before Emmy ushered the children out into the rain and into the car, she turned once more to Frank.

"I know which side I stand on, Frank."

"And what side is that?"

"Whatever one means I'm next to you."

Frank watched the car pull out into the road, the water hovering like mist around it as it crashed back off the black road. Closing the door behind him as he walked back into the empty church, Frank walked slowly down the aisle before falling to his knees. Feeling more alone than he had ever imagined possible, he longed and prayed for God Himself to speak to him, to send him some sign of His intentions. For an hour he stayed steadfast in that position, his eyes shut tight and knees sore against the damp stone floor. Eventually a deafening, violent boom that reverberated across the cavernous space around him, followed by the sound of metals and wood crashing and splintering, jolted him out of his trance. Stunned and stumbling, Frank stepped out into the gale, the rain now coming at him horizontally, and moved around towards the west side of the church. The closer he got, the more the earth around the church seemed to give way beneath him, the water now rising above his ankles. He was greeted at first by the site of the scaffolding collapsed upon the ground. Behind the mass of contorted steel branches and plastic-covered earth, the freshly constructed foundations of the new west wall had been half washed away, the pressure causing a trench-like split through over twenty feet of masonry. Frank backed unsteadily away, his mind reeling at the vision before him, until finally his feet found firmer, surer ground. The rain, it seemed, had come to divide them all.

6. A Wolf in Lamb's Clothing

When my grandfather spoke it often felt as if the people in his story had silently congregated in the room around us. They seemed to twitch and glimmer in the corner of my eye as they presented themselves again and again in Frank Marlin's tale, before dissolving themselves into shadow once more. So vivid was each sentence, so beguiling was he as an orator that you could practically feel the damp cold floor of that church, see the rawness of his knees, sense the desperation implicit in his heaven-bound prayers. Having lost our father, my sister and I could not help but tap into that deep vein of sorrow that passed through his young life. Through that bond, we were gradually absorbed by Grandfather, his narrative somehow changing our own histories and future. As the ghosts circled, Mother sat staring into some unfathomable distance. Yet at every point my Grandfather became impassioned, she would claw at the collar of her dress, her taut knuckles resting against the top of her swollen bosom, her gaze momentarily burrowing deep into our own. Her new-found sense of devotion and serene acceptance of the tenets of this faith was something I felt duty bound to replicate. It was clear to me then that we were all connected by far more than mere blood.

The name of Eldridge St. Clair was clearly still an open wound in Frank's mind. Each time he was obliged to say those words he uttered them with an unchecked hostility and disgust. I am certain he longed for a way around St. Clair's place in the story of his life, but there was none. For St. Clair, and Minister Earl, were the pivots around which his whole life had moved, and this had been predestined to be so. It was God that moved the pieces on the board and Frank ultimately had no cause or belief to question why.

Now as he reached the tail end of his story, he had once more decided that evening to go no further. Despite a captive, desperate audience, the sentences had begun to set like concrete in his throat, each one harder to deliver than the next. With his energy spent and will retreating, he gave the impression of a performer unable to carry out his *coup de grace*, the encore that would send the crowd home happy. Frank moved to the window and stared into the darkness of the fields. For a second I could see in his reflection what I thought was a smile, but the glass quickly misted as the cool Midwestern air met his breath.

'Let me tell you something, girls. The past is never behind you. If it's not walking by your side, it's waiting for you a little ways down the road. Isn't that right, Josephine?'

Mother did not reply. Though she nodded her head in agreement, she shot him a troubled, unsettling look. The weight of things unknown to us pushed upon her, and her mask, for the last time, momentarily slipped. Unable to quite gather her composure, she knocked a glass over as she stood, and ushered us both to our beds. Grandfather cupped his hand beneath the water spilling from the table before finally letting it fall through his fingers.

Though in truth, it was really never a question of my grandfather's ability to continue. As with all great actors, it was a matter of timing. Though exhausted, he knew, more importantly, that we needed to digest what he'd said, for it to slowly seep through our minds over the coming days and weeks. With time, the significance of each part of the story to our own lives would grow, its meaning would deepen. Frank was also aware that for his tale to ensnare what was left of our hearts he would need to wait for the correct circumstances to present themselves, circumstances that would assign the maximum gravity to the conclusion.

And Frank, being Frank, had every conviction that those ripe conditions would come to pass.

Surely enough, they did.

Three weeks quickly went by, the days becoming indistinguishable from one other. Study and chores were the foundations of our hours. There seemed no single minute when we were allowed to do anything else; the control of our time had become so absolute. We folded laundry, and then we read Corinthians. We swept the porch, and then we were lectured on why the Almighty has no love for the un-elect. Even the weather followed an unseasonable pattern; dank grey mornings, with the sort of chill that freezes your insides, imperceptibly transformed into the kind of sweltering afternoons that make your skin feel as if it's melting. Ann and I either shivered or baked. Mother in this time had grown full to bursting. Her due date came and went, which seemed another sign of the unchanging nature of the days.

The repetition was shattered by a single phone call. Grandfather had spent his morning looking at the property sections of local newspapers, impatiently drumming his fingers as he failed to find anything we could afford. You could sense the edge of his anger, his frustrations building with each turn of the page. Mother did her best to keep them at bay.

"That one looks fine, Daddy. It's a lot bigger than this place."

"We can't accommodate any one else in that. There are people on their way, Josephine. Where's Cousin John going to stay? He's coming from New damn Mexico to be here. Or what about Michael and Ramona? Maybe show them the barn or the chicken run? There are *people* on the way!"

It was the first time I had heard we would be joined by others.

The full implications of this would not dawn upon me for a while.

"We've just got to be patient. When we sell this place, you'll get the money that's coming to you."

"I've been waiting too long already. That smart-mouthed lawyer of mine is too tied up in the law to actually do anything about it. I swear if I hear the word 'procedure' from him one more time..."

The shrill burr of the phone was almost lost amid my grandfather's consternation, so I took it upon myself to answer it. A solemn, matronly voice greeted me at the other end and asked to speak to my grandfather. I cupped the receiver and waved frantically to get his attention.

"Well, who is it, girl? A man's got to know who wants him."

I had forgotten to ask.

"It's a Mrs. Clarke."

"Oh Lord above. And *where* is she calling from? Josephine, they should know better by now. You need to be schooling them on this kind of thing. If the wrong person calls, we could-"

"She says she's calling from Valley Stream. Valley Stream Care Home."

For a brief moment he looked dumbstruck, completely unable to process the information he had just been given, before he finally leapt from his chair and raced over to snatch the receiver from my hand. Within ten minutes of the call ending, we were all strapped into his car and heading as fast as Frank could go down a route that would lead us across state lines.

We drove for ten hours in near total silence, stopping rarely because of traffic or to refill the tank. As to the purpose of the trip, Grandfather would only confide that we were going to visit Emmy, our grandmother, as her last moments were upon her. A sharp pang of guilt swept through me as I realized I had given no thought as to what had become of her. She had gone from an unmoving, frightening figure trapped in a wheelchair, to nothing more than a character in a story. When the ghosts of that tale appeared to me, they had all seemed long dead. Yet now, having never left the Midwest or ever been this far west of my home, we were hurtling across the country to witness her last breath. When I began to ask what had happened to her, I was told not only that she had suffered for a long time, but that I should never concern myself with the details of disease. They were, after all, the mere minutiae of God's plan for us all: He wished to take my Grandmother to His side, and without her being placed in care, Grandfather would never have been to save me, my mother, or our family. Her illness was a means to a literal end. Within the context of our faith, the logic was unassailable.

Ann and I took turns to say out loud each new town or place name we saw a sign for, but our interest waned as the states we passed began to merge into one. The freeway stretched in impossibly straight lines into hazy distance and the same, unending flat plains and farmland appeared again and again at our side, their differences displaced by our speed. As the violent summer sun relented and my mind tired, I grew convinced I had seen the same houses, barns, and people earlier that day.

With night time encroaching on the day, and knowing we would not get to our final destination that day, Grandfather swung the car out at the next exit that came and followed the signs advertising a motel. The last thing I remembered was Mother complaining of pains in her chest she attributed to the seat belt in the car. I awoke the next morning in a strange bed, drenched in a pool of sweat, the temperature having already reached dizzying heights. The door of our room was open and outside,

Grandfather was belting Ann into the backseat and packing our case in the trunk. She desperately wound down the car window to release the stultifying air trapped inside, her tiny lungs gasping for cool air. Grandfather strode back in, his silhouette caught between the streaming sun and the dirt-grey walls of the room.

"It's time to rise, girl. We've only got 200 miles before we reach Denver. Your grandmother's waiting."

It was the first time I heard where we were actually going.

"Does Grandmother know we're coming?"

"Laura Jo, I don't think she knows her own name any more. In that way, she's been gone for quite a while now."

Scared at what we would find in Denver, I told him I did not want to go. I strongly resisted as he tried to lift me from beneath the covers.

"There's no choice in the matter, Laura Jo. You cannot simply cower, or shrink before the situations God places before you. At the other end of that road out there, my wife of thirty-eight years is dying. Her mind is as blank as those walls, and her suffering has been great. But do you see a man racked by fear? Do you see a man filled with sorrow?"

"No… but I don't want to see anyone die."

Death's what you're worried about?! Death is not the end for us, like it will be for others. How many people in this motel do you think God will ultimately save? Though your Grandmother's mind may be lost to the teachings of the Lord, He will not have forgotten her or how she has enabled us to be together. It was His will after all. It's our job to ease her into His long embrace. Now move yourself before my patience leaves me."

Head bowed and feeling foolish for my fear, I followed my

grandfather out into the harsh light. With each step, I attempted to dispel the image of my father's truck plummeting over the edge of the ravine.

When we finally entered Colorado, the landscape began to change dramatically. Though the lush plains remained on one side, the rolling hills on the other gave way to the looming splendor of the Rocky Mountains. Never had I seen ranges so vast; it was almost as if there were a rhythm to their peaks and elevations, a design and point to every crevice and crag. Purple rivers of rock cut through riots of orange and yellow, which quickly gave way to swathes of dense wooded green. Though summer was reaching its apex, the very tips of the peaks were still studded with crystalline snow. Distant streams forged their way down between the rocks in the vain hope of joining a sea that was not there. Ann sat practically across me for the rest of the journey, her head pressed against the glass and filled with wonder at the immense beauty of the mountains we moved alongside.

Momentarily I was distracted from the world outside the car by my mother's quiet display of pain and discomfort. She grimaced and sucked the air in around her as if there would soon be none left. The woman I once knew -- the gregarious, combustible woman -- would have made every ounce of fuss possible over the situation she found herself in: her husband dead, her baby due, her mother dying. I longed to comfort her, to fling my arms around her neck, knowing the deep pain of losing a parent only too well, but that emotional creature had long left us. She sat there now like an iceberg, slowly dissolving into the deep around her; the embodiment of stoicism and patience.

Before long we pulled inward from the mountains and headed for the suburbs surrounding Denver. Having broken the speed limit along the motorway to get here, it felt as if we were moving in slow motion once we turned onto the gridded rows of residential streets. Lawns hissed or burned in the summer haze, brass door handles glinted amidst the whitewashed brilliance of large town houses, and hedges formed perfect right angles amid an unreal postcard scene.

At the corner of a crossroads, Grandfather suddenly pulled the car over to the side of the road. Telling us to wait in the vehicle, his door was opened by a man in a crumpled beige linen suit, who had walked down the wheelchair ramp of the building to our right to greet us. His balding head was reddening in the early afternoon sun, and his face covered with sweat, which he wiped away on the back of his sleeve before embracing my grandfather like an old friend. In his hands he clutched a stack of documents, which he manically began to flip through. The car window on my side was rolled down just an inch, and through it I could just make out their conversation.

"I've been through this with a fine toothed comb, Frank. It's water-tight. Looks as if you're finally going to get what's yours. Feels like we've been waiting for this forever."

'We're not quite there. You know they're going to dispute this.'

"Let them do it. You're her husband. He made that will originally, and then she made hers. They'll laugh it out of court if they try. No contest."

"Isaac, I trust you. You've been my lawyer for fifteen years… but you'd better have done your homework on this. Everything depends upon this money. I can't do what I need to do without it. My plans are bound to it, and it's been sitting there unused for Lord knows how long, taunting me."

'Relax, Frank. Relax. That's why you pay me. And that's why we picked this place.'

'No questions.'

'Right. No questions. I've got a nurse -- Dorothy Leary -- lined up as a witness. I've greased that particular wheel, so she'll stay true. You just need your daughter to co-sign and we are *golden*.'

'How long?'

'Minutes, maybe hours. I'm surprised you made it before the end. It'll look even better.'

The lawyer loosened the belt on his trousers, his exaggerated paunch straining to break free from their confines, before telling my grandfather they had better go in. Calling on us to get out of the car, Mother took our hands and pulled us towards the large goose-grey paneled building.

'Now girls, there's no need to be frightened. Mama isn't who she once was, but she's still family. And we're here to say our goodbyes. I'm asking you to be big girls and stay strong for your grandfather. She's going to a better place. The Lord decides who to take and when to take us. It's not for us to reason.'

We were quickly buzzed through the reception area and entered a wide corridor with dozens of adjacent rooms. The whole place was drenched in that sickly, institutional air. No sunlight seemed to penetrate its interior, which only served to accentuate the drabness of the dozen poorly done paintings that clung to the walls. A rowing boat that seemed about to sink and drown its passengers; a cityscape of buildings whose foundations looked about ready to collapse; a bird that looked ready to peck out the eyes of anyone who neared; each more imposing and frightening than the next. A thick, nauseating mix of cleaning fluid and medicinal chemicals made me almost wretch as it worked its way into my lungs. Through a half open door I could see an elderly man in a maroon silk dressing gown slumped in a bedside chair. Bar a slight tremor in his right hand he looked already dead. By his side sat a canister of air. He shakily placed a gas mask over his face and twisted the top of a canister, causing a sinister hiss of rushing air to come forth. The death rattle of his chest and desperate gasp made me sharply turn away, so sure was I it would be his last moment. Yet I could hear the echo of his shuddering wheeze as we walked on. In another room a nurse sat spoon feeding a woman sat upright in bed, her eyes staring at something beyond the walls of her tiny room. A locked door to our right muffled sounds of a metallic object crashing to the floor. The voices of two nurses imploring an agitated, shouting man to get back into his bed seeped through, before one triggered a 'help' buzzer, a light immediately flashing above the door outside. A nurse raced past us and entered the room, a readied syringe in her hand. At the end of the corridor we were met by the manager of the care home, introduced as Mrs. Krause, who led us through the day room. A few scattered residents sat in a vegetative state before a cartoon flickering upon the television. These people existed in a place between life and death, and their sallow, grey faces saddened me so.

As we reached the door behind which my Grandmother Emmy resided, Mrs. Krause took one of my mother's hands in both of hers. Behind the rimless spectacles she wore, her eyes conveyed a well-practiced pity. It was an automatic gesture reserved for those whose relatives lay slowly expiring in the 24-hour care section. Though my grandfather had coaxed her back into some semblance of normal, everyday existence, Mother still barely left the house, so it was a shock to see her standing beside another woman. Compared to the highly groomed and tailored Mrs. Krause, Mother seemed so stark and unkempt. No trace of make-up adorned her, and her hair, though clean, looked dry and untamable. I was sure that the streaks of grey that I saw in it had appeared almost overnight, and her skin looked as if it had never been touched by sunlight. Mother quickly removed her hand, clearly irritated by Mrs. Krause's studied lines of condolence. In a symbolic attempt to shield herself, she moved Ann and I in front of her, Mrs. Krause noticing our presence for the first time.

"Your Mother, in her more lucid moments, has spoken of you. Those moments aren't very often now, I'm afraid."

"Will I have any time with her?"

"Some. She's forgotten how to breathe twice now. It does that to you. It's a terrible disease. With the onset of pneumonia on top, she really can't have long."

"What if she forgets to breathe again? I can't...."

Grandfather interjected.

"Then that's the will of the Lord. I do not want her kept alive artificially. Do you understand me?"

"Well, there are consent forms you'll need to sign in that case."

"Isaac, I thought we'd already signed a billion of these clauses and waivers. You best get that form, Mrs. Krause. I don't want our beliefs or my wife interfered with again. There's only so much my daughter can take."

The lawyer held his palms up to Mrs. Krause.

"Now, this is the kind of detail we've been paying you a great deal to take care of. I want this form now. We made it *abundantly* clear."

"Are you suggesting..."

Mrs. Krause froze as Ann began to cry at the raised voices. She suggested that rather than waste any more time we go in and see my grandmother.

"Maybe we should let the little ones keep their memories of their grandmother the way she once was."

Mother's reply contained an unmistakable note of venom. "They have no memories of their grandmother."

Mrs. Krause turned quickly away and opened the door. So cramped were the proportions of the room it was almost impossible to fit everyone inside. A nurse, who had clearly been dislodged from slumber by our entrance, was sent to fetch the appropriate forms. The journey through the care home had set my expectations of horror and I was not disappointed. My grandfather was well into his 50s at the time, and she was only a couple of years his junior. Yet the woman on the bed before me had aged beyond all logic and reason. Her warped, dry skin had shriveled tightly to her skull. Her eyes seemed to have been replaced by glass, reflecting the blankness of the ceiling above, and no trace of color remained in her hair. Mother reached out to touch her hand, but recoiled as she neared Emmy's brutally skeletal fingers. Below the oxygen tube pumping air into her nose, her mouth hung limply open. Her body was the mere residue of a human being. When Mother began to try and speak, she was interrupted by Frank.

"She's gone, Josephine. You'll simply be shouting into a void. The hours I've spent here. The hours I've waited for some sign, for some form of recognition."

"I know. But I've missed her for so long."

Ann reached a hand up and clasped her fingers around my grandmother's fragile wrist. The contact triggered a change in Emmy, who slowly turned her head to look at Ann, her face a study in confusion. She began to scan around the room, her eyes searching mine for a fleeting moment. When she came to my mother, she paused.

"Mom? Momma darling, it's me, Josephine. I'm here with Daddy. Can you hear me?"

Emmy looked back and forth between them, some vestige in her memory picking up on the tone of my mother's voice, but her mind was unable to process anything she saw. The minutes felt like hours as we stood with bated breath, hoping for acknowledgement. None came. Unable to take the tension anymore, the lawyer suggested we all adjourn to the relatives' waiting room, leaving my mother to spend time with Emmy. The nurse returned and Grandfather hastily began to sign the forms, not even bothering to read their contents. As he did so, Emmy, her lifeless eyes staring into space, became to quietly speak.

'You keep away from him now. Never come back. You stay away from him. You keep safe.'

The exertion of speaking saw her fall into an immediate and wretched sleep, and we left her alone with my mother, ignoring the nonsensical ramblings of a woman ravaged by disease.

Once in the waiting room, we did not have to wait long. Within less than three hours, my grandmother had passed to the other side. Grandfather had returned to the room shortly before Emmy died, and led my weeping mother out within moments of her last breath. I sat numbly watching my mother in pain once more, the lawyer asking her to sign as witness to her mother's will before her body was even cold. Grandfather gave no outward indication of emotion, which I simply interpreted as a stoic acceptance of God's will and His greater plan for us all. When I later asked him what, if anything, Grandmother's last few words meant, he reminded me that the tongue is a fire, a 'world of inequity' that no man or woman could control. It was, he said, the final dregs of poison escaping from her mortal body, devilishly warning us to try and resist God's grace. That resistance being something we knew was not possible.

Once he had obtained nurse Leary's signature, we soon found ourselves back outside by the car. Dusk was descending upon the Denver suburbs, and it felt as if we had just stepped from a terrible dream. Looking back at the care home as we drove away in the suffocating evening air, it seemed as if the entire building was little more than a monument to decay. It had already been decided that we would bury Grandmother in that very state, the cost of transporting her body being far too great. My grandfather, as a legal minister, would preside over the ceremony himself. The lawyer, who gave the distinct impression he was using every ounce of restraint not to smile, booked us into a local motel while funeral arrangements were made. It was at the motel that first evening that, after we'd completed our evening Bible study, that Grandfather decided to return Emmy to our presence once more and finally reveal what became of those two great pillars of his life.

***

Frank had watched Emmy take a call from her father, her face ashen and eyes reddening as the minister demanded she recount everything that had happened. The line broke up just as she began to explain that a great deal of damage had been inflicted upon the church. She stood there shaking as she repeated 'Daddy? Daddy?' into the receiver. Unable to hear any more of her sobbing, Frank walked over, grabbed her hand and placed the receiver back down upon its cradle.

"We made our choice. No point crying about it now."

"It doesn't have to be that way, Frank. You've got to make it right with Daddy. And I... I didn't speak in front of those people."

"But you didn't stop me. There's a reason for that. I saw that reason in your face. Looking down from up there I didn't just see worry and fear. I saw understanding. What I said made sense to you, like it did to others there. We all felt His irresistible grace. This was supposed to happen."

"We are *supposed* to be a family, Frank. You don't treat family that way. He's been like a father to you. He took you in."

Grandfather pointed to some unfixed point in the heavens.

"I know who my Father is."

Telling her to make herself scarce as the minister would soon return, Frank sat and calmly waited at the Peaks' dining room table, as the minister had once done for him. He had left the front door that opened to the hall wide open. From where he sat he would see the minister the second he crossed the threshold. His mind pored over the sermon he had delivered, and more than ever he felt the design of God is his actions. His body had been crippled by nerves, and he had given no real thought as to what he would say when he stood before the congregation. But each sentence that left his mouth had felt pre-ordained. It had flowed from him in a perfect torrent, almost as if he were reciting scripture itself. The fevered reaction of many in the congregation had made him feel alive in a way he never had before. Frank had surrendered himself to his fate and faith completely. Emmy's words were not completely lost on him. Caught up in a sense of his own righteousness, toxic feelings of guilt swirled around inside of him. Never had he dreamed of biting the hand that had fed and nourished him in such a public manner. Conflict was a certain consequence of his actions though, and he steeled himself in preparation for the tirade the minister was sure to unleash against him.

When Minister Earl finally walked through the door, Frank jumped to his feet. He felt short of breath, his lungs seeming to move upwards to his throat. Unable to look at the minister approaching, he winced as each slow, echoing step got closer, their methodical thuds rebounding through the old house. Half expecting the minister to strike out at him, he gripped the edge of the table to help absorb the force of any blow. Frank's head remained steadfastly bowed, his eyes scanning the floor in the hope of a hole that would swallow him. The silence suffocated the air around them. Frank tried to summon every shred of spiritual strength he could to ward off the shame enveloping him. Pictures of Eldridge St. Clair defiling the young stranger spun through his mind. Frank could see him waving from beneath the corpulent mound of flesh that writhed upon him. His internal battle was ended by a sharp crack on the table before him. A half crumbled brick greeted his eyes, as at last the Minister spoke.

"Look at me, Frank. Look at me."

It was the softness, the openness of his voice that made Frank finally turn to him. Strands of the minister's usually immaculate hair were matted across his forehead. Gone were his glasses, exposing his bloodshot, sleepless eyes. Patches of mud stained the kneecaps of his black trousers, his hands caked in the very same earth.

"Is this what you wanted, Frank? Have you longed to divide our community, to drive a wedge between each member of our flock, between me and you?"

"It's not about me or you, or anyone else. Can't you see what we were all becoming?"

"Son, you had no right to stand before them. And you want to tell *me* about the community I've lived in my entire life?"

"I want to tell you that we were losing sight of the very things you've had me learn and study. St. Clair is depraved, and yet we stand with our hands out for another check, embracing him as if none of what we believe matters. So don't stand before me now and act as if you're the only one who's been betrayed."

"Young man, I have just watched my mother die. The agony of her last breaths is something that will live with me until my own end. I've returned home to find my church falling apart at its very foundations, and the boy I took in to the heart of my family, attempting to commandeer my flock. You have no idea what you have done. The wildness that once defined you, that deep-seated need to destroy, has once again taken control. Frank, you're out of your depth on this, son. Did you even think to ask me for my reasoning? Do you not think the Lord has sent us St. Clair for a reason? He is the means through which we can continue to grow, to reach out beyond the borders of our town."

"Ask you? You were never prepared to listen, only to instruct. Forget the town, forget the damn church. What does any of that mean next to what we know to be right, to be true? It's you who's strayed from the path. Because... because the Lord has not persevered within you."

The minister could not help but laugh.

"You think the Lord has not set me apart, yet you are now his right hand? Your vanity knows no end. It's not too late though, Frank. I know you want to feel important, to be at the center of God's work, but betraying what we have done for you is not the way. We can turn this around. We'll go back out into the community together, atone for any mistakes we've made, and reach out to Eldridge-"

"Save your words, sir. This was not my plan. It is His grace and will that guides me."

"Such devoutness Frank, such devoutness. Yet all I see before me is a boy that believes himself to now be a man. But you're right, I should have been paying more attention to the things I've been taught. Truly, a man's enemies will be the members of his own household."

My grandfather looked defiantly into the eyes of the man who had become his father. He would say that in that instant, some essential fire within the unkempt and desperate minister died. No longer would he see a figure of influence and authority, but a man who would increasingly become a shell of his former self. As the minister walked away, Frank bellowed after him, his voice cracking with rage.

"They stumble because they are disobedient to the word, and to this doom they were also appointed!"

Pausing as he reached the door, Earl Peaks seemed unable to respond or even turn around, as if he would turn into a pillar of salt if he did. The earthbound part of Frank wanted to call out for forgiveness, but he too was unable to command the words to come forth.

***

Frank retreated to his room, certain in the knowledge that he would be asked to leave the Peaks' household. The minister would surely not be able to exist within the same four walls as him, seeing as he had not so much crossed a line as set fire to one. With little money and no accommodation, Frank would be forced to go door to door in the community in the hope that one of his most fervent supporters would grant him temporary lodging. But home or no home, he was determined to form a new congregation, away from the crumbling walls of the minister's church. He knew this was his true calling and that the minister and his family had been a means to this end. Yet as he was packing his meager belongings, Mrs. Isabelle entered the room and told him to stop what he was doing. Frank looked on, dumbfounded.

"You didn't think he would give up on you that easily, did you?"

"Mrs. Isabelle, I'm not going to change my mind. I'm truly sorry, *truly sorry* to have caused this conflict. But I can't run from my belief."

"The minister still wants you under this roof. He loves you, Frank. He knows you'll find that common ground again."

Not having the heart to argue his point with her, he smiled, stopped what he was doing and returned his things to their place.

Over the next week, he neither saw nor spoke to the minister. In his place each day, Earl Peaks sent a new visitor to try and make Frank understand the terrible mistake he believed he had made. Whether it was one of the Peaks' children, a disapproving member of the congregation, or a teacher from his Calvinist seminary, he respectfully repelled each one and dismantled their arguments with the calm conviction of the Chosen. No emotional infant's plea, local logic or scriptural proclamation could move him an inch. As Sunday approached, Frank began to fill his days preparing for the birth of his new church. With what little money he had, he hired a hall right in the center of town; a statement of intent to be both seen and heard. He then set about rounding up his flock, visiting anyone who had seemed to respond well or who had stayed in the church that previous Sunday. Though a handful of citizens had clearly developed grave misgivings about their support for Frank's foundling church and refused to even open the door to him, almost everyone else he met assured him of their attendance. Flushed with the success of his stumping, Frank even enlisted some of the Peaks' children to help him write out sermon sheets.

When the day of his first service arrived, Frank, not wanting to cause a commotion, had decided to rise before any of the Peaks family would normally be up. Yet as he descended the long, wide staircase that led to the front hall, he was greeted at the last step by Minister Earl. The minister's face seemed drawn and grey to Frank, his face sporting a day's stubble. From a few feet away, he could smell the noxious stench of stale whiskey on the minister's breath. Behind him lay the dozens of scattered leaves of paper. In the Minister's hand was one of Frank's sermon sheets.

"I guess you'll be needing this. Well, I hope you enjoy shouting into empty spaces, son."

"I believe when people give me their word, they'll be there."

"If your faith in your 'congregation' is going to be based upon their word alone, then you've one heck of a fall coming. Folk have been attending our church their entire lives and you think they'll give you that loyalty over a matter like this?"

"Yes. Yes I do."

"Well I guess you'd better run along then, you don't want to keep the legions waiting."

As Frank walked over the paper scattered floor, he realized they were not more sermon sheets of his.

"What are these papers, Minister?"

"Those? That's just a building survey telling me that if the damage to the church gets any worse and I don't find the money to fix it, then it will probably have to be condemned. But that's not for you to worry about, is it?"

On the way to the hall in town, Frank felt sick to his stomach. As he walked past the minister's church he was unable to bring himself to look at it. He wondered if this was how Lot felt as Sodom burned behind him. But unlike Lot, he needed no angels to guide him; he was certain in his heart that this was a sign that a new church – his church – would need to be built from the ashes of the old. The anticipation of seeing a swollen sea of faces before him as he delivered his sermon made each step swifter than the last.

Frank was soon to feel crushed. He stood behind his makeshift pulpit in a sparsely populated hall. A mere couple of dozen people had sheepishly taken their place before him, a sense of discomfort washing through them as the lack of numbers became apparent. Undeterred, Frank delivered his sophomore speech with all the passion of the first. Yet he knew that few were in his thrall. They congregation looked everywhere but at him, the men checking their wristwatches every few minutes, desperate for the ordeal to be over. When Frank brought proceedings to a close the townsfolk hurried towards the door. They hastily made excuses for their quick exits or offered up half-hearted goodbyes. The last person to leave was elderly woman. Frank quickly caught up to her as she shuffled towards the door.

"I know what you going to ask me, son. And the answer's no."

"What was I going to ask?"

"Whether or not I was going to attend next week."

"Yes. That obvious, was it? And why, Mrs. Wesley, won't you be coming, if I may ask?"

"Son, now I've no time for St. Clair and his ways, or the manner in which Minister Earl ingratiates himself with him. But he wields an awful lot of influence in this town. You think you and the minister are the only ones who've been going door to door? The difference is that St. Clair owns half of this town; you don't. He's close with the mayor; every lawyer working here's a personal friend of his; and he's on more committees and boards than you've got fingers and toes. Half the folks in this room are afraid he'll raise the rent on their house or see to it that they're no longer employed in one of his factories or establishments."

"They're scared of him?"

"They're practical. People gotta stay dry and people gotta eat."

Frank couldn't hide his rage.

"Then the Lord moves in none of them. They'll all be damned."

"That's right son, together they have become useless."

Crestfallen, Frank watched her turn and make an agonizingly slow descent down the steps of the hall's entrance. He called out as she reached the bottom.

"And what about you, Mrs.Wesley?"

She straightened her small black hat and looked back up, straight into his eyes.

"Me? I figure I've lived a good, God-fearing life. At my age the fear doesn't seem so important anymore. If I'm not chosen now, then I don't suppose He'll be getting around to that anytime soon."

The sight that greeted Frank when he walked back into the Peaks household was one of destruction; shards of glass and china shimmered in the dim light of the central hall. All of the Peaks' children were down on their knees, sweeping up the wreckage as fast as they could. They froze as Frank stepped between them, all unable to look at him, bar Emmy.

"He's been drinking, Frank. Hardly anyone came. The folk who were there didn't want to be there. He won't even listen to Mother. She tried to pull him back."

Minister Peaks appeared at the top of the staircase, a nearly empty quart of Bourbon in his hand. Sweating and disheveled, he tried unsteadily to navigate the stairs, spilling the alcohol as he descended.

"Is that the prodigal son I see before me? What a *vision* on this wonderful day. There – pick it up. A little bit more of your inheritance on the floor. You've spent everything else I've given you."

The youngest of the Peaks' children, David, began to cry.

"You're scaring your children, sir."

"You want to discuss fear with me? An empty church that's damn well falling apart is something to fear! What price a child's tears by comparison? Tell me, what price?"

"This is not my doing. I understand my place in His world. You've forgotten yours."

The minister began laughing so hard he had to bend over to catch his breath. He dropped the bottle as he did so, letting it crash down the last few steps.

"You've not come to repent then, to ask forgiveness from your loving father? That's as clear as the glass at your feet. Well I'm sorry son, there's no fattened calf left here to kill for you. In fact there's going to be nothing much left here before long."

Minister Peaks stumbled down towards Frank, his face contorted in anger. Emmy stood up and placed herself between them both, sheltering Frank behind her.

"Daddy! No!"

"Oh come now, would I lay a finger on such a sainted head! Surely my darling, surely you should be protecting me from him?"

Isabelle Peaks came rushing in from the dining room.

"Earl. That's enough. Where's the man I married gone? You're still the cornerstone of this community. In God's name act like it."

She began dragging his great form towards the kitchen, his resistance gone. Laughing aloud once more, he mockingly made the sign of the cross as he went.

"In the name of Frank Marlin, amen."

***

Grandfather would often describe the next few months as a time of refusal and denial. Within the Peaks household he cut an isolated figure and was forced to look on as both his and the Minister's separate lives and plans unraveled even further. Eldridge St. Clair had instigated and then orchestrated, by means fair and unfair, a town wide embargo of attendance at both the Peaks-led church and Frank's fledging mission. Though they were twinned in their misery, Frank was simply able to walk away from his situation and be at no risk of monetary loss or social ruin. This was part of God's greater design for him, the weeding out of those within whom His Grace had not persevered.

Minister Peaks' whole life and family were bound to the town and financially chained to the crumbling edifice of the church. After being pressured by St. Clair, the checks many townsfolk had written out towards the restoration of the church began to be cancelled before Minister Earl had gotten around to cashing them, or they simply threatened to sue should their money not be returned. St. Clair was doing all he could to force the resignation of the minister and had even begun negotiations to buy the land on which the Calvinist seminary school stood – a place Frank was no longer welcome to attend. The minister desperately tried to finance reconstruction himself and began selling off whatever household items and family heirlooms he could uproot. Almost every morning, Frank awoke to find movers transporting yet another piece of antique furniture as Mrs. Isabelle stood by and wept. Soon the huge house seemed stripped bare, its innards seemingly eaten away by swarms of starving insects.

But whatever money he recouped from the sale of possessions, it was nowhere near enough. With each rain that came, more damage was inflicted upon the church, leading the minister to unsuccessfully try to borrow money against his family property. No local bank would lend him the money; Eldridge St. Clair sat upon each Board of Trustees and stored his personal fortune within them. As the situation worsened, the minister turned to alcohol to ever greater degrees. It was rare now to see him without a glass of bourbon in his hands, or searching through the house to find where he had misplaced his open bottle. Still he could not bring himself to let Frank go, or accept that the town had shown their back to him. His days were consumed by pleading Frank to rekindle their partnership, or pleading with St. Clair to end his campaign against his church and family. Neither would relent; one through faith and one through pride. Frank's calmness and St. Clair's delight in the face of his desperation sent him spiraling ever downwards.

Frank was only ever to come into contact with St. Clair once more: as he walked hopelessly around town he came across St. Clair stepping from his automobile, its chrome fins gleaming in the deep afternoon sun. With a winning postcard smile etched upon his face, he simply declared 'Well, good day to you, sir, *good* day!' He turned his back upon Frank, struck out his cane and walked off, quietly intoning the words to "I'm sitting on top of the world."

Glory, hallelujah, I just phoned the parson,

"Hey, Par, get ready to call!"

Just like Humpty Dumpty,

I'm ready to fall.

St. Clair had won the battle for the town. Frank could do nothing but accept this. As an outcast within his own church and community, my grandfather had taken it upon himself to continue his education. He devoured every text he could and prayed with an even greater intensity. Frank knew that events were not his to shape, and patiently wanted for God to reveal the course he should follow. While chaos reigned in the Peaks household, he grew closer still to Emmy, heartened as he was by her desire to protect him from the anger of her father. Moreover, he came to depend on her company, for only she would now listen and learn from his unwavering convictions. Her spellbound attention to him spurred on his belief that one day many would hang as devoutly off his every remark, despite his rejection by the wider congregation. In his naivety, he believed Emmy's interest in him was solely the result of faith, of her unconditional election by God. He was soon proved wrong.

When he woke in the middle of one night to the sound of scraping and banging beneath his floorboards, he was startled to find her sitting on the edge of his bed, quietly watching him. In the bruised-blue light, she cut a ghostly figure.

"Daddy's removing the lighting fixtures from the hall ceiling. He says they are worth a small fortune. He's drunk again and Mother finally made good on her threats. She's taken David and Dorothy to friends of hers in town. We older ones are supposed to meet her there tomorrow. I've never seen her so angry. I... I don't think she's coming back."

"Lord help him. I guess your mother figured they'd be nothing left to sell but his children if he carries on. I hate to see him so desperate."

"He's about drunk enough to sell us all off tonight."

"Maybe we should find where he's hiding them and start… what are you doing?"

Emmy had pulled back Frank's cover and lain down beside him.

"It's killing me being all alone and listening to him. And I'm cold. Don't you want me here?"

"That's not the point."

'I'm plagued by thoughts of you, Frank. Thoughts I know are wrong."

"What… what do you mean?'

'Thoughts of us being together in ways that we shouldn't. I'm scared Frank, scared of what I want to do."

As he stuttered to speak, she silenced him by kissing him, her hands desperately moving on him as she did so. His head felt as if it were melting, the moral urge to stop her conflicting immediately with his basest desires. Finally, he pushed her away from him.

"I want to be yours, Frank. Whatever happens I want to stay with you."

"Emmy, this has got to stop. You're 15, and it's against the-"

"I'll be 16 next year. There's going to be nothing left for us here. What's left for us in this town? Daddy's drinking himself into the gutter, and Mother won't take us away from it. Will you take me away from it, Frank?"

A scream and a crash came from below. Frank and Emmy raced

out of the room and along to the top of the staircase. Earl Peaks lay squirming beneath the ladder on the floor. The light fitting lay in pieces on the floor. As Emmy began to cry, Frank put his arm around her and they made their way down the steps towards the pathetic form of the minister.

"Minister, are you hurt? Maybe we should get a doctor."

"Shut up, boy! Get your damn arm off of my daughter!"

Earl Peaks rose unsteadily to his feet. The left lens in his glasses had shattered and blood dripped from the ear on the same side. For a long moment he studied them as if they were under a microscope. Drunk as he was, he instinctively sensed a difference in the way they stood there together.

"Why are you here together? Have you been in his room? Have you?!"

Her stunned silence spoke volumes.

"Did he touch you, my darling; did he make you do anything?"

"I haven't done anything. Minister, you have to stop this. It's over."

"Your poisonous presence in this house is what's over, boy. If you've touched her... I want you gone by morning!"

Emmy exploded into anger.

"Then I'm going too! You're going to make us all leave. Where's my father gone? Where is he?"

"Nobody's leaving but him."

"Haven't you even noticed that Mother's already left?!"

Rage incarnate, he staggered forward and with one terrible movement crashed his fist into Frank's temple. When Emmy stepped in his way he pushed her aside and rained a shower of blows down on

Frank until he stopped moving. Earl Peaks grabbed Frank by the collar of his nightclothes and began dragging him across the floor, all the way through the hall and into his study, which he bolted behind him.

Frank woke some minutes later, still limp and only semi-conscious, seated before the minister's desk. The minister sat across from him, devouring the last remnants of a bottle of whiskey, his shirt wet from the rush to pour the alcohol down his throat.

"Behold, the self-anointed one awakes!"

His mouth swollen and bruised, Frank could not speak without great pain. But he felt compelled to speak when, as his vision started to clear, he noticed a revolver on the desk in front of him, its barrel open and all of its chambers empty.

"I'd turn the other cheek, minister, but it seems you've hit me on both. Is this how you want to treat you family? You beat someone you've likened to a son in front of your own daughter?"

"No, you're no son of mine. I thought the Lord had sent you to me. A lamb in wolf's clothing, who would help lead this town to its salvation. How wrong I was! How very wrong. All you have accomplished is to tear this town in two, to scare the flock away from its shelter. Look what you've done to us, Frank. It seems you were a wolf after all."

"Your family has fled from you, but I'm the destroyer? I've followed my faith to the very letter, the faith you introduced me to, and now you blame me for what God has predestined to be so?"

"You're right in a way. I see things clearly now, Frank. You were the real test all along, and the ultimate proof of my election. Everything goes back to that moment in the bank. Jimmy was supposed to pull the trigger. No *bullet* would have left that gun. I would have been spared. We've merely delayed the inevitable."

Frank knew what was coming.

"And this is how you're going to test your faith?"

"It's how we're both going to."

Earl Peaks pulled open the draw, from which he took a single bullet and loaded it into the barrel of the revolver. He spun the barrel before flicking it closed, mid-turn. Slowly he raised the gun and aimed it directly at Frank's head.

"This will only prove how far you've fallen."

"It will prove you're the Devil himself."

Frank could not help but smile. He neither panicked nor showed fear, and offered himself up quietly to the will of the Lord.

'The difference between us is that I have accepted whatever fate God has for me. Your faith is a house of cards. I pity you. So go ahead and shoot."

Frank sat serenely, his display of contentment clearly infuriating the minister. Sweat began to pour from him as he cocked the revolver and willed himself to pull the trigger.

"What if God, wanting to show His wrath and to make His power known-"

"Be quiet!"

"-endured with much longsuffering the vessels-"

"I said shut your damn mouth, boy!"

"-of wrath prepared for destruction, and that He might make known the riches of His glory…"

The minister squeezed his finger, only to hear the dull click of the weapon. Shock and confusion engulfed him as Frank continued, as if he were not in the room.

"...on the vessels of mercy, which..."

Pointing the gun at the side of his temple, the minister looked up towards the heavens, certain of his moment of delivery. A second later, Frank sat covered in the minister's blood. Earl Peaks' lifeless body rebounded back off the chair and slumped forward onto the desk, his shattered skull facing my grandfather. Wiping the blood from his face as best he could, Frank moved around to the minister and whispered into his ear.

'...He had prepared beforehand for glory.'

By the minister's right hand lay an open copy of the Bible. One passage -- Isaiah 34: 16 -- was marked by blood: 'Look in the scroll of the LORD and read: None of these will be missing, not one will lack her mate. For it is his mouth that has given the order, and his Spirit will gather them together.' Behind the padded door, he could hear Emmy screaming. It was not her Father's name she called aloud, but his own. Frank knew from this point on that he would lack for a mate no longer.

7. We Seed Each Twisted Bloom

Two days after she died, we buried Emmy. Her final resting place was to be a cemetery just outside of a mountain town called Ward. Past the half-burnt signpost of the municipal border, we were greeted by rows and rows of abandoned or broken cars and farming equipment. Amid this endless metal junkyard, I noticed that there were no door numbers on any of the houses. Ward, it seemed, was a place you came to be anonymous, or came to hide - a faceless town in the middle of nowhere. The few folk we saw watched us with an intense, instinctive distrust, before quickly retreating into their grim, dank houses. It was the perfect place to bury someone without any questions or interference, the perfect place to put a grave that no one would ever visit.

As we drove ever upward I began to feel dizzy; the thin air and suffocating gloom of the endless vista of grey rock and stone left me reeling. It seemed as if the whole mountain had somehow been frozen in mid-avalanche, and that the smallest amount of pressure would trigger an almighty collapse. Try as I might, I could not suppress the thought that this was the kind of road on which my father had met his end. Upon passing the last few isolated houses on the mountain road, we pulled off into the cemetery. Once out of the car, you could see the steam rise from the earth among the wild, overgrown foliage that strangled lines of crumbling crosses and tombstones. Her tiny piece of land was wedged into a darkened corner of the cemetery grounds, the surrounding copse blocking out almost any natural light. The lawyer had apparently bought the plot months in advance, and it had patiently awaited the body of my grandmother ever since. My grandfather had decided to dispense with a formal service, his reasoning being that there were no local Calvinist churches and no one worthy of conducting her ceremony but him. I had expected a long, elaborate eulogy. Instead he delivered a terse, impersonal prayer in a manner that was stripped of any emotion. Beside him, my mother wept as the casket was lowered by two cemetery workers into the damp earth; it was the last time I would see her cry. Grandfather pulled the workers aside and I watched as he handed them each a roll of dollars. When we finally walked out of the unsettling murk, it was Emmy Peaks that my grandfather whispered goodbye to, as if Emmy Marlin had never existed.

In truth, it was hard to find a cent's worth of emotion for someone that I did not know. Each time I had been in her presence it had been a truly horrifying experience. I was happy that she had been chosen and would now be with God. Though I was perhaps more relieved that I would never again see her trapped in that wretched halfway house between life and death. It was for my mother that my heart bled. With each twist and turn down through the ranges, she became ever more agitated. Small convulsions rippled through her body, and a grey sheen cloaked her skin. When we were finally greeted by open plains once more, her discomfort became unmanageable. She clawed at the seatbelt, pulling it away from her stomach. Rapt in agony, she then gripped my Grandfather by the shoulder, forcing him to slide the car to a screeching halt off the side of the road, the dust blooming in great sheets from under us.

"What in the name of God are you doing, woman?!"

"She's coming. She's coming. Not here, Lord not here!"

She pointed towards a pool of water that had dripped off the seat and settled at her feet. Grandfather sat dead still, momentarily stunned, before he unbuckled her belt and told us two girls to get out of the car.

"Momma, you're scaring me!"

Grandfather shot a fierce look at Ann that sent the words in her mouth into retreat. Frantically, he looked along the roadway for a telephone or even a stranger's assistance, but could see nothing but miles of empty roadway, heat and dust. The temperature had jumped as soon as we left the mountains and the earth now cooked beneath out feet.

"Ann, I want you to listen real careful. Your mom is having her child. There's no one around for miles so I need you to stay here with your sister while I take care of the situation. You dare not move from here. This is what God has chosen for us."

He moved us onto the grassy bank before he drove the car off the road into a wide meadow. From a distance we watched him fold the seats down and open the trunk of the hatchback, placing our mother inside. The wind would occasionally carry her cries of pain over to us, Ann wincing each time. Time passed as if someone was trying to force back the hands of a clock. Our skin became livid red and blotched as the sun beat remorselessly down upon it. We could practically ring out the sweat that seeped into our dresses.

"She'll be alright, Ann. You heard what Grandfather said."

"But what if-"

"There's no 'ifs' about anything. God wouldn't let her die like this. There'd be no point. He says our family is here for a greater purpose. Don't you believe that?"

"I do, I do. I just want Mom."

"I do too."

Holding each other close, we continued to wait, with nothing but a lone circling bird or passing car for company. After an uncertain number of agonizing hours, things unfolded before us as if in a dream.

Frank Joseph Marlin stood in the center of the meadow with our newborn sister held aloft to the dying sun. In a single day my grandfather had been both the escort of death and the receiver of life. Ann and I sat and looked on in wonder. Here he was once again, the principal figure in a momentous act, as if such circumstance were irresistibly drawn to him. Though my mother was the one giving birth, she seemed almost incidental to events, the vessel through which Frank could prove his prominence once more.

***

The realtor sped away behind us. In my grandfather's hands were dozens upon dozens of keys, which belonged to three converted barns he had just leased. The forest seemed to grow outward from their great structures before finally giving way to the clearing we now all stood in. I had never seen him so happy, a grin like a crescent moon sat unmovable on his face. Above us, the sky was saturated in an all too perfect blue, as if played on an endless movie reel.

"This is the start of everything girls, the start of everything!"

"Why, Grandpa?"

"Because, my sweet, we have the means. And soon we'll have the people. Our people are on their way!"

Grandfather knelt down beside me and Ann. He emanated a sense of complete triumph as he pointed towards his newly acquired empire.

"You know our history well, girls. It's long been God's will that I have my own ministry, my own flock to govern and watch over. My patience and resolve on this have been sorely tested, but the saints have

123

preserved in my life, and God has finally cleared the path down which I need to walk. Down which we all must walk. My plans will take root like never before. Starting right here. Right *here!*"

He slammed his fist into the dirt beside him. Mother clasped us both tightly to her.

"Now girls, you're going to be a big part of those plans. We all are. Outside of this family there's nothing but sickness and sin, and we've done our best to protect you from it. But we're not going to do that anymore. You're old enough now to see people and their sick ways for what they are. This family is finally going to take a stand, finally establish out place in the order of things. Your grandfather needs your faith, your conviction. He deserves it after all he's done for us. There'll be things we have to sacrifice. But those sacrifices will be for the greater good of our flock. "

Frank would remind us time and again that there was no sacrifice we could make that was as great as Christ's sacrifice for the chosen few. We were indebted to him, so the time had come to put his teaching, and our faith, into practice.

Duly, the chosen few began to arrive. Where they came from, I did not know. Accent was certainly no reflection of their origin: despite the Louisiana drawls, the clipped New England phrases, these folk could have been from anywhere and nowhere. Some were introduced as blood relatives, others as friends, but all were straight away called family. The deferential manner in which they all greeted Frank Marlin was a sight to behold. Some barely held back their tears, the sheer relief of being around him once more all too much. If the king's heart is in the hand of the Lord, Frank was undoubtedly the king. It was obvious that this first wave of strangers had known my grandfather for a long time, and had waited and waited to be here with us. Judging by the speed with which they were able to arrive after my grandmother's death, many had obviously been prepared to leave the place they had once called home at a literal moment's notice. They each had crammed their worldly possessions into a ramshackle collection of RVs, cars and trailers. As quickly as the vehicles were unloaded, anything unneeded was shipped into town and sold off. Every new arrival would immediately be allotted rooms in one of the barns. By the end of the week there were nearly thirty new faces waiting to greet us as we stepped from our quarters. As the direct descendants of Frank Marlin, we were granted a prestige like no other. We were the first to be served at the communal dining tables, the first to be asked to read at our morning prayer meetings, and our names were spoken in hushed, reverential tones. In fact our very presence could conjure silence from the younger members of this newly swollen flock. I sought and indulged this new-found celebrity, as did my mother, whose quiet demeanor was quickly beginning to erode. People would congregate around my newborn sister, Beth, and constantly give Josephine gifts for her, like some strange, modern nativity.

Among the first to arrive was John Murphy-Wood, who would forever be known to us as Cousin John. Though he was 'family,' from the very moment I met him, he troubled me. Standing before me, his great, bulky frame absorbed the air around him. For reasons known only to him, he was dressed as if he was about to go hunting; he wore heavy terrain boots and a camouflage jacket, whatever the weather. Sometimes he even sported a faded orange vest over it. He reached down and moved my chin slowly up until I was looking straight at his eyes; eyes that were forever hidden behind dreadful round, brown-tinted glasses. They always seemed far too small for his bloated, mottled face. Cousin John spoke as if he had met me before.

"Well, looky here now. Haven't you gotten all grown up? How old are you now? Twelve, thirteen?"

He gently squeezed my face, causing my lips to part.

"Cat got your tongue?"

"Ten. I've just turned ten."

"Now I could have sworn you were older than that. Thought the last time Josephine sent me on a picture you were... all grown up. But hey, you kids grow up quickly nowadays, don't you?"

Where age was concerned, Cousin John was probably in his late twenties then, though he looked as if he could have been forty. It was impossible to know his true age; years of poor living had seen to that. There was always something possessive in how he spoke of me in those early days, but I was yet to be told why. But despite my instinctive misgivings, I was merely a child, and unable to define what I felt. Moreover, I was child who was always compliant and ready to please anyone who had been chosen, especially a relative, and a leading individual within my grandfather's new ministry.

John was typical of a certain kind of young man who my grandfather amassed around him. A sense of entitlement ran through their veins, a cocksure knowledge that they were destined for a special place in this kingdom and the next, and a willingness to do whatever it took to make that remain the case. This meant they subjugated themselves entirely to the whims of my grandfather. It was a civil contract of sorts: in return for their unquestioning obedience, their surrendering of any independent thought, and indefinite commitment to our cause, they received a place at the left hand of my grandfather, and the right hand of God Himself. They had probably been the troublemaker in their class at school, the disruptive child who had refused to learn or listen. Deep inside they raged against the constraints imposed upon them by youth, authority and circumstance. The systems and ways of the world were beneath them. No doubt they bullied and abused as they themselves may have been dominated or put down, their anger at not being heard or respected becoming almost uncontrollable. These arrogant, disenfranchised young men would often take the path down which violence led them. Or they would end up at the door of someone like Frank Marlin. With him they found a justification for their innate sense of superiority; with him they were able to nurture it. He would hear their despair, channel their anger and impose a divine framework upon their existence. In Frank, the likes of Cousin John also saw an older version of themselves. There was, however, one key difference: Grandfather was smarter than all of them. He was always careful to keep a certain distance between his own powers of intellect and those of others.

Michael and Ramona Chance were a different sort of person entirely. Life had clearly visited misfortune after misfortune upon them. The stench of failure, of emotional and financial poverty hung upon them. I saw them for the first time from the high, tilting windows of our sleeping quarters. They greeted my grandfather like children returned from years in the wilderness. Poorly dressed and ragged, they resembled a pair of gutted buildings, entirely hollowed out by the cruel hand that fate had given them to play. In the months following their arrival, I would overhear snatches of conversation among the adults detailing Michael's bankruptcy, his loss of the one good job he ever had due to an incidence of fraud by a colleague he had trusted, his failure to find proper employment since, and how overwhelming debt had caused them to lose their house.

Ramona had struggled in vain for years to conceive children, only to finally find she was as barren as a desert. Endless cycles of depression had punctuated their nomadic wanderings from state to state, the fading hope of a future driving them on. All that remained in them was a nagging sense of desperation, and a desire to find the reason for the tragic state of their lives. Enter Frank Marlin with the promise of a better, richer life. Once he had established his new ministry, he would provide them a permanent base from which to be at peace, both financially and spiritually. And here he was, making good at that promise. Now they could abdicate any responsibility for the day to day running of their lives. They would be told what they should eat, how to dress, when they should pray, how they should make money, and what to believe. Michael and Ramona would be finally made to feel valuable, their worries evaporating like early morning mist through Frank's blazing sun. Should anything go wrong, they, in many incidences, would no longer be seen as culpable. Michael and Ramona's vulnerability was both their sweetest characteristic and their greatest failing. Frank's power over them hinged on it. Inside his ministry there would be protection, sustenance, an unwavering vision of the world to come. Outside, the thousand humiliations and endless grind of their past lay in wait, ready once more to become their present. There was no real choice for them. They were ripe and ready to be saved.

Ramona, especially, spoke to me and Ann as if we were angels that had fallen to earth. Whenever we were in her company her gaze barely left us. Not long after they had arrived, Mother declared that she had to go to town to attend to preparations for our new ministry, and Ramona surreptitiously tried to take over the washing and dressing of us.

As I stood on a stool to see into the bathroom mirror that morning, her reflection slowly came into view behind me. Despite my protestations, she began to get me ready for the day.

"You have such fine hair, Laura Jo. It looks almost silver in this light. All of you girls are the sweetest creatures on God's earth."

She turned her eyes away from me. A veil of sadness had drifted down upon her.

"If… if I have children, you know I'd want them to be just like you."

"I'm old enough to wash myself now, you know. You really don't need to."

"Aww, darling, isn't it nice to have someone looking out for you though? I know you're a big girl. But everyone needs a little care, right?"

"I guess so."

"We'll just keep it between us then. Our little secret."

I suppose it was a taste of everything she had wanted. She simply could not help herself, despite our presence being both a pleasure and an utter torment. It was no secret either that Ramona believed that she would still one day have children. Frank did everything he could to encourage that belief. Regardless of her advancing years and frigid womb, Frank would tell her to ignore those perverse, calculating doctors, and all those charlatan-scientists with their bankrupt ideas on the origins of humanity. It was His will that governed whether she conceived or not.

For some, joining the burgeoning ministry was a willing fall into the spider's web. Others were unaware they were in a web at all, or even that the spider existed. Over the years, Frank had developed an instinctive sense of whom to ensnare. It was to the margins he looked, to the downtrodden, and to the socially excluded. Among us there were students, cut off from their familiar surroundings, open to extreme ideas and a different way of living; ex-military personnel unable to deal with the lack of regimentation and discipline in everyday life; lonely divorcees, estranged from their once tight-knit families and longing for company and comfort; those unable to shake off the wretched grip of bereavement, their days spent hopelessly searching for meaning in the death of their loved ones. Then there were those who felt they had hit the limitations of their own religious upbringing. Whatever spiritual values they had once believed in no longer satisfied the deep, puritanical fault line opening within them.

***

By the time the very last of my grandfather's followers had arrived, the rooms in the barns were swollen to bursting point. Despite the cramped conditions and the fact that children accounted for at least a third of our population, there was already something unnaturally ordered and quiet about our tiny mock town. And like any town, there were rules that were required to be followed. Grandfather had tasked me and Ann with delivering a letter to each and every adult member of our congregation, which detailed the limits of our consumption and interaction with the outside world.

There was to be no personal use of television. The one TV was to be in the communal building, and only certain channels would be made available. No newspapers except those distributed by the newly created ministry council, upon which sat my grandfather, Mother, Cousin John, and a one-time lawyer called Edward Gant. No books were allowed to be read, bar a list of religious texts that anyone could freely obtain. No music was to be played at any time and stringed instruments were completely banned. There were to be no visitors to our property of any kind, unless specifically sanctioned by my grandfather. A strict curfew of eleven o'clock was put in place. Every family or individual would have to contribute financially to the ministry. All accounts were to be centralized, with the new ministry overseeing the deployment of funds. Any existing land or house ownership was to be declared and submitted for assessment. Alongside these rules, a dense handbook was then sent out. Within it, the fundamental articles of our faith were listed in minute detail, our belief system distilled to its perfect essence, and key points of American law outlined within the context of faith. We were expected to carry it all times. A twenty-four hour amnesty on newly outlawed materials and goods was declared, and designated spots for each kind of possession to be left were listed. A forest of televisions, stereos and musical instruments quickly mushroomed in the communal dining room, all ready to be sold on. A miniature mountain of books, newspapers were soon set ablaze in the clearing beyond the barns, as were any toys that had been either declared idolatrous, or were seen to clearly promote homosexual values. Bar the odd teary child, whose favorite plaything was now a black, smoldering mass, no one complained or protested. These people had not come to continue their lives, or take a holiday from them; they had come to free themselves from their previous existence. They willingly changed their lifestyles, gave up their domestic goods, and signed over their pay checks from the local jobs they had quickly found. Each step was a deliberate act of liberation.

With our basic rules in place, and the whole encampment a hive of frenetic activity, Grandfather declared that May 4th, 1997, would mark the start of our Eternal Campaign. Now we were settled and our physical numbers and finances were strong, the moment was coming for us to reach out, to declare our beliefs to the wider world. To this point, the only thing that had brought us together was Frank Marlin, and our faith in him. Now, for the first time, he would address us as one. We were all ordered to gather at 9 am in the central barn, its floor having been emptied of furniture. The whole congregation jostled for space before a makeshift stage, on which stood Mother, Cousin John and Gant. You could feel the collective fervor of the room as we awaited the arrival of Grandfather. Neither I, nor probably any of the others, had ever experienced such a feeling of anticipation. Behind me there was suddenly a commotion, and a wave of people parted as Frank strode solemnly into the room, his eyes fixed above all of our heads. A round of spontaneous applause broke out and people shouted "Reverend Marlin's here!" as he took to the stage and stood in the middle of the ministry council. When he raised his hands to both acknowledge and quieten us all, the immediate silence became electric.

"Tell me, friends, why are you here? Have you come to live like frightened mice? To meekly go about your existence, waiting for the crumbs to drop from the tables of others? Perhaps it's an easy life that you seek. One in which, like children, you'll play make believe with your faith, dressing in its finery whilst your actions, your conviction runs counter to the image?"

People around me shook their heads, or clutched at their chests, the tension overwhelming.

"If that is the case, then God has offered you no eternal security, He has not called you to communion with Himself. But I do not think that this is the case, no, not at all! As I look out across you now, I see those that, like me, have been set apart by the Lord, in whom the saints have persisted. Yes! We are bound together by His sovereign will."

The silence was shattered by another cry of exultation.

"Yet we are also bound together by a more solemn task, my friends. For outside of the walls of our family lies a nation in the clutches of depravity, a festering cesspool of degradation and sodomy. Our nation promotes and accepts homosexuality, it normalizes such behavior. It practically teaches it in our schools and colleges! It is utterly damned. And God will bring destruction upon them. For in every ancient culture, 'faggots' are pieces of wood designed to burn for great lengths of time, to fuel nature's fire. I tell you know, those who flaunt their venomous, filthy lifestyles will be enflamed by God's anger."

His words drifted down and radiated among us. We felt guiltless joy, and the bond of a common purpose.

"But let us be clear. We are not here to save these people. They cannot be saved, or save themselves. We are here to hold a mirror to their perversion; our anger will be a reflection of His anger and disgust. Though I must tell you what they're going to label us: extremists, fascists, *intolerant* bigots. They will hate us, vilify us, and besmirch our family's name at every opportunity. But will we bend? Will we be made to tolerate what is the opposite of what we know to be God's law?

A ferocious cry of "No!" leapt up around me.

"The same corrupt Semites that killed Jesus Christ himself will turn their ire on you and your children. They will crucify our reputation; they will accuse us of untold ills. And every filthy Catholic and Lutheran, with their bankrupt, junk theology will point their sodomite fingers at us on the streets and in court. But we will triumph because God and His texts are on our side. Our invertebrate government and its army of media whores will defend their queer lackeys and their sodomite public. But we will not bow in the face of their pressure and consternation. We will simply point and say 'Thou shalt not lie with mankind as with womankind; it is abomination.' They cannot defend the indefensible. It is still God's immutable law, regardless of what they do to us. Our road is a long, arduous one, and I, as your reverend, will always be there to lead you on, to channel the will of the Lord himself. Come with me on this journey. We must remain organized and steadfast; put your trust in the council before you. Come with me on this journey. Do not falter or doubt, or let your heart be deadened by the poison of the wider world. Come with me on this journey, and I'll promise you one thing..."

Cries of "What?!" and "Tell us!" ricocheted around the room. "Salvation."

And with that, he walked off the stage and out towards the clearing beyond our town, the near deafening sounds of our euphoric ovation following after him.

The tables were arranged in the gloaming. They formed a rigid pyramid shape with Grandfather at its apex. This was to be the scene of the first great Confession. There was no month in which this gathering did not take place until that of our destruction. The Confession was one of the many mechanisms through which Frank Marlin would establish and maintain control over his followers. His method was simple and direct; no magic or sleight of hand was involved. Frank, with the other members of the Council, would call forth one person and ask them to stand before them. A wave of silence would wash over the congregation as Frank would unflinchingly stare at whoever he had chosen until a sign of deep discomfort or outright fear manifested itself. The one chosen would inevitably begin to search the faces of the congregation around for an ounce of understanding and sympathy, but would be met by dozens of glares conveying nothing but condemnation. No one wanted at this point to be associated with this person, even if it was their wife, husband or child.

Thomas Goodman was the first ever lamb to be called for slaughter by the Council.

His body seemed to contract and wither as he edged towards Frank, his face shot through with confusion and nervous ticks. He stood there, not knowing what he done, or what was expected of him. Before Frank even uttered a word it was like he had burrowed deep into Thomas's mind. When the silence had reached a deafening crescendo, and Goodman looked as if each intake of breath was an act of suffocation, Frank Marlin began his three part play of interrogation, accusation and reconciliation. Raising his hand towards the heavens, he began to solemnly reveal the nature of the situation.

"Friends, until our last days these gatherings shall be called. This is our Confession. Our time of truth, through which those chosen will be brought forth to relieve themselves of their indiscretions, their selfish longings, and every sin they thought to shield from His eyes. It is to remind us that these sins are part of His grand architecture, and determine your continued election. Discussed and acknowledged here before your brothers and sisters, they will matter no more."

Thomas came from old money. He had continued to make more money still as a tax attorney in Manhattan, and had lived a life in which every available social privilege had been thrust upon him. The rumors had spread since his arrival that a complete mental breakdown, brought on by the pressures of the corporate world, had triggered him to take permanent leave of that cossetted world. Grandfather had met him through a contact at a drug rehabilitation center. Thomas' cocaine habit had been so bad that he had had to have surgery to fix his nasal cavities. Grandfather had offered an escape from Thomas' familial and societal expectations. Looking at him at that moment, however, it was clear he still carried many of the affections of his former life around with him. His manner and dress reeked of weekend lunches on New England lawns, of the polished oak tables of executive boardrooms. As he stood there, nerves unraveling like a ball of wool, Frank began to dissect him.

"Thomas. Tell me why you are dressed today as if you are going to work?"

"My work?"

"Your previous employment."

"I guess it's what I feel comfortable in."

"You feel comfortable in that world?"

"It's what I've always known."

"And that's where you want to be right now, isn't it? Setting up some offshore accounts, making the big decisions. Sipping a scotch and back slapping with your Jew friends. Planning a luxury break for your wife and kids. And yet God's work, the work He has chosen for you through me, has not even begun!"

"No Frank, I-"

"You stand before me in your $300 shirt and your woven tie and plead that you want to be here?"

"I gave it up, Frank. I gave up that life to be here!"

"And yet you dress in that way still. Because in your heart that's where you want be. You want your brothers and sisters to know that's where you really belong."

Mother interjected. "Do you know what your clothes tell us, Thomas Goodman? That you think you're better than us."

"Of course I don't. I had opportunities. A life mapped out. I rejected it!"

Frank's laughter boomed out across the field.

"That was God's choice for you. Yet still you fight and deny His will. He takes you from the clutches of the same race that crucified his only son, those stealers of the wealth of others, and *this* is how he is repaid"

Thomas' voice had cracked. Barely a recognizable sound could leave his mouth. His small sons had begun to cry as they sat at a nearby table, as they watched their crestfallen father ridiculed before them.

"Thomas, do you know what you have done?"

His response was pitiably meek. He dragged the words out as if they were heavy as boulders.

"Yes… yes I do. I haven't shown the proper commitment to my faith."

Grandfather hushed the whispering among the congregation.

"Thomas, dear Thomas. The saints have persevered in you. All is not lost. You are able to hold a mirror to your actions and understand the shadowland within which they exist. We are all here for you, Thomas. But if your mind and intentions lead elsewhere, for what purpose do you serve Him?"

Thomas clawed at the hot tears falling from his cheeks. His self-worth and confidence had taken the bluntest of public blows.

"Come to me now, Thomas. Leave your sadness there. The Lord will clear a path for you, through me."

Thomas Goodman stumbled as if a zombie towards Frank,

whose great hands pulled his head deep into his chest as Thomas continued to weep.

"Cast your minds to what is written in scripture: "For it is by grace you have been saved, through faith - and this is not from yourselves, it is the gift of God." This is as true for you all as it is to the man who embraces me now. Your brother Thomas has returned to his place in our flock. Stand now and reach out to him.""

A cacophony of noise erupted around us as people clapped and cheered for Thomas' brave admission, and his journey back into the heart of our congregation. No one among us wanted to be in his place. They would all know now that it could be them. That each month the cycle of blame and praise, the transition from leper to loved one would be endlessly repeated. As I had sat there watching pieces of Thomas' very soul being sliced away by my grandfather's surgical words, a current of joy passed through me. I had an unshakeable sense of belief that my exulted position with this congregation would mean I would never have to face this bear pit. How could I, a point in the holy lineage between Frank Marlin and God, the elect among the elected, ever be offered as raw meat to the flock? How foolish I was.

Yet right then, we stood on the cusp of our golden age. The light had risen on my Grandfather's house, and he would not waste the dawn. He had the means, the people and an unflinching will. Thirty long years of his frustration would pour out in an unimaginable torrent of condemnation, hate and death. The days and years to come would stamp the name of our family in the consciousness of a nation. It reverberates still.

8. Formative Years

Within the walls of our compound, Josephine would one day build a special room. In it you could trace the modern history of our family and our church. The 14ft high walls were adorned on each side with hundreds of framed newspaper clippings that detailed our movements and actions across the nation. It was a grand hymn to our impact and influence, and a shrine to my grandfather and mother's vainglory. In my mid-teens I would make regular pilgrimages to this hallowed space and spend hours trying to find my own face in the pictures of the yellowing pages. Those grainy images revealed my rapid transition from girl to young woman. I had aged among the lurid headlines, vitriolic editorials, poisonous profiles, and the isolated dispatches of support. The reputation of our organization changed and mutated before our eyes. You could see our language growing ever more extreme as our notoriety mushroomed. I was spellbound by the swirling mass of information and would consume it until it became an overwhelming blur. Lines of scripture, lines of hate. Faces contorted in joy and anger. Crosses and placards. Crying housewives and furious bikers. Guns and police. Funerals and demonstrations. State buildings and court houses. Abortion clinics and synagogues. All life had become manifest through the prism of our belief.

Yet, amid the media maelstrom, it was a single newspaper article that changed our church forever. For this well-crafted, law-bound conflagration of words would point towards a burning compound and the deaths of dozens. This is not to say that the writer was to blame for our fate. Those words were inked by Daniel Riley of the *Ohio Star* in good faith, with the noblest of intentions. Its significance was that it was the first piece about us - the stealer of innocence, and the harbinger of possibilities. The danger lay in what it represented to both Frank and Josephine: a secular framework within which to defend our very existence and the very air upon which our fire could live and grow. The piece would appear a few weeks after my grandfather's mauling of Thomas Goodman, and no words would ever prove as important to our congregation as its title: This Is Still America.

Years after Daniel Riley submitted that piece to his editor, he would write another nationally syndicated piece recanting and retracting all that he had outlined before. He would argue for the slaying of a beast he had helped breathe life into. It was a hopeless, forlorn plea that would fight for, and fail to get, attention in an ever swelling sea of discourse about us. By the time it hit newsstands, mailboxes or the screens of computers, we had long moved on to a place where bad press was far more vital than good, and would only be measured by the prestige and size of the publication or media source.

Riley was a seasoned reporter for the *Star*, and had stumbled upon us by chance. A detour to get a cup of coffee on his way to another assignment way out in Salina had led to him being given a leaflet by a small blond-haired boy, a little older than nine years of age. Upon the piece of paper he took from the smiling child were the words "Jesus didn't save you. Come find out why!" It gave a date and time, and listed the meeting place as a lawn in front of a church he had never heard of. He likely stuffed it in his pocket or even a trashcan, and went about his business. But something about those vague words stuck in his mind. They were not an invitation as much as they were an affront, a provocation. It must have gnawed at the edge of his mind all week, until that part of him that really needed to know what those words meant was itching. And like an old fashioned newshound, his gut sensed the possibility of a story.

***

Having decided that we must go out into wider society to lay down the markers of our belief, Frank Marlin knew that the right target had to be found for our fledging church's public demonstration. He had scoured the soft underbelly of the state's hundreds of churches and settled upon the Holy Trinity Church in Marion. It met his exacting criteria completely and was reflective of so many late twentieth century Christian institutions. Those who attended services would be presented with a benign Lutheran Christianity that skimmed around the merest surface of belief. There was no fire, no brimstone, and a doling out of well-worn weekly homilies about Christ's love for all humanity. In all probability, the middle-class folk who formed the congregation were largely well-adjusted citizens, liberal in the broadest sense and saw their participation as a rite of passage at what was little more than community center or a place to be seen with and integrate with their neighbors. This was religion as wallpaper, a decorative covering over their beautifully manicured lives. And Frank Marlin intended to rip it from the walls, hold a mirror to these men and women of little substance.

All week the children aged over eight in our congregation had been sent out onto the streets of downtown Salina. We were bussed in by Mother from the outskirts of Shawnee County each morning, alongside the turbulent surface of the river, its sides occupied by wild grass at the height of summer bloom, to be greeted by an alien forest of concrete. After organizing the rest of the children into small groups, we would set off among the Wendys, the Chick-fil-A and Bob Evans, and begin street by street to hand out leaflets to anyone who would take one. We had been strictly instructed to avoid vagrants. As I wandered among the shop fronts, I felt entranced. Each one glowed with exotic possibilities; objects for which I rarely knew the use, and brightly colored advertisements with slogans that I did not understand radiated from behind glass. It was as much as I could do to not constantly stop and stare. My memories of even being taken to a restaurant by my father were so dim that they seemed no more than a flight of the imagination. The smell of a burger joint or the malty hum emanating from an open bar doorway seemed to drift in from another time.

The mission itself was very easy to complete. Few of those we tried to hand leaflets to would refuse. They townspeople of Salina, on their way to work or browsing the shops, would eagerly reach out to take the piece of paper from our little hands, surgical smiles playing upon our faces. Their delight would quickly transform into confusion or horror when either they glanced at the text on the flyer, or we added for effect as we walked on "Thank you! Jesus didn't save you." Or "Sorry you're damned!" Frankly, the only issue was stopping the younger children giving them out to just anyone. John Maybanks was by far the worst: his desire to be done as quickly as possible so he could play and mess around was infuriating. I would always follow him closely.

"John. Your bag is nearly empty. You couldn't possibly be done so quickly."

He would screw his round little face up in mock anger and try to protest.

"I just met a lot of people by the bus station. They all wanted one!"

"Don't lie to me, John. I've watched you. You dumped ten in the hands of a homeless man, most of which blew off into the street. On your soul John, how many times does Reverend Marlin have to remind you? Why do I have to be your nursemaid?"

He could not take being chastened in any way and would invariably cry. Mother would pick us after two hours and ask each child for a run-down of the type of people we gave the leaflets out to, and the reactions that they had engendered. You could see how flushed with pride she felt as we laid bare the shock of our paper gifts to Salina. She and Frank did not expect anyone to come. That was never the point. It was an exercise in infuriation, a first shot across the bows. Like Daniel Riley, if they did turn up, they would soon regret that their interest was ever piqued.

***

I can still remember the smell of the flowers that dotted the lawn in front of the Holy Trinity church. The Jack-in-the-Pulpits jostled for space with the Blue Sage and filled the air as our congregation fought for standing space beside each other. The church itself was at the edge of a quiet suburban neighborhood, the kind that was docile, clichéd and tranquil as you could imagine. A local school that was no doubt the pride of the area, a row of independent, artisanal shops not too far away, beautifully kept common land which all the residents paid towards, and a well maintained playground for the children. It was perfectly anywhere. We arrived way before the members of the church had finished their breakfasts in their bright and airy kitchens, or strapped their children into their station wagons. Our instructions were simple: to approach and talk to churchgoers as they walked in, and to react, in accordance with our beliefs, as impassioned as could physically manage to Frank's remonstrations and statements. The man we would soon realize was Daniel Riley stood 20ft away to the right of us, beside the shaded stone walls of the church. In his top pocket, a tape recorder protruded and a notepad and pen stood at the ready in his hands. Frank, of course, has already noticed him, and quickly realized he might be playing to an even largely gallery than he had expected.

The minister of Holy Trinity Church was a softly spoken Irish-American called Michael O'Connell. Looking and sounding as benevolent and nondescript as the worship he practiced, he approached us in a welcoming but entirely bemused manner.

"I take it you ladies and gentleman aren't here for today's service! Glad you're making use of the lawn, I suppose."

Frank knew before he spoke that he had the measure of the man.

"No, sir. We are not."

"So, well, I guess that only leaves one question: what exactly *are* you here for?"

"We're here to explain to you that God has little purpose for you and the trash you peddle as faith will not save you. We're here to tell you that you're little more than a wet-nurse for these liberal sops, and their grubby little lives of perversion and greed."

Michael O'Connell's mouth looked as if a train could pass through it. Despite Cousin John and Edward Gant practically laughing in his face, he eventually managed to gather himself.

"That's an interesting perspective you have there. Now I'm not going to ask you to leave. This is a public space. But I would ask you to leave my congregation alone."

"This isn't a perspective, minister. This is about your ignorance of God's immutable laws. They come here for a dog-and-pony show at the county fair. Well when your flock parades up and down here I'm afraid we're duty bound to explain just how damned they are."

O'Connell clawed at the collar of his shirt, pulling it away from his skin as the morning heat and rising anger caused him to half choke on his words.

"I won't have you harassing anyone! This is not the way decent people behave in this nation. Who are you people? What's your name, sir?!"

Edward Gant could not help but contribute. "You'll know his name soon enough. It's what we know about you that you should worry about."

The distinct note of threat in his voice saw O'Connell slowly back away, still facing us, towards the church, his face a violent shade of red.

"I've tried to be civil. But as you've no interest in anything but hateful words, you'll have to explain yourself to the police."

"I have no one but God to explain myself to. So I think I can reconcile myself to dealing with local law enforcement."

As I made my way to my grandfather's side and took his hand, he smiled at me in sheer delight, like a child on Christmas morning. It had struck me that our congregation had no name, nothing to identify ourselves by or bond us further. Edward Gant's words would have carried more than just a vague sense of menace if we had.

"Grandpa, why haven't we a name? It feels strange that we don't know what to call ourselves. We're not the same as anyone else, after all."

"Your brain is as sharp as a barber's razor, child. The same thought just struck me. Maybe I've been too busy organizing everything else to give it the thought I should."

When the congregation began to arrive *en masse* we descended upon them like a swarm of wasps. Children moved among them and thrust leaflets into their hands. The adults in turn began to greet them with a barrage of faith as we knew it, the air simultaneously pierced by the noise of an approaching police siren.

"I hope you enjoy hot flames on your skin. That's what you and your family will be getting for eternity."

"You know you let your children attend schools and churches run by sodomites?"

"That mealy-mouthed minister in there will not save you. He will not absolve you. No prayers, no good deeds will save you. It is down to God's will alone."

The words spread like a poison through the stunned churchgoers. Their disgust at the disturbance of their Sunday routine was palpable, their faces crumpled up in horror and heads shaking with contempt. It was all too much for one of this flock, who looked like a straight up Jersey mobster. Pushing Cousin John aside as if he weighed nothing, he turned his anger upon us all.

"I don't care if this is holy ground; get the fuck out of my face. You keep troubling our peace and I'll put every last one of you on the floor. Are you clear on that, you fucking nut-jobs?"

One of his sons smiled at me as they were dragged past us. I had to try hard to not smile back. I was happy I could at least let him know I was sorry his father would burn in Hell.

Frank corralled us into a group once more and began to hold

court, his right fist clenched and held up as if sparring with an imaginary opponent.

"Now you've seen it with your own eyes. The mockery made of God's works by those unfit for purpose. This is not His house, but a wretched place inhabited by those who were born into sin and have remained there ever since. Look at who this 'minister' lets walk through these doors. Look at who he tolerates. Look at the behavior he condones. You saw with your own eyes the *kind* of men that have entered this filthy pit. The kind of men that the book they now read from declares an abomination. As a con-"

A police officer had placed his hand on Frank's shoulder, bringing his sermon to a grinding halt.

"Yeah, OK. I think we've all had enough of the freak show. You've had your fun; you've ruined these peoples' days and you're crossing a line. You need to gather up your possessions and your children and make your way off this property. And just so we're clear: we don't ask twice around here."

"We know our rights, son. Maybe I need to remind you of them."

The officer moved his great bulk closer, sighing as he brushed his hands through his grey and white buzz-cut, lowly murmuring to Frank.

"Is that so? I tell you what: Fuck your rights. I told you we didn't ask twice. You don't get to behave like this here. Get on your fucking knees, grandpa."

He signaled to the other officer, a young Latino.

"Carlos, cuff this son of a bitch and read him his rights for disturbing the peace, for God's sake. I can't take any more of this crap this morning. It's giving me an ulcer. I've barely digested my Apple Jacks."

Frank did not struggle. He seemed very well practiced at this routine. On his knees he was still taller than me. People from our church began to curse the officers, and cry shame at their actions.

"Look on, friends. This is always how persecution starts. No modern country is more repressive than the good old USA. Does anyone wonder why God has abandoned this nation? Edward - you know what to do. Now everyone, stay calm."

They led Grandfather away, forced him into the cramped back seat of their car, and drove off. Mother hushed the angry congregation, and reminded them that Frank had asked for order.

"We knew this would happen. It was inevitable. This is how it's always going to be. Don't kid yourselves that it will be any different. It's the price we pay for our beliefs. Now let's go home."

As she walked away, the man I had seen watching us with the notepad and pen approached my mother, his right hand extended to greet her. His arm around her back, he walked her over towards the shadowed wall of the church, the little red light on his recorder flashing on as he did so.

***

Waves of relief swept through our camp when Frank returned the next morning with Edward Gant. Christina White, a relatively new member of the congregation, was the first to see him. She had knelt in our field and had prayed all night, her eyes bloodshot with fatigue and worry, and her cries of joy had alerted us all to Frank's release. As he strode through between the barns he lifted Christine's child, Heather, onto his shoulders as we gathered around him, her hands lifted into the air by Frank like a triumphant boxer.

Christine's faith in and love of Frank was further proof of the devotion he inspired. He had met her on a recent trip in a diner on the outskirts of Connecticut. She was sitting in a booth trying to get her two young children to eat their pancakes and blueberries instead of pulling each other's hair and fighting. Frank watched as she gave up trying to control them and wistfully gazed at the highway beyond. Instinctively he sensed something in her manner and look, a void waiting to be filled. I don't know exactly what he said, but between introducing himself on that day and a brief exchange of letters thereafter, he persuaded her to leave her husband, home, and life. Her husband would have returned one day to find one of his children alone and crying in her bed, and a terse note of goodbye from his wife, who had taken their eldest with her. She would literally have disappeared into thin air, having smashed his world into sharp little pieces. The remnants of their domestic bliss would haunt him until the day he stopped breathing. I suppose Frank offered Christine what he had offered the rest of us – the promise of a greater life, a life of eternal meaning. Perhaps her old reality was simply too average, too staid, the responsibility and rigors of domesticity causing her to question her entire existence. Frank had found a perfect nuclear family waiting to destruct. The terrible elixir of words he had decanted into her head achieved their goal with ease. No resistance, no discussion, but unquestioning acceptance. From a housewife making the school run, to a face on a missing poster, to a devotee of a man she had met once in roadside food stop, all in the space of a few months.

It was apt that Christine was the first to see Frank that day, as

behind him followed another new recruit. On his night in prison Frank
had convinced, with the guaranteed promise of food and a place to lay
his head, a man called AJ Smith to return with him. Smith had spent a
few days in lock-up over the illegal ownership of a military-issued
firearm. The kind of charge Edward Gant had found it impossibly easy to
get dropped. Hailing from Wyoming, Smith was jobless, itinerant and
purposeless. Bar a brief time in the National Guard, from which he was
dishonorably discharged, he had been drifting like tumbleweed from
state to state, unable to put down roots. I would come to know him as the
most genuinely paranoid man I had ever met, his hatred of the American
government and its institutions so raw and pure that it would take the
average person's breath away. This worldview became even more
frightening when combined with his absolute obsession with firearms. AJ
Smith would quickly ascend within the ranks of our congregation, once
my grandfather had bolted on a religious resolve to his civil fury.

The next few weeks would follow an identical pattern. We
would decamp onto the lawn of the Holy Trinity church, engage with and
protest against its flock and their doomed beliefs, and leave with one of
our members having had an altercation with, or been arrested by, the
local police. With each visit our confidence in what we were doing grew
and grew. We could feel and see the anger of those we spoke to rising,
the number of children attending services dwindling, the minister
O'Connell being driven to near breakdown and threats of litigation by
our continued presence. In the midst of one of these hours of frenzy,
there would appear literal signs of what was to come. Inspired by the
brightly colored adverts and billboards that had so enamored me in
downtown Salina, I had made a crude placard from a broken fence post
and a square piece of solid cardboard. I had used a mix of paints to

construct a colorful and direct message. Vibrant yellows, reds and blues screamed out a message in childish writing 'Jesus didn't save you!' as little smiley faces grinned from each corner. Mother had told me it was the best thing I had ever done; Grandfather would state to all that I had set an example of true conviction to the rest of the flock.

It was the image of the placard that would feature most prominently in the column that would appear in the *Ohio Star* in the third week of our protest. As our congregation passed plates back and forth over breakfast one morning, Mother called for quiet, and then slowly distributed a newspaper to the head of each family. She then held aloft her own copy, opened up to a full page article on the events we had initiated. It was a seminal moment in our existence, and its words burn inside my head still.

This is still America

By Daniel Riley.

The French philosopher Voltaire is often wrongly attributed with writing "I may disapprove of what you say, but I will defend to the death your right to say it." Whoever misinterpreted the old Parisian, it is a phrase that has echoed down the ages and found a home in the languages of all major western democracies. It, perhaps too neatly, summarizes what is, and what should remain a fundamental principle of this nation of ours, and all those like it. For there are indeed moments in all our lives when the views of others stand in direct opposition to the things we believe or understand to be true. The ability to tolerate those opinions so virulently hostile to our own, despite the anger or upset or disgust they may cause, is one of the high water marks of our nation.

In both our public and private lives, it is easy to forget that our deluge of differences, and the scorn, vitriol and derision that surround them are not, in fact, signs of a malfunctioning society, but the very glue that helps bind it together. We lose ourselves in the polarizing rhetoric of our major political parties, the warring words of opposing scientific and commercial lobbies, the cultural, economic and racial divides that still haunt us, and the million domestic dramas unfolding behind closed doors. These are in reality the signs of our rude health.

I was re-awoken from my own slumber to this centuries old notion by events that have unfolded outside the doors of Salina's Holy Trinity church over the last few weeks. The tranquil grounds of this average, suburban place of worship have been transformed by what can only be described as a modern day biblical siege.

For the last three weeks a 50-strong band of Calvinist fundamentalists have taken it upon themselves to protest what they see as the 'degradation' of God's words by churches here in Ohio. Led by the towering, charismatic figure of Frank Joseph Marlin, they have harangued, insulted and harassed those attending services by reverend Michael O'Connell.

Mild in manner and nature, with a church that is 'open to all' regardless of their race or sexual persuasion, Reverend O'Connell would be undoubtedly seen as a pillar of a thoroughly modern local community. The same could never be said of the man that has driven Reverend O'Connell apoplectic with rage and forced him to seek recourse to state law: Marlin is the kind of figure libertarians have sweat-filled nightmares about. He and his followers are hateful, homophobic, and vicious in their condemnation of those whose beliefs are different to their own. For instance, anyone attending the Holy Trinity church recently would have been treated to hearing how they were damned to spend eternity in hell by children not old enough to have their second set of teeth. They may have been told with a smile that their love for another man was a disgusting abomination and that Jesus categorically did not die for them. I watched as tempers were lost, minor scuffles broke out, and, inevitably, the local police were called to restore a semblance of order.

The level of fury this has generated in the local community is astonishing. After the initial shock towards Marlin and his followers' protests had subsided, a general feeling of bemusement and anger at what the townsfolk are describing as "un-American" and "illegal" has set in. The air of illegality has been aided by at least one arrest of Marlin's pack every day. People simply want it stopped and Marlin silenced so they can go again normally about their daily lives.

And every one of the people who think that is entirely wrong.

The basic facts are simple: our First Amendment rights grant us all the right to say the most 'un-American' things, to air the most preposterous marginal beliefs, and the sickest, darkest thoughts that enter our minds. Vigorous free speech - even a variety so extreme - in the open hall of ideas is one of the few treasures we have as citizens. The congregation of the Holy Trinity, Reverend O'Connell, as well as the readers of this newspaper all have to remember this most salient fact. Given the numbers of arrests, this has been clearly lost upon the misguided Salina Police Department. I have seen no more 'un-American' act than people expressing their right to say what they believe being carted away in patrol cars. While of course our sympathies lie with O'Connell and all those abused going about their daily business – who, to all reasonable thought, have done nothing wrong - it is their duty, and ours, to tolerate that abuse for the far greater good. We must, as Donald H. Kirkley put it, accept it "up to the last limits of the endurable."

Josephine Marlin, daughter of Frank and nominal spokesperson for the group, makes a further valid point from the perspective of her flock.

"These aren't 'our' views. They are written down in God's good works. It's there in the plainest black and white. We're doing this in accordance with His laws. Did we make it up that man should not lay down with man? No. Did we decide that these people can do nothing to affect their salvation? No."

We could call them dangerous extremists or outright crazies, but on a rational level, their interpretation of Christian doctrine holds as much value as any other. Though we may recoil at the expression that "Sodomites burn in hell" they can quickly reference a biblical verse that supports just that standpoint.

Amid the vortex of anger generated by such divisive views and language, we simply *must* remember that this is still America: The right to free speech is this nation's holy frontier. History repeatedly warns us of the kind of nation that exists beyond those boundaries. Those mid-20th century shadows loom large. So for all the unease, tumult and ferocious opposition it may cause, it is a frontier we must defend and expand at all costs.

This 'opinion piece' would set in motion of chain of events that would determine our future. Its first major impact was on the very way we defined ourselves. Both Frank and my mother would be found clutching that copy of the *Ohio Star* as if it had been stitched to them. Copies of the page were plastered over every surface imaginable. Through the window to his makeshift office I'd watch Frank pace, his body bent in the cramped space, his hands gesticulating wildly as he over-enunciated words and phrases from Riley's article. After three whole days of this, he called for attention as we sat down to our breakfast. I had rarely seen him happier as he gently hushed the congregation, my mother tapping a knife on the side of a glass as he did.

"Friends, let me first apologize for my distracted state of mind. The wonderful furor we have created has swept me before it. Between that church, the courthouse steps and the local jail, I have been torn all ways. But, as in all things, this is His plan for me. He needed these things to pass, and the article that you've all seen in the newspaper to be written. Each one is a sign; a sign that the law, despite its recent stranglehold over us, is how we can and must sustain ourselves. We must become intimate with its every nuance, its every vagary, until it becomes a shield before us from the likes of the Salina City Police Department. It was a sign too that we can no longer afford to fall under the broadest banner of Calvinism: we are a band apart, our future mapped out along the lines of no others. All my adult life I have subsumed myself to the word of the word of our Lord, to each sentence of our canon. But I have come to understand that those works are not the only way He communicates His wishes."

He held the newspaper aloft as if it were the very cup of Christ itself.

"It is our fate to be the great mirror of these times. To become this, we must differentiate all that we are from the thousand sects whose rotten worship and barren morals dilute and corrupt everything we believe. My friends, our name should burn and glow from these pages. It should solder our message into their minds, and open a shaft of light onto their sorry world. They must know that we are the vanguard, the very edge of His blade. Our name must define our pu\rpose. From this day we know ourselves as the Frontier Saints. From tomorrow, the state of Ohio will..."

The sheer volume of noise that erupted seemed to shake everything around me. Children were lifted into the air as if they might fly from their parents' arms, their chests straining as they hollered. AJ Smith, Edward Gant and my mother walked among us and distributed an explanatory leaflet on how and when our name must be used. People gathered around my grandfather, all clutching this new holy text, their fingers stretching out to try to get their merest touch of his clothing or skin. He stood serenely in our center, his power over us expanding as each moment passed.

***

The euphoria was soon punctured. Alongside our joy, Daniel Riley's article had brought with it the flip side of such exposure. It had enraged the wider local community and led to anyone holding any kind of religious grudge to seek us out. We began to wake each morning to emptied piles of rubbish strewn between the barns. The remnants of roadkill were hung from doors, their maggot-ridden carcasses swarming with squadrons of flies. Graffiti was emblazoned in foot high letters on the side of the housing structures: "Fascist Scum," "Burn in Hell," "In passing judgment on another you condemn yourself – Romans 2:1-3". I explained to Mother that the children in the camp were terrified, and asked if Grandfather was going to stop these people. She looked at me, clearly disgusted that I had even countenanced such a thing.

"Were you raised to be dumb, child?"

"No."

"Then why ask such stupid questions? Do you not think we're letting this happen for a reason? The vermin that enters these grounds each night are just reminders that we are on the correct path."

She pointed to the rotting corpse of an indeterminate animal.

"This will only drive us closer together. This is our proof to the likes of Daniel Riley that it is *we* who are in fact persecuted for our beliefs. We cannot give in to this. Now you calm those children. You know they listen to every word you say."

Though give in is what we ultimately did. It was not just the handiwork of a few local crazies that would drive us out, but the threatening behavior of the Salina police, who were clearly incensed at their name being dragged through the mud in the press. The entire congregation was awoken to the draining screech of police sirens in the early hours of the morning for over a week. When a posse of men, led by AJ Smith, followed the noise to its source at the entrance of our encampment, the sound would suddenly stop. They would be greeted by a dozen officers standing in front of four police cars with the hazard lights on full beam behind them. They would tip their hats, all wearing sunglasses in the middle of the night, gun handles gleaming at their sides. It would take Grandfather a long time to calm down Smith, to get him to stop proclaiming that he'd shoot the next "uniformed bastard" who set foot on our land. An article duly appeared in the *Ohio Star* on the desecration of our property and a reminder of our right to believe, worship and protest as we saw fit, but this merely seemed to escalate things. Rocks were slung through windows, car tires were let down, and when we returned a few days later from what was to prove our last protest at the Holy Trinity church, we were met by the burnt-out mess of the storehouse we used for food. If Grandfather was looking for portents of things to come, then this was surely the greatest.

The Council dined separately from the main congregation that evening. Only my sisters and I were privy to their conversation as once again our relationship to Frank brought with it special privileges. A sense of agitation hung in the air: Cousin John stabbed at the chicken on his plate as if it were not already dead, and AJ Smith sat sulking like a toddler, refusing to let a single morsel pass his lips. Edward Gant was the first to offer an opinion on the negative turn of events.

"I think we need to be done with that church now. We've made our point. It's not as if there aren't worthier targets."

Mother looked sharply at Gant.

"Targets? You of all people should know better than to use language like that. My father picked that so-called house of God for a far greater purpose."

I did not know if she meant Frank or God himself.

"Josephine, sooner or later they're going to throw a charge at us that sticks. There'll be nothing I can do, and we've wrung every piece of juice we can from this situation."

Cousin John was infuriated at the prospect of such helplessness.

"Then so be it! Let them lock us up. Maybe a martyr's just what we need."

Frank sat silently listening, his hands clasped together in semi-prayer. AJ Smith finally slipped away from his temper.

"The fact is we can't defend this place. Edward's right. We've brought the trouble back here and they aren't going to leave us alone. Anyone can enter this space from almost every side. There are no barriers to the outside world. And if folk can get in, then this pressure is bound to start driving some of folk out. I don't like being defenseless. Pretty soon every nigger and spick from downtown will be up here trying to take advantage, looting us wholesale – the whole goddamn rainbow brigade will be picketing us outside our own doorstep."

Frank stood and silenced everyone.

"Now I've listened to you all. And while I understand your concerns for out congregation, it's not ourselves we must listen to. This was never going to be our final destination, never our final port of call for Him. Our name may now be fixed, but as a church and a place we are not. Do you really think this is where we should be?"

Cousin John tried in vain to protest.

"But there's a battle here now and we can't just up-"

"You passed through Mexico City once, John. Do you know how that sprawling mass came to be?"

As ever, Cousin John was comfortable in his complete lack of knowledge and understanding about everything beyond Calvinism and whatever hot-headed emotion he felt at the time.

"It exists because of a vision. The Aztecs, animals though they may really have been, at least had a devoutness of faith. Through their God Huitzilopochtli they were presented with a prophecy, a prophecy of an eagle resting on a prickly pear cactus. In its claws it held a snake. They were told that vision would come to pass and that when it did this was the land on which they had to construct their empire, their home. That's where Mexico City was born. God will show *me* when we come to the place from which we must lay down foundations. He will send us the time, the money and people to do this."

They knew immediately that the decision had been taken. They were certain this event would come to pass.

***

For the next few years we would drift slowly from state to state. Our trail of anger and hate illuminated Minnesota, Missouri, Nebraska, North Dakota, Ohio, and Wisconsin before, like blood trickling through snow, we migrated up the eastern seaboard. Each town we lit upon quickly took on the air of the plague-infested; its residents galvanized and united by their mutual horror at the arrival of our cortege.

The changes that took place to both the church and me in this time were monumental. First and foremost, we had come to understand the power of being properly prepared. In those early years of protest, so few of our adversaries acted out of anything other than blind rage. They were all easily bated, and easily argued against. Every aspect of our demonstrations was properly detailed and controlled. Not one member of our group attended a protest without being drilled to within an inch of mental exhaustion as to why they were there and what they believed in that context. Grandfather had given Mother and me the task of overseeing the production line of banners and placards that were often created specifically for each new protest. We fed upon the vitriol their swirling mass of color and incendiary words created. "The land of the freaks" was written over American flags as we protested upon on the steps of a courthouse in Maine over the corruption of the American legislature by queers and their liberal agenda. "Killers of prophets" and "Sons and daughters of Satan" were plastered over hooked cross Star of Davids as we engaged in a running battle with a small community of Jews in upstate New York. Given our ever escalating notoriety, TV crews would regularly descend with their cameras transfixing on the lurid signs held by such angelic Aryan children. Mother's skill at utilizing and manipulating the media's attention was a sight to behold. She endeavored to give us a human face, explaining our plight in the face of hostility for sharing our beliefs. She would touch the reporter's arm, ask them where they were from, how long they'd been in the industry, and smile as she told them it was not our fault that the Jews scarified Jesus for their own preservation and blood lust - it was written right there in the Bible after all. Josephine would do everything she could to make that personal connection, and drag that ounce of sympathy from them. Effectively she was the warm-up act for the great orator, Frank. After whipping up their interest to fever point he would deliver another searing monologue that would rattle the spiritual and emotional foundations of those who heard him. When delivered by someone as charismatic as Frank it was television gold, or manna from print heaven.

One way or another, his words and image generated emotion, in his believers and in those who instantaneously hated everything he was. People could not help but stop and rubber-neck our constant car-crash of ideas and provocation. While most folk we protested against reacted with decency and dignity, we eagerly collected the physical trophies of success when the decency was thrown aside and the confrontation became physical. Bricks and stones were thrown and scattered around our feet. Urine in glass bottles was tossed at us. Paint and feces was slung at on our vehicles. These were gifts for our growing media star, and signifiers of our persecution.

In each state we erected our own temporary town, and within that town our time and movements became increasingly governed. After Grandfather's morning sermon, reinforcing one of the five main messages of Calvinism, those adults not at work that day would participate in what Grandfather had dubbed The Education. This process involved formal teaching by committee members such as Edward Gant, whose role was to provide each of our congregation with a deep understanding of their constitutional rights, the specific actions to take in the event of arrest and the reading of the Miranda rights, and the legal specifics of each protest that we decided upon. Could we stand on the court steps or inside the lobby? Could we freely enter the abortion clinic or synagogue, or was there a minimum distance we had to keep to avoid arrest? We had to know how far we could go. Mother would give what amounted to a media performance class. Given the growing press interest, the way we behaved in front of the cameras or before the voice recorders of journalists became ever more important. She knew that we could, in part at least, control our own image. In her class I was her favorite guinea pig, her partner for a recital of a protest. Though I knew these rules inside and out, I would each time feign ignorance of how to act, before supplying her with the pitch perfect performance she required for the class. She would hand me a placard and send me to the center of the room.

"Now Laura Jo. I need you to imagine this scenario. You're in an urban environment, and there are police and media watching. We are protesting a street carnival for queers. They are *everywhere*. And these godless cretins hate you. They'll spit at you. They'll call you a fascist. They are going to push their filthy fingers into your face. Show us how you'll engage them."

With the placard above my head reading in fluorescent yellow and blue that "The United States of Sodomites", I would screw my face up into a parody of anger, and shout at the top of my lungs "You're a disease. God is the only cure."

Mother would then face the class. "So what did Laura do wrong there? Well, let me tell you there was more than one problem. For a start she screamed out the words. Learn to communicate loudly and clearly without it coming across so harshly. Unlike those who'll scream back at us, we are not animals. Just look at the way the blacks and Mexicans conduct themselves on the news. Always shouting, always distasteful, with their slang and their curse words. That is not how we represent ourselves. Did you see Laura Jo snarling? That is unbecoming. There is nothing, absolutely nothing more disarming than a smile. We deliver our message firmly but with grace and decency."

The layers of irony which revealed themselves in this moment were lost on us all. It existed in a place somewhere beyond both comedy and tragedy. As I then gave the correct rendition, our audience would begin to participate. A dozen people would stand and practice saying "God is your enemy," "God hates Jews," orthodontic advertisement smiles playing upon their faces, their voices the false, cheery tone of a cable TV game-show host. They were grace and decency incarnate.

Grandfather also began to give special classes. He announced early one Spring that, given the possibility of arrest and detention by the sodomite-loving authorities, he would begin conducting intense one-on-one spiritual workshops. As part of his succession planning he would select, after great contemplation or a sign from the Lord himself, one individual to study and learn with him for an indeterminate period of time. They would live, eat and drink with him in whatever quarters he had at the time. There was, he told us, no other way to truly develop a closer communion with God. This led to a great clamor amongst the congregation to be chosen by Frank for such a special honor. The sense of anguish that ran through those not selected each time was palpable. It was the men of our church who would come to be most disappointed, for Frank only ever chose women. His first dedicated pupil was Christine White, who was already certain that Frank was the medium through which God spoke. Immediately this elevated her position among us, as she stuck to him like a leech for the next two weeks, tracking his every movement, living or dying on his every word. She began to look at Frank in a way I did not yet understand: a strange mix of awe and intimacy. It was a look I would only truly comprehend when Jackson Tait entered my life. After Christine, a pattern was set, and Frank would invariably select an unattached female for his personal tuition. When there were no more single women left to choose, he began to cast his attentions to those who were married. But there were commonalities between all the women he picked; they were pretty, years younger than him, and they were never the same after they had spent time with him. None of those who were single ever attempted to form relationships with other men, and those who were married acted as if their spouses had been replaced by strangers. Frank had informed his students that they were never to discuss their teachings with each other, as it would break the individual bond between them and God that had been created. Every husband whose wife spent time with Frank acquiesced without complaint. It was all for the good of the congregation, all for a greater purpose.

The only person that I knew who ever questioned his behavior was Ann. I had screamed at her after she has asked why a lady was staying in Grandfather's quarters.

"She's there to deepen her understanding of God, of Calvinism. Don't undermine your grandfather."

"But I haven't read anything that says that says this is how people should be taught."

"What do you know about it?! Grandfather studied for years at seminary school – none of us have formal training. That's the whole point. Where would we be without his guidance?"

She had then tried to tell me that she thought she has seen him sharing a bed with one of his married students. She had peered through a crack in the door of his quarters in the half-light and swore she had witnessed Ramona laying next Frank. I laughed straight in her face, dismissed her stupid notion outright and told her I would be asking Mother to organize a sight test for her. Ann looked crushed but accepted she was undoubtedly mistaken. I gave her no other option.

Through the cracked mirror of hindsight, this was the point at which our congregation began to slip away from the moorings of doctrine. It was the time when the word of Frank and the word of God became irrevocably blurred. He had laid the foundations not only of complete control of our daily lives, but of his ability to act with impunity, to exist on a different moral spectrum to that in which we believed. Through Calvinism he could find ways to justify it all. The Frontier Saints had become a sect within a sect, a holy elite with a purpose unlike any other before us. Frank would remind us incessantly of this separation, this divine mission, and even began to teach us that specific Bible verses were references to our coming to be. We had become 'the chosen people, a royal priesthood, a holy nation, a people belonging to God...' and Frank was the apex.

Though our numbers had grown to almost one hundred after four years of itinerant travel, and our public profile had been astronomically raised, there came a point where Frank dismissed any notion of the Frontier Saints becoming a larger movement. This was partly a natural result of our belief in limited atonement. It was also because Frank needed personal control over all those around him. He was unwilling to cede that power to anyone else. To maintain his complete governance of us, Grandfather would isolate us from values of the outside world by turning ever more of that world against us. The list of those who would not be saved, of those who we were taught to despise, therefore grew ever longer. Though homosexuals and Jews would always retain a special place in Frank's well of hatred, he added to this list public health workers, government officials, the military, the police, Mormons, Presbyterians, Lutherans, Anglicans, Baptists, and most of all Catholics and Muslims.

Catholicism to Frank was little more than an organization set up to facilitate the buggery of children. The Pope himself, Frank declared, was the supreme ringmaster of pedophilia, who watched on his debauched administration set about sodomizing the most vulnerable in their flock. "Donate to Catholicism: pay for the rape of children!" read one of our finest placards. They were a vampiric breed, trashing the souls of a billion misguided believers. Even their idolization of the Virgin Mary was reprehensible to Frank. She was, he declared, 'little more than the human vessel chosen for Christ's arrival."

As for Islam, AJ Smith and Cousin John were arrested for burning the Quran in front of a makeshift mosque in Wisconsin. Mother had alerted the media as to our whereabouts and plans, and ABC News helpfully obliged by sending along a camera crew. Grandfather, in his best suit, stood before a cartoonish effigy of Mohammed and the charred remnants of their holy book, just as AJ Smith was slung headfirst into a vehicle by half a dozen officers.

"Mr. Marlin, can you justify your actions here today? I'm sure you can agree that if this was Muslims burning a Bible, there would be a public outcry."

"You can't compare the Bible to a work of satanic fiction. That's plainly ludicrous."

"Surely people are entitled to worship wherever they-"

"And what are they worshipping? It's an idolatrous, evil piece of trash. It's a 300 page cacophony of lies and deceit. Have you ever read it, son?"

"No."

"Well I suggest you do before you question my civil right to protest against its distribution in our schools and colleges. Unless, of course, you want Sharia law to be instituted in Wisconsin."

The beleaguered reporter stared blankly back at the camera, pausing for a couple of seconds too long.

"And... it's back to you in the studio, Jim..."

9. A Living Sacrifice

As we travelled the country looking for our final resting place, the Frontier Saints were organizing over two hundred and fifty protests a year. The people, the places and times of our demonstrations appear in my mind as an endless, fantastical blur, like a play whose continuity has been cast to the wind. One protest in particular stands out in this time as a high-water mark of our infamy, the moment our church went from a local or statewide concern to a national one. The sort of concern that people spoke about all week at office water coolers, and at the family breakfast table, half in disgust and half in delight.

It was early autumn, 2001. We had left Cleveland as a result of the threat of litigation from a synagogue we had protested outside for two weeks. Its members just so happened to include one Abe Franken, Senator for the state of Ohio. Edward Gant had rightly convinced Frank that we would find ourselves quickly out of our depth in that particular fight. We couldn't match the financial muscle of such a powerful synagogue, and would likely end up with a 'Jewry instead of jury,' given the corrupting influence of the US Senate. Besides, we had already seen victory in that arena: our funds had been swollen by around $300,000 as the result of successful civil lawsuits against the city of Salina, and Fremont in Nebraska. Gant had argued that they were responsible for failing to 'provide sufficient protection during our protests' as well as 'unlawful arrest.' Both judges had declared us victors with a look on their face of a man who had just found out his house was aflame. Frank wasn't prepared to fritter that away defending our name against the descendants of those who killed Christ. It was, he announced, 'beneath us.' Gant had also registered us as a non-profit organization, and this was acknowledged and ratified by the federal government; we were therefore exempt from paying taxes. Grandfather's glee over this fact was immeasurable. The very mention of that status would see him almost cry with laughter.

The decision was therefore taken to migrate south to Youngstown. It was a typical rustbelt settlement that had never truly recovered from the hammer blow to the industrial economy in the 1970s and had been trying in vain to recover its steel glory days ever since. Its population was still made up largely of tough as nails blue collar workers, as it scraped along on the remnants of steel, coal and automobile manufacturing. It gave me the impression of being an unforgiving kind of place, though it did have its pockets of culture. This was why, after having short-term leased a small enclave of houses on the outskirts of town, Mother set her sights upon demonstrating outside the McDonough Museum of Art, the Mahoning Valley's center for contemporary works. Having gone through its brochure proudly declaring its ongoing exhibitions from national and international artists, it was clear to her that it was little more than a shop window for homosexual artists. Worse still, the museum actually belonged to YSU University, which had no doubt been turned into a hotbed of homosexuality by their 'liberal' arts manifesto.

We arrived to set up our picket line on a day that was saturated with greyness; the sky and the buildings morphed into each other, and the roads seemed to lead out towards dark, threatening trees whose knotted branches locked and grappled together across two whole lanes. The damp, lung-prickling air slowly gave way to a fine rain that began to cause some of our freshly painted banners and placards to run with

colors, the words melting into each other. Within minutes the sign for
"Liberal Ass College: an education in buggery" was practically
unreadable. Mother pointed to the sky, and shrugged at me. There was
simply nothing we could do. By her side stood Beth, now six years old
and the living image of my dead sister. We waited patiently as the
student body began arriving. Watching their sense of freedom as they
pulled up in their own cars, or were dropped off by their parents caused
my stomach to flip, but I willed that feeling to dissipate and reminded
myself they were damned regardless of what they had or did. As we
began to spread out along the sidewalk, our voices at the ready, it rapidly
became clear that something was not right. Usually our very presence at
such an institution caused an immediate response; students tended to get
organized quicker than other groups and actively seemed to enjoy the
tension and trouble that we brought. I suppose it broke the monotony of
their study, and played perfectly into the surging mass of hormones
cascading around their bodies. All that energy and passion had to find
somewhere to go. It was almost enough to respect them. On this occasion
they did not seem to notice our existence. They congregated in great
packs in front of the main administrative building, their faces expressing
concern and shock; some among their number were inconsolable, with
tears staining their faces as friends and classmates endeavored to comfort
them. Ever sensitive to events, Mother called for silence.

"OK, quieten down everybody. Clearly we're not in on the
reasons for their group therapy session."

She weighed up the options as if she were a hawk watching a
rabbit from afar. Eventually she turned to Ann and me.

"Girls, I want you to go on a little fact-finding mission for us.
They likely wouldn't speak to me. But I doubt they'll not talk to your

pretty little faces. Be polite. Look a little sad if you can."

Taking Ann and Beth's hands, we made our way across the road and onto the lawn, the grass luminous in the drizzle. Behind us Mother called out.

"Let Ann do the talking, Laura Jo. You be the concerned big sister, looking after Beth!"

We stood around 15 feet away from the students, our arms folded in contemplation. The abrasive noise of their grief caused Ann to wince and mockingly place her fingers in her ears.

"Who should I speak to?"

"No point in talking to one who's crying. You won't get a sensible word out of them."

She pointed to a guy in a blue and black lumberjack shirt. "How about him?"

"No. He looks like he's there as an opportunity to touch girls he never usually has the chance to. Anyway, he seems a little retarded; he's almost smiling. Pick a girl. Anyone with dry eyes will do."

Slowly, we moved across the neutral zone between us. Ann tugged at the shirt tail of a girl whose hair resembled a Medusa-like mass of snaking curls. Heavy black makeup around her eyes made her look all the more intimidating. She looked at us as if we'd just arrived from another galaxy. Perhaps it was our matching outfits that caused her startled glare.

"Are you girls with the circus?"

"No. We're with them."

Ann pointed towards the congregation and our now dripping placards, which now more resembled the abstract art on display at the museum.

"I'm Ann and this is Laura Jo and Beth. We just wanted to know why you're all upset."

Amid the wailing and gnashing teeth of her friends, it finally sunk in as to who we were.

"Oh. Jesus. You people. Of all the days. Don't you watch the news or read the fucking papers? Are they banned in your house?"

"We just got into town yesterday. We can watch TV normally. Well, we watch what Grandfather says we can."

"Who the fuck is Grandfather? Why do I even care? You just thought you'd come over and make an already bad situation worse, right?"

She ran her hands through her hair, despair etched in her face. I jabbed at Ann with my elbow.

"No, we just wanted to know what's going on. It's just awful seeing you so sad."

Ann made a face as pure as driven snow. The girl stuck her tongue under her top lip and clenched her fist as if wanted to punch us. We had begun to attract the attention of her friends too; a phalanx of girls was momentarily distracted from their emotional meltdowns and began asking our new friend who we were. She raised her hand as if to say 'I'll deal with it.'

"Taylor Watkins, that's why. You can do your own fucking homework. Can you leave now, please? Take the rest of the fucking hicks with you, if you wouldn't mind."

Ann was on the cusp of asking her who Taylor Watkins was when I dragged her away. Medusa could not resist one more parting shot, her Kohled-eyes boring into our backs.

"Hey, girls: Halloween isn't for a while yet."

Ann couldn't help but laugh.

"And I thought *she* was dressed kinda funny…"

***

Taylor Watkins was a 19 year-old sophomore at YSU University. The newspapers described him as an 'intelligent boy,' who was 'much loved' by his family. He had hoped to graduate with a major in music and wanted one day to teach grade and middle school kids that very thing. Taylor was also openly homosexual. This was a fact his devoutly Catholic parents, Ken and Mary, had struggled initially to accept, but had 'deep down' known it all along and had finally made peace with it. There was not a person upon campus who had a bad word to say about Taylor Watkins; he was a genuine popular young man, classically handsome and was active in both college sports and extracurricular art classes. Indeed he had had several works displayed at the McDonough Museum. It was also noted that he was often to be found surrounded by beautiful girl friends, which had the consequence of making him all the more highly regarded among the straightest of guys. Upon reading this, Grandfather quickly deemed him to be an 'All-American Queer.'

Taylor Watkins' body had been found beneath one of the bridges that spanned the Mahoning River. A group of children had been playing on the roof of a small, disused warehouse on the opposite bank. To the right of a low tree whose branches bent like an ageing ballerina into the muddy, lapping water, they had convinced themselves they could make out the half-naked figure of a man. Little under an hour later the police had cordoned off a two mile stretch of the 113 mile river and had identified the corpse of Taylor Watkins. His wallet had not left his pocket. Two things became immediately clear: the boy had been murdered, and this was likely the spot upon which the murder took place, given the amount of blood found surrounding the corpse, and that the flow and currents of the river would have seen him deposited much further along into the county. Forensic tests had revealed that his death was the result of a number of blows to the head with an unevenly shaped heavy object, most likely a rock that had been cast into the river thereafter; the entire back of his skull had been caved in. Whoever killed him had continued to strike him even after he was dead. The murder itself had a sexual element. Taylor Watkins had been found with both his briefs and pants around his ankles, and the presence of semen in his anus confirmed that intercourse had taken place not long before his life was taken. Police, however, thought it likely consensual given the lack of marks indicating any kind of struggle, and the complete lack of drugs or alcohol in his system. The wrought-iron supporting beam of the bridge, which rested just yards from where his body had lain, became a makeshift shrine; flowers and cards, and objects of great sentiment were scattered at its foot and were taped to its sides. The entire community of Youngstown banded together in collective misery over this utterly heinous act. Helplines were set up for YSU students affected by the murder, and services were held at churches of most denominations to mourn his passing.

The entire situation was almost too perfect for the Frontier Saints. A young catholic homosexual attending a college famous for its support of 'liberal' arts had been slain in a manner that would turn the hardest heart. Frank knew that we had to capitalize on the event - it perfectly summed up the vision he had been espousing of a doomed America, whose population was predestined to damnation. At a Council meeting just a day after the murder itself, an extraordinary new step for our congregation was swiftly decided upon. Not only would we picket the funeral parlor in which his body lay in state for viewing by relatives and friends, but we would picket the funeral itself.

Two days later I found myself staring into the casket of Taylor Watkins. As the rest of our congregation began consolidating their positions at the entrance to the driveway of the parlor, I felt a compulsion to see the boy whose face had been in constant rotation on the TV news. A tall, solemn man with tiny rimmed spectacles told me he was sorry for my loss as I made my way through the inner door of the hallway. I am certain he took my emotional blankness as deep, inexpressible grief. In the viewing room I was alone, but for an elderly woman sitting with her hands clasped in prayer in the corner. She barely moved other than to occasionally adjust the string of pearls that shone against her dour black dress. It was as if they were strangling her. In the hushed reverence of the room, a soft light covered the corpse of Taylor Watkins. As I moved over to the coffin I felt nauseated by the overpowering smell of lilies and pine. I had never seen a dead body before, but as I stood there, transfixed by this wax-like, rouged parody of life, a rush of long-buried memories of my father flooded into my mind. I felt something akin to sympathy for all those who were suffering as the result of Taylor Watkin's death. Immediately I felt disgusted with myself for entertaining this feeling. Trying not to cry, I repeated over and over under my breath 'God gave them over to a depraved mind, to do those things which are not proper.'

As I began to back out of the room, I began to think about Taylor Watkin's killer. On the previous evening the police had arrested a 44 year-old steel worker called Mike Kozlowski. He was a married man with two children, and had confessed straight away to the slaughter of

Watkins. The police had been led straight to him by finding his wedding ring on the ground near where Watkins' body lay. Inside the ring, an inscription read 'Michael and Cynthia Kozlowski Forever' alongside a date. There was only one Mike Kozlowski in Youngstown married on that date. In his confession he blamed Taylor Watkins, whom he had met in a downtown dive bar, for perverting his mind, for tempting him into a homosexual act and therefore endangering his marriage. He claimed he had never before experienced homosexual feelings, and that his anger and disgust after being taken down to the river, was so great that he wildly lashed out at the boy. Kozlowki, a catholic of Polish origin, said he was sorry for the boy's death, but that he also hoped that he rotted in Hell.

When I thought of Mike Kozlowski's family it made it easier to engineer hate for Taylor Watkins. When I walked back out into the chilly morning air, two men were confronting Cousin John and AJ Smith. They had left their car engine running and doors open on the slope up to the parlor and were literally begging us to leave. Inside the car, a woman sat sobbing uncontrollably.

"Please, for the last time, be reasonable. You've made your point. None of us like this. But his parents are coming soon. They're distraught enough. Please, act like decent human beings and go."

His eyes were swollen through crying, and his neck and face had taken on a deep puce color. The man's arms were raised in an open fashion; every part of his action was conciliatory. Cousin John simply grinned back at him.

"There's no such thing as decent human beings, sir. Least of all those who commit acts like that boy in there. The wages of sin are death. He's paying the price for his actions. He's no child of God."

The man's peaceful resolve collapsed; fury stung him like a dozen hornets.

"You fucking *people*. You call yourself Christians. What a Goddamned joke. Standing here, shitting on people's grief. That's someone's son, someone's brother. You fucking sick bastards. A bullet's too good for you."

He leant forward as if he was going to strike Cousin John but was held back by his companion.

"This is a peaceful protest, sir. We have every right to be here. Everything we're saying is in the good book. Leviticus 18:22. Leviticus 20:13, Corinthians 6:9-10. You can argue all you like. It's there in plain English."

"Fuck your god, you son of a fucking bitch!"

As AJ Smith smiled and exclaimed "Don't forget, dear sir: There will be no Sodomite sons of Israel!", the weeping man was dragged back to the car, his fists clenched in anguish. He was held onto the woman for dear life as the car slowly made its pathetic 30ft drive to the entrance of the funeral home.

The next few days passed in a firestorm of media activity, and full scale public outrage. In their complete naivety, relatives of Taylor Watkins did our work for us by calling every news outlet in the county. They were certain it would drive us away and shame us, but found to their cost that they had merely poured gasoline onto the bonfire. Mother was in her element; she barely had time to join in the actual protest herself as she was in such high demand in front of the cameras. The entire street was made near impassable between the news vans with their satellites protruding from their roofs, the small battalion of state troopers and local officers who had been sent not only to keep the peace but 'protect' us in our right to protest. Youngstown wasn't the kind of place that could afford a big civil lawsuit. Anybody who wanted to actually see Taylor Watkins had to navigate this unholy gauntlet: once they'd be vetted by the police, had microphones thrust in their faces by NBC or Fox News, they had to contend with us telling them that God himself had orchestrated their loved one's terrible death. The student body had, to its credit, gathered its composure and was actively protesting our protest. Even Grandfather could not help but be amused by their placard that read "If God existed, it's you he'd hate". In my near 15 years I had never encountered such a level of profanity. AJ Smith reasoned that maybe Fuck was actually one of their first names and they were not talking to us at all. Oh, how we laughed. Each day that passed brought a rash of tawdry headlines, and an outpouring of disgust at our actions. TV debates were held on the legality of our demonstration, and questions were asked as to whether we would picket the funeral itself. Trashy profiles of my grandfather and our family adorned a few low-rent scandal rags. The mayor of Youngstown, Gary Swaine, fought for air time with Mother. His quote that we were "the most despicable organization in America" quickly went primetime. It would stick with us forever. There he was on every network castigating the laws that bound him from doing anything about our "gross intrusion upon the private grief of a traumatized family". A host of rent-a-quote 'experts' offered up their psychological profiles of Grandfather, whose 'cult of personality' was essential to his control of our organization. Yet they found almost no information as to his whereabouts or life prior to 1995. All this did was imbue him with an even greater sense of mystery and power. Mother's decision to keep Grandfather away from interviewers seemed ever more a masterstroke. She had quickly realized that nobody really cared if she endlessly repeated the same quotations she was giving to other papers or networks. They simply wanted to make sure they received a piece of the controversy. Her interview with ABC was a particular high point.

"Ms. Marlin, how do you respond to Mayor Swaine's comments that you're the 'worst kind of Americans'?"

"We take that as compliment. Frankly, we despise everything this nation has become and Gary Swaine can sling whatever empty phrases at us he likes. He simply needs to remember what sewer he's shouting from; there's none filthier than the one that houses our government."

"And what about Ken and Mary Watkins - have you no sense of shame as to what you're putting this family through?"

"What's happened here was not our choice. Taylor Watkins' homosexuality is the root of all of this. As it is written "those who practice such things are worthy of death." And God found him worthy. We're simply here to remind you people of that. "

"Surely Jesus's message was one of love and forgiveness?"

"Clearly you're reading a different book. Jesus didn't die for these people. He died for the few his Father chose. We are the few and we will be forgiven. The rest of you will rot."

"How do you answer the charge that your views are not acceptable in modern society?"

"You think we should listen to the politically correct rubbish of a decadent, dying culture over the 2,000 year-old words of God? Our mission is to preach this word – it rises far above the trash that is your so-called morality. It's this morality that enables the behavior of people like Taylor Watkins."

"Taylor Watkins' family are deeply religious themselves, practicing Catholics."

"That's exactly our point: Taylor Watkins habits' are typical of Catholic practices. We expect nothing less from a church whose leaders actively promote the corruption of children."

One and on it went, scathing soundbite after scathing soundbite. It was undoubtedly Mother's finest series of performances to date. As soon as the camera went off air, she was politeness itself, schmoozing each journalist, asking them if they got what they wanted, and whether she came across OK. By the third day they were calling her Josephine, making small talk about their kids, and complimenting her on the hair she'd started to have done professionally. The tragedy that had befallen the Watkins family was pushed aside to make space for the newest freak show in town. They had implored the police to move us along, but were told there was nothing they could do. And so they trudged hopelessly behind our vicious wake, their dignity in tatters. The drive and short walk to the body of their dead son, brother and nephew had become an almost unendurable journey through a hostile, unforgiving, wasteland.

On the day of the funeral things became ever more surreal. In their desperation the Watkinses and their relatives had hired private security to shield them as best they could from our congregation. Mayor Swaine had tasked his whole political apparatus with coming up some measure or by-law that could force us as far away from the church as possible. Not only could they find no way around our First Amendment rights, but they felt the cold clasp of key members of the Ohio State General Assembly upon their necks, who admonished them publicly for even attempting such a measure. We were therefore free to take our protest as close to the Our Lady Of Mount Carmel church as we liked.

We had parked our bus and cars half a mile away, as Grandfather had decided to lead us in constant 'prayer' as we walked along the road to our destination. Passing motorists were forced to drive around us and either honked their support at our placards and banners or bellowed a long list of obscenities. Our congregation had never been so cocksure in our own eminence, never so confident and righteous. As the church came into view, delight swept through our number. This was to be our crowning moment.

But beyond the lines of waiting media, security and police a low, intense growl of engines could be heard. The noise grew quickly more intense and through the early morning haze three dozen motorcycles came roaring towards us. One hundred feet before they reached us, the leather and denim-clad platoon on the bikes briefly cut their engines. They maneuvered themselves into lines three to four bikes deep, before restarting their engines and slowly driving their metal blockade towards us. Grandfather stopped in his tracks and we froze behind him. AJ Smith and Cousin John shot each other knowing glances. Smith patted down the left side of his chest as if he had forgotten something. When they had almost reached us, along with a photographer who had quickly caught up with events, one of the bikers at the front unfurled a large American flag. The picture of our two opposing sides would be the one that hit the newsstands the next day. While they were hardly Hell's Angels, and were almost all safely into middle age, this chapter looked grizzled and dangerous enough to my young eyes. They opened their engines in a threatening manner as they moved nearer, startling the children among us. Finally, a lone biker rolled forward to speak to us. I could see the reflection of our placards in his mirrored sunglasses. He scratched his nails through his greying beard as he reached us, sizing us up and down, assessing his approach. Raising his hand in the air he waved his index finger in a circle and the mass of engines fell dead.

"I respectfully ask that you turn yourselves around."

Grandfather shook his head at the heavens as Edward Gant and Cousin John walked to his side. His language shocked me.

"You want to fuck with our constitutional rights, boy? I'll serve your peckerwood ass papers quicker than you could read them. Who the fuck do you think you are?"

"You're not passing, sir. Not today. Serve any fucking papers you want. You're still not passing. It'll literally have to be over our dead bodies. So I suggest you and the rest of your brainwashed clan turn yourselves around."

Cousin John began to walk forward and bellowed in the man's face.

"You and your faggot loving friends best back off now. There's no one stopping this congregation."

Grandfather pulled John away.

"John, your temper won't do us any good. Calm yourself."

"You better listen to the old man there, Tex. That boy's funeral is going to be just fine without you."

You could almost see the cogs churning in Frank's mind.

"It's funny. I bet in different times we would have got along well. You want to stand up for what you believe in. I admire that. Son, we're just trying to live by the word of the good book. Deep down I bet you boys are sickened by what that boy did with his body. We're not unalike."

"You reckon so, do you? I've done some pretty fucked up things in my life, but if I was anything like you people I'd find the nearest bridge and throw myself off. Now, back the hell off. This is America, not some Middle East shithole where they stone people. You can't get away with that here."

"You're right, son, this is America alright. In all its vile glory. You see, you're worse than them in a way, because you condone their perversion. You wave that tattered flag like it actually means something."

He began to try to squeeze through between their machines and signaled for us to follow. Some rushed to the outside, some tried to force through the mass of vibrating metal. But they moved their bikes closer, and a flaying mass of tattooed arms shot up to hold us or push us back. AJ Smith was the first to react: he grabbed the helmet chin strap of a biker and attempted to yank him from his machine. A volley of curse words and threats hit the air and children began crying and screaming. The biker who detained me apologized profusely and told me to let him know if he was holding on to me too tightly, as hurting anyone was the last thing they wanted to do. I smiled in resignation that there was nothing either of us could do. Yet the situation quickly spiraled out of hand: in the midst of the melee a sharp, fear-inducing crack ricocheted across the road, causing two bikes to crash slowly into each other. Grandfather shouted for us to make our way back to the bus, and as we separated out into two clear opposing lines, Thomas Goodman came crawling on his hands and knees after us, blood pouring from what could only be a gunshot wound to his shoulder. Edward Gant ran to drag him off the floor. For once my grandfather looked dumbstruck. AJ Smith took his hand, his voice strangled by fury.

"This is what happens when we don't protect ourselves, Reverend. We're fucking target practice! We might as well paint 'shoot here' on our asses. I told you, I've warned you!"

Frank roughly grabbed him around the back of his neck and pulled his face to close to his, Smith's features contorting in fear.

"Not here, not now! This is not your call."

The lead biker shouted across the divide.

"You gotta get him some medical attention, man. That's not our doing – not one of us is armed, for Christ's sake! You people are fucking insane. We're not going anywhere. Not one fucking inch."

In five minutes we were gone, the bus carrying the greatest number of our congregation quieter than a tomb. We had never experienced such a setback, or been so forcefully repelled. The sense of defeat clung to us like dank air. Every time we hit a bump in the road, Tom would whimper from the back seat, the entry and exit wounds on his leg covered by a sodden towel. He stared at Cousin John as if he wanted to kill him. John could not look him in the face. But from the depths of this despair, Grandfather rose up.

"Why the sad faces my friends? Do you not realize what has just happened? That was no defeat. That was everything God wanted for us. Those imbeciles just etched the name of our church into the conscience of the nation. We not only were denied our basic civil rights, but one of our own lies here bleeding. It's our moral triumph. Once again we've shown them for what they really are – Godforsaken. Let them hate us. We will take strength from it. Our path becomes ever clearer. We cannot fear such little men."

As ever, he proved to be right. The evening news and next day papers were festooned with reports and images of the event. Some treated the bikers as 'heroes,' others cited a breakdown in legality and added a question mark after the word. Most were simply revolted by us.

Controversial, dangerous, radical, controlling, hateful were all adjectives that were used in conjunction with Frank and the Frontier Saints. It had truly elevated us into the wider public consciousness. Though the nation was starting to turn its bile and disgust towards us, the Watkins event had elevated us to the level of celebrities. We fed upon it all. People knew who we were, what we stood for, and their attention and interest took our faith in ourselves and God's teachings to new heights of narcissism. The Watkins funeral seemed almost incidental to proceedings. Our message of Calvinism had become little more than window-dressing for the hatred we felt for anyone who had not been chosen like we had. The Watkins protest had led to my conviction in our beliefs deepening ever more. Through it I became a more vocal member of our congregation, my relation to Frank already guaranteeing me an esteemed place in the order of influence. I was more certain than ever that Grandfather had a direct line to God, that his every utterance was unimpeachable. I took every opportunity to remind our congregation that everything Frank had outlined had come to pass.

Thinking about Taylor Watkins now is enough to bring me to my knees. We may not have been his killers, but we brought his passing back to brutal life each day and murdered him afresh. In his transition to a better place than we will ever deserve, we dragged his families' souls through the gutter of our disgust, forever spoiling their chance to lay him peacefully to rest. I will not allow that shame to subside. To do so would be to forget what we were, what we became. They were the very definition of 'decent human beings' and my pain, my own end, is nothing compared to how we made them suffer.

Looking at those pictures of myself, caught up in the madness of the Watkins' situation, I began to realize that I'd started to change. I paid so little attention to the physical world that I could not, until that point, have described myself to anyone. The first signs of womanhood were beginning to transform me: you could see the outline of breasts protruding through my starched white dress, and my face had begun to lose its childish qualities. They may as well have been pictures of a stranger. It was around this time that my periods began. It was as if they were jolted from their slumber by the events of that week. It made me feel conscious of my body in a way I had never thought possible. Each cramping sensation triggered a rush of questions and feelings. I had never been so aware of my own biology, so aware of the consequences of my gender. Lying on my bed, my stomach knotted and angry, I felt between my legs for the source of my pain. The sensations it caused in me flooded me with shame. As I pulled my hand away and held it to the light, I saw that tiny smears of blood covered my fingers. All I could do was stare at its dark red mystery. Mother had for years intermittently asked me if my curse had started. She was concerned, I had first believed, that it was so late in coming. I could not bring myself to tell her at that time. Clearly, I could not let go of the child in her eyes. I vowed to tell her once we had found and built our lasting home.

Her true motives for wanting to know would open the ground beneath my feet.

The event that would ultimately drive us to the land that the Frontier Saints would call home occurred on the day my first period ended. The Council had met early to determine where we should head to next. We had wrung dry everything Youngstown had to offer, and Mother was of the opinion that a 'bigger stage' was needed. This, at least, was the advice she had gotten in a telephone call from one Michael T. Jones. Jones was the host of a nationally syndicated LA radio show and was the bête noir of liberal America. His views were the verbal equivalent of shotgun blasts and, like ours, often seemed constructed merely to offend. He had recently been fined by a radio watchdog for saying that women who had been made pregnant as a consequence of rape should have no recourse to terminating the child's life. It was, he proclaimed, usually the fault of the woman in the first place, with her 'loose morals, loose legs, and loose screws.' Not unlike Grandfather, he was a handsome and charismatic man with a wicked way with a phrase, and he had formally invited Mother to speak at some point on his show. They had talked for over an hour and he had expressed his admiration for the Frontier Saints for defending what he called the "true American values of individualism and free speech," and was certain his loyal listeners would 'lap up' everything we had to say. He thanked us also for reminding people that this was a Christian nation. Mother had been unable to talk about anyone or anything else since, and her face became flushed with color whenever she did.

On this particular morning, September the 11th, 2001, she was busily prognosticating on Jones' belief that we should establish ourselves in one of the big ten cities. She had proposed Chicago or New York. Frank had quickly rebutted the idea of both. Where, he reasoned, would we find the space to construct our home so near to those swollen metropolitan hellholes? As she desperately tried to convince him it was possible, Thomas Goodman came stumbling through the door, his whole face bathed in sweat from running 50 feet. Having found himself bedridden and cared-for by members of the congregation for over a week, boredom had driven him to summon the energy to go and watch TV in our makeshift communal space. Within moments of turning it on he could not believe what he saw. He thought at first he was watching the footage of a hoax, or had caught the tail end of a disaster movie. When finally he was convinced of its reality, he raced to Frank.

"You've got to come and see this!"

Mother was not pleased to have her latest Jones-inspired diatribe interrupted.

"Have you taken too many painkillers, Thomas? This is Council business. What the hell is it?"

He looked both drained and exhilarated as he incoherently pled his case. All the motion had caused blood to seep through his bandages. He did not notice.

"Please. Look, I... I can't even begin to explain it. You need to see it for yourself."

Minutes later they stood with their mouths open as they witnessed the second plane fly headlong into the south tower of the World Trade Center. Grandfather called for the rest of the congregation at home that day to join us. We huddled *en masse* around the small television set, the endless replays of the initial plane impacts glimmering in our eyes. Yet there was no human response to the horror we saw, no sense of revulsion at the events unfolding before us. Grandfather nodded in triumph, and kept raising and waving his fists above his head. As I looked across the room, most of the congregation was smiling; some cried what could only be tears of joy. This was what had been foretold, the prophecy of a doomed nation made immaculately real. Smoke bellowed from the buildings' gaping wounds, bankers threw themselves to their deaths, trapped workers left desperate and dying messages with helpless emergency services before the towers finally collapsed, their vicious detonation of dust, concrete and steel consuming all around and inside them. A sound of pure, unadulterated joy erupted around me.

Grandfather could contain himself no more.

"This, my people, is the start of the end of days. These are God's actions. This is the sign of his wrath and disgust with everything this nation has become. Look on! Look on! What do you see? I..."

Grandfather looked overcome with emotion. His voice wavered and his hands shook. Perhaps he was more shocked than the rest of us that his divination of national ruin had unfolded; like Frankenstein, he was stunned when the monster opened its eyes. Behind him, the TV continued to transmit scenes from the nascent apocalypse. Bloodied, dirt-covered men and women had cameras thrust in their faces. They spoke of the end of the world they lived in; the dead had risen and were walking through the streets of lower Manhattan. Finally, Frank gathered himself, his lungs sucking in air as if he had resurfaced from the depths of the ocean.

"And I will show wonders in the heavens and in the Earth: blood and fire and pillars of smoke. Here are your pillars of smoke! The pinnacles of American finance reduced to burning rubble. And who controls that finance? Watch the little Jews wave from the windows. Watch them shout for mercy as they fall. Where is their God now? Where is he? I thank our God for this day. The east is *dead*. There's nothing for us there. I know where we need to be."

The next few days blurred into one; it became a rolling, endless celebration. Every detail that spewed forth regarding that event further consecrated every ideal we held dear: the incompetency and corruption of our government; the ever rising death toll; the nineteen Islamic terrorists. Armageddon had visited these shores and was here to stay. Grandfather was delighted when I suggested that we create a banner that declared "9/11: the twin towers of Sodom and Gomorrah". When we eventually unveiled that touching tribute to the murder of 3,400 innocent people, it would align us with the Devil himself in the eyes of the public.

***

In a grand meeting six months later, it was announced by Mother that we had purchased eight acres of land in California. The west, Mother explained, was the last moral frontier. Not only did California house that Jewish factory of nightmares, Hollywood, but it contained the grand republic of sodomy, San Francisco. It was the ultimate playground of debauchery, the sewer into which every American sin would naturally flow, the nation's black, black heart laid bare for all to see. Like the old wagon trainers, we would head out to this wilderness and lay down our foundations into its crumbling earth. The land we had purchased was located in an 'unincorporated' area. This was important in that it meant we would not fall under the governance of the local municipalities, and would fall under the jurisdiction at the more remote state level. As secluded as the land was, it was only a 70 minute drive away from the very center of San Francisco – which was to become the main focus of our fury. This alone had led to angry debates between the Council members. Ann informed me that she had witnessed Edward Gant and Cousin John almost come to blows.

"Cousin John doesn't think we should go to LA. He says some nigger from Watts or Compton will end up shooting at one of us."

"If you say that word again, I'll drag you to Mother myself."

It was on a tiny list of words that were banned at all costs. Mother had been told by Michael T. Jones that it was a certified way of bringing the kind of 'heat' and attention to us we couldn't deal with so easily.

"I'm just repeating what he said!"

"What else did he have to say?"

"He said if the blacks didn't mess everything up, then some wetback probably would. That we'd be pissing in the wind in Mickey Mouse land; we'd just be joining the freak show. Edward says it's a cash-cow. It's the most litigious place in the world. What does litigious mean?"

"It means we could get more money…"

Not that money was an issue. To finance both the purchasing of the land and the construction of our new home, Grandfather had asked every member of our congregation to sell whatever assets they had left. They bent to his will like willows in the breeze: a dozen houses and apartments, cars, farming equipment, stocks, bonds, antiques, pension plans, and life savings were all sold, cashed in, transferred and donated to our non-profit organization. Though many of these assets were sold under market value to guarantee a quick sale, the Frontier Saints were soon sitting upon a fortune beyond their wildest expectations. And now our flock had surrendered all their wealth to Frank, they would become all the more dependent on him.

Before the ink was dry on the land deal, Edward Gant had employed architects and builders to construct what Grandfather was calling our 'ark,' our refuge from the drowning world. Though it would use some modern materials, Grandfather's central command was that the buildings would look like it had stood for centuries: weathered timber would give our compound that old-time feel. The compound would in fact be dominated by two identical buildings, 300ft in length and 75ft high, that would face each other, their arched timber roofs sitting upon three deep stories. They would protrude out at opposite right angles at their south end, and almost touch, the narrow gap leading to the church that would sit proudly in front of our complex. At the north end the two wings would abruptly end, their shadows looming over a surging river that acted as a natural boundary to the land now owned by the Frontier Saints. A ten foot fence would run around the perimeter elsewhere. To save costs, much of the internal finishing, plumbing, and electrical work would be done by our own members – there were few trades that did not exist among us. We would live in temporary housing next to the construction site, and watch as our fortress was slowly raised.

The journey to California was long and laborious. Indiana, Illinois, Missouri, Kansas, Colorado and Utah passed in a haze of steadily rising heat, the freeways stretching into a never-arriving distance. We struggled from state to state to find motels that could accommodate our huge number. The endless parade of beige walls, stained carpets, malfunctioning ice machines, and filthy, drained swimming pools were enough to sap the soul of feeling. Nevada's orange dust plains offered little respite from the sun: it malignantly shimmered in the dead blue sky, its rays laying waste to the dry dominion below. Looking out across its fractured valleys, and ancient outcrops of rocks, a sense of desolation swept through me. I had never been that far west, and though we passed through populated towns and cities, it seemed to me a godless, abandoned place. We were stopped twice by the police, no doubt bored and listless in their no man's land outposts, and bemused by our ragged convoy. Flat tires and spluttering engines also conspired to regularly grind us to a halt. It was a blessed relief by the time we reached Lake Tahoe, its water-cooled air reinvigorating the entire congregation. It had been our own biblical journey to the un-promised land through the wilderness of the desert towns of America. Mother smiled for what seemed like the first time in days as she looked out upon the ponderosa pines and conifers that straddled the landscape. With most of the state falling behind us, Grandfather broke what had been a week-long silence to address the congregation on the bus.

"Make straight in the desert a highway for our God…and that's what we are going to do in this state my friends, in this desert of the minds…though I'm sure we're not going to miss that heat – I nearly left myself to the vultures out there!"

It was a rare moment of levity from him. He unfolded a piece of paper about 4ft long, which contained the plans for our complex. In the middle of certain sections the letters M, W, and C had been scrawled in marker pen.

"Take a good look, my friends. This here is our new home. It may just be lines on a page right now, but this is the place He has led us to. He has brought us the security we have for so long needed. Soon our feet will rest on its land."

As people hugged each other and clasped hands, I turned to Mother.

"What do those letters stand for?"

She gently stroked the side of my face. "Trust you to notice that, Laura Jo. Nothing gets past you, does it? I guess they stand for change, sweet girl."

"What change? What kind of change?"

"You can't go through this life expecting nothing to alter. You're of an age now where you need to start taking a greater responsibility for those below you. It's for the benefit of us all."

We would soon be told that those letters represented men,

women, and children. Depending on each families 'circumstance,' and moreover the whims of my grandfather, the sleeping and living quarters would be arranged upon these lines. It would represent a new level of control; a tearing down of the traditional family unit until there was but one family under Frank.

***

Standing upon the green pasture which we could now call home, as the California sun etched its warmth into my skin, I felt one last unadulterated moment of elation as a member of the Frontier Saints. Grandfather stood before us, a shovel raised to the heavens above his head, his mouth silently intoning a prayer. The congregation clasped each other's hands and called out my grandfather's name as he sunk the shovel into the earth with almighty force. He bent to his knees and grasped a handful of dirt, before rising and letting it fall slowly through his willowy fingers.

"Into dust. As far as your eyes can see, all will return into dust. All except the land of the Frontier Saints, which God, in his wisdom, has led us to. We have here a chance to maintain the purity of our election, to feast upon the milk and honey He has provided, while around us the world falls away. We must protect the children among us from the cancerous longings of those who seek to defame our belief. How, I hear you ask, should we do this, Frank? We do this by keeping those who have lain with no one else within our own flock."

Frank had become ever more cryptic, his references and commandments to our flock, like us, drifting ever further away from absolute Calvinism. Only the Council would know what he meant. As he signaled for us to all to follow him down towards the river, Mother called for our attention.

"I want all the girls over twelve to come forward to me now. Come along, don't be shy, my darlings."

She mouthed at me to come forward, knowing all would follow. As I moved past the congregation Frank waded, fully clothed, up to his waist into the river; he had to use all of his strength not to be knocked from his feet. Seven girls followed behind me. Mother ushered us forward into a line before the water. One by one Frank called us by name, Mother pushing us towards him in the water. I was to be the first: kicking off my shoes I edged down the bank and into the cold flow, a shiver ricocheting down my spine and breath pausing in shock as I tiptoed towards Grandfather's open arms. He began to say aloud a baptismal prayer, and plunged me backwards into the water for what seemed like an eternity. As I came back into the light, Cousin John stood waiting by the bank, ready to haul me out, a smile so wide on his face that it scared me. Grandfather bellowed to the watching mass.

"Let this be the first example. Here stands my own flesh and blood. The fruit of the fruit of my loin. Now He asked us to offer our bodies as a living sacrifice. This, He said, is holy and pleasing to him. This, He said, is true and proper worship. And do we adhere to the word of the Lord?!"

A fierce cry of 'yes' echoed from the flock.

"And do you wish to please the Lord?"

The affirmation was deafening.

"Then we must sacrifice our bodies. And we must maintain the purity of our election. He decreed that each man must take a wife. So those who will soon reach maturity must be paired with those who already have. Those who have been elected must be paired with the elected. So here is the first."

Grandfather turned to me once more, one hand holding the back of my head, the other placed over my face.

"Laura Jo, I commit you now, upon turning 17, to John. This is your sacrifice to God, and to me. Go to him now to seal this pledge."

He let me go and I dropped, unconscious, into the water. Minutes later I came to, wet and shaking upon the verge. John's cold, calloused fingers clawed the hair from my face as Mother looked curiously on. I tried to turn my face away from him but Mother took my jaw and moved me back to look at him.

"Laura Jo Marlin, you cannot turn your back on God's will, or on your responsibilities to this flock. In time you'll accept that John has been chosen for you – you have two whole years to accept this inevitability. This is a lifetime's commitment. To God, to this church, and to John."

"I… I don't want to. This isn't fair."

"You think God gives you a choice? The saints will persevere whether you like it or not, sweet girl."

John cleared his throat. His dead eyes loomed behind those wretched tinted glasses, and what would become a familiar look of desire crept slowly onto his face.

"You've nothing to fear from me, Laura. In God's name I'll treat you right when our time comes. This is what the Reverend wants. He's never led us wrong. We need to stand strong together behind him."

"Listen to John, Laura Jo. You don't think I'd let my own daughter come to harm in any way? That I'd allow my first born to be pledged to someone who wasn't worthy of her? Answer me, girl!"

"No. No you wouldn't."

Looking into her stark glare, I could feel her draining away my initial resistance, forcing me into resigned acceptance of this coupling. I knew it was the ultimate sign of commitment to God and Frank, and Frank who was God. Yet I was naivety writ large about all things concerning intimacy and had not seen this coming. Mother's constant querying about whether my periods had begun suddenly made sense; John's daily remarks about my appealing appearance no longer seemed casual or polite. It was obvious even then that I had no means of controlling or understanding the tangled mess of emotions that led to my body shutting down completely. I would have twenty-four months to come to terms with him becoming my husband. Twenty-four months to accept that a man who had forever made me uncomfortable would be able to place his hands anywhere upon me. I resolved to bury my dread deep within me, to not question Frank's will.

In the river I could hear him continuing to call out the names of the children in our flock. Each girl over 12 was assigned a future mate. Ann quivered and cried as she was embraced by Kenneth Letts, a relatively new 24 year-old member of the Frontier Saints. With his greasy hair and unkempt clothes he looked at her in a way that made the blood freeze. Running his hand across her cheek one more time, he sent her off back to Mother. My own problems, for a brief moment, faded into insignificance. The daughters of the Frontier Saints had been auctioned off and their parents did nothing to stop it. They simply beamed with nervous pride, and blindly agreed to proceedings. Only one couple had the temerity to try to stop their daughter from entering the water. Rose and Marcus Sullivan, with matching looks of disbelief, had called out for their daughter Jennifer to come back to them. AJ Smith immediately dragged them aside and began to harangue them for their outburst. Marcus Sullivan protested wildly, his arms flailing around as his wife choked back tears. Mother strode over and within moments had them cowed. Their card was marked. Still prone on the ground, I began to fool myself that a peaceful, happy acceptance of my future was somehow possible. As the madness of our baptism continued to unfold, I saw myself walking again into the river. After one last breath I felt the suffocating rush of the water into my lungs as Grandfather pulled me sharply under, his face a demonic scowl. Soon I ceased to struggle, in the realization that he was never going to let me back up. I saw the body of a child drift away. A small fracture had opened inside of me.

10. Upon the Picket Fence

The endless waves that broke on the shoreline clawed at the sand, the water fizzing and foaming in the egg-yolk light. The constant rattle of highway traffic could do nothing to spoil the vast tract of ocean to my left and the gorgeous green netherworld of the park to my right. Gulls circled above the frozen windmill; I followed their path across the road, over my head and out along the rocky buffs that caressed this stretch of coast. Frisbees, kites and the excited cries of children filled the air. Teenagers sat contentedly blowing smoke from joints into the descending blue sky. They sprawled on the pale sand like resting seals, their heads moving in time with the sounds that escaped from their portable stereos. As the gentle wind brought the smell of salt and herbs, an elderly Chinese woman performed Tai Chi at the edge of the waves. As they passed, people paused for a second to admire her slow-motion grace. Ageing hippies and old enough to know better skateboarders bumped into each other on the congested sidewalk, their faces a picture of amusement, and hands a blur of high fives. Random weekend strangers asked me about my day, what I was doing later on, whether I'd watched last night's Giants game, and wondered aloud if I'd ever tried salt and pepper squid at Yuet Lee's.

This was the destination point of what had become, over the course of eight months, my fortnightly pilgrimage. After being dropped off into town in the early morning, I would take the 21 bus to Hayes and walk to Alamo Square. There were few tourists at that hour, and I would gaze at the pastel row of wonders that lined Steiner Street. I would speculate as to who lived there: where they were from, where they worked, what they ate, how they filled their days. I imagined that I too was part of their lives. Taking Geary to Division, I'd walk the dozen or so blocks to Haight Street. Up the slope I would stride, the brownstones blocking the light, before the road levelled off and a riot of clashing color saturated the senses. It was at once a dilapidated dream of the 60s, a Victorian studio set from a movie, and a magnet which drew every tattooed freak, tripped-out voyager, or lost cause towards it. I was a perfect fit.

Fake legs hung from windows, smoking apparatus shone from behind glass, and bleach blonde surfer kids slung weed from the first floor balconies of grey painted houses and shouted out after me.

"Hey! Yo, Blondie!"

"Yes?"

"On the dawn patrol again - I see you around. I'm Justin. What're you doing?"

"Just walking."

"Just walking? Come up here and you can walk and smoke with just Justin – no grommets up here... don't leave me hanging now."

"Sorry. I have to go."

"Oh, man. You closed me out. A deal for you though, Blondie, any time."

Past the murals, ornate awnings, vintage clothes shops, junkies, graffiti and buskers I wandered, swallowed by the cacophonic vision. Outside the Magnolia pub, I would stand just before the doors and wait as great blasts of rock music filtered through when they opened, the smell of chargrilled burgers, chicken and beer drifting deliciously onto the street. Through the doors of Amoeba Music I'd walk, ghostlike in my white dress, breathing in the rich odor of plastic and dust from vinyl records I had no knowledge of, their covers and content an alien world.

My feet would lead me then to the edge of Golden Gate Park. Across its grasses, through its bushes and bramble, and into its tropical hideaways I'd go. Regardless of whether I faced sun, rain, wind or snow, I'd explore its tea gardens, and moss green lakes. Scrambling among the foliage, my dress would catch on branches and pine needles as I fed through a dirt path to Rainbow Falls, then up to the top of the hill off of JFK drive. Stretching 60ft into the air was the Prayerbook Cross. Placing my body and face against its cool sandstone surface, I'd listen intensely for a sign or sound from God. I heard nothing but the noise of people in the valley below. Heading further west I'd watch the buffalo graze through the wire fence, before looping around the Dutch flower gardens amid parents attempting to stop their children trampling over the tulips. Across the road awaited the ocean.

Sometimes I waited for people to vacate that exact spot of wall I always sat upon. And as I did, the same feeling bludgeoned its way into my head: a hatred of this city for making me love it so much. San Francisco had surreptitiously crawled beneath my skin, and had infected my thoughts. I fought and fought off its call, but such a loving, warm bug was hard for any host to refuse. Once, I had walked past a grand old house on Russian Hill. On the windowsill sat a plaque with a quote from Mark Twain that read "I have always been rather better treated in San Francisco than I actually deserved." After the best part of a year, I knew this to be true. Given that we had had to divert the attentions of many of our senior leaders to the construction of our home, more responsibility had fallen upon me. My time had therefore been almost entirely devoted to either organizing or leading picket lines against this beautiful city and its sinners. My day in the city was supposed to consist of banking duties, food orders, and reconnaissance for future protests. Yet now these tasks would be crammed into an hour at the end of the day; the hypnotic pull of the rhyming hills, the mists that appeared as if from dreams, and the neighborhoods that teemed with exotic life proved too much. It, and the future that was Cousin John, had slowly muddied the clarity of my thought. My duties and the Frontier Saints' protests had, on occasion, suffered.

The obvious target that summer had been the annual Pride march. With Grandfather and Mother busy directing the construction of our home, I had led the sixty-five strong group to a pivotal point of the carnival route and somehow had expected to bring the festivities to a stinging halt. Yet our protest was doomed from the start and quickly descended into farce. After leaving our buses, we had walked from Ellis Street to its intersection with Market and stood, to a person, · dumbfounded at the sights and noises that greeted us; almost-naked black men with gold lightning bolts painted on their chests blew whistles in our faces; dance music pumped from floats carrying drag queens in jewel-laden bikinis; lesbian cycling club members sauntered past on symbolic tandems; cowboys wearing only chaps openly kissed each other, bottles of alcohol raised to the sky as they chose random people from the crowd to rodeo dance with them. We could not be heard above this layer of hell, our brightly colored placards were ignored and lost amid the sea of rainbow flags, pro-queer banners and lurid hoardings. They refused to take us seriously, and attempted to undermine everything we believed. The frustration mounted as the parade swept along. Just before I was about to lead everyone back to the buses, I thought we had at last managed to achieve something, however small. A Latin man dressed like Marilyn Monroe danced ten foot away from us but stopped dead still when he caught sight of our multi-colored mural of hate. For a brief moment he looked as though he was choking back tears, his fingers clenching as he swallowed hard. However, he gathered himself, straightened his dress, and walked over to us.

"Oh baby, we both got white dresses on, but it's gonna take a big gust of wind to lift that thing. Bet you got nice legs under there too. Come on, gimme some ankle!"

"Sir, God will not save you. What you do is-"

"Honey, God got the day off today. Why are you wasting that lovely face on those ugly words? They do nothing for your complexion. Didn't momma teach you to be nice to strangers?"

He squeezed my cheek affectionately.

"Man should not sleep with man. This isn't our-"

"Baby, we all God's children."

"No, we are his cho-"

He held his hands out by his side, his fingers pointing inwards.

"Listen now – who else could create something this fabulous but God? Tell me that's not the truth, honey!"

Romona shouted from behind me.

"When you die, you will not be at God's side. What you're doing is an abomination."

"Everybody loves a good abomination now and again, sweetheart. Even God. Maybe a dance with Carlos will make you feel less angry at yourself?!"

Carlos took my hand and graciously twirled himself around.

"There you go, baby. You getting it now. The sun is out, the celebration is on – and I feel sorry you don't understand me, honey. I feel sorry you don't understand who you are. You can't hate me or yourself forever. You on the wrong side of history, baby."

Another man appeared behind him, his hand wrapping around Carlos' waist, a fake handlebar moustache half falling off his face, and Aviator sunglasses hiding inebriated eyes. Behind me the congregation screamed at them even more ferociously.

"I leave you for a minute and you go and sweet talk pretty girls. You're fucking outrageous. But that's why I love ya!"

He gave Carlos a tender kiss, and Carlos blew me one in return.

"You take care now, Goldilocks. Carlos has to go entertain these lucky people. They're not much different than you…"

I reconciled myself in that moment to accepting the duality of loving the place and hating the people. But, as Carlos forewarned, in time even that would prove impossible. I couldn't help but admire his elegance in the face of such hostility. For a brief second, I wished that he would be saved.

We had far greater success when picketing smaller scale targets like city clinics. Edward Gant had reasoned that not only would we draw a reaction from those coming out from being tested for sexually transmitted diseases, but hopefully deter and shame a great number of people from going in. As men entered health centers in the Castro or Mission we would hand them leaflets that read 'The wages of sexual sin is death,' or 'God created HIV for YOU.' Gant was a master of provocation: I have never seen someone more skilled at the generation of rage in people. One fog-shrouded morning at a clinic on 17th street, a man in his early thirties left the walk-in center. Gaunt and anemic, with worry etched upon his face, he froze in his tracks as Gant called out.

"I hope it was positive."

"What? What did you say?"

"I said that I hope it was positive."

"You have to be fucking kidding me. What sort of sick person are you?!"

"No, it's you who is probably 'sick.' That's why you've had that dirty blood tested."

"How do you fucking sleep at night?!"

"I sleep very well, sir, knowing that every day one more of you people is taught a lesson."

He ran at Gant and crashed his fist hard into his nose; blood exploded onto the sidewalk and Edward momentarily stumbled. When he corrected himself he simply began to laugh. A member of the congregation had already called the police. When they arrived we had four dozen witnesses to the 'assault,' which he would no doubt be charged with, and would likely spend a day or night in jail. It was the perfect outcome.

***

The construction of our home had begun and continued at a searing pace. After only three months, the skeleton of the complex had been erected. A mere two months later, the complex was water tight and the electricians and plumbers had gotten to work alongside the interior fixings. It was not long after that that we were able to move from our temporary dwellings into the relative grandeur of the gleaming new complex. Each wing had a great southern gothic-styled hall at its middle, with communal cooking, eating, and meeting areas being accessed from each side. The sparse sleeping quarters populated most of the upper two floors on each wing, alongside storage space. My grandfather had what was effectively a full-size apartment at the end of the west wing on the lower floor, sealed off to all but him. Beneath the floor of the east wing a great steel reinforced vault had been constructed which only Council members could enter.

Unlike the ground-breaking ceremony, we were taken to our new residences with little fanfare. The change, however, was stark. It was the first time I had lived apart from Mother, and all along the first floor east wing corridor there was nothing now but children, of which I was the eldest and expected to maintain discipline among them all. With the few possessions I had thrown onto my bed, I stood in my doorway. Children passed with confused and excited expressions, others in tears, and some stricken with fear. The smallest bunked together and at least had each other. Like little boats set adrift from the shore, they looked at each other for an indication of what to do next. With most families, bar a lucky few, separated under the direction of Grandfather, the dynamics of our flock immediately began to change. With his focus on 'One Family Under God' – a message carved in wood in the west wing's hall – the normal bonds and patterns of family interaction were altered completely. Wives quickly became estranged from husbands, the rift in their emotional intimacy growing wider with each day. Brothers became distanced from their younger sisters, and everyone focused ever more on desiring and earning Frank's love and approval. The children were the responsibility of everyone, though a special responsibility fell upon those who had been promised a bride. On that day I had escaped the attentions of Cousin John, but Ann had not been so lucky. She walked solemnly into the room next to me, Kenneth Letts' spidery fingers upon her shoulder. I attempted to follow them, but as I reached the door he closed it in my face, the bolt sliding across. Outside, a sense of panic raced through me, but no matter how much I strained only silence emanated from behind the oak walls.

My inertia was broken by Mother's voice.

"Leave Ann be, Laura Jo. She's getting to know Kenneth. He's helping get her room straight and proper."

"Why can't she stay with me? She doesn't want to spend any time with Kenneth. She's 13. He's too old."

"What has age got to do with it? He's perfectly respectable. This family is interested in Bible law on marriage, not state law. She'll get to know him whether you like it or not. Like you'll get to know John."

"Tell me where it says in our canon that we should live apart like this? We're supposed to be together."

"What do you think we're building here? We are the elected, and our purity is all. How else can Frank maintain that without being able to oversee these important aspects of our lives? He's the head of this family. Maybe you shouldn't let that little fact escape you so easily."

"Why don't you want to listen to a word I say?! I'm your daughter, for Christ's sake!"

"Lady, you need to watch your damn tongue. Where is this disrespect for your grandfather's wishes coming from? I don't understand you lately, Laura Jo. You come home from that squalid city late, as if you've been sleepwalking, and worse still, your work's getting sloppy. We'll need to adjust your thinking if you don't buck up that attitude."

"I'm... I'm tired is all."

"How can a girl your age be tired?... Oh, has it started? I want the truth, now."

"Has what started?"

"Your monthly."

I knew that if I said no once more she'd begin to inspect my laundry every day, or worse still take me to see Dr. David Harding, our very own qualified physician. The thought of his hands inside me made my hands tremble.

"Yes, yes it has."

"Oh you poor lamb, you should you have told your momma. No wonder you've been out of sorts."

As she stroked my arm, it finally dawned upon me how different she looked. How entirely glamorous. Even at the happiest moments with my father, the thought of applying so much make-up would have been decried as an affront to humanity. Yet here she stood, her grey dress gone, her face artfully decorated, a citrusy scent of perfume on her skin. Once more I looked upon a stranger, and my face betrayed my thoughts.

"I'm dressed like this with good reason, Laura Jo. Take a look into the quad."

I walked into my window and pressed my face against it. A thick-set man in his 50s, with sculpted grey hair, and teeth whiter than icecaps paced the shadows of the wing.

"That, I'll have you know, is Michael T.Jones. He's come all the way up from LA to see our good work first hand. He's what you'd call impressed. This is business, darling."

"What kind of business do you do dressed like that?"

"The kind where we get airtime on national radio. The kind where we make friends who defend our rights. I'm sacrificing a little of my time for our cause. There's a game we all have to play; don't be so naïve, Laura Jo."

Moments later, I watched through the window as she greeted Jones. He bent and kissed her hand in an exaggerated manner, his eyes never leaving hers for a second. Arm in arm, he escorted her like an old friend towards the northern end of the quad, and out into the open plain beyond the exit.

It was amazing how quickly our new living arrangements were normalized. In our hermetically sealed world, separation through routine and repetition became the natural order. Our congregation found fulfilment and purpose in regimentation. The pressures that feed upon an individual in the outside world evaporated once you stepped inside the grounds of our home. The isolation helped further warp our sense of reality. We learned to function and thrive within its strictures and embraced Grandfather's arbitrary decisions as to whom, how and when kith and kin could meet. In truth, the traditional connections of marriage and blood had withered away under his stewardship; when people did see their husbands or wives, the passion and intimacy of old was largely gone. 'Family' was now an amorphous concept, the only fixed point of which was Frank; our father and teacher. When he would remind us that it is written 'you shall have no other God before me,' it really meant that no relationship was more precious than that which you had with him or with your faith. It was belief – a belief that had drifted ever further away from pure Calvinism - that truly bound us together and we could no longer live like those who had not been chosen. Within the complex our time and emotions were micro-managed and any infraction caught by, or passed on to, Council members would quickly lead to being ostracized at one of our great Confessions.

Violations of Frank's word were rare. But to maintain discipline and focus, regular scapegoats were necessary. Fear of reprisal and punishment were essential to keep the flock in check. When you found yourself stripped of the meagre comforts you were allowed, or were forced to go without human contact for days on end and were forced into ceaseless prayer in our chapel, your spirit was broken. However, not everyone was broken so easily, and the scale of punishments found a new level in the case of Rose and Marcus Sullivan. They had been stopped from leaving the compound, in broad daylight with their daughter Jennifer, by AJ Smith and Thomas Goodman. Raised voices echoed down between the buildings as Marcus Sullivan attempted to push his way past them. A crowd soon gathered as Frank was called to 'reason' with them.

"So, you've decided to walk away at our moment of greatest need. After everything we've given you."

Regardless of the moment, Frank always declared it to be of the greatest need. Marcus's hands shook by his side.

"Reverend, we... we need to live as a family again. It just doesn't feel right for us being here anymore. I don't know, maybe the saints have not persevered with us. We'd just be getting in the way of your work."

"It's for God to make that choice. Not you. I'm clear of your purpose and it's to stay as part of our family. You know what is going to happen in the world out there. It's going to fall and burn, and you're walking that sweet child straight out there into the flames. Is that what you want? To give up your seats at the right hand of God? Come, Marcus, let's me and you talk alone.'

Grandfather frog marched Marcus away towards the chapel, his arm crushed tightly around him. At breakfast next morning he was nowhere to be seen. Three days later he finally appeared, unshaven, unwashed and looking and squinting as if he had not seen sunlight for days. He was physically sick when he tried to eat. When he lifted a glass of water to his gaunt face, his shirt sleeve fell down and revealed a chain of vicious black bruising on his wrist. Around his neck lay the small cross made of ivory I had never seen him without. His fingers shook as he lifted it before him. It was as if he had never set eyes upon the object, its presence entirely foreign to him. At the other end of the hall sat his wife, Rose. She clearly wished to rush to him, but fear rendered her prone. Marcus could only summon the energy to sadly and oh so slowly shake his head at her. I never knew if this was a warning, an act of defiance, or a sign of resignation. That was the last time the Sullivans were seen together. They disappeared from our midst after Marcus was caught attempting to get into Jennifer's room in the middle of the night. All of the children awoke in time to see him swinging her door into the face of Kenneth Letts, before attempting to punch and kick his way past all those who arrived to restrain him. As Jennifer screamed inside her room, he was brought to heel by the barrel of the gun AJ Smith placed against his skull.

"Just fucking shoot, then. Do it. Go on, you fucking cowards. I don't care anymore. You won't have her. You won't get away with this if I leave here without her!"

Edward Gant pulled down Smith's gun.

"We're doing this for Jennifer, Marcus. She needs to be protected from you. You know what you and Rose have done."

"What *we've* done?! You're all utterly, Goddamned insane! Take me to the Reverend! Take me now!"

Gripped by hysteria, he laughed until he choked. Smith smacked on the front of his knee with the handle of the gun, causing him to fall in agony onto all fours. Gant and Smith then grabbed an arm each and dragged him off screaming down the hallway. Grandfather informed us the next day that Rose and Marcus had been exiled from the Frontier

Saints, and that Jennifer was now solely in our care. They were born to sin and remained its prisoner; their only purpose in life was to bring their daughter to our loving arms. Yet nobody had seen the Sullivans leave. It was a lesson for every family there.

***

Where the Frontier Saints were concerned media-wise, familiarity may have initially bred contempt, but in an era of twenty-four hour rolling news, it soon bred boredom and dwindling interest in our activities. Of course our first year in California had set the airwaves, internet and printing presses ablaze like the wild fires that so often consumed the state. The pink press set upon us like rabid dogs, their exasperation with, and vilification of our existence reaching fever pitch at our targeting of proponents of the proposed Domestic Partner Rights and Responsibilities Act bill. Mother's face, with childishly drawn-on devil's horns became a popular anti-Frontier Saints image, after she had told the waiting media hordes on the steps of the California State Capitol building that there was no bill of rights for queers that would be passed in Heaven, so none should pass on Earth either. Grandfather's press release decrying this attack on the 'sanctity of Christian marriage' played perfectly into the clenched fists of conservative commentators already imbued with a hatred of California's liberal establishment.

However, in a state created in the cutting room of a studio, the tiny attention spans of the press hounds were easily diverted to newer scandals and shocks. The reporters stopped calling, the column inches shrank and the bile was directed elsewhere. We needed an angle with national bite, something that would send us once more into the stratosphere of public hatred. And as this was America, the land of opportunity, we didn't have to wait to long for one to present itself. When the President addressed the nation from the Oval Office on March 19, 2003 to announce the invasion of Iraq, Grandfather clasped his hands together and thanked God for sending us such a gift. Not all the Council felt his elation. I had sat in on the Council meeting to take notation of action items in place of Mother, who had flown to LA to 'work' with Michael T. Jones for a week. It was clear that AJ Smith, ex-Guardsman that he was, had a natural sympathy for the soldiers going into battle.

"Reverend, I don't get it. These guys… well, these guys might not have been elected, but in comparison to the queers downtown, and the politicians we've spent the last six months harassing every day, they're not that bad."

"Are you wilfully being blind, AJ? They're doing the bidding of the very same politicians who want equal rights for queers. You need to see the bigger picture. They suffer because of their masters."

Gant interjected. "But how do we exploit this? It's happening in some dried-up desert thousands of miles away."

"We wait for the bodies to come back."

Smith may not have been brightest spark, and it pained him to comprehend and agree, but the Reverend Frank Marlin's logical was simple: every dead soldier was God's punishment for the United States' moral perversion. Each mutilated carcass, each black plastic body bag, each flag-covered coffin was His sign to us that this nation was doomed. And, as the family of that soldier was laid to rest, we would be on hand to tell that person's family just how much in vain was their son or daughter's death.

We did not have to wait long for military planes laden with this horrific cargo to start arriving back in the States. It took a mere two days for the war to serve up its first American victim on a steel-encased platter, and the banquet of the dead would roll on endlessly; though the main conflict in Iraq was over quickly, the peace, for which they did not prepare, imitated war most effectively. No month would pass without fresh meat to picket in California. The first funeral we chose to 'attend' proved to be a real showstopper – it took away the breath of even our staunchest apologists. As the ceremony for 19 year-old Army Private Jimmy Mayweather took place, we were confronted with absolute disbelief from the on-looking mourners and the press we had so graciously invited. With smiles on our faces and passion in our hearts, our noise drowned out and disturbed almost all of what was said by the pastor at the boy's graveside. Though standing beneath banners that read "No place in God's house for American soldiers" and "The Stars and Stripes is the cloak of sin" even Edward Gant looked nervous.

"Jesus, Laura Jo. There are more guns there than I've ever seen."

"It's a military funeral. It's not like they can shoot us."

"No? Funny, as that's what they're trained to do. *I'd* shoot us."

His fellow comrades were remarkably restrained. They gave impassioned speeches about how this boy had died bravely when the helicopter carrying him was shot down in the vicinity of Nasiriyah, of how he was preserving our right to protest like we were today. We told them, with the *utmost* respect, that he was going to Hell.

The headlines that followed proved we had hit the ultimate nerve, and had moved to a position of infamy from which there was no return. This Molotov cocktail of politics, Islam, homosexuality, and military conflict was guaranteed to cause an explosion on some level. Mother and Frank were particularly proud of the *San Francisco*

Chronicle's one-word declaration on us: "Sick". Frank's response to the paper in a follow-up interview was as cutting as ever.

"What's sick is a society that tells its citizens that its ok to defy God's will and breach the laws of nature and then expects there to be no consequences. And what's more, the reaction to us is another example of our First Amendment rights being violated. Free speech? That's the preserve of liberal newspaper editors. People don't want to recognize the truth. And the truth is that this war is simply another mechanism by which God has delivered His verdict upon you."

The third soldier's funeral we chose to picket would be the most fateful. Every moment of it comes back to me unblemished, sealed in a formaldehyde dream. A normal day in the Frontier Saints diary of protest and anger became the point at which the direction of my life began to vehemently veer from the chosen path. Lance Corporal Carey Tait was killed in action in southern Iraq. He had been protecting an oilfield when an enemy mortar had sent him careening into the air, his left leg ripped from his body, and internal organs crushed against his rib cage. Carey Tait was not killed at that moment; after being evacuated to the US camp's medical facility, he died after ten hours of surgery. The reports of his death revealed him to be an all-American archetype. Tait had a face of calm, chiseled beauty, and a muscular, tall physique. At college he was both a celebrated defensive lineman, and a 3.8 grade average student, majoring in economics. He had given his country two years of perfect military service, and in San Francisco he had a beautiful fiancé, and loving middle-class family awaiting his return. Now in Iraq he had been reduced to a wreck of bleeding tissue and splintered bone, his life ebbing away among smoking wells of black gold. It encapsulated everything Frank had declared about this war. Why else would such a human being suffer?

It was a crystalline May morning as we pulled up at the grounds of the Neptune Society Columbarium in San Francisco. The elegant neo-classical form of the Columbarium shone a brilliant white, its oxidized copper roof hinting at the colors of the beautiful grounds around it. Mourners, as yet unaware of our presence, moved in crow-like flocks, the California sun consumed by their jet-black attire. His remains were to be interred in what was one of the only non-denominational facilities in the area. His parents, though Christian, were not regular churchgoers, and had been quoted as saying that their son had died for all Americans, regardless of religion or race, and that the Columbarium was therefore a fitting last resting place.

Outside of the sickly claustrophobia of our compound I felt once more a clearer sense of purpose. Surrounded by the full contingent of the Frontier Saints, it was once more us against the dying world, as we stepped off our buses and made our way along the crescent path to the Columbarium's entrance. All except Ann, who sat gloomily fastened to her seat and had refused to come with us. Nothing Beth or I said could change her mind.

"It's a beautiful day. Come on, Ann, the service will probably be quite short. There's clearly press waiting too."

"Just leave me alone. I don't care who's here. I want to go home to my room."

"You need to put aside your personal problems right now – Grandfather expects us all to do our part."

She locked her eyes with mine, her face a portrait of immaculate sadness.

"My problems? You have no idea. Run along and play God."

Unsettled by how much older Ann seemed and sounded than her 13 years, Beth and I made my way to the rest of the congregation. We had been pushed back 40 feet from the Columbarium's door by the police, who with interlocked arms had formed a human barrier. Angry relatives shook their hands and shouted 'shame' at us from behind them. Mother was infuriated and rounded on the officer organizing the chain.

"We've every right to enter that building! Move aside, or we'll slap your office with a lawsuit faster than you can say 'dead soldier.'"

He looked as if he wished to spit straight in her face.

"While that boy and his family are in that building, you'll go no further. I've got a temporary injunction in my pocket that stops you from doing so – you'll get a copy soon enough."

Cursing under her breath, she turned to us.

"We're going to have to turn the volume right up so they hear us. Let them be under no illusion as to how pointless and empty that boy's life was. Louder! Raise those voices, lift those banners high!"

Cries of "Thank God for mortars!," and "Thanks God for IEDs" shot past the officers, who winced in fury at every slogan. We had never sounded so united, so righteously indignant, or been so narcissistically in love with the awful noise that our combined voices made. The line of police bodies and our banners thrusting up into the cobalt sky behind them played wonderfully for the cameras. It was further evidence of our oppression.

I moved back a little way from the rest of the congregation to soak in the entire scene. With my placard resting against my chest, I felt satisfied with our day's work, and took no small pleasure in the reddened faces of those who left the Columbarium to voice their anger at us. To the east of the building, I noticed a boy sitting atop a small garden wall.

Based on his clothes I couldn't tell if he was a mourner or not, and wondered why he sat alone, watching our every action. When he noticed that I had drifted apart from the rest of the Frontier Saints he pushed himself off the wall and began to walk towards me. Every few strides he took, he had to push the bangs that swept across his forehead from his eyes, or adjust the too big suit jacket that looked like a hand-me-down. As he drew near I tensed and prepared myself to face a barrage of abuse. I was disarmed somewhat by how handsome he was; his slightly tanned face was beset my freckles across the bridge of his nose, and though hidden somewhat by his hair, his large, opal brown eyes pierced right through me. With his casual demeanor, and one corner of his rosy lips turned up in what seemed to be an amused grin, he did not give the impression of someone about to unleash every ounce of pent-up fury in his body. He stopped a mere three feet from me.

"Hi, I'm Jesus."

I could barely hear him above the din of the congregation. "Excuse me?"

"I said hi, I'm Jackson."

"Oh. I thought you said something else entirely. That your name was Jesus."

"Well, I do know a Jesus, but he got busted in school for having a big bag of pot in his locker. So Jesus doesn't come around much anymore. I think he's working in a vineyard up in Sonoma. He's helping to turn grape water into wine."

"So, Jackson, what do you want? Information about our church? I can give you some leaflets, or point you to our website."

"You know, I'm good for the literature. You've all given such a great account of yourselves today; I've got a pretty fair idea of what you're about. I guess I just wondered what your name was."

"Our congregation is called The Frontier Saints."

"No, no. Your name. Who are you?"

"I'm Laura Jo Marlin, granddaughter of the Reverend Frank Marlin."

Jackson Tait laughed and shook his head in weary fashion.

"Well now, isn't that just fate?"

"How so?"

"We've heard all about the Reverend. My folks have been trying to avoid seeing his face or reading his name, but there he is every day in every paper, on the television, radio. You people are kind of – what's that word? Ubiquitous."

"Whatever Grandfather says is based on tenet. People are so lost within their own sin they cannot deal with the truth he bears witness to, and-"

"Yeah, it's hard for us sinners not to be lost on a day like this, you know, what with the choir of angels behind me. Do you ever feel lost, Laura Jo? "

"Why would you want to know that? Why would you want to know anything about me?"

"Well, you'd taken a break from shouting so I guess I'd like to know why someone who looks and speaks like you comes to think and behave how you do. What drives you to come to the funeral of someone you've never even met to holler damnation and hate? I guess that takes a special kind of person, right?"

"The way I look and speak? What way is that?"

"I've got to go sit with my parents. It's a hard day for my family."

"Hold on, wait a minute. Who did you say your parents were?"

"Mr. & Mrs. Bill and Jean Tait."

"Tait?"

"You got it. That's my brother being cremated in there…and this is his jacket. Looks like a tent on me, I know, but hey, it's something real, you know? See you around, Laura Jo Marlin."

My placard dropped to the floor and I stood open-mouthed as he moved around the line of police officers, flashing them his driving license as he went, and walked up the steps of the Columbarium, never looking back once.

***

Soft voices and the rolling hum of the river echoed across the quadrangle outside, as a hostile army of thoughts plagued my mind. As I tossed and turned in my bed, a flickering image of that wretched boy danced around me. In the suffocating darkness, with the bed sheet wrapped around my neck like a noose, I dipped deep into my unending reservoir of hate and loathing. I reasoned that the callous trick he played upon me was a sign of his abasement in the eyes of God, and that he too would suffer in ignominy like his brother. Who was he, unchosen, made from the basest clay, to mock me? My nails dug fiercely into my palms as I imagined the boy to be dead, his smart tongue gone, eyes pinned open with fear, as I, the elect, stood over him. Incanting a terrible curse over and over, I wished misfortune on all those who knew him, as I tried to shut out his knowing, sarcastic voice and cull that conversation forever. Yet a different image of him would also appear, causing a knot to form in my stomach, and frightening warmth to spread through me that I could not control. There he was with the waking sun behind him, his hands pushing his hair away once more, and a sniper's gaze fixed upon me. There was no reference point for this alien feeling. It was, I told myself, the onset of a sickness that would pass, a feeling that would soon be unmasked as an imposter. A secondary sensation lay behind this turmoil: at the edge of my consciousness I could feel the sharpened blade of guilt awaiting me. It took all my strength not to run onto it and concede to the notion that our congregation was in some way wrong in its actions. The temptation to understand what he and his family must be feeling was almost overpowering. When finally the dawn came, it seemed simultaneously a relief to know that I would never have to set eyes upon him again, that the haunting presence of that devil would fade, and also an unthinkable, dreadful possibility that I would not see him again. He had generated fury and disgust in me, and yet also a need to know more about him than I did. How I wondered, did he look when not a funeral? Where did he go to school, and what did he like to study? At breakfast I went as far as imagining him next to me, his hand upon mine; I pushed it into the pointed corner of the table until the swelling pain laid waste to such a terrible notion.

The following weeks were ones of near unrestrained success for the Frontier Saints. Our decision to picket soldiers' funerals had re-ignited the media's interest in us and had drawn level of condemnation from all corners of public life; mayors, councilmen, senators and veterans associations all took turns to vilify our presence at such events and in the state itself. We were an "appalling affront to decency in America," "a malignant cancer in California," and "the evil extremists in our midst." Yet they could do nothing. The law and those staunch protectors of our First Amendment rights were firmly on our side, not least our own nationally syndicated ally, Michael T. Jones. Mother's bravura performance on his show took a swift axe to flimsy accusations against us.

"Extremists. Fanatics. Christian jihadists. That's right, listeners – once again our great state of California has seen fit to jump all over our civil liberties. This week the California-based Frontier Saints church was widely condemned in our oh-so-liberal media for protesting at the funerals of a soldier who had died in the war on Iraq. Or as we like to call it, 'Another fine mess we've gotten ourselves into, Stan.' Well, shock, horror, that's reasonable, you may well think. These are the guys fighting to protect our country. They're giving their time and lives to do this. But hey, this is your host Michael T. Jones saying wait a minute now, it's not as simple as that. That's the line pedaled by every lawmaker who wants to crush your voice, listeners. So I'm joined once again by the lovely Josephine Marlin of the Frontier Saints. Josephine, thanks for coming in again, and I have to say, looking and sounding every inch the extremist."

"Ha, well thank you, Michael. It just seems a case of history repeating itself, doesn't it? As the Reverend Marlin, the head of our congregation, always says, if this is a Christian country, why does it seek to penalize those who seek to practice Christianity?"

"Exactly the point, Josephine. Now folks go to church, they read the good book, but we then get chastised like school children for following the word of the Lord? "

"Michael, we consider ourselves within the context of our faith to be a moderate, progressive church. Quite frankly it's those who want to suppress our ideological beliefs that are the real extremists. We peacefully demonstrate, yet every day face a barrage of death threats, legal threats, and are constantly harassed by the authorities. We've broken no laws. It seems the so called 'keepers of the flame' want to extinguish it for everyone else."

"Now many folks might recoil at the military focus of your latest activity. But here's the rub, Josephine, these guys join up to protect the rights we have to free speech, even if what we say concerns them."

"That's exactly right, Michael. What people fail to realize is that God is not some benign, take-every-Sunday-off creator. He is active is our world and every one of our actions has a consequence. That's why these men are returning home in the state they are."

"Now my listeners know full well my views on allowing homosexuality within the military itself. This is another aspect of that same argument."

"If this is allowed and encouraged, what does that say about what we have become, in God's eyes, as a nation?"

Mother was not lying when it came to the level of threat against us. Edward Gant had announced our intention to the *San Francisco Chronicle* to picket the funeral of Sergeant William Walsh, a native of Ventura County, who had been killed when a rocket-propelled grenade hit his convoy in Assamawah. Travelling back up from the city after filing a lawsuit for defamation against the mayor's office, Gant was set upon by four men in a side street off of the Tenderloin. His left arm was broken in two places, the fingers on his right arm stamped upon and shattered, and his face left a map of bruises. Mother rushed pictures of his injuries as he lay semi-conscious on a hospital bed to the newspapers and posted them online. This was followed by a visit to our property by the Contra Costa County sheriff's office investigating a disorderly conduct charge against Michael Gray, the oldest member of our congregation. A 'witness' claimed to have seen him forcibly stopping a woman from entering an abortion clinic during a picket line. He was released without charge after two days of questioning.

A feeling of unease and embattlement gripped the congregation. So much so that Grandfather was finally convinced by AJ Smith that we needed to be able to defend ourselves in our own home. A small cache of weapons were easily obtained through various members' existing licenses. Assault rifles, shotguns and various semi-automatic pistols were stored away in a vault built beneath the east wing of our home. Male adult members of our church were to be trained in their use in the event of an attack. Every other Saturday morning would from now on be punctuated by the sickening crack of bullets fired at trees and fence posts on the other side of the river.

Caught up once more in the tidal rush of my life in the church, I tried to stave off the presence of the unwelcome guest in my head. Jackson Tait, I thought, was now confined to a memory. I almost managed to convince myself that our meeting had been something I'd imagined, that he was a monstrous ghost of my own creation. That was until, at a picket we had organized outside an abortion clinic, the apparition reappeared from nowhere. A small group of us stood swathed in winter coats to protect against the freezing fog that had descended, as the weather sometimes did in San Francisco, in the middle of spring. My hands had turned as blue as the letters on the placards reading "Baby Killers," "Pro-Choice: Pro-Hell" and "Elective Murder." It was easier still to stop young women from going in or out of the Women's Options Center. The guilt they already felt at their actions intensified like never before when asked by us if they enjoyed the sight of the blood that was now, or soon would be on their hands. A young Latino woman screamed abuse back at us and called her mother in tears, a well-dressed white woman ran back down Potrero Avenue as soon as she saw us, her hand covering her face as she went. Medical staff taking cigarette breaks outside the entrance looked at us with disgust. We were sure to remind them that God would not forget what they had been part of: "Cursed be anyone who takes a bribe to shed innocent blood." They flicked their cigarette butts towards us and stuck their middle fingers in the air.

As the blanket of fog began to lift, Beth pointed to a lone figure walking towards us, a placard that read "This Is A Sign" slung over his shoulder.

"Isn't that the boy you spoke to at the soldier's funeral?"

I froze. It was the first time anyone else had confirmed his existence. When he waved at me as if I were an old friend, my face turned quickly from frozen to molten. As he drew near I moved away from the other members of the congregation so they would not be able to hear us. I could feel the anger surge inside me.

"What are you doing here? Don't tell me – your sister's got an appointment at the Options Center."

"Nah. No sisters. I've got a little cousin called Billy though. Not much chance he'll get pregnant. Though miracles do happen, so I'm told."

"You really do think you're smart, don't you? You stand there, reeling off your clever lines and yet have no idea what's in store for all of you."

"All of us? Oh that's right, I read we're all doomed, right? Except you, of course.

"That's right. Except us."

"So explain something to me I don't understand. Why do you

even bother to picket this place? If not a single one of those unborn kids has got a chance in this world, why bother? If they aren't chosen, why do you care?"

"Because it's better that they realize and accept their damnation. From the moment they are born they enter into it."

"You don't see the irony of this? You're protesting to save the lives of children you'll then claim aren't the children of God. Because they're born into sin, right? Which they can't escape themselves unless your God, if He's in a good mood, might, just *might*, save."

"Our scripture says-"

"You mean the same scripture that I could pick a hundred passages from that say how all children are blessings from God? That scripture?"

"I think my grandfather knows a little more scripture than someone like you."

"So clear this up for me. Your grandfather, does God just whisper inside his head when he talks to him, or does he use a phone. If so, there are quite a few people who could use that number. Makes you wonder, doesn't it?"

I wanted to strike out at him, claw my hand down his face until it bled. It was all I could do not to cry. When he saw this, he looked genuinely saddened.

"Look I'm sorry. I didn't want to upset you. I just don't understand how someone like you… Guess you're not allowed to do a lot of thinking. I'm sorry for that. I'm sorry for you. Really. "

"There's nothing to be sorry for. Why be sorry for someone who's been saved?"

"Maybe you should come and see what the rest of us live like.

226

That'd answer more things than I could. Anyway, I made this for you. It's pretty descriptive, but meaningless all the same. Kind of like the ones you have."

He gave me the placard, and backed away, just as a beautiful young black woman was crossing the street to enter the clinic. She stopped halfway across the avenue when she saw us, cars crawling past either side of her. Before she had another second to change her mind, Jackson Tait walked up to her between the traffic, murmured something into her ear, placed his arm around her shoulder and walked her slowly into the clinic, talking constantly as they went. It was as if we had become invisible, the noise of our congregation entirely muted. I had never felt so barren, useless and angry, nor been so jealous at the sight of an arm around a woman's shoulder.

11. Alive In My Transgressions

Jackson Tait became a pervasive presence. Regardless of weather, time or distance, he began to appear at almost all of our demonstrations. Be it outside downtown synagogues, gay bars in the Castro, or soldiers' funerals in neighboring counties, Tait would materialize as if from nowhere. He was never there when we arrived, or began protesting; he would shimmer into view when our protest was at its most strident and vocal. During the first week of his attendance, my heartbeat would jolt and my mouth would lose its ability to form sentences as this specter shimmered into view in the corner of my eye. He would casually wave at me, his expression not reflecting the discomfort of my own. I would mouth for him to go away and silently ask what he wanted, but he simply smiled back. Alongside the placard he made freshly for each protest, daubed with surreal messages that derided the Frontier Saints, he would bring sandwiches wrapped in aluminum foil and a steaming polystyrene cup of coffee. During lulls in our picketing he would once more approach me and a ritual of disparagement and mocking would begin.

"I don't know why you're here again. You've no right to be here."

"Don't tell me you're going to call the police? I could be arrested for protesting your protest. That'd be amazing. You should definitely call them. No, seriously, go ahead."

"Maybe you like what we have to say too much. Perhaps you're beginning to understand what we say to be the truth."

"Yep, you guessed it, I'm a convert. I was waiting in line at In-and-Out Burger down at Fisherman's Wharf, watching the tourists picking the worst things on the menu, and it struck me that the Double-Double was The Chosen One."

"Did your Mother pack those sandwiches? I guess she has one less person to make them for these days."

"Jesus. Who knew such words could leave such a pretty mouth. But I guess that's why they push you to the front, right? You're the sweet icing on the cyanide cake. Don't forget to smile for the cameras!"

"Oh, she sent you dessert too?"

He raised a clenched fist and begun to take imaginary pictures of me, his index finger moving down like a dead weight.

"Well, I guess she doesn't want me to go hungry. I can't be a starving spectator at the feast. Aren't you starving, Laura Jo?"

"For what, exactly?"

"Something other than this. Standing on street corners screaming at strangers, telling them they're going to Hell. Doesn't sound so appealing when you put it like that, does it? I guess it's what you choose to believe, right?"

"Belief is not a choice. You are chosen by God, or you are not. If the spirit moves within you, acceptance of your faith is not an option. It's not something you can question"

"Yeah, you're right, Laura Jo. You've never had choice. But it wasn't God who denied you that choice. Take a look around you to see who did."

I could not help but laugh at him.

"What's so funny?"

"You're like a mosquito. Frank Marlin could crush you whenever he pleased. You're just a minor irritant. Whatever victories you have, you'll only ever draw a little blood."

"He's not at your demonstrations much these days, is he?"

"He certainly doesn't have the time to deal with somebody like you, to listen to your pointless questions."

"You know, my mother, who made me those sandwiches, told me when I was little that it was important to question everything. She said if Christ could question his own father when he was dying, then why the hell couldn't she? I guess that helps her get through each day. Maybe she doesn't feel quite as guilty asking God why he took her eldest son from her. I'd say that was kind of important, questioning. You'd like my mother. Her name is Jean."

"I don't care what her name is. It's of no consequence to me, or my congregation."

"Her name is Jean, Laura Jo. She's a real, live human, not a mosquito like me. But that's the funny thing about mosquitos, Laura Jo, even they have a purpose. It's what they pass on that's the danger."

As the weeks passed, the manner in which we interacted began to change. On the odd days that Jackson Tait did not appear I would catch myself forlornly scanning the sidewalk and the entrances of surrounding buildings in the hope that he was there. I consequently felt a sense of relief flooding through me whenever he returned the next day. It was as if anything I said during our protest was somehow lacking without him, and my conviction only reappeared when he did. Though we would still intensely pull at the loose threads in our belief, we became more gentle and hospitable in our conversation.

"Is that the best you can do? 'God Hates Signs'? It's not your finest work."

"Everyone's a critic. It's a variation on a theme. God hates signs, the Frontier Saints, and the fact that Christmas decorations go up earlier and earlier."

"I suppose the more pressing question is 'what's in the foil today?'"

"Chicken. Again. That's three times this week. I was promised tuna, but hey, I'll live. Tastes pretty good still, though. You want one?"

"I'd better not. I have to eat with everyone else. Rules are rules."

"Those rules, hey? What would you do without them?"

"Eat chicken sandwiches?"

"Ha. I was hoping for a more profound answer, but…what kind of coffee do you like?"

"I've only ever had it black."

"Just black? That totally sucks. We'll have to do something about that."

"Totally sucks? You know sometimes you're so Californian it's ridiculous."

"Guess it's hard to escape where you're from, right?"

"I guess so."

For the next week he brought me a different coffee each day. Caramel lattes, espressos and mochas came forth. I decided that I liked cappuccinos best, which Jackson Tait then bought for me whenever he came. Of course, his constant presence did not go unnoticed by the rest of the Frontier Saints. I half-truthfully informed them that I was attempting to educate him as to our beliefs, and outright lied that I was constantly telling him to stay away. They believed me implicitly.

As the weeks progressed, Jackson Tait burrowed deeper beneath my skin. My thoughts rarely strayed from him, whatever I was doing. I sat through a great Confession, as my Mother and Grandfather drove another of our congregation into the ground, and could only think of him.

I taught a Bible studies class to two dozen members of our congregation and delivered each word to Jackson. When I saw my shadow in the sunlight, it was his form that it became. His scent seemed to saturate my own. Even more difficult to process were the thoughts of his mother and father. Their suffering must have been absolute. I was haunted by the idea of them watching their son's casket being lowered down to meet the crematorium flames. It was becoming harder to reconcile the depth of their sadness with the joy my grandfather had taken from the whole ordeal. That wretched human part of me tore at the cloth of my religion.

Yet I did all I could to curtail and contain the emotions swarming inside me. On a cold early summer's day, two months after we had met, I found a note slipped into my jacket that read:

"Laura Jo,

I spend my days wondering what you look like without a banner in your hands. I also wonder how many of those identical white dresses you have, but that's just how my mind rambles. Come meet me away from the noise? Y for yes…you know for no.

Jackson."

I slept with the note pressed against my skin, in the hope that the words would seep into me, and that I would awake with the courage to act upon them. But I could not countenance the idea. The trouble it would bring was too immense to imagine. I consoled myself with the idea that he had merely been sent as an object of temptation. This was the moment to see if the saints had persisted in me, my time in the wilderness to suffer the enticements of those who would be cast adrift at the end of days. And I had been promised to another. When I burnt the note I may as well have carved off and crushed a piece of my own heart, such was the anguish that it brought me. But the thought of standing before my grandfather in the center of my own great Confession was enough to steel my senses.

Though once I had decided to distance myself from Jackson Tait, to treat him as a doomed stranger, everything changed. After a long day of picketing an all-boys Catholic school, which Mother decreed was run by teachers engaged in the sexual abuse of their pupils, we were visited by Michael T. Jones. Mother had arranged for him to give a rousing speech to the congregation that evening. I heard little of what he said. My mind was preoccupied with replaying how I had ignored Jackson that morning. When he had approached me I had looked past him as if he no longer existed, and the searching look that formed on his face as he backed away ripped my insides to ribbons. Once more he raised his hand to take imaginary pictures of me, but instead shook the camera and shouted 'no film left' over the din the rest of the Frontier Saints were making. It was only the noise that erupted around me as Jones reached his grand finale that tore me away from that corrosive memory.

"...and my friends, do not forget, do *not* forget, that you are the real American freedom fighters. And when the quasi-liberal hordes turn up banging at your door, with the full force of the *heathen* establishment behind them, that God is standing behind you. That's right! Behind you! For it's the Frontier Saints who uphold the finer traditions of this nation, that exercises the right to protest and free speech that brings God closer to a people that have often lost their way. For that, all true Americans will thank you. And in Michael T. Jones, you've always got a friend."

Frank rose and with one wave of his hand brought silence to the congregation, as if a switch had been flicked.

"Words cannot express our gratitude for all the support Michael has given us. It gives us strength in our darkest moments. And make no mistake, we are entering that time. For every true voice like Michael's, there are two dozen who would like to see us vanish from the face of the earth without a trace. Do not doubt that those who misunderstand our cause and seek to destroy us *will* come, and when they do, we will not go silently. I would rather perish on the land we have made our own than bend to the will of such men. And you must be prepared to do so too."

The pressure valve of noise was released. Mother held Jones' arm aloft in the dewy night, before he ran his hand all too tenderly down her side, the three bulbous rings on his left hand glinting like the shells of insects. I knew in that second that he had known every part of her.

As the crowd dispersed I began to walk towards the east wing, my legs heavy as bags of sand and mind a whirlpool of disgust and confusion. Jackson's face and that of the father I had long been told and taught to forget began to interchange, one resting on the head of the other's body. It was in the middle of the courtyard that I felt the meat hook hands of Cousin John clench down upon my shoulders. He leaned close into me from behind, the stench of sour bourbon on his breath, and rough beard against my cheek.

"Slow down there, missy. John's just wants to walk you home, what with it being so dark an' all outside."

"I think I'll manage the walk, thanks... cousin."

"Now I'm trying to be a gentleman here. Is that any way to be? You ain't a child any more, Laura Jo. Why you gotta be so smart all the time?"

He pushed me towards the entrance to the wing and then up the tight, spiral staircase towards our bedrooms. As I fumbled to open the door in the all-encompassing blackness of the landing I felt John's hand smother mine and push the handle down hard. The door jolted open as he swung his shoulder into it. Before I could even turn to say goodnight, he had corralled me into the room, and pushed the door shut with his foot behind him. He pulled my back into his huge chest, our eyes adjusting to the blue miasma of light that penetrated through the window. Slowly, forcefully, he began moving his right hand across my breasts, his left arm holding down my arms across my stomach. When I opened my mouth to scream, nothing but air escaped.

"I've been waiting for such a long time Laura Jo. We deserve this, don't we? It feels so right. Don't you struggle, just relax into it."

When with one hand he started to undo the buttons at the top of my dress, and with the other beginning to pull the bottom of it up as if it were a net from a trawler, I willed myself to speak before my last ounce of courage drained away.

"John, John, please… you have to wait. I know I've been promised to you. It… it can't happen like this. I'm not ready."

"You'll never be more ready than now. Just shush your noise and let it happen."

I began to struggle against him, my fists flailing into his thighs and an elbow finally jagging back into his ribs. As bone hit bone, my arm going instantaneously limp, a scream that literally shook the rafters surged from me. Behind us the door opened, the harsh light casting his Minotaur shadow across the floor. Releasing me, we both turned to see Ann standing before us. Cousin John looked back down at me, his features caught between a smile and a snarl. Raising a finger to his lips, he then calmly flattened down my ruffled hair, and, as if nothing had happened, wished me goodnight and left. Beneath me my legs buckled, and I collapsed into a sobbing, sprawling heap. Ann closed the door and laid her small body across me. We did not move for an hour.

***

Ann and I lay awake in the ink-black dawn. Our heads gently rested against each other on my pillow. Despite her comforting presence next to me, I could still smell the wretched chemical stench of John's cologne on my body. The inside of my bottom lip was bloody and swollen, as I'd bitten down upon it during our struggle. It was impossible not to feel soiled, as if an invisible mark signifying my defilement had been placed upon me. Sleep was not an option: an endless montage of the night's vile events awaited me the moment I shut my eyes. Outside, the birds were reaching the crescendo of their morning conversation.

"It's beautiful isn't it?"

"No. Not really."

"You used to love that sound. When you were really little, you would spend ages trying to spot which bird was making what sounds in the trees behind our house."

As I said those words, Ann seemed far more mature than I had ever been. The world sat wearily upon her shoulders as she considered every word of her response.

"Well I know differently now. There's nothing sweet about it. They're warring."

"Who told you that?"

"Kenneth."

"And what does Kenneth Letts know about nature?"

"Plenty. About all kinds. He told me the dawn chorus was basically a quarrel. Each male bird protecting his space, making threats to the others about his territory, or his mating rights."

"I see. I guess that would spoil it for anyone."

"He's pretty good at that."

Ann placed her hand on mine to stop me clawing at my skin, in the hope of removing John from me.

"There's nothing you can do about it, you know."

"What do you mean? I'll tell Grandfather. He'll punish him. He'll throw him out."

"No. He'll do nothing at all. His bond to Cousin John runs deeper than his bond to us."

"How can you say that? We're his family, his flesh and blood."

"That just means we're convenient, Laura Jo. It won't be long before we're officially bound to those we've been promised to."

"That's years away for you."

"Kenneth says it might have to happen sooner."

I could feel every muscle in her body contract inside her. A hidden history of sadness momentarily forced itself into a pained expression on her face, before the blankness that permanently consumed her these days returned. I knew in that moment I had ask the questions which had circled and taunted me ever since Ann had stopped fully engaging with the work of our congregation. Visions of her silently holding placards, her mind elsewhere amid the maelstrom, came flooding to mind. The words set like tar in my throat.

"Has Kenneth Letts touched you?"

"You're asking that now? After John?"

"I need to know. Ann, please. I'm your big sister."

"For whose sake do you want to know? What difference will it make how I answer it?"

"I can protect you!"

"Laura Jo, you can't even protect yourself. Anyway, it's not a question of that. This is our fate, what God wants for us. Grandfather made that clear to me in no uncertain terms."

"What did he say?"

"That the outside world does not exist. That we are defined by a different moral order, that we all have no choice but to accept and not question. These are the burdens of being a Frontier Saint."

"Ann, stop this, please. Just tell me if he's touched you. This isn't right."

"Right? It's a little late for right. I just need to sleep for a while. Let me be, Laura Jo."

She refused to murmur a single other word about it, no matter how I cajoled or begged her. I had not felt so sick and alone since my father passed. The earth seemed to shift inside of me, the tectonic plates of heart and soul heaving together in desperation, fear and longing. Regret sent its sharpest pangs to mind as I remembered how I'd burnt Jackson's note. Leaving Ann alone in my room, I began to head towards the workshop. Once there I would write a small 'Y' in the corner of a placard. When the moment came later that day, for the first time, I would not raise those brightly scrawled words to sinners I had never laid eyes on. They would be solely for me.

***

As the street blocks gave way to the coast on Point Lobos avenue, the veil of mist that had greeted me off the bus began to evaporate. Before me the ocean moved like liquid grey glass; the waves' relentless argument with the rocks that blocked their path produced a muted cannon-fire that echoed in my ears. On the right hand side stood Louis' Diner, its façade the same color as the rusting hull of a boat. Half a roof sat squat upon the front of the building. Once inside, the place seemed trapped in amber: the last few decades had barely made a dent in the décor. School canteen-style cutlery sat on Formica-covered tables; a row of barber shop swivel chairs grew out of the bar; and a sign proudly declared that Louis' did not accept credit cards. I followed the wooden slatted walls and lampshades to the end of the largely empty diner. In the corner booth by the window, reclining into a leather banquette, was Jackson Tait. He stared out through the window down towards the strange man-made pool of water built into the rocks. Over a plain T-shirt he wore an unbuttoned mint green short sleeve shirt with white polka dots, as if he had consciously tried to look in-keeping with the restaurant's mid-century scheme. I watched as he nervously fiddled with the sleeve of the brown corduroy jacket he'd slung over the back rest as he waited on my arrival. When he finally turned around, he did not instantly recognize me.

"So… what happened to the dress? I thought you were going to ask me if I wanted more coffee. You look… different. I mean, good. But, you know… different."

In Union Square I had bought a cheap pair of dark blue jeans and a charcoal blouse. They were the first clothes I had ever bought for myself, with funds borrowed from one of the Frontier Saints' many accounts. Inside the department store the shop assistant – having seen the look of terror on my face - had bypassed asking 'can I help you?' and had insisted that she did. I let her hold clothes up against me like a mannequin and was grateful when she decided what I should buy. When

I stepped back out onto the street wearing my new clothes, I felt thrillingly invisible among the crowds.

The dress that Cousin John had contaminated was folded in a plastic bag, which I lifted to show Jackson.

"I guess by now you realize I didn't ask you to meet me here for the food. I'm pretty sure their cooking oil dates back to the pilgrims' arrival. Some view though, isn't it? We may as well both enjoy it."

Shifting along the banquette, he pointed for me to sit where he had been. I couldn't, in that moment, remember ever facing the same direction as him. Jackson signaled over my shoulder and asked for some coffee for us both, and a piece of pie to share.

"That's Sutro baths. Well, what's left of them. There were seven pools under a huge iron and glass structure that the ocean could sweep into. Now there's nothing but stairs and passageways that go nowhere, rotting ladders and crumbling walls. My brother Carey pushed me in there once. Dad threatened to drown him. Once he'd fished me out, of course."

"It's still kind of beautiful, despite how tarnished it is."

Jackson unglued his gaze from the pool and looked straight at me.

"You know, I was thinking exactly that."

We sat in satisfied silence as the coffee chased off the chill of the day, our forks fighting momentarily over the last piece of cream-laced pie, before he conceded defeat and let me have it. Before I could steal it away from the plate, he announced that there was one small caveat: I had to tell him about my whole week, from start to finish without leaving out a single detail. Before I even swallowed the pie I began to tell him everything that had occurred. He sat, for the most part, impassively listening as I outlined our morning prayers, how Wyatt Ford had been viciously dragged over the coals during the latest of our Confessions, the scouring of local news for the subjects of our protests, organizing our picketing timetable, avoiding the noise of afternoon target practice, our special afternoon classes on media representation and this week's special lecture by Ramona on why the Jews were more to blame than the Romans for Jesus's death. I neglected to tell him that I had almost been raped by the man my Grandfather had promised my hand in marriage to, or that I was certain my Mother was having an affair with Michael T. Jones. When I was finished he drew a sharp intake of breath.

"So it seems like your grandfather has really hit pay dirt with the soldier's angle. He's got more column inches than the war itself this week."

"I've never seen so many articles get framed to go up. We've got a room you see. Every clipping gets a place."

"I wish I was surprised by that. You know they're thinking of a law change, right? Banning anyone from being a certain distance from funerals?"

"Frank says it will never happen. That it'll make a mockery of the constitution."

"Well, my dad – that's Bill – says that the kind of people whose attention you're attracting now aren't going to give a fuck about that."

I had never heard him curse before; it carried just a hint of buried rage and it scared me. Before I could ask what 'kind' of people he meant, he suggested we get some air. As I got up, his jacket fell onto the floor beside me and small brown bottle of pills rolled under the table next to us. Jackson quickly scrambled around on the floor to retrieve them. He did not speak to me until he had paid and we were alone out on the

Land's End trail that runs along the coast.

"In case you're wondering, that's Prozac. And I can tell by your face you have no idea whatsoever what that is. You really have no idea about the world at large, do you? It's like being born again."

"What do they do?"

"They're supposed to stop you feeling sad."

I could feel the wind whip up and carry the spray from the ocean, the tide forcing itself upon every available piece of shore. Jackson watched as I began to shiver. He placed his coat over my shoulders and stood facing me.

"I won't take them. I just keep them on me. It's a reminder, I guess. They've signed me off school too. Not that I'm missing too much. I get to follow you around though. I'm also available for weddings and bar mitzvahs."

He practically spat the words out, his face reddened and his left fist closed tightly.

"You seem angry too."

"You think? Maybe that's because my brother went to some fucking dustbowl half way around the world to fight some two-bit dictator and came back in little pieces. Maybe it's because sometimes I go home and hear my father lock himself away in our garage and sob like a child, or hear my mother talking to my brother as if he's still alive while she puts his clothes on to wash. Maybe it's because your family decided to take our sorrow and shove it down our throats until we couldn't breathe. Every night I go to sleep and I dream of him dying. And you know what? Every time he does, he can't speak. I watch and he tries to move his mouth, he's desperate to make a sound - any sound. But he can't. So I'm speaking for him. And yeah, I'm a little angry."

I stood there, frozen and ashamed.

"I'm sorry."

The words burned like acid in my mouth. Part of me screamed out in indignation over why I had apologized to someone who had not been chosen. The other part wanted to pull him tightly into me, until the barriers between us disappeared.

"Don't. Don't say it. I don't want to hear that. Standing there you could be any girl I know; a high school kid with the same problems as the rest of us. But there's nothing average about you. Maybe I wouldn't be interested in you if you hadn't been taught to believe in what you do."

He reached out, took my hand and we walked slowly along the path. I could feel his pulse jolting as he rubbed his thumb back and forth across the top of mine. We gradually ascended, the view becoming more panoramic and beguiling behind us with each movement. The fragments of sun began to burn ember red and split the creases in the clouds and chase away the goose-bumps on my skin. We stopped to look out to the frayed horizon.

"What does 'interested' mean?"

"It means..."

Whatever he wanted to say it disappeared as it hit the borders of his mouth. Shaking his head, he turned sharply to me and kissed me softly on my lips. A warm, narcotic surge drained through the top of my head and then downwards through my chest. The scent of his skin, and the slow caress of his tongue as our mouths opened and joined hit me as if whiplashed by the waves below. He pulled away slightly and took my head in his hands, his face just inches away.

"What's been allowed to happen to you... I can't even find the words for it."

Jackson backed away down a path to our right. I felt as if the coast was about to crumble into the sea, and me with it.

"Just walk straight on. It'll take you to your bus. Check out the view to your left at the top of the road. Don't be a stranger, Laura Jo."

I watched him move off into the bluff, his head tucked into his chest and hands thrust into the pocket of his jeans. With his jacket still draped over my shoulders, I began to walk towards the road as if I were crossing quicksand, each step an immense struggle. A solitary car meandered along Lincoln Highway as I crossed it. It was then I glimpsed a lone white figure just beyond the line of trees, his head forlornly bowed to an unseen God. With his haunted, stooping stance, and ragged clothing, I expected him to move towards me; until, that is, I finally registered that he was a statue. The man stood beside two high white posts, and as I moved closer the barbed wire that connected them came into view. His right hand hovered just above a length of wire, the white paint chipping off him in places to reveal his copper interior. Behind him a group of ten white figures lay sprawled on the floor. Their horrific, entangled mass of limbs was disorientating, and the starkness of the concrete wall that part encased them was enough to imbue a sense of entrapment. In the hand of a woman, her face and body corroded and blackened by the elements, was an apple. In the center, a child stared into the heavens, its mind stripped of dreams. One figure stood out more than any other: as I studied its benign form, its arms stretched out wide as if crucified, its face betraying none of the horror of the others, I saw Christ before me. I reeled away, unable to look. In the wall a stone tablet protruded, declaring this to be a memorial to the Holocaust. The only lines I seemed to digest were those that read "We will never forget the martyrs of that evil abyss in human history." Looking back at the figure of Christ I began to sob, a deep sense of regret and anger at what had happened with Jackson running through me. He had led me towards this monument to shame and humiliate, to place me firmly on the other side of the barbed-wire fence. This was how he saw me. I convinced myself in that moment to tell my grandfather all.

***

The words seemed to fall from the page. Every time I tried to make them resolute in my mind, to fasten them onto the remaining tendrils of my belief they evaporated before me. Over and over I whispered 'God is faithful; he will not let you be tempted beyond what you can bear.' Yet I could no longer endure the things I felt. The merest thought of Jackson Tait brought with it both a suffocating rage and an overwhelming desire for the basest of pleasures that I struggled not to act upon the moment I was alone. Passion and guilt had become inseparable. I would curse him for the caverns he had helped create from the cracks in my world. Now I doubted each day whether the saints had persevered within me; that I was never chosen and had cast aside into un-original sin. Nevertheless, life within the congregation was emptiness exemplified; a hollow procession of rites and rituals. Morning prayers became meaningless, Frank's sermons little more than noise, our picketing a performance by out of work actors.

Jackson had not attended our protests for nearly a week. And every time I reached the point of acknowledging that he would not appear, some little death occurred inside of me. This devil, sent to plague me, had an immovable foothold in my life. If it was a test by God, I was failing. If it was a trial, I was condemned. It seemed to me that every one of his actions had been designed to fool and entrap me, a grand act of revenge against my congregation. He had made me care about the very people whose unimaginable sadness I had mocked. I had been led to the pinnacle, from which I had been prepared to cast myself down, in the understanding that nothing, no man nor heavenly being would stop my fall. But it was not all the kingdoms of the world that I coveted; just the presence of that boy beside me, devil or not. No matter how much hate I summoned from the deepest of reservoirs, it was met headfirst by empathy and longing. My life of absolutes had been absolutely destroyed.

Staring at the leather-bound Bible I had carried with me for eight long years, I could not help but feel I had never *read* it. In dreams the book came before me: a man's body lay under an American flag, the wind slowly moving the cloth to make it seem there was life beneath it. Only the arm of the man was visible. In his hand lay my Bible, its edges charred and burnt, my face reflecting in the untouched golden cross on its cover. Pulling back the flag, I would reveal the face of Carey Tait, the empty blackened holes where his eyes should have been looking right through me. Waking once more in a cold sweat I would question why God would want me to bring persecution to those who had already suffered so much. If, as my grandfather had proclaimed, we were the chosen few, why had God gone to such lengths to populate the world almost entirely with those who he would discard like trash? It was as if I could suddenly pick a page at random and find lines of scripture that refuted everything I had come, or was taught, to believe. Love, forgiveness, choice, love, forgiveness, choice. These were the lessons that leapt from the ink, the very things that did not exist in my life. Had I so wilfully ignored these teachings, thrown them aside and failed to grasp their meaning? Or had I been force-fed their opposite, like some dumb animal?

In those moments, Jackson Tait's cloven hooves disappeared and he became once more beguilingly human; a beautiful, damaged, grief-stricken human. Even so, I could not help but reason that that sense of humanity was maybe the greatest trick the devil could pull. Circling around and around, I would always come back to the same thought: who was my God, and who was I to him? One of his chosen sons and daughters? His granddaughter? The un-elect? His would-be lover? Jesus, Frank, Jackson: the unspeakable triptych of God, devil, and man. I could not tell them apart, or what name belonged to what form.

What I could not escape is that I had consciously chosen to ignore what had been happening to Ann. Like the words in the good book, I had chosen to interpret what I saw in ways that suited my beliefs. Now each morning the uneven steps, and deep, droning voice of Kenneth Letts that rippled through the wall sent me into a state of paralyzed hysteria, and a yearning to bring him violently to his last breath. It was as if I had been transported back to the cornfield I hid in as a child. This time, however, I knew that the wheat thresher was coming, and knew exactly what that sound meant. Yet to help Ann it was I who had to stand up and walk back onto the path. To save myself, it was I who had to confess all to Frank, so that he might reset the misaligned compass of my thought. I was certain too that Grandfather did not know of my Mother's betrayal, and that I'd have to confess her sins as well as my own.

It had been a full week since I had seen the face of Jackson Tait. Outside, the darkness had finally prized away the fingers of the long summer light, and I lay thinking of the bag containing the clothes I had bought to meet him that lay under the bed. Before I threw them away, I decided to look at them one last time. As I removed each item a small piece of paper dropped upon the floor. On it, in Jackson's writing, was the address of a house. Though it was too late to change my intention of confessing, at least, I realized, he had not abandoned me. Leaving the jeans and top laid out upon my bed, I slipped into the pitch black hallway and made my way down the stairs and out into the courtyard. Visiting Grandfather at this late hour would be the only way I might have gained an audience alone with him. Moving quickly across the courtyard, I could see a dim light emanating from the window of his private chamber at the end of the west wing. Fear over what I was about to do began to make every nerve and sinew convulse as I ghosted along the passageway that separated his accommodation from the rest of the building. I would fall to my knees and beg forgiveness. I would plead for guidance, and for Kenneth Letts to be removed from our congregation forever.

The door to his room was slightly ajar; I pushed my face against it and caught the smell of burning candles in the air, and could hear the muffled moaning of what I thought to be a woman coming from within. Tentatively, I began to push open the door, one slow inch at a time. In the dull amber glow of the room, a naked woman was bent over the high bed. Frank Marlin stood behind her, his clothes neatly folded on the chest at the bottom of the bed. One hand gripped her hair and pulled back her head as he thrust his great body into her. Her mouth and eyes flashed open and closed with each rhythmic collision. Clawing at the sheets beneath her, she said nothing but the word 'God.' To the right of Frank, another man knelt, facing the corner of the room. Instantly I recognized the figure of Thomas Goodman. Fully clothed, he shook from the very core of his being, rocking back and forth, his hands locked in prayer as if he were a chastened child. The back of his shirt was sodden with a great patch of sweat as he quietly, but dementedly murmured lines of doctrine.

"And those whom he predestined, he also called, and those whom he called, he also justified, and those whom he justified, he also glorified."

Looking back at the woman, I finally grasped that she was Thomas Goodman's wife, Mary. My Grandfather pushed her down hard into the bed and forced himself into her one more time, before collapsing in a heap upon her, his breath heavy and eyes wild. Finally he looked up, his arm stretching out for something beyond his reach on the desk against the back all. Tied around the body of a small lamp was a cross made of ivory. The very cross I had last seen around the neck of Marcus Sullivan before he had been dragged away like rotten meat.

Closing the door, the darkness engulfed me once more. A sickness began to cascade around inside my stomach, and begin to tear its way up through my throat. Back out into the cold evening air of the courtyard, I half ran, half stumbled towards the river. Falling onto my hands and knees at the bottom the sloping bank, I vomited into the rushing water. I did not stop until I could taste blood in my mouth. With my hands covered in mud, chest burning with acid, and a hitherto unknown desire to die surging through me, I knew this was start of the end of everything I had known.

***

1520 Seacliff Avenue stood waiting to swallow me. Though every window of the house was bathed in beckoning light, I was scared beyond words as to how I would be received. Reaching out to steady myself on the cold metallic trunk of the car that sat on the inclined driveway, I watched a man gently place his hands on a woman's shoulders and bury his head in her neck. She closed her eyes and placed her hand on the side of his face, her smile failing to hide the sheer depth of her sadness. A sprinkler rose from the lawn that curved out from the house and spat water onto the hem of my already muddied dress. The flowers and shrubs it nurtured seemed too perfect to be real, like the painted background scenery of a play. Wooden steps led to the veranda and the entrance to the house. Given my terrified state, those steps may as well have been a mountain, the lawn a vast, black desert before them. When finally I summoned the courage to walk, I moved as if covered by a diving bell, the floor beneath transforming into wet cement. The noise of some unknown song drifted out into the street from an upstairs room and met with the sea-scented air. It seemed to give me the final spur I needed to knock upon the door.

As I backed a few steps away, the man who I had seen through the window opened the door. I recognized Bill Tait from the newspaper pictures of his son's funeral and our protest. Adjusting his thick-framed spectacles, he squinted at me in the half light of the veranda, clearly bemused at the bedraggled mess that stood before him.

"Hello? You look a little lost, young lady. Can I help you with something?"

He walked close to me, scratching the tight, salt and pepper curls of his hair as he did. When he could clearly see my red-raw, tear-stained eyes, the filthy state of my dress, and the sorry-looking plastic shopping bag I carried, he knew all was not well.

"Oh, dear. Are you in some kind of trouble? Why don't you tell me you name? Do you know Jackson, my son Jackson?"

Amid the tears that once more started to flow, my lungs rendered all sound stillborn, and all I could do was nod.

"Oh, God. It's another Friday in San Francisco. Don't worry, young lady, we'll sort out whatever this is."

Turning his head back toward the open door he shouted out to his wife.

"Jeanie, you'd better get out here pronto, sweetheart."

She arrived at the door as Bill Tait removed his tweed sports coat and placed it around my shoulders and began to usher me inside.

"What in God's name is going on here?"

Jean Tait emanated a natural elegance. With hair shorter than her husband's, and an angular, crystal-cut face, she looked at least a decade younger than her fifty years. Only the faintest web of worry lines around her eyes signaled her true age. The powder-blue dress she wore enveloped her as if it had been crafted to fit every single line and curve of her body. Her husband, with his arm around my shoulder, blew out his cheeks in exasperation.

"I think you'd better get that boy of ours down here, now."

As Bill Tait ushered me into the hallway, his wife called up the stairs to my left for Jackson, before taking hold of me from him. While inspecting my ragged appearance, and attempting to straighten my matted hair, she kept glancing down at my stomach. Pictures of their family were scattered across the walls and ornamental table; I watched Jackson morph from toddler to young man and tried as best I could to stop the pure, untroubled gaze of Carey Tait dissolving what was left of my soul.

"Laura Jo?"

Crouching down and peering through the banisters of the stairs was Jackson, his shirt half undone and a towel in his hand.

"What are you doing here? I mean, I figured you might write to me."

His father's voice hit a tone somewhere between anger and fear.

"Son, if you've got this young lady… in trouble, your mother and I are going to damn well excommunicate you."

Jackson bounded down the final few stairs and took my hand.

"It's nothing like that, I promise. Laura's my friend."

He looked pleadingly at me for confirmation.

"Right?"

I meekly smiled and murmured yes, to the obvious relief of his parents; Bill Tait sat on the bottom of the steps, a sudden weight lifted from him.

"Christ, I think this family's been through enough lately. So, to be sure, you're not… right?"

"Dad, just relax, she doesn't need this. Have they hurt you, Laura Jo?"

His mother interjected. "OK this family is turning into the Spanish Inquisition right before my very eyes. Enough. Laura Jo, you come with me, darling, I'm going to sort you out. Have you any spare clothes?"

I lifted out the jeans and top from the bag, and she took my hand and led me upstairs. We entered a bathroom to our right; a large free-standing bath rested on wrought-iron animal legs in the middle of the room which she immediately began to fill with water. It rose rapidly, as if filled directly from the sea that was visible from the window. She laid down a clean towel and a robe on the long grey slate sink top that went the length of one entire wall.

"Now, you get in here and just soak for a while. It'll chase that chill right from you. Use anything you need in here. Clean away the day, OK, honey? I'll come and get you in a bit. We'll all talk together."

The warm water colluded with my utter exhaustion to send me into a semi-comatose state; I curled up on my side into a fetal position and listened to the raised voices coming from below, before finally I drifted off into a sleep a mere step away from the dead. I woke thirty minutes later, completely disorientated and unaware of where I was. It was only the hushed roar of the ocean outside that brought me back to reality. After bathing, I dried myself, slipped into the robe, and made my way through the maze of rooms below until I found Jackson and his parents.

They sat closely together in the dining room, Jackson at the head of the table and his parents either side of him. He bit nervously at his nails, his face flushed from anger or embarrassment. Bill Tait slowly spun a tumbler of whiskey around on table as he stared at his wife, worry etched upon his face. It was obvious enough that Jackson had told them who I was, and that they would want my sick presence removed before it infected their whole house. When I spoke, my voice seemed dislocated from my body, as if I'd just learn to speak again after a terrible accident.

"Mr. and Mrs. Tait. Thank you for your hospitality. I'm sorry for disturbing your peace this evening. I'm going to leave now. I owe you an apology I don't think I'll ever be capable of doing justice to and..."

Tears tried to form in corner of Jean Tait's opal eyes but she fought back their tide, as her husband stood and walked around to her side of the table and pulled out the chair next to her. The crushing weight of the sadness that consumed them filled the silent air for what seemed an eternity. Finally, she gathered herself.

"Laura Jo, the only thing you owe us right now is some of your time. Though given Jackson has told us exactly what you're part of, and that you're actually related to that… man, if I was to drag you out of the house with my own hands and throw you into the street, I think that'd be understandable."

I closed my eyes, ready to let her do just that.

"But then, that wouldn't exactly be a Christian thing to do, would it?"

She walked to me and took my hand.

"You'll come over here, sit down, drink some tea while I dry that hair of yours, then we'd like you to tell us everything about you, and your family, and your church. We need to understand why you did what you did to us. Do you understand that? For our own sakes and for yours too, we want to listen."

She turned to face her son.

"Now that boy of mine there, though he's in some pretty hot water with me and his father, it's clear he cares for you. He wouldn't do that if he didn't see anything worth salvaging, some seed of goodness. You've come into my house, a house filled with pictures of my son, Carey, and for you to find the strength to do that, to be desperate enough to do that, I've – we've – got a sense there's something badly, badly wrong in your world. And I'm going to need you to tell us what that is, however painful that might be. All this family has known for the last few months is pain, but we'll open our arms to yours too."

I was led to the seat like a willing lamb, my last defenses shattered by the bare humanity of her words. Such unbridled kindness was at once disturbing and soothing; the opposite of how I had been taught to act, but the single most nourishing thing to touch the remnants of my soul in more years than I could recall. Bill Tait threw a towel across the table into the hands of his wife. She pulled my hair from out of the collar of the robe, and ran her fingers back through it. Jackson reached out across the table, his fingertips touching mine as his mother began to dry my hair. For the next two hours I performed open surgery on my own mind, taking a scalpel to its every recess and letting the contents spill out, raw and unfiltered onto the scene of domestic comfort, this refuge from my wretched reality. No denial, no construct, or hidden memory was safe from this purge. I laid out the full cast of characters in the twisted puppet show of my life in the hope that they and I would understand how I became this shell of a person. I started with the death or my father and my grandfather's re-entry into our lives and did not stop until I reached his physical liaison with Mary Goodman. Throughout our conversation my father moved before me, his long buried image resurrected within the four walls of the Tait's dining room, his presence provoking me to finish what I had begun. Intermittently the Taits would all ask questions about the doctrine in which I believed, and ever so gently continue to unravel the already torn fabric of that faith. The longer I had gone on the more bleached and drained their faces became, Jackson withdrawing his fingers from mine the moment came to the funeral of his brother. Yet I could not bring myself to divulge quite what had happened with Ann and I. Bill Tait braced himself to speak. Holding what was left of the bottle of whiskey up to the light, he poured it over the ice in his glass, and swigged it quickly back, the cubes clattering against his teeth, his lips sucking in air as the alcohol burned through his chest.

"Where does someone start on a story like that? Laura, I'm not going to pretend I can sit here and eloquently argue with someone who shares your Calvinist faith as to its merits and intricacies. I'm no theologian, no scholar of religion. But I do know a little about human nature, a little about desire and motivation. That's my job, you see. It's what I do every day. I'm going to apologize in advance if any of what I'm about to say offends you."

Those words actually brought a smile to face.

"Please don't apologize. I've spent a lifetime trying to offend people. There's not much chance of me taking offense now."

"Well you've been honest enough with us, so I'll be blunt straight back."

He leaned across the table and rested his palm on top of mine.

"Your grandfather, Frank Marlin, is a cruel, twisted man. As far as I can see, your faith, or his take on it, allows him, and him alone, to behave with absolute impunity. There is no kind of behavior he cannot justify, and no consequences for the behavior of those that he favors. Yet he can use the very same rules to punish those he does not. The only thing that man desires is power; power and control of others. He has…"

Every syllable seemed like broken glass in his mouth, so gentle was his disposition as a man, so anguished was he to say this to me.

"Go on, darling. Laura needs to here this."

"He manipulates the weak, and latches on to the vulnerable - children, the destitute, the depressed or lost. He takes their money, steals them away from their families, and promises them a better life, here and eternally. But all they end up doing is serving Frank Marlin. It's an old trick to pull; people have been doing that to each other since we lived in caves. Now I don't really know if Frank Marlin really believes he is a god on earth, or whether the church he has built was just a means to money, and influence and notoriety. Or maybe he's been doing it for so long that he even believes his own lie. But what I do know for certain,

Laura Jo, is this: he is not holy, or righteous, or God's chosen one. He is a fraud, a fantasist, and a dangerous, dangerous, man."

Jean Tait took my face in her hands.

"We consider this to be a Christian house in our own way. We don't attend church very often, or believe half of what's written in that book, and I'm sure that throughout our lives, both Bill and I have acted in ways that were un-Christian to say the least. But that's because we're human. We're flawed, and contradictory, and we don't understand half of the things we've gone through in this life. And that's ok; it's how it is for most people. But though we have our own individual beliefs, it's very hard when you bury your own child to maintain even the slightest conviction that there's some higher power out there. I've cursed His name on a daily basis. I've threatened and warned Him. If something exists, it knows my anger."

I had known only anger *on behalf* of God. My pitiful, stuttering attempts to apologize were quickly hushed.

"But here's the thing. If you or your Grandfather could prove the God you believe in existed, I'd stop believing in it that very second. It'd destroy whatever faith I have left. That so-called God is a hateful, spiteful, petulant little child. There's no goodness, no forgiveness in his heart. Like there's none in your grandfather's. Laura Jo, I'm looking at you now, and the state you're in and I know there's something else. We made a deal, Laura Jo. Why are you in my house?"

The room dissolved and reformed before me. All I could see was the face of Kenneth Letts, and the ivory cross of Marcus Sullivan.

12. The Pattern of the World

Gulls stood huddled together across the eroding promontory, their heads bowed as the icy morning air swept off the ocean before us. The churning, sickly green blanket of water seemed to poison the sky above it; nothing flew or fluttered in the empty expanse. I imagined taking the twenty short paces to the shore's edge and slipping, unseen, into those freezing fathoms, my body drifting down like a bag of lead weights. Up above and behind me the Tait's family home glimmered in the dank light. Inside I had left Bill Tait nervously watching the street as he waited for the authorities to arrive. Jackson and his mother had left before we had both woken. Bill had explained that since Carey's death, Jean had sought every opportunity to spend time alone with her remaining son. The way she spoke to him it was clear that she needed to relate to him, his dreams and desires, as a fully-fledged human, not just as her child. She would never know Carey in that way, and would not risk the possibility of that happening twice.

"And I was so looking forward to taking a dip with you."

His steps camouflaged by the harrying swell of the sea, Jackson had crept up behind me. Though his lips just were just inches from my ear, his words were barely audible in the breeze. Turning around, I prodded him gently in his sternum.

"You convince me to stay and then this morning you're nowhere to be found?"

"We went shopping for you. Mom's bought you some new clothes. She couldn't believe that what you're wearing and those old dresses were all you owned."

I looked away, embarrassed.

"I'm not some kind of special project. Why would she do that?"

"Because I asked her to. Because she realizes how much I care for you."

"You care because you want to use me. That's what I am to you, isn't it? – a means of revenge after what my congregation did to your family. You need me to get to them. I know what it is to target the weak. Why else did you lead me to that place at the end of the trail in Sutro? You kissed me, made me feel things I'm not supposed to, and then walked away. And if they notice I'm missing… I'm scared of what they'll do."

"It's not about what you've done to my family. Not anymore. It's about what your family's done to you. It's my choice to care. Everyone in my house needs something to care for right now. Maybe I won't walk away this time."

"Choice. I don't understand choice. I'm not sure if I ever had any choices, or just didn't make them."

Jackson silenced me by running his thumb slowly across my lips from left to right. He moved his hand behind the top of my neck and pulled me into him as our mouths greedily met, his hot breath chasing mine into the cooling sky. I could feel myself letting go, readying my body to be consumed by his every touch, pushing his hands down across my behind, and up towards the cup of my breasts. Our absorption in each other was shattered by hearing what sounded like his name upon the air. Jackson's father stood up above at the edge of their garden fence, beckoning us back up the path to their house. As we walked, Jackson's hand rested upon the small of my back, instinctively knowing that without his steadying force I would likely turn and run. We paused when through the gap between the houses we could see the driveway crammed with police cars, the blue stars on their sides throbbing ominously amid the greyness of the day.

Awaiting us in the Tait's front room were four black-clad police officers, three of them holding their hats in their hands, their batons and guns protruding from their sides. The youngest of the officers spoke to Jean and pointed respectfully to the figures in the photo of a football team that rested on a side table.

"That's me, ma'am, just three left of Carey. He was something else on the field. My dad said he'd never seen a better Tight End at that age in all his life. I just can't believe that... well."

"Listen, Mike, I'm just so happy you could share some of your memories with us. It helps us keep him alive."

She took his hands in hers, before telling them all to drink their coffees before they got cold. To a man, they obeyed her. Bill Tait entered the room with another older officer, his thin-rimmed spectacles and greying hair giving him more the air of a librarian than a policeman. Behind them strode two officers sporting khaki pants, green jackets and black ties. The stockier of the two had distinct Latin-American features, his thick, dark eyebrows and moustache curving like bridges across his face. In direct contrast not a single hair could be seen on his head. He called the officers into a huddle.

"Gentleman, we've just had to discuss some jurisdictional issues, and I think we've gotten it straight. Now, we've got an indication of the general nature of the crime that may have been committed, and while, given it's in Contra Costa County, that comes under our remit, we're going to take up Jim's kind office of tactical support on the matter – he's got some resources and experience we haven't. How'd do you want to play this, Jim?"

"Maybe we better ask the young lady, see what she's comfortable with."

Jean Tait stood behind me, her hands on my shoulders, as they turned to introduce themselves.

"Hello Laura Jo, this gentleman here is Sergeant Jim DeNapoli, and he's with the Richmond branch of the San Francisco Police Department, and I'm Deputy Sheriff Javier Martinez, based in Costa Contra County, where I believe your home and – let's call it your church – resides. Now Jim here has some experience of dealing with your congregation, so he'll be sitting in on our discussion. We'd prefer it if it was just us alone with you, but that's your choice."

"I'd like Mr. and Mrs. Tait to stay with me. Jackson too."

"I'm not sure Jackson hearing this would be-"

"He stays or I say nothing."

Martinez waved his hands in defeat as Sergeant DeNapoli ushered his men into the adjoining room. With moments, the officers sat before me, a recorder on the table. Martinez ran his hands across the stubble on his face, his eyes darting over me, searching for a reason in my every movement.

"Before you tell us your story, I'm going to lay my cards on the table here, Laura Jo. In the last few days we've been inundated with correspondence from a lady called Angie O'Dowd. Mrs. O'Dowd is the mother of Rose Sullivan."

The temperature in the room seemed to fall ten degrees.

"We've already begun preliminary investigations as a result of her claims that her daughter and son-in-law are in some kind of trouble. She had been receiving letters and calls from them since they joined the

Frontier Saints on a regular basis, and in the last few months the tone of that communication changed. They alluded to both problems concerning their daughter, Jennifer, and being forced to sign over large amounts of money they had inherited. Mrs. O'Dowd claims that just as they expressed a desire to leave the church, any type of correspondence ground to a halt. She hasn't heard from them for a substantial amount of time. Can you tell me, Laura Jo, if the Sullivans are still with your congregation?

"No. They're not. I mean… Rose and Marcus aren't. Jennifer is still with us."

"You're saying that only their daughter is there?"

"Grandfather… Frank Marlin told us that they'd left her in our care."

"OK, so they just upped and left?"

"Not exactly. They'd try to leave with Jennifer before. They were convinced not to."

"And why did they want to leave?"

I dug my fingers fiercely in between the bones of my left arm until the sweetest of pains ran through it. Jean Tait moved my hand away.

"Laura, darling, you need to think of this girl now. Nothing else really matters."

With five pairs of expectant eyes upon me, and tears beginning to sting my own, the dam inside finally gave way to the pressure

"Jennifer was promised to a man in our congregation."

DeNapoli leaned in towards me.

"Can you tell us what 'promised' means, Laura?"

I explained that eight girls of non-consenting age had been

'promised' in marriage to much older men, and that that number included my sister and I.

"Rose and Marcus were deeply upset over this. They tried to stop Jennifer being given to Bryan Whitmore. It's not like anyone was expecting this. It was nothing we'd ever learned about. I guess you could say that the rules that govern our life there have moved somewhere far beyond scripture."

Martinez asked me about Whitmore, his background, how he interacted with Jennifer, and what had happened next to the Sullivans. DiNapoli and his counterpart shot each other a troubled glance when I began to outline Marcus' first three-day disappearance, and the following incident in which he was dragged away, struggling and screaming, never to be seen again.

"And do you believe that they just left?"

"No."

"What reason do you have to believe they didn't?"

"They would never leave Jennifer. And I've seen Marcus' cross hanging inside my grandfather's room. I've never seen him without it."

They took down the details of the cross, its exact place in the room, before turning the conversation back to the Sullivans' daughter.

"When was the last time you saw Jennifer?"

"Yesterday. All the children sleep in a different part of the compound. She's on my floor."

His hands gripping his knees as if to steady himself, Martinez carefully thought through the next words he would deliver.

"So this brings us back to why you called us here. I'm going to say for the record that I hope you realize the trouble you can get yourself into over false accusations. Just think about that. Now, Bill told us that you suggested that these girls who have been 'promised' are in trouble. What kind of trouble is that exactly?"

Slowly and calmly I began to express how I was certain that at least some of the girls were already being sexually abused by their future husbands; that Kenneth Letts was spending entire nights in the room of my thirteen year-old sister.

"Have you ever seen anything directly that you can attest too?"

I struggled to think of a single incident and could only say no.

"Laura, now take your time when answering this. Have *you* at any point been inappropriately touched or molested in any way?"

Bluntly answering 'yes,' I recounted each minute, terrible detail of how Cousin John had attempted to rape me. Jackson seemed unable to look at my face any longer, and moved to the window, his lungs sucking hard on the salty air. His mother's face had developed a sickly pallor, which she tried to hide by putting her head on her hands.

"And that last event was what caused you to come here. I see. Laura Jo, I'm going to advise you to not go back to your congregation. If the things you have described are taking place then you'd be unnecessarily putting yourself in danger. In the coming days I think it's pretty safe to say that this will become a certified investigation and your congregation will be receiving a visit from the combined forces represented in this room."

"I'm going back. I can't leave without my sisters. If I don't go back now they'll know it was me who told you. And there's…"

Jean Tait began to furiously protest.

"Laura, you cannot return to these people. The police will deal with this situation; they'll put it stop to it. You have to trust them – trust us – now."

"They'll stop it, will they? You really don't understand. As much as you'd like to believe that we – they - are little more than a bunch of dumb, disaffected hicks, they're not. They are organized, they are devout, and they'll use the full weight of the law against you. It's what they know how to do best. Sheriff, please *listen*, you can't just walk in there."

"Why is that, Laura Jo?"

"Because it's private property and they've been stockpiling weapons and ammunition for months. There's not any one over fourteen who couldn't shoot a sparrow straight out of the air."

His brow as furrowed as a winter field, Martinez gestured for a radio from the officers in the adjoining room. DeNapoli grasped the thread of discussion.

"What makes you think they'd take to violence? Now we've looked into their background with the whole situation surrounding Carey, and while the arrest sheet is long, the number of convictions stands at precisely zero. There's no previous, and no evidence right now."

"Isn't my word enough?! I'll get you whatever you damn well need. But just don't think for a second you can blindside my grandfather. Deep down he knows the end is coming, one way or another. He's said as much to the congregation. And there's little you can do to stop that."

"Frank Marlin explicitly said that?"

"He doesn't need to be explicit. I suppose he's been preparing us for this since we began, in a way. That's what it means to be the chosen few: it's inevitable that we'll eventually part from the rest of you. We can't coexist. When the law fails, and it will, he'll still have the laws as written in that book. They usurp anything you have, and he'll die by them. And there's barely a man, woman, or child who won't act upon his any and every word. If he says jump, they'll be no way you could talk them down from the ledge."

"And do you believe your grandfather is really a man of God? That he's acting in accordance with his beliefs?"

"What difference does what I believe make right now? Maybe he has a phone with speed dial to God, or maybe he's a fraud and everything he's accomplished has been based on a lie. I'll have to somehow live with that. But even if he's been lying for all that time, he's made the lie a reality. It's become the means to a greater truth."

Bill Tait broke the silence that followed.

"What I believe Laura is trying to say is that he will not back down. He can't afford to break whatever spell he has on these people, or himself. If he moves one little inch, the whole house of cards comes tumbling down."

Over the next two hours I began to detail the history of our congregation, including my grandfather's story of election, before supplying a police cartographer with the particulars of the entire compound, from room to room, floor to floor, from entrance to river. I passed on the bank account details of the Frontier Saints and noted down as best I could the list of the people and the amounts that had made been made out directly to our organization. They would need clear evidence of financial infringement to get permission to gain access to it. Most importantly, they wanted information on the most powerful individuals that surrounded my grandfather. While I felt nothing while divulging intimate details about Edward Gant, Cousin John, and AJ Smith, I found it nearly impossible to tell them about my mother. I would have preferred to have my teeth removed with no anesthetic. It was only the thought of Beth and Ann that allowed my words to spill forth, a sense of betrayal clinging to them like a boa constrictor around its victim. After their final pleas to not return to the Frontier Saints, they warned me to not say a word about where I'd been or what I'd said. If I blew the operation I would automatically implicate myself in any wrongdoing occurring within the confines of our congregation. Concerned about the reaction of my grandfather and Mother as to where I'd been for the last thirty hours, they provided me with a copy of an arrest sheet and police warning for disturbing the peace outside St. Dominic's Catholic Church in Lower Pacific Heights. I would simply have to sell them the lie. In case the lie did not hold water, for my own sake, they refused to tell me when they would pay Frank Marlin a long overdue visit.

***

I crept back into our compound that afternoon amid a biblical deluge. Once the heavens had opened, an ocean of rain poured forth, the sky itself a colossal collage of bruised clouds as the wind whipped across the fields and rolling booms of thunder threatened the earth below. Dozens of frogs lay squirming on their backs at the entrance to the Saints' ground, as if placed there as a warning sign, or marking the start of a pagan ritual. The curved run-off ditch that connected to part of the river at the other end of our land was almost full of water and was promising to turn part of the road that led to our home into an impassable bog.

With some of my 'new' clothes hidden away beneath my mattress, I went directly to find my mother, my face a fake contortion of anger, peering from beneath a mass of wet hair and clothing. I found her in the Council's office in the middle of a telephone interview with a newspaper based in Nebraska. Edward Gant, who had been listening in on another line to vet the journalist's questions, called for an immediate halt to proceedings as he saw me sobbing my false tears at the doorway. Mother's immediate rage at my disappearance soon turned to disgust at my treatment by the police, and she began discussing the legality of holding a minor in such a fashion with Gant. My performance was so convincing that I managed to generate a distant relation of sympathy in my mother, who still could not wait to tell me how worried Cousin John had been. Grandfather's reaction was less certain. After I had been unceremoniously taken to find him, he studied me for what seemed an eternity with his hooded, vulture eyes. Before I could even deliver my fiction he asked for the report and called the station, his gaze never leaving me for a moment. Panic swept through me at the fear that the veneer of our little ruse would be quickly rubbed away, my hands shaking beneath the blanket that Gant had draped over my shoulders. The answer he received from the desk sergeant seemed to pacify him somewhat, but it did not stop him interrogating me as to what the cell I was held in looked like, who I had shared that cell with, and why I had taken it upon myself to confront people outside St. Dominic's. A short display of fiery disgust over the imaginary sight of two men holding hands just outside the church grounds seemed a winning, almost too perfect, excuse; I watched him recoil then rejoice, his transition from anger to delight a rapid one as I detailed one of the men's attempt to physically assault me – the dark contusions on my skin given to me by Cousin John were still ripe enough to use as stage props. Frank promised he would make both the church and the police suffer for their actions. We would organize and attack, and drag their 'good' names back down into the sewer of their origins. Though the touch paper of relief was lit inside me, I could not help but pray that the imminent arrival of the police would bring the Frontier Saints problems of a different scale entirely and consign this matter to irrelevance. When he brushed the wet hair from my face, I no longer had to feign disgust. All I could picture were those hands upon the naked body of Thomas Goodman's wife.

For the next three days I waited expectantly for the squall of sirens. I lost myself in the notion that this would all soon be over, that Martinez and his officers would sweep through our home like white blood cells pumped into a disease-ridden body. Ann, Beth, and Jennifer and every wretched soul who scraped their knees in prayer to the plastic deity of my grandfather would be saved. Caught unawares, the police would surely find the evidence they needed to remove each brick from Frank Marlin's monument to corruption. And all the while I ignored what this meant for me. Had I not helped him to erect his empire? A web of guilt was unfurling inside me, its spidery silk wrapping itself around every waking emotion and action. Untethered from the sun that I had for so long orbited, choice brought nothing but anguish and discomfort. I would not only be responsible for betraying my mother, but my sisters and I would have no home. State care would take us and separate us, though this, I rationalized, was a lesser horror than the alternative, which was to remain.

Yet my naïve expectations were brought crashing down around me. The arrival of the police did not herald our moment of redemption and safety; the cavalry that came through the gates would be crippled before they sat foot on our soil. Though the fickle sun had returned, the road was a sodden mess. Just after dawn, Michael Chance and David Hollow were attempting to drive out to a nearby town to pick up food supplies for the coming week. Hollow sat infuriated in the passenger seat as Chance slowly attempted to navigate the battered old Ford pick-up through the mud and water-logged stretches of dirt-road, warning him to go faster than the 5mph he was managing. With his faded denim shirt, choppy shoulder length hair and oversized glasses, Hollow looked as if he'd stepped from an old hippy commune, but his nature was anything but peaceful. He banged on the dash and screamed at Michael as his warnings came to pass: the truck stalled right at the end bend of the road and the vehicle's back wheels immediately began to settle firmly into the thick, welcoming mud.

As the engine turned helplessly over, the water spraying out around the car with the frantic spinning of wheels, Hollow suddenly reached over and cut the engine. Out across the harvested fields a line of Contra Costa County sheriffs' cars, tailed by those of the San Francisco Police Department could be hazily seen. The two men sat immobilized, watching in shock as the metal cortege made its way past the thousands of butchered crop stumps. Finally Hollow snapped out of his trance and grabbed Chance by his lapels, warning him to run the 350 feet back to the compound. Dropping out into the mire beneath the truck, Chance began to run as fast as his unfit lungs would allow him, his hands wildly attempting to attract the attention of the figures he could see moving towards our church for early morning prayers.

Once Martinez and his fellow sheriffs reached the rusting bulk of the pick-up, they could not move its leaden mass. In between abusing them, Hollow had thrown the keys of the truck far into the field beside them, leading to his arrest for obstruction. He fought the officers as they attempted to cuff him, knowing that this would further delay and distract them, and also that they now were forced to walk the remaining distance to the compound, eliminating once and for all any element of surprise.

When they passed through the gates, arrest and search warrants in hand, they were greeted by only the men of our congregation, my mother, and me. When Michael had stumbled, half shouting, half gagging for air, back into our grounds I sprung towards my bedroom window and had watched as he rushed to clasp hold of AJ Smith, who stood mending the frame of a window. Smith threw his tools to the ground and began screaming at the children outside to move together into the communal dining area. I scanned their distant faces, attempting to pick out that of Jennifer. As Ramona Chance dragged and cajoled the frightened huddle of children indoors, I thought I recognized the dark reddish hair of the Sullivans' daughter. Having not seen her since my return, I ran along to her room, which stood empty. The sheriff had made me swear to stay away from proceedings, but at that moment, I knew I had to make a show of solidarity with the church, so I raced from Jennifer's room and into the melee of the courtyard. The noise and panic had summoned Frank out onto the grounds, his feet bare and shirt buttoned only half way up. Brushing his great mane of silvery hair back across his scalp, he stretched himself out, rotating his shoulders, and flexing the muscles in his neck as if preparing for a boxing bout. After calling for quiet, he began to dictate orders to the foot soldiers around him. Smith was sent to open up the weapons cache and distribute armaments. Mother, who had been giving this morning's sermon in church, walked to each group of men, and began telling them to remember that silence was the watchword of the hour, her finger clamped to her lips in an exaggerated fashion. When Gant appeared, Grandfather whispered something close to his face. Our lawyer raced toward the dining hall and re-emerged a few minutes later, just as Martinez and his men came into clear view.

Frank stood in front of the assembly, a great number of whom now had either handguns tucked into the waistbands or rifles slung over their shoulders. Martinez swiftly ordered his men alongside him in two great flanks. Dropping his sunglasses into his hat, which he then passed to a deputy, he began a cautious walk toward my grandfather, his hands up in a submissive fashion.

"Is this really how you want this to play out, Frank? I can call you Frank, right, Frank?"

"You can call me Reverend, *sir*. This congregation is not one that plays."

"Well, *Frank*, the warrant for the arrest of Kenneth Letts and Brian Whitmore might indicate that the County Sheriff's office isn't here for breakfast. Not to mention the one that says he can search your premises for any member of the Sullivan family."

Sheriff Martinez thrust the papers into my grandfather's hands.

"You can read those at your leisure. But in the meantime why don't you be a good sport, and tell your men to put those firecrackers on the ground. Then you can make our lives easier by getting Letts and Whitworth to step out here. It's called aiding and abetting a suspect, Frank. I get to lock you up because of it, so don't force my hand."

"There are no felons here, Sheriff, just men and women of God. Whatever any of my flock has done in the past served only to bring them here, to lead them to the word of God. You can only offer the security of a cell and bars, sheriff. It hardly compares with the eternal security that they've been granted."

"I didn't say felons, Frank. I said suspects."

"I deal in sinners, Sheriff. We're born to it."

"Right now I'm trying to stop you committing some sins as

outlined by the State of California, Frank. I'm trying to save you from a certain fate."

"You're looking at the only people who've been saved, Sheriff. Whatever you do to us is meaningless by comparison."

Blinking as is someone had flashed a light in his eye, Martinez began to look around to the upper windows for signs of life.

"Have you got sights on me, Frank? Is that what I'm sensing? I'm going to give you one minute to tell them to disarm or there's a chance they'll be thanking God personally for being saved a whole lot quicker. I don't want that. That's everything we want to avoid. Nobody here wants that, right Frank?"

I could not help notice the tone of uncertainty in Martinez' voice as to whether this was want Frank wanted or not. Tapping his watch in rhythm with the second hand, sweat had gathered on his forehead, a clear outward sign of his internal fear.

"You listen here, friend. This is the land of the Frontier Saints. You and these heathens are nothing but a cancer upon it. You'll all burn out there, away from the only holy land left in this Godforsaken country. This place shall be green and full when everything beyond has become dust, and bone, and rubble. In God's eyes, you're vermin. Nobody died upon a cross for you."

"Take a look at those charges, Frank. Child abuse. Holding a minor, whose parents have been declared missing, against her will. I'm guessing we'll be able to throw a few weapons charges your way too. This isn't some First Amendment rap. And you can quote your fire and brimstone at me all day, but there's not a judge in the county who's going to give a shit about that, given the nature of these allegations. Time's done."

When Martinez began to step away, Frank signaled to the men behind him to lower their weapons to the ground.

"Kenneth. Please offer yourself into the custody of this man."

As Letts stepped forward in robotic obedience, the officers swarmed among us like wasps, and thrust him to the ground. One cuffed his hands as the other held his face into the soft grass, the Miranda rights echoing between the buildings. Grandfather knelt down beside his follower, his voice spiked with wrath as he spoke.

"This is all part of His plan, Kenneth. She will not speak. She will not speak. 'Remember the former things of old: for I am God, and there is none else; I am God, and there is none like me, declaring the end from the beginning, and from ancient times the things that are not yet done, saying, My counsel shall stand, and I will do all my pleasure.' My counsel shall stand, Kenneth, it shall stand!"

He spoke once more to Martinez.

"You'll find neither the Sullivans nor Whitmore upon this property. They left of their own accord a long time ago."

Mother and Gant took hold of the warrants and began to pick over them, desperate to find some infringement that would see Martinez and his fellow sheriffs escorted from the property. The painstaking search across our compound for Whitmore, Jennifer, and any sign of Marcus or Rose Sullivan was begun. After emptying the dining room, and discounting Jennifer's presence among them, they moved through each room, pictures of the girl in hand, hoping to find a trace of her. Each officer would call out her name as they opened cupboards, closets, and crawlspaces. They peered under beds, turned over our storehouse, checked floorboards for any signs that they had been recently moved, and sliced through the blackness of our attics with their torches and found precisely nothing. Marcus Sullivan's cross was not recovered from my grandfather's room and whatever meager possessions had been in Whitmore's room had been disappeared into the ether. By the time DeNapoli and the child care unit arrived, Martinez' disappointment was evident. Bar Letts, they had nothing to show for their investigation. With other members of the congregation out of earshot they approached me, concern etched upon their brows.

"I'm telling you she's *here*. Why have you stopped looking?!"

DiNapoli tried his best to console me.

"Laura Jo, be reasonable. We believe you. You know we do. But Javier's men have gone through this place with a fine toothed comb and there's more chance of finding Jimmy Hoffa than Jennifer at this point. Short of pulling up the floorboards and taking down dry walls."

"So pull them up, tear them down. Do whatever it is you need to do!"

Hearing my raised voice, Mother came and pushed me behind her, her lioness instinct roused and ready.

"You have no idea what you've done today. I hope your lawyers have had a great summer vacation because by the time we get through with you, you'll both be sent on a permanent holiday. You stay the fuck away from my daughter."

"Ma'am, it's not Laura Jo we need to question. It's Ann…"

With that, a stream of the vilest obscenities I had ever heard came flooding from her mouth. Thomas Goodman was watching and, just as she began to throw an awkward punch towards Martinez, he rushed over and restrained her.

Martinez, unruffled by events, was handed back the hat he had taken off hours earlier by another sheriff, which he tilted over his eyes, tired of the relentless afternoon sun.

"Guess we hit a nerve there."

Once they had identified Ann, the two dozen officers began to walk back out of the main entrance. Following behind them, I watched DeNapoli take her small hand in his gentle grip. She turned back just the once, her face utterly uninhabited by any hint of human emotion. Desperate to let her know I was there for her, I shouted to her to 'tell them everything.' As they placed her into the back of the squad car, she looked through me as if I was nothing more than figment of her imagination. The sheriff and police convoy moved away amid the haze of steam now rising from the drenched fields, and with them went my last remnant of hope.

***

These were the days of Salem. Hysteria gripped our congregation as Frank Marlin and my mother unleashed an unstoppable wave of blame, accusation and retribution. The rooms and minds of each and every man, woman and child were unceremoniously ransacked in the hope of revealing and punishing the demon in our midst, the absolute source of our betrayal. Kangaroo courts were hastily convened in a near blackened basement in the west wing of the compound. AJ Smith and Cousin John would drag whoever Grandfather had chosen into this wretched pit to be vilified, chastened, and in the case of Len Mathers and Michael Chance, beaten until they confessed whatever solemn sin they believed themselves or others to have committed. They roamed the compound after their ordeal, their eyes vacant, and skin the shade of decaying meat, acting as visual reminders of the failure to comply with the standards of obedience expected by Frank Marlin.

A deep paranoia swept plague-like through the ground, every conversation becoming infected with the language of conspiracy; families and old friends began to turn on each other, and folk began to go in droves, the kindling of allegation in their hands, to profess their certainty of their neighbors' wrongdoing. I waited and waited for my turn to come, to feel Smith's rough hand around the back of my neck to pull me into the bowels of the building, but it never came. Though Grandfather's rage was disciplined and directed with purpose, Mother's was a bushfire consuming all around it. No one was safe from her ire as she stormed and sobbed through the hallways, a floundering specter at our feast of hate. Ann's 'incarceration' with the Child Protection Service had loosened the tethers of her sanity, and her decline was only arrested by the arrival of Michael T. Jones. She practically fell at his feet upon his arrival, amid his grand declarations of support for our groundless victimization by the state's authorities. As he was taken by Mother to the Council's office I latched onto her arm, a look of deepest sympathy and concern etched upon my face. When we reached the door, she looked down at me.

"You and Ann look so much alike. Even your voices are similar. She's a strong girl, isn't she? She wouldn't... harm us in any way? "

"She'll do the right thing by us, I'm certain."

The words lay ambiguously between us and I attempted to leave them to their business with Grandfather. She grabbed my arm a little too tightly.

"No, no. Your grandfather wants to see you."

Frank sat slumped upon the chair behind his desk. He sat with his head bowed and features indistinguishable in the half light, as if they had been rendered flat with a hammer and chisel.

"So Jones, I was just telling young AJ here how this desk reminded me of the one my old mentor had. It's uncanny. The same legs, same shape, same finish, same wood. I didn't consciously choose it."

"And what happened to your old mentor – is he still with us?"

He banged his closed fist down hard on the left side of the table.

"Let's just say he couldn't keep pace with my convictions. The saints did not persevere."

"Of course, Frank, such devotion is hard to maintain. But let me tell you, the volume of calls into my show this week expressing sympathy for your plight has been unprecedented. Once again the heavy hand of the state comes crashing down on the civil liberties and fundamental choices of normal folk. Listen, maybe we can try and raise some cash through the show, start a legal fund-"

"Money is not the question. Gant's tried everything. We don't have a leg to stand on. There are no loopholes, no issues with protocol, no administrative problems with their warrants, no precedents."

A stalking hyena at the boundary of its prey, he scanned the room, looking at each of us in turn.

"They knew far too much about us and our methods. The way they moved through this compound, the places they looked first. There's a fox in the hen house, make no mistake."

"Come now, Frank. Your friends, your congregation has not deserted you, there's still hope. Let us remember Psalm 58:10 - The righteous will be glad when they are avenged, when they dip their feet in the blood of the wicked. There is countless support for your campaign among so many right-minded Americans."

Grandfather left him and everyone else in no doubt that the end of all we had built may be upon us.

"Jones, it's our blood they want. One word from that silly little girl, or a falsified confession from the boy Letts, and they'll ready the bulldozers. I've foreseen this. They won't rest until my head sits on a stake. They'll hoist it up for every wretched sodomite and liberal to see. But if it comes to pass then that's the will of the Lord. I'll welcome the end with open arms, ready the congregation for one last sacrifice. It's inevitable. When you twist the tiger's tail, you'd better accept that you're his next meal."

"Frank, Frank, this isn't you talking. Where's that tower of strength gone, the energy that keeps this community together? You just have to let this blow over. These charges will never stick. Just keep it all on the down low for the time being and we'll let the Lord's justice take its course."

We had no choice but to do so. The situation inevitably forced us to retreat further still into our hermetically sealed world. It had been decreed that we would not for the time being go out into the community. No protests or media outreach of any kind would take place for the foreseeable future. A bitter sense of defeat hung heavily in the air. I had never seen them all so forlorn, so hopeless and it sent a jolt of exhilaration through me. Despite this, his wits had not left my grandfather, as he caught the trace of a smile upon my face.

"You've always stayed true to me, haven't you Laura Jo?"

"Yes, sir. You're my very blood. How could I not?"

"That may be the case, but blood has its limits. There's nothing you want to tell me, Laura Jo? Nothing you're harboring deep down inside in that pretty little head of yours?"

"No. Nothing whatsoever."

"Why haven't you told me about the boy then?"

I stepped almost imperceptibly backwards, and tried in vain to push the image of Jackson back to a place in my mind he could never discover.

"What boy? I don't know who you're referring to."

Cousin John interrupted.

"The same little fool who keeps appearing at every demonstration we hold in the city. I've seen you talking, girl. Everyone has."

My hatred of him came rushing from my mouth.

"God *damn* you, John. I'm not your property. Some piece of meat to throw to the dogs. He's just a kid who's interested in us. He might well been chosen, just like we all are. But what would you know about that?"

I pointed to Michael T. Jones.

"And what about him? Is he chosen? Why is he here, in *our* home?"

Mother shook her hands free of Jones and reared up towards me.

"How dare you Michael's presence. After all the support he's given us. You've got questions to answer, young lady! "

Grandfather bellowed at the top of his voice for us all to be silent.

"Who is or who is not chosen isn't for any of you to decide, is it? Now, here this, Laura Jo: you made a solemn vow to John here. There are consequences for breaking that."

"I know. I know. I've broken nothing."

The door to the left of my Grandfather opened. There stood Edward Gant, his hands upon the shoulders of Jennifer Sullivan. It took all my strength not to scream, to run to her and grasp her as tightly as I could. She had materialized from nowhere. I had no idea where they had been keeping her. Even the vault has been empty. Grandfather walked to her, bent to his knees and placed his palm on her cheek.

"Edward, does she understand what's been happening? Does she know we've done all we can to find her mommy and daddy and that it's for the best if we keep her safe for now? I know it's lonely down there, but you're a brave girl."

"That's right, Jennifer knows Uncle Frank and the rest of the congregation love her and are all looking out for her."

The child nodded her agreement and put her arms around Frank to hug him, and in that moment I saw my own young self, and pitied everything that I was, and everything I had become. I would tell Martinez about her when, surely, he and the rest of the Sheriff's Department returned to take my grandfather away. I left the room knowing that as soon as I was gone they would begin to discuss me.

Two days later my every hope lay in tatters. As I walked out into the chilly morning air, I saw the unmistakable figure of Kenneth Letts walking towards me. People began to gather round as he loudly declared that he'd been released with no charge. Fifty feet behind him stood my beaming mother, my sister Ann beside her, who were both soon swept up in amorphous mass of our delighted congregation. I backed away from the terrible sounds of joy until I felt a hand grasp my shoulder. Grandfather leaned down and whispered.

"You know what this changes, Laura Jo?"

He turned me around to face him.

"It changes nothing."

I woke in the early hours of the morning. As I struggled to open my eyes, Grandfather's sermons and commands flittered around inside my mind, like a horde of unrelenting wasps attacking each clear thought. The plan was simple: get out of the compound unnoticed and get to Jackson, from where we could contact Sheriff Martinez. Given I had heard nothing from him since Letts' reappearance, I was angry and frustrated and ready to declare him and the rest of the police to be little more than useless errand boys. I had not risked everything only for my sister to return. When I moved back the covers, someone stopped me.

"You don't understand."

Ann stood above me.

"What don't I understand, Ann? Let me move. I need to leave."

"You don't understand about Kenneth. He loves me."

"He loves you? You're thirteen. He's not allowed to love you."

"Not in the world out there. But since when have we ever paid any attention to what others believe?"

"Ann, for God's sake, this isn't what we are taught to believe!"

"Are you jealous of what I have?"

"Ann, I love you, and he is abusing you. Can't you see that? You shouldn't be going through this. I'm trying to make it stop."

"It was you who told them, wasn't it? What if I don't want it to stop?"

"You don't have a choice in the matter."

"But he wants to take care of me, to have a family one day. He talks to me, he listens. He wants to be around me."

It was clear that an emotional shift had taken place in Ann. After months of suffering her fate, followed by months of blank acceptance, she had managed to somehow empathize with her abuser. Her logic and perspective had been shot to pieces by the unceasing humiliation she had faced. Now even the smallest act of kindness of the part of Kenneth Letts registered as a shockwave of undying love.

"Ann, please! Please go with me now. It's not safe here. He's using you. Everybody's using us. We're nothing but bodies to them, bodies they can fill with whatever filth they desire. We can tell the sheriff everything. We can tell him the truth this time."

"I won't say a word against Kenneth. Even if I wanted to I wouldn't. Because then you know what will happen to Mother. That's not something I can live with."

"She'll deserve whatever she gets. She's offered us up like meat to these people. We were abandoned, Ann. Abused and abandoned. I know people who can help us. The Taits will look after us."

"The Taits? As in Carey Tait?"

"Yes, I've become… close to them."

"What are you doing?! If Grandfather finds out there's no telling what he'll do."

"I'm pretty certain he's only a few steps away from piecing it together anyway."

"Then stop now before it's too late."

"It's already too late. He knows it too."

My tears and pleading were delivered into a void, for she would neither listen nor move. With first light threatening to chase away the dark, I would miss my window if I didn't go now.

"I'm not giving up on you, Ann. But promise me at least that you won't tell them. I've never asked much from you, but please promise me this."

Though she agreed and solemnly vowed not to, the conflict

within her was clear. As I dressed and left the room the last ounce of trust I had in my family seemed to fade within me. Passing through the narrow bap between the two wings of the compound I heard somebody whisper my name. In the frame of the window sat Christina White. She wore a negligée that looked torn on one of the straps, and had the composure of someone who'd not long sunk a bottle of vodka. We stared for a minute at each other, some glimmer of recognition passing between us, before she mouthed the word "go," and ushered me with her hand out towards the main gate.

***

Jackson and I sat next to each other in a coffee shop just off Columbus Avenue. The place was quiet, bar the random cursing of the Italian-American owner directed at the baseball game that played soundlessly on the television, and the strained warbling of some second rate soprano from the radio behind the counter. As we waited for Martinez to arrive, Jackson held my hand while simultaneously ripping to pieces the blue napkin that lay on the empty plate before him. His nerves seemed shattered having spent the last few says slowly driving himself insane over what might have happened to me. When he opened the door to his house he had greeted me as if he'd not seen another human being in years. We had phoned the Sheriff's Department straight away to demand an audience with Martinez, but were informed he would be out of the state until the late afternoon. An hour later they returned our call and asked us to meet him where we now sat. Jackson did his best to calm my agitated state, but my temper over the authorities' failure to make good on their promises would not abate.

"Don't you think we should call your parents too?"

"Look, they're under enough stress. We can handle this until we see them later, OK?"

"I wouldn't be surprised if they didn't believe a word I've said. After all, what's changed?"

"Laura, please. Just calm down, this isn't the end. Things rarely happen that way. Nothing's straightforward. How could this situation ever end easily?"

A shadow moved across our table.

"He's a smart young man, Laura. You ought to take heed of what he just said."

Sheriff Martinez stood over us, a toothpick rotating in the corner of his mouth, and a line across his head where his hat had been resting. He shouted over an order for a coffee and an omelet and squeezed his huge bulk onto the other side of the table, resting his hat and glasses neatly next to him, like they too were expecting food. A whirlpool of anger and desperation span in me as I tried to speak, only to be quickly silenced by his great, soft hand coming down upon mine.

"I know. I know, kid. You feel abandoned and let down and probably think that no one believes a word you've said now. I would too. No one who should be in jail is there right now. We've not been in touch since we let Letts walk out of our station. Nothing's changed."

There were those words again, hanging in the air. They ran through me like nerve gas, paralyzing the remnants of feeling inside.

"But that's not the case, Laura Jo. *Everything* has changed. It really has. Now you're going to have to accept my apologies about the lack of contact. I'm afraid it was necessary on two fronts. Firstly because any attempt to contact you would have placed you in danger, and there was little we could do to protect you while you were isolated like that. Secondly, because we need your grandfather and his congregation to believe - at least a little - that we've failed and aren't coming back. What this operation has bought us is time."

"Time?! My sister hasn't got time! None of us have."

I could feel the first forays of a panic attack begin to rise. Seeing my rapidly developing state of agitation, he asked the owner and three glasses of bourbon appeared on the table.

"Yes, I'm breaking the law. But I'll look the other way this time; you just need to both sip that, and try to be calm."

No alcohol had ever passed my lips before. Its burning warmth had an immediate sedative effect.

"I just want you, for a moment, to think about the scale of our nation. From the deserts, to the mountains, to the cities, a man can lose himself several times out there. He can migrate from place to place, each one unique in its laws and customs, and, if he knows how to, he can reinvent himself each time. When people say there are no second acts in American lives, they're very wrong. That's what Frank Marlin's done his entire life. And no one's ever taken the time to step back and follow the trail he's left, to connect the dots and discrepancies. That's exactly what I've been doing. In the last few days I've been to Kansas, Missouri and Colorado, and I could have gone to a dozen other places where Frank has left a footprint of some kind. It's when you start to look down from above at all the pieces that a very different picture begins to emerge. In the last week I've come to know many versions of the same man; you could say I've picked up the skins he's shed along the way. It seems he's been this version of himself for quite some time now, perhaps since the late 70s. This one's his greatest work, like all those other attempts to reimagine his self were simply trials for this one."

The sheriff pointed towards the drinks that rested in our hands and gestured for us to lift the glasses to out our mouths once more.

"Here's the deal: no matter how many times you transform yourself there's a thread that runs through the soul of a man that you can never destroy. It's his essence, the thing that truly determines the life he leads. And the kind of life Frank has led has been one that's left a trail of destruction in his wake. He's a narcissistic, immoral human being but what makes him special is just how driven he is. What he's always craved is power and influence, and almost everyone who has ever come to 'know' Frank has become a means to that end."

"Like me."

"Exactly like you. Like your mother, your sister, his wife, and his own brother."

"Jimmy Marlin?"

"Jimmy Ray. Your grandfather was born Frank David Ray. He became Marlin in about 1969, a year after Jimmy began a four stretch at Missouri State Penitentiary, or The Walls as its residents call it. He never left that place. They didn't call it the bloodiest 47 acres in America for nothing. In 1972 he was stabbed in a dinner line as he waited to get served chicken. It took him days to die. Now I'm certain you know the version where Jimmy died in a hail of bullets in a bank, over ten years previously."

"It's part of Frank's story of election."

"Story: the magic word. That's the right way to rewrite your past, you see. You keep enough of the truth in there to make it believable, even to yourself, and twist what remains to suit your needs."

Jackson finally broke his silence.

"And they wonder why our generation doesn't believe in much. All history's fiction, apparently."

"In a way, son. It's just that some, like Frank's, has far more fiction than others. And the genius of it all is I'm still not sure what bits are real and what bits are created. Take Jimmy's story: he's lying there dying, his insides all messed up, and he dictates a confession that, for the second time, he's taken the rap for his brother. He'd been jailed for strangling his sister-in-law Emmy, your grandmother. Now he pled guilty at the time to assault and battery on the pretext that he'd been accused by her of physically abusing your mother, Josephine. Disgusted at her claims, he set about her. In his testimony he claimed that it was actually Frank who had been seen throttling the woman, and Frank who'd been abusing your mother. The passing motorist who had witnessed the event picked him out of a line up because he looked so much like his brother; he was only there because Frank, who dominated and controlled him his entire life, had forced him to take the fall. Just like he'd done at the First National all those years before. It was Frank's plan, Frank's concept, and his weak, gullible older brother had been forcibly hauled along for the ride. Jimmy says he froze in the bank and that was the only reason they got caught. But then, you'd be taking the word of a convicted felon against a man who has no real criminal record."

"And what about Minister Earl? Did he even exist?"

"Very much so. Once again, it's sown with the seeds of truth. Now the documentation surrounding the death of the minister wasn't exactly kept as well as it should have been. But these are the facts: Earl Peaks did take in your father after the bank incident. There was no gun used by either brother in the attempted robbery. It was two teenagers with no real clue as to what they were doing, which is why, ultimately,

Jimmy's sentence in his first go round with prison was relatively short. Then there's a declaration of bankruptcy filed by the minister. And finally Minister Peaks' death was recorded by the coroner as an open verdict. Suicide was possible, but he couldn't tell if the minister had died at his own hands because of the strange trajectory of the bullet, and the position in which he was found dead. In between those three things is a collage of fact and fantasy that seems impossible to separate. On the one had there's Frank's version you told me and Sergeant DeNapoli. On the other, there are claims by the Peaks children that Frank was hired not as a potential protégé but as a laborer around the huge estate of the minister. And as time moved on, resentful of his menial position within the family, and driven by jealousy and greed, he found a way to blackmail the minister for large amounts of money. They also claim he consequently forged the minister's last will and testament so that what was left of his estate and the land on it would go to Emmy upon his death, which the Peaks' relatives are certain Frank had a hand in. They each stuck to that belief until they died. Up until your grandmother's death a couple of years back, that property and land was still in her name, and was worth a small fortune. And then it passed to Frank."

Jackson placed his arm around my shoulder, and pulled me in closer to him. He was having as much trouble trying to process this as I was.

"There's one more little detail I didn't mention. It's the sort of thing that, given the history of your congregation, you can take in a dozen ways. Frank Ray was arrested for suspected homosexual activity in the very early sixties, when such laws were still in place. Frank of course denied any involvement, and through various mitigating factors, the charges were dropped. Though I suspect that Frank's co-defendant had something to do with that. And you both know all about Eldridge St Clair."

In that moment someone may as well have taken a scalpel and opened me up from the neck downwards. The pain and humiliation would have felt just the same. Through a fog of tears and a burning sensation deep in my gut, I could see the window to our collective past shut. In a few short months I had gone from God's own blood, to perhaps little more than the summation of a history of lies.

With my eyes tightly shut, I felt Jackson's fingers wipe away the wetness on my cheeks.

"You're not him, Laura Jo. You can't hold yourself responsible."

"How am I any better? Tell me *how*?!"

Looking directly at Martinez, he cleared his throat and briefly avoided my gaze, the moment having gotten to him too.

"Listen, kid: how you're behaving right now, and the actions you've taken, are the things to focus on. Over the decades Frank's been a spiritualist, lying to old ladies desperate to receive message from their long dead relatives while he lines his pockets with their cash. He somehow became the mayor of a little town in Wyoming. Until they discovered, after a year or so, a hole in party funds you could have driven a convoy of trucks through. Some years later he started an investment firm in Maine, all built around fake connections to old money families in the north east, and managed to use the law to abscond with thousands of dollars of his backers' pension funds. What he's done to his own family is not much different. He's promised the earth, and sometimes heaven beyond, before he's snatched it clean away."

He began to sadly laugh, a puzzled, disbelieving look on his face.

"You know, I wouldn't be surprised if at some point he had a medicine wagon that sold snake oil out in the prairies. His life has been something to behold."

After all the things Frank had attempted or pretended to be, he had ultimately revisited his time with Minister Earl. It was through the beliefs of Peaks that he finally realized the method via which he could become something more than all those around him; it would take him to a place beyond the stifling limits of mere humanity.

Jackson leaned in towards the sheriff.

"So what you're saying is that he got away with all of that? You've not told us *anything* that's going to make us believe this is going to end. How the hell are you going to stop him, and stop the rest of them too?"

"I'm getting there, son. By my count there are half a dozen counts of fraud and embezzlement charges still open against the various personas Frank has adopted over the years. Something is going to stick, no matter how big or small. The law has a long memory. In all these places he had assumed identities, a tailored backstory, and a different name. He's just been too good at disappearing, keeping it on a scale where the ripples weren't felt beyond the local county. Until the Frontier Saints, that is. It's as if he couldn't contain the demand of his ego anymore.

"There are still charges being looked into over the physical abuse of minors within your congregation. There are at least two individuals with priors from underage sex offences. But proof is what we still need on that front. Beyond those issues, DeNapoli and the Federal agents he has spoken with are pretty certain that when they get permission to open up the can of worms that is your congregation's finances they'll be able

291

to throw several books at your grandfather, Gant, and your mother. The misuse of the not-for-profit status alone would sink them. It's a matter of time before we get the green light to take a peek into those accounts."

I thought of my own role in the money trail.

"Why are you so certain you'll get permission? I suppose that's what you need me for the most."

"Yes I do, Laura Jo. Especially as I'm guessing you sometimes carried on cashing checks long after people had left the congregation, in one way or another. I guess that brings us full circle to our original conversation: neither of the Sullivans had, until three days ago, been seen since they left your compound. Picture the river that runs behind your homestead. It goes out beyond the county and rushes, at full pelt, deep into the next. That's over a 25 mile radius. If you follow the road that runs parallel to it about half a mile away, it meets the river where it widens out. Two days ago someone's dog dug up the partially decayed body of a man as it waded back out of the water with a stick in its mouth. He'd been purposely buried there down in the silt, when the water was at low tide. Whoever did it didn't appreciate that the silt and mud there would do a fine job of preserving the things that make it easier to identify someone. Giving the clothing and personal artefacts found on him, we're pretty certain that we've found Marcus Sullivan. There's enough circumstantial evidence, including what you've seen, to take this back to Frank and his associates in terms of an investigation."

Sitting there motionless next to Jackson, I had the same feeling that comes when you dream you are falling from a great height and need to wake yourself to stop your descent. Yet nothing could stop this fall, or, it seemed, Frank's.

"So when I said everything had changed, Laura Jo, I meant it.

The sun is setting on the church of the Frontier Saints."

13. The Object of His Wrath

We were swallowed by the oppressive heat as soon as we stepped outside of the cafe. The sun seemed to have un-anchored itself from its orbit and was slowly filling the horizon, a red giant moving steadily down its path of destruction, incinerating all before it. Twenty feet away, the owner of the bar complained in turn about the local kids and the weather to Sheriff Martinez, his hands gesticulating wildly in that grand Italian manner, as he stamped out the cigarette that had withered between his fingers. Jackson had his arms folded as if he has encased in a strait jacket. I brushed the damp hair from his forehead and separated his arms, moving myself in tightly between them. He had not yet lost that tender scent of youth, the skin on his face as soft and hairless as a pre-teen. Though it was obvious he wanted to be with me in ways that I could not yet quite offer, he intoxicated me in ways I could not describe. Perhaps it was that he offered no physical threat, or the sliver of feminine grace that ran through him and resisted the full bloom of manhood. Maybe it was because he seemed able to locate a vestige of goodness in me, when I myself had surrendered that place to shame and disgust.

As I stared into the road, the cars' metal surfaces harshly refracting the light back into my eyes, there appeared a sight I was, at first, convinced must have been an illusion. An arm dressed in green camouflage rested in the windowsill of a white pick-up truck as it slowly rolled past. I followed it open mouthed: in the wing mirror I saw what I believed to be the ruddy, bearded face of Cousin John, his empty eyes hidden by those awful tinted glasses. A few minutes later I came to on the sidewalk, a blackness having covered me. Jackson knelt beside me, his hand under my head. Amid all the things Jackson was, I knew in that moment he was also the tiny drop of blood in the ocean that would see the sharks converge around me. And that it was too late to stop it being spilt. Above me the sheriff's mouth moved in what seemed slow motion. Finally my ability to hear and move returned, like an unspooled tape snapping back into place.

"No, no I don't need an ambulance. It's the heat... and the alcohol. I'm not used to either."

Jackson lifted me to a sitting position, his hand shading my face from the heat.

"You looked as if your own shadow had walked away from you. Just when I thought you couldn't get any whiter..."

"I thought I saw... it's just the light playing tricks. I'm fine."

Martinez took one of my arms.

"We all live with ghosts, Laura. Now let's get you up and home as we discussed."

As Jackson and Sheriff Martinez hauled me to my feet, I was completely unsure as to whether I had seen what I had seen, or if it was simply a case of mistaken identity. If it was Cousin John, then he must have followed me, or was told by someone where we were to meet Martinez. In the grip of that moment's dense paranoia, it seemed entirely possible that Frank's influence spread financially to individuals within the Sheriff's Department. There was, after all, almost no legal threat to our congregation that he was not entirely prescient about. Coincidence and chance were outliers that had to be discarded. I had placed myself and everyone one I cared about in danger and I knew I had to get back to the compound as soon as possible.

Martinez' plan was simple: I would spend one more night with the Frontier Saints, so as not arouse suspicion of the imminent arrest of over a dozen members of our congregation, within which time they expected to have the confirmation back that they had found the body of Marcus Sullivan. At that point they would take me into either state care, or if the Taits agreed, I would temporarily live with them, abandoning everything I knew, my sisters included. The sheriff had placed in my hand a mobile phone on which they would contact me. Never having used one, Jackson had to show me how to work its most basic functions. Martinez' number had been programmed into it and I was to call should I find myself compromised in any way. We would meet, regardless of what happened the next day, with Jackson and his parents at 5.30 pm outside the Contra Costa County Sheriff's station.

Having walked the last mile to where our home stood, I was greeted with the site of Abe Magill and Nate Ramsey guarding the entrance to the grounds, rifles slung over their shoulders, and cartridge belts around their rotund middle-aged guts. Magill took a few moments to register who I was, his sight corrupted since birth by his albinism. His shock of white hair gave him a ghostly menace in the fast falling dusk.

"Laura Jo, this place is in lockdown. Everyone's been summoned. No one's to leave. Your mother has been searching high and low for you."

"I had to buy some new clothes in town. I'm growing out of my dresses."

They looked disapprovingly at my choice of outfit, and passed back and forth little knowing gestures to each other.

"Well, I'm sure your mother will have something to say about that."

Brushing past them as they began to bolt and padlock the gate, I walked between the wings to witness a hurricane of activity. A wooden podium, four feet off the ground, had been erected in the center of the grounds. Upon the front of the pine surface a black crucifix had been crudely painted. Sad streaks ran down from it to the base of the platform, giving the impression that the structure was decaying. Mother was agitating for people to stand before the podium, but the second she set eyes upon me she raced over and grasped me forcibly by the wrists. I yelped and pleaded for her to let go. She began to drag me towards the east wing and then up the stairs towards my room. Inside she threw me upon the bed and began to pull and tear at the clothes I wore. The more I fought her, the harder she pulled, before finally she struck me with the back of her hand across my face.

"You get these things off now! How dare you wear these things inside these grounds? You look like a filthy, disease-ridden whore. It's for the boy, isn't it?! Tell me!"

Tears flowed across her face, her mascara running like the paint on the podium.

"It's for *me*. You're a hypocrite. Look at you. I've seen you with Jones; I've seen his hands upon you. Do you think we're all dumb and blind?"

"What would you know about the things I've had to do for this congregation? The things I've had to sacrifice. I hear nothing but lies from the mouth of an ignorant, deceitful child!"

"Child? You have no children left. You killed the child in me a long time ago. You fed us to these people and you stand before me preaching righteousness? All the nights you've spent away from here with him, all the nights I've known he's lain in your bed."

She ripped the underwear I had on from me. She stuffed my panties into my mouth as I lay there naked and vulnerable before her, choking upon them.

"The way Michael T. Jones has supported this congregation and this is his thanks? It was God's will that brought us together. The same will that brought you and John together. Why couldn't you have ever let John in? He's beside himself with grief over your betrayal. You could have been happy. Like Ann is happy. Jesus died so we, only we, could be saved and taken into God's loving grace. And you think your grandfather would let you reject that gift? You ungrateful, disobedient wretch. You're the dregs of your father. I see that now."

Just as I began to feel the last gulps of air escape from my lungs, my skin turning a gangrenous green, she stepped back and reached out to touch the wall. The desperate sound of my gasping for breath brought Ann to the door.

"*These*. These are closing in around us. We do nothing and we will be crushed. Better it be on our own terms."

My mother opened a drawer, and threw several of the exact same dresses at me. The bitterness and anger in her voice left me cowering.

"Choose *one*. You have two minutes to dress and join the congregation downstairs. I will drag you down those stairs by your hair if I have to."

In her state of rage, Mother had not found the phone upon me; I had heard the dull thud as it fell from my back pocket and landed between the wall and the bed. Ann helped me put on my dress and took me, still shaking, down to the courtyard. Mother had all but confirmed that John had indeed been following me. It was impossible to know whether he had connected me to the sheriff. As Council members lined up beside the podium, the congregation nervously crowded before them like penned-in sheep. On top of the brutal methods employed by the

Council to repress and interrogate them, the almost total isolation from the world outside in the last week had left them frightened and circumspect. Poisonous asides, and murmurings of discontent disseminated from person to person; it was clear that for at least some of those around me, the awe and respect they once held for Frank and his faith had been replaced by a distilled fear. Moments before Frank Marlin took to the podium, Cousin John stood whispering into his ear. When John had finished, Frank clasped his eyes shut, his general expression informed by some internal agony. He raised his arms out wide and began to offer up a prayer only he could hear as he finally ascended the podium steps.

"Friends, it was written that in the last days there would be times of great difficulty. That the Lord would steal in like a thief and that the heavens would pass away amid a great noise. Do you see Him among us and hear that noise, the sound of seven trumpets? It was written that our holy bodies would be burned up and disbanded, and the earth, and the things we have accomplished on it, would stand here exposed, ready for His judgment. The flames are waiting. Look around you at the monument to God we have created. Are we not ready? I know the troubles and turmoil of recent times have been hard upon you. But to inflict these tests upon our nature and character was necessary to our very survival. Believe me, I have suffered in this process too, suffered more than you can imagine. I would not spare myself the same measures. And through that suffering I am clear in my mind of our path, clear of the things God wants for us. Outside these walls we stand vilified, vilified for revealing the rotten core of existence, the putrid, diseased state of so-called humanity. Those sick faggots; the Jews, for who money is the one true God; the degenerate Muslim hordes, the perverted sodomite

Catholics, the police, those bastard handmaidens of every filthy law: they all conspire to bring us to our knees. They do not want us to exist and will not stop until this comes to pass. Some of you before me have chosen to lend the unelected the rope by which they intend to hang us. The sons and daughters of Judas, the friends of Pilate, have betrayed this flock. Our Day of Salvation approaches and in that reckoning they will be the first to be summoned."

The malcontent that had been breeding in the crowd burst forth; they began to call upon Frank to tell them just who those people were. He did not need to reply. Like all baying mobs they singled out those themselves who seemed the weakest and least necessary. Two families, the Adamses and Wilsons, were indicated as the source of duplicity. The members of those families quickly banded together, their outrage at the accusations clear. Yet as the crowd hollered abuse towards them, the threat of physical confrontation growing with each second, Frank did not intervene. He ignored their coarse, angry pleas and with a turn of his head and an upturned palm, he condemned them as guilty. It did not take them long to realize the danger they faced, and they began to move in a tight huddle towards the exit of the compound. Attempts were made to grab their children, which only stopped when Stephen Wilson pulled a pistol from his waistband and fired it into the air, just over the heads of the pursuing group.

"We want no part of this anymore. Move back or I swear I'll shoot the first fucking man who gets within ten feet."

Grandfather called out into the frenzy before him.

"Let them go. Return here to me. They cannot outrun the fate that God has for them. The harvest is the close of the age. They were not sown by holy hands. So let them go. It is we who wear the armor of God.

The poisoned blood that seeks to soak the land of the Frontier Saints must not be allowed within these walls. When they come to our door they must be repelled. I ask you now: do you have the will? The will to do what normal men cannot?"

There were those in our congregation who shook as if the Holy Spirit had entered them. Frank pointed at some unseen stigmata upon his hand.

"Is this flesh what you truly value? Is this bodily vessel the thing that stops you from taking that final step towards the Lord, from enacting the will of the Lord? We must reject its borders. Our lives will live on in a state of bliss unobtainable to all those out there. Friends, this is our inheritance. And the flesh, be it now, tomorrow, or the next day, will ultimately be our sacrifice. Do not fear it. He will be there beside us. He will work through me."

The long knives of his fingers cut through the air in front of him and stretched towards the gathering, before pausing on a person of his choosing

"Michael. When you and your wife found yourself destitute, who was there to comfort, support and guide you?"

"You were, Frank."

"AJ. When you sat alone in that cell, facing your third and last strike and a lifetime behind bars, who released you?"

"You, Reverend, you."

"Thomas. Who saved you from the pit of greed in which your family swam? Who accepted you when others would not and gave you a place at this holy table?"

"Only you, Frank."

"Christine. Who took you far from the loneliness and desperation you felt, and has cared for your daughter as if she were his own?"

Christine cut a pitiable, sad figure. It was likely she had not washed for days. She had reached the end of whatever journey she had been on and loathed the place at which she had arrived. But right then she had no option but to respond positively to Frank.

"That would be you, Frank."

On and on he went through his flock, reminding each member of the overwhelming debt of gratitude and deliverance they owed him, dismissing them with orders to stay locked in their rooms. With the congregation dispersed, and only Council members remaining, he at last came to me.

"Laura Jo. Flesh of my flesh, blood of my blood. Have we come to this? Where you choose the company of a stranger, of one who will perish, over the loving bosom of your family? You've still a chance not to fall from God's grace, Laura Jo. Do you really think the Wilsons and Adamses will survive out there for long? That you could do the same? God is not full of mercy. He cares not for your empathy, your desire, your hopes and needs. He is vengeful and spiteful. He will not set you free. He will level everything you hold dear. Renounce the boy."

"There is no boy."

"Liar."

Frank placed his hand around my throat.

"Renounce the boy."

"There is no boy."

"Liar!"

I could feel the pulse in my neck throb as his hand began to tighten around me.

"You've been *seen*. Let him go; commit yourself to John!"

"I'd..."

The words could barely break through the barricade of my throat.

"I'd rather die."

"Perhaps then, all those years ago in that field, I should have let the machine finish its work."

He let me drop to the floor. My mother stood there impassively, the faintest hint of pleasure on her face. Vitriol and disappointment consumed my grandfather. As he raged at the night, his mouth foaming, and hands beating upon his own body, he confused lines of scripture; they bled together to form a new, impenetrable language only he could understand. Though Grandfather was never far from control; he knew that the world around him was falling apart, but also that he would do anything to make it fall apart on his terms. He found once again the benign center of his storm. The fact that for so long I had been his most apt and dedicated pupil was maybe the only reason he did not finish me there and then. I was only thankful that it was others he blamed for bringing the authorities to our home. Frank turned to Smith and Gant.

"Lock her in her room. It seems, yet again, the saints have not persevered. The few get fewer. "

Mother stood over me.

"You really are your father's daughter. I can't believe you came from my womb."

When Gant and Smith began to lead me away, Frank took hold of Cousin John, whose fury was obvious to all.

"She was supposed to be mine, Frank. She was promised to me. I've waited so long. We should have done something about that boy. We should have done something."

"John. Dear, faithful John. There is still much we'll do. But clearly, she was destined for more common use. She's kindling for the fire. A greater promise awaits us."

***

The power in the east wing of the compound had failed or had been purposely switched off. I flicked the light switch up and down as I leant against the door, the key to which was sitting in the lock on the other side. Nothing I tried would dislodge it. Hours had passed like days as I tried to find reception on the phone they had given me. The orange glow of the screen blinked forlornly at me, my arm reaching upwards out of the small gap in the window, as I desperately hoped for a satellite up there in the nothingness to drift my way. Giving up, I let it slip from my hand onto the floor, and I realized that the dozen text messages I'd tried to send - pleading for Martinez to come and get me, for Jackson to go to the station - would likely be read when I was already gone.

The contents of the drawer my mother had emptied lay strewn across the room. Picking up the last of my meager belongings, I began to fold them, pack them back into their space. Amid this sea of cheap cotton I came across the oldest dress I owned of this type. Lifting it up by its narrow shoulders, a small object dropped from its folds onto the bed. By touch alone I knew that it was the small figure of Christ that my father had carved for me. It was relic of pre-history, an artefact from a time that had been chased from my memory by the will and whims of my grandfather. Yet it meant more to me in that moment than anything ever had. Pulling back the covers, I lay down upon the bed. As I clasped the tiny figure to my chest and prayed for a God to exist, other than the one that I knew, I imagined Jackson sitting on the porch of my house talking to my father, James. I saw him put his arm around Jackson and call me towards them, but I could not picture myself moving any closer towards them. When their forms finally began to dissolve in my mind, I closed my eyes and made peace with the fact that they would not likely open ever again.

Yet as the night began to release its grip, they opened once more. The sound of the key slowly turning in the lock had awoken me, the door opened to reveal the silhouette of my sister. She beckoned me quickly towards her, her head twitching like a rabbit expecting the imminent descent of some bird of prey.

"Just put your shoes on and leave. They're going to be coming."

"The gates are barred. How am I supposed to leave?"

"You drop from Jennifer's empty room on the opposite side of the wing and make your way out across the land or you cross the river and pick up the highway half a mile away."

"I'll break my leg falling or drown."

"They're both better options for you than staying."

"So take that chance with me."

"I won't leave Mother. She's still here somewhere."

"She left a long time ago, Ann."

We entered Jennifer's room. Looking out of the window into the rolling land beyond, the drop from the first floor was perhaps twenty feet. I climbed onto the sill and slipped off until I held on to the edge by my hands. Still fifteen feet from the ground, loud male voices echoed from the hallway and out above my head. My feet dangled helplessly as Ann urged me to let go, her eyes awash with tears and grief. Falling through the air for a matter of moments, I hit the ground with my heels first, then flat onto my back. It was as if a spike had been riven through me, the searing pain taking my breath away. Yet I could still move my limbs, the soft earth having cushioned the blow. Once dizzily on my feet, I turned and ran eastwards as fast as my concertinaed body would let me into the early morning light. Around one hundred and fifty feet away, I glanced back towards the compound, expecting to still see Ann. Instead the neon hunting vest of Cousin John loomed out of the window, the scope from the rifle he had aimed at me glinting before him. Dust kicked up from a bullet that ricocheted off the earth just beside me. I could not tell if it was a warning shot or a bad shot and, absorbed by terror, I did not wish to find out.

Countless miles from where I needed to be, I crossed the undulating landscape in an attempt to stay off main roads and avoid suburban centers. Through the burgeoning heat of the day I passed a tapestry of dead vineyards, reservoirs, crumbling outhouses, golf courses, and wooded hills. The dominating vista of Mount Diablo reared up to the west, its parched sides exposed to the sweltering heat. Local laborers, bandanas tied around their heads beneath their Mexican cowboy hats to keep the sweat from their eyes, and random red-faced hikers waved hello to my spectral form as I moved through the countryside or rested against the greying wooden boards of a barn. It was midday before I realized I had left the phone Martinez had given me back in my room. Either way I could not make my way back to Jackson in San Francisco. The distance was too great, and I would not blindly lead Cousin John, or whoever else was undoubtedly looking for me, to him. If I made my way towards the sheriff's station I could just reach it at the time we had agreed. In a car on the long open stretches of country road it would have taken thirty minutes; staying out of sight and crossing this terrain meant hours.

Above and before me, the shape of the sky shifted as phalanxes of cotton clouds gave way to darker hues of pure blue. In the distance I could see the slow arc of a Ferris wheel, its bright red and yellow carriages drawing me instinctively towards it. Signs for a County Fair smothered telephone poles as I came across and blended into great crowds of people. There was simply no way to avoid them. Kids sat high on their father's shoulders, and swarms of old ladies in pastel pant suits and sun visors complained about their long dead husbands. My disheveled image passed beside me in a hundred parked car windows, the lurid smell of candy floss and hotdogs permeating the air. The sounds of bumper cars and carousels intermingled with a voice announcing the start of a prize sheep competition. Men wore clothing as white as the animals they paraded back and forth, the audience inexplicably cheering each one. The twitching, frightened animals' heads shot nervously around, the strained leashes around their necks the only thing stopping them from bolting. It was impossible not to pity the poor creatures. They were all fattened for breeding, fattened for eating, or fattened for show. Wandering through the blitz of color and sound, my paranoid imaginings saw members of the congregation scattered among the fair-goers, each one searching and waiting for me to make myself known. When a voice exclaimed behind me that it was nearly half past four, I began to push on through the fair, out of the exit and back out across the twisting hillside roads, keeping in unison, where I could, with the roads that would lead me almost to my destination.

Just under an hour later, the sun was readying itself for its gradual descent. I had finally moved from the maze of country roads and pathways to the planned order of the town. Moving from Ward to Main to Escobar, I watched as office workers slunk into bars, gangs of children crowded the sidewalks outside fast food restaurants, and all normal life took place. Halfway along Pine I saw Jackson. Sunlight forced its way through the leaves of the umbrella of tree branches above him and dappled across his body. Rubbing his forehead with the side of his hands, the cuffs of his shirt undone, he looked as if he had aged since I last saw him. It was as if the trouble I had gifted him had somehow seeped through to the surface of his skin, his face ashen and creased, his eyes drained swimming pools. While he nervously checked his watch, a car pulled up across the road and into the sidewalk. Jean Tait leaned out of the driver's side window. Jackson bent down to speak to her and she took his face in her hands. She began to talk forcibly to him; you could practically see the tension rise from him and fade into the air. I watched them, an uninvited guest in their tender moment, as she mouthed to her son that she loved him. It was in that moment that I knew I felt the same. He embodied every hope and desire imaginable to me, and there was nothing I would not do to stay even the smallest part of his world. When the Taits' car finally began to move down the street, I walked, as if unseen by anyone, towards Jackson. From behind, I placed my arms around him, and pressed my cheek against the top of his back.

"I'm almost too scared to turn around in case it isn't you."

I reprimanded him in the manner of a southern school mistress.

"Jackson Tait, you better darn turn around. You'll have to get used to this face."

"I see it every day."

He spun me around and we stood facing each other. I ran my finger along the tiny creases beside his eyes, and the dim purple patches beneath them. We stood for a time simply looking at each other, embracing every aspect of that moment. The road we stood next to doglegged about two hundred yards down, the sheriff's station another two hundred and fifty yards to the right, but visible as the crow flies across a stretch of park land. In that distance we saw the Taits walking towards the low hung sheriffs' building. They were joined not far from its door by Martinez, who greeted them as if they were old friends. He shortly began walking towards us, waving his hat in the air as a greeting. We began to cross the road, Jackson's hand lovingly crushing mine like it was the last thing he would ever feel. It felt in that instant that this was how it would finally all end, my past, present, and future distilling to a perfect second in time. This was the Hollywood denouement, the cinematic sunset. This was the winning run in a college baseball game, the crowd cheering themselves hoarse from the bleachers. This was our ticker-tape parade through the streets in an open topped car, my smile caught by the shutters of a thousand photographers' cameras.

Yet when Jackson began to speak, the future would recede in a terrible moment, and my past would be nothing but present.

"You know, I was worried when the sheriff told me you called him to ask where we were meeting again."

"I... I didn't call him."

Nails fastened my feet to the black tar road as he grabbed me by my arms, the sidewalk an elusive few feet away.

"What do you mean you didn't call him?! He said you spoke to him, that you were upset and hard to make out."

A groundswell of fear overcame me.

"I left the phone there. I didn't use it. I didn't call. I didn't call!"

It was instantly clear that it had been Ann. They had used her like a living marionette, strings attached to her flesh, forcing her to pretend to be me. I knew too that they would take a hammer to her crystal-glass heart and make her suffer for helping me. The world seemed to warp: I could see Martinez, now just ten feet away, begin to run towards us across the park, his features electrified in panic, his great hands beckoning us towards him, his mouth screaming 'move!', the violent sound of a vehicle gunning its engine to breaking point filling the air. Looking back down the road, Jackson's mouth dropped open in horror, his body tensing to prepare for an impact he could not escape. It was both a split second and a lifetime later that the sheriff pushed us both over and out into the road; falling backwards he watched as a white pick-up truck careered straight into him, pinning the lower half of his body between it and a parked vehicle just behind him. It was a scene of unfathomable carnage: steel impaled flesh, flesh embraced steel; a spray of blood on glass, a shower of glass on concrete; the piercing screams of alarms and passers-by; a pall of acrid grey smoke and buckled waves of metal; the inhuman cry of a man alive only from the waist up.

People rushed around us, absorbed with the horror of the mutilated, convulsing sheriff, his blood segueing into the dark red hood of the car behind him, and luminous on the white one before him. Jackson's face glinted with small shards of glass as he tried to lift me up. Under great duress, the driver's door of the pick-up was thrown open. Cousin John stepped unsteadily from the vehicle, a rifle clasped between his hands, the knuckles of which carried roads of black bruises. An open wound on his head saw blood drip down onto his filthy orange vest. He waved his gun across the gathering crowd, eliciting great screams and no end of panic as people ducked under the point of its barrel. Finally he lowered his rifle to my prostrate position on the road.

"You come to me now Laura Jo, you come to me. Didn't think I'd let you go that easily, did you? In God's name, you belong to me.

Me!"

His words were washed with the blood he spat out onto the floor. The vicious nature that my grandfather had both suppressed and nurtured in John had finally reached its crowning moment. The clandestine, monstrous desires that infected our entire congregation had seized conscious control of him, his fury, vanity and errant righteousness collapsing in upon themselves as he slid back the bolt of the gun. The image of John disappeared as Jackson stood and covered me. I could hear his mother's cries for him to step away. A shot rang out as I reached up towards him. The bullet passed clean through the upper part of his chest, a mist of blood still hovering in the air as Jackson span to the ground, his body a limp, dead weight. Before I could even scream, John placed the rifle under my chin, pulling me to my feet. Its cold barrel began to choke me as we rapidly backed away down the empty road. Nobody dared follow us. When we reached the T-junction a short way away, he swiveled the rifle to point through the windscreen of the first car that had the misfortune to come our way. A small Asian man raised his hands in surrender behind the steering wheel, his panicked pleas muted by the confines of the vehicle. John moved around to open the car's door, pushing me to the ground as he did so, placing his knee on my back. He dragged the terrified driver from the seat as if he was lighter than air and forced me to clamber across to the passenger seat. John brought the butt of the rifle down in a forty-five degree arc against the face of the vehicle's owner, who sat intoning some unintelligible prayer on his knees. A fountain of blood came back across John, as the driver's nose bent into an obscene new shape. Slipping the car into gear, John began to move the car forward as if we were on a scenic Sunday drive. The carnival of misery we had left behind began to recede in the wing mirror. People scurried like a multitude of ants around Jean Tait. She was stillness incarnate as she slumped over her son, oblivious to the panic surrounding her. The colony queen was at one with her dying offspring. Over my shoulder I could see a group of sheriffs racing towards the obliterated body of their colleague, the cars unable to get through the extensive mass of people and vehicles that had stopped to rubberneck.

Within ten minutes we were out onto the freeway. Ambulances slalomed between traffic on the other side, their sirens piercing right through me. With the rifle resting upon his lap, John's hands shook upon the wheel, the cavernous gash on his head causing him to constantly wipe blood away from his eyes, the vehicle swerving slightly each time. Unable to comprehend the sequence of events that had taken place, I could not stop looking at his disgusting form. This had pushed me to a point far beyond mere pain and anger; an incandescent, beautiful rage was spreading through me like a cancer, from cell to cell, vein to vein, thought to thought. It was ready to govern and enforce my every decision, become the epicenter of my will and conviction. Somehow I felt an absolute sense of control and purpose once more, a needle-sharp point of clarity on who I was, and what I must do, beyond anything I felt as a member of the Frontier Saints. I had reached the house where no one but death resided, and, with nothing but the image of Jackson's body to illuminate their way, I would usher the whole congregation into my new home. They would be welcomed with open arms. Neither Cousin John, my mother, nor my grandfather would decide my fate. It was I who would decide theirs.

"Why don't you kill me now, John. You know you have to."

"Be quiet. Frank will know what to do. He'll make you see."

"Did he send you, John? If he didn't you may as well kill me now anyway. I'm already dead you see, John. I'm still his granddaughter."

"I said be quiet! I'm taking us home."

"That's what I want to do John, take you and everybody else home. There's nothing here for us now. It seems like the saints did not persist. Not in me. Not in you. Not in any of us. How could He save a wretch like you, or me?"

"Just shut your fucking mouth, I can't even see with this crap in my eyes!"

"Why don't you keep them closed, John? Just press your foot down. Close your eyes. It'll only take a second. We won't feel a thing."

"God damn it, shut your fucking bitch mouth up. I've told you!"

Enraptured by his anger, he almost missed the turning that led to the land of the Frontier Saints. With blood dripping down again onto his face, his eyes blinking rapidly and hands crossing over the wheel as he swung the car off the freeway, I made a desperate lunge for the rifle. The back of the vehicle swung out and down into a light slope as he slammed upon the brakes. John's disorientated, injured state caused him to let out an animal yelp, as the car stalled to a shuddering halt. Before he could even react I had pulled back the bolt of the gun, and stuck the tip of it into his wound.

"Every time you move your head I'll push it in deeper. If you move your hands one single inch, I'll move my finger the inch it takes to pull this trigger. You speak, I'll do the same."

With my left hand I reached behind me and opened the door, the rifle swaying in my other momentarily. Slowly, I made my way from the vehicle, the sight never living his skull for a second. In the pocket of the door was a box of matches and a crumpled wad of dollars. I took them both.

"When this shuts, you drive back home. You stop, turn around, or deviate in any way, I'll open fire. They'll be coming for you soon enough."

As the rusting blue Buick pulled off into dust and made its unsteady way forward, I brought the rifle down to my side and held it under a long fold of my dress. Not far back along the main road was a gas station. When I reached it, the attendant, who immediately became suspicious at my unruly state, was distracted by an old lady looking to put some air into a flat tire. As he bent down to inspect it, I slipped past him to a pyramid stack of gasoline cans, and took two from the top, wedging the money under the next can down. Turning behind the station I walked out and headed inland to the fields beyond. I was going home.

***

It is here I find my own reflection, here that I step back into the footprints that marked the end of the beginning, the beginning of the end. Yet she is me and not me. Her truth is mine alone, but also belongs to all she knew. Even the path on which we both walked was not the same: the steps led to a place that she and I had never seen nor understood. For this was where we came to meet our Father; where he ultimately drew us, to be raised up on the final day.

In the half an hour it took me to get to the compound, I had imagined working my way through each floor, the gasoline pouring forth around me, the matches in my dress pocket clamoring to ignite. Once lit, the flames would quickly ravage and illuminate every dark, dead room. And, until the fire consumed and nourished me too, I would ask myself the question that Frank Marlin had proposed all the long: What if God, in choosing to show His wrath and make His power known, bore with no patience the objects of his wrath, and prepared them for destruction? I would finally understand, as our whole world burned down, that the answer was all around me.

But when the east side of the building came into view it was as if my vision had escaped from my mind, rushed its way across the fields, and mutated from dream to reality. The immediate sense of wonder and delight at the trident of smoke that belched from the compound quickly gave way to revulsion. Under the thickening mushroom cloud, my family and the congregation that had been my entire life could be dying. Sickened by own sense of retribution, I ran the final stretch towards my home. In the middle of the compound the windows were molten hot and ready to give way, but one nearest the river was cooler, and already slightly cracked. Dropping one of the gasoline cans in the sparse, bed-less room, I opened the door and let in fearsome wraiths of black air. Through the semi-darkness I felt my way along the wall towards the far exit to the long courtyard. Above me, I could hear a hymn being sung; the strained, tearful voices slowly transmuting into cries of pain. A cascade of fresh air hit me as I collapsed out on the grass and entered and walked through a man-made hell: the rooftops swirled with the madness of the fires; shadow-figures choked in the prisons of their rooms; a child's charred body poisoned the river; the burning effigy of Cousin John fell before me; and the disfigured bodies of my mother and sisters lay together, their wounds glistening with the very blood that ran through my veins, and hands clasped together in a prayer no God would receive.

All that was left was my Grandfather and I. The kingdoms of this world had become the kingdoms of his land. And now both that land, and we, would perish. That old serpent, the dragon that would be cast out, had called my name. At that moment, standing on our own twisted Golgotha, he would bring down the curtain on our theatre of the absurd, and take my life. Through the dark black barrel of his rifle, that rod and staff of the sick shepherd, would come the light that took mine from me. Though Frank Marlin would tell me that God had never entered my heart, the truth was simpler still: the God of his creation had left it. Looking up beyond the melting pictures of my mother and I, up beyond the blistering rafters of the buildings, one tiny patch of sky was incandescently bright and clear. As the sound of sirens drew near, I fixed my eyes upon that heavenly point, and let the last remnants of hate slip from me, and waited for the dark to come.

Yet before Frank Marlin could become the author of my end, the blackened beam above him burned free from its once immovable frame and broke his neck under its terrible, crushing weight. The fire spread further across the room, overwhelming the worthless objects of our religion. My grandfather lay in its center, the beam horizontal across his motionless body, the flames and I the only guests at this wretched crucifixion.

Voices beckoned me towards the cavalcade of flashing blue lights, and through the fountain of death that was my home. When I reached the arms of a stranger, I looked back into the fury and heat and saw that I'd left behind the girl I knew.

14. Death Forever Swallowed

I am twenty-six years old.

It seems to me that I have lived several lives in that time. I was born Laura Jo Carter, I became Laura Jo Marlin, and I exist now as Laura Tait. The hair that was once almost white has darkened with age, my eyes have taken on a greener hue, and the delayed arrival of true womanhood has added both height and curve to my physique. It is almost as if my body has consciously chosen to move away from who I once was. On the tenth anniversary of our congregation's end, the *San Francisco Chronicle* interviewed me and the few other surviving members of the Frontier Saints. On the table before me the journalist laid out the photographs they were considering running with the article; an article that would dissect the sorrowful unfolding of events, now that time's arrow had moved us far enough away. Staring at the dizzying array of faces, those frozen frames of anger and disgust, it was a puzzling test to recognize who and where I was. This, I suppose, has been my great struggle: how to reconcile those versions of myself, how to assimilate them into my everyday life. Those years with the Saints take on the form of an unedited movie; as the scenes play back, I have to fight the temptation to embellish, falsify or completely remove parts of it. The truth of who we were and what we did is something I cannot live without. Each day I read the words inscribed on the memorial I was once led to; in remembrance is the secret of redemption. I have remembered my truth, at least. As the years have passed I have shed the layers of conditioning and control that were woven into to the very fabric of my soul. It has taken longer still to admit my own complicity in proceedings, and, more importantly, to forgive and pity the child who was never really given much choice. Yet I will never fully let go of that flickering pulse of regret and anguish that lights up, on occasion, from the depths. Without its piercing, painful call, I could not steer myself clear of the familiar, deadly rocks that lie in wait for us all.

I had spent most of my childhood with no access to books, so the four years I spent at college began a journey into a sea of words, ideas and concepts from which I hope never to reach land. With every conversation and interaction, every point of view and perspective, through each book, and film, and piece of art or music, the shape and substance of the rest of the world has slowly become clearer.

Jackson and I were married not long after we graduated. His proposal was the only thing that has ever felt truly predestined in my life. Standing on the shore by the Sutro baths, fresh from breakfast at Louis', it was the kind of day in which San Francisco sends all four seasons at once. We stared out into the tumult of the ocean, our lives far removed from the first time we shared that view. Having circumnavigated time to return to this point, he asked me to become his wife. Under the hiss of foam, with the light dissecting the clouds, and my hand slipping beneath his shirt to rest upon the scar from a bullet, I said a near silent yes. The beautiful accident that is our son, Henry James, followed two years after I began teaching grade school kids in northern San Francisco, a position to which I have now returned. Plans, it has been said, are the things that make God laugh, and the thought of not having Henry James in our lives is one that neither of us would like to comprehend. He has my father James' arresting eyes, and the graceful beauty of my mother, Jean. When he crawls into our bed in the early hours of the morning, and presses his face deeply into my chest, I wonder about the man he will allow himself to become. I resolve myself once more to finding out what it is he truly wants, so I may only advise him to act upon that.

Last summer I returned alone to the land of the Frontier Saints. Crystalline blue skies hung above Contra Costa County, and as I touched the rotting roots of a post that once formed part of the entrance gate, I thought of the avalanche of words that where mentioned in connection with this place. Through the noise of 'cults' and 'abuse,' 'murder' and 'bigots,' 'tragedy' and 'suicide,' there are a small few who, in relation to Frank Marlin himself, would rather utter 'conspiracy,' 'martyr,' 'misunderstood,' and, most alarmingly of all, 'prophet.' Be they a follower, an academic or reporter, when someone enquires as to who Frank Marlin was, I try, in my fractured, distant way, to convey that he was nothing but the most terribly human of men. Indeed, for a year after the compound was razed to the ground, it became a pilgrimage for those with a ghoulish fascination for what had happened there. Banners and placards in the style of which we once used to protest would be found scattered among the ruins, some reflecting our beliefs, some denigrating us for them. It was no small wonder that the Sheriff's Department, who had lost one of their own amid the carnage, soon sent in the bulldozers and trucks to level and remove what was left of our former home.

Once the fires of the Frontier Saints had been finally extinguished, the authorities report was both stark and bleak. John Murphy-Wood, on his own volition, or under instruction from Frank Marlin, murdered Sheriff Javier Martinez and shot Jackson Tait. After first taking Laura Jo Marlin hostage, he returned alone to the compound of the Frontier Saints and informed Frank Marlin of what he had done. Frank Marlin, who had already predicted the imminent end of the congregation, and knew now that the authorities were closing in around him, decided to put his final plan into action. While, most likely, Edward Gant, AJ Smith and Murphy-Wood spread gasoline across the compound, eighty-two men, women and children were locked, willingly or unwillingly, into rooms in the east and west wings and were slowly burned alive. Gant and Smith then took their own lives in a fire strewn downstairs west wing room, from which Murphy-Wood then briefly escaped. Josephine, Ann, and Beth Marlin were shot at point blank range in the courtyard of the compound. There were no signs of a struggle, and based upon the bullets from the weapon that was recovered from beside the still smoldering corpse of Frank Marlin, it was probable that it was he who had killed them. The evidence Martinez had collected against Frank Marlin, Frank Ray and several other identities he had taken was passed to the relevant authorities from state to state. Without prompting, the police force that had first investigated the death of my father, James Carter, reopened the case, and concluded there was sufficient evidence to rule that the brakes of his truck had been tampered with. By whom, they could not determine.

Standing on the space that used to be our courtyard, I could feel the weight of history that had sunk into its soil. Thinking back to that day of destruction I wondered whether I would have doused the walls with the gasoline from those cans myself, had our home not already been aflame. Looking at the field of green beneath me, and the rampant spread of summer to every point on the horizon, I knew then it was an act I would never have been capable of. For though this earth was without form and void; and darkness was upon the face of the deep, the spirit of God moved upon the face of the waters, for I was returned to the family, to Bill, Jean, and Jackson Tait, who had taught me forgiveness and compassion. It would seem that in a life once caught between devout dream and waking nightmare, I received no revelations but these: no God is worth believing in who would not allow you to save yourself; no God is worth praying to whom would not have died for all.

Outside at this moment, Jackson is leaning on the hood of our car. He is lifting Henry James up into the tender rays of the morning sun, making a sound like a rocket ship as he does. The boy's face is immersed in delight, his arms outstretched through the air, reaching for a place that only a child could see. When I exit through that door I will leave this congregation forever. And my family and I will go to church.

ABOUT THE AUTHOR

Jamie McDuell was born, and still lives in London. He studied modern history at Queen Mary College, University of London, and has since worked in various institutions as Dark Lord of the Internet. A JG Ballard, Scorsese, Nick Cave, and Bowie obsessive, he is as influenced as much in his writing by music and films as he is books.

Printed in Great Britain
by Amazon